THE FALL IS ALL THERE IS

C.M. CAPLAN

THE FALL IS ALL THERE IS

by C.M. Caplan

ISBN 978-1-7372095-3-9 (paperback)

ISBN 978-1-7372095-1-5 (ebook)

Cover Art by Fay Lane

Edited by Noah Sky

 Created with Vellum

To Tim Quigley

I told you I'd finish it. RIP.

Richard: He's here. He'll get no satisfaction out of me. He isn't going to see me beg.

Geoffrey: Why, you chivalric fool, as if the way one fell down mattered.

Richard: When the fall is all there is, it matters.

—James Goldman, *The Lion in Winter*

PART ONE

CHAPTER

ONE

I was six years old the first time Mom threatened to sew my mouth shut. She got the needles out and everything, I swear. In her defense, I was a chaotic little shit at that age.

And while this incident never managed to convince me it was worth it to shut the fuck up, that afternoon I spent with the back of my head pressed against the cold basement cement *did* teach me I had to get away.

From her. From Dad. My siblings. From Mercy House.

I was eighteen before I found the kind of courage I required, but I got there. Eventually. I ran away to Blackheath House and everything.

The rest of the family didn't like it, mind you. They all sent letters and missives my way expressing their disdain, telling me how I was embarrassing them. There were no shortage of attempts to fetch me over the first few years. But soon enough they found new conflicts, new trivialities at court to snap at and chase after.

I had five years to build a life without them. To stay out of the spotlight. To realize I didn't need them.

Until—*well*. Hm. How to put this?

Let's say you get a letter for the first time in a while. Let's say the people sending the letter are angry. Let's even suppose they might have valid reasons to be angry because you've been avoiding them.

So! When you knife the envelope open and find they're making demands—when you find that they're threatening everything you've worked five years to build—all because you refuse to embroil yourself in their insipid games...

Hypothetically.

Can you see how I'd be upset?

Honestly I was surprised it took them five years to find the words to express exactly how much and in what ways they wanted to hurt me for leaving, and how badly they wanted me back.

Maybe surprise isn't the right word—the letter inspired something closer to *fear* and *alarm* and *sheer fucking panic*.

It's a funny thing, panic. It's got a way of getting you on your feet. Making you want to move. Like your body wants to match the speed of its thoughts.

But sometimes those thoughts are stuck on hamster wheels that spin and spin until you're sweaty and exhausted and you can't breathe because your heart is clogging up the hollow of your throat—and then you look around and realize you never actually got anywhere.

I couldn't figure out what to do on my own. I needed help. Advice.

I had to talk to Avram.

I navigated Blackheath House's labyrinthine hallways, the twisting corridors, the limestone tunnels, with my mind snarled in hysteria.

The whole place was built inside the structure of a

gigantic lizard skeleton. Big wooden doors were set in between the skull and jawline. Steel and iron and concrete clung to it—the meat between the old bones.

I hurried through the furrowed hallways of the right ribcage, passing windows reinforced with orange plasma. They hummed softly. Helped keep the ghosts out. As I passed, one of them eked out yellow veins that sizzled as the ghostfog outside breathed against it, frying the spirit-air into smoke and black vapor.

They wavered softly when the wind howled, bending inwards to receive it; growing big distended bellies every time wind swelled against them.

I slipped past chamber doors inset with heraldry. Fesses and gules. Chevrons and bordures. Scutcheons. Archways reinforced with cyborg bronze. Ribbed marble hallways with electric panels.

Until a small white door stood out, completely blank. I knocked insistently. My knuckles buzzed with the impact. I don't know how long it took for Avram to answer my insistent pounding. Time was runny round the edges while I did it. Clarity only bothered to show up when he did. He was wearing nightclothes and looking ludicrous without his glasses. He squinted, eyes adjusting to the hallway light. "Petre?"

"Maunders." It was the first time I'd spoken since I'd received my siblings' threats, which meant my mouth still had to catch up with my thoughts. I wished I'd practiced what I would say to him. "Come with me. I need injections. Quickly."

"Petre, I—?" He rubbed his eyes and blinked at me. "Your injections? What?"

"The IMI," I blurted. Intramuscular Memory Injections.

"I know what your injections are," he said. "You're not due to get them until tomorrow morning."

"I need them now." I needed to be able to coordinate myself before tomorrow morning. Without them I was about as physically adept as a wet paper bag. IMI could at least bring me up to the baseline of the average athlete before breakfast time tomorrow. "I need them *now*."

"Petre, it's dangerous—you can't—why—?"

I knew he needed more information, but I was struggling to array my facts on the fly. Instead, the details fell from my tongue in haywire fragments. "It's important. I just got this letter and I read it and my sister's about to host a coronation feast and all my siblings are reaching out to me about it and I've been thinking about it for a while and I haven't had a chance to tell anyone before you now but I was thinking maybe if you got me my injections I'd be prepared to deal with them and I think I can get them to cooperate if I just see them in person so then it'll be okay and nobody will be the wiser and I think maybe I can—"

"Petre," Avram drawled. "Slow down. Take a breath, Mercy."

"I just—"

He put up his palm. "What did I just say? You'll wake up the whole fortress at this rate."

It's funny, you know? It's not like he told me anything I didn't know. I knew I had to fucking breathe. But somehow when he said it—I don't know. He made it sound a lot more reasonable than I ever could.

So I obeyed. Only then did the noisy carousel of my mind begin to slow its spirals. The letter, crumpled up inside my pocket, still felt heavy and demanding. But I could breathe.

"Again," he said. "I want to hear you."

I did it again as Avram slapped himself awake, calloused hands sliding against blond stubble. "Alright. Alright. Alrightalrightalright. What's the problem, Petre?"

"I—"

"Actually. Don't answer that. You said you needed your injections?"

"Yes." The word burst out of me. I had too much to do. I couldn't waste time standing here and talking. My fingers made their way around the crumpled paper in my pocket. "Someone's coming tomorrow and I want to be prepared."

"Are you sure that's a good idea?"

"Depends."

"On what?"

"Are you asking if I think getting my injections is a good idea or are we talking about the thing I have to do after I get them?"

"Whatever it is you have to do."

Damn him. I knew clarifying would hamstring me. I owed him honesty. And he knew it. And I knew he knew I knew. "Not even a little bit."

Avram looked at me, scrutinizing the panic written deep into the contours of my face. "Tell me what's going on."

"I—"

"Slowly."

I swallowed. "Oh man. Where to start? I mean I just got another letter, but—"

His eyebrows shot up. "What do you mean *another* letter?"

Sometimes the more you worry the harder it becomes to convey what you're worried about. You spend enough time picking at the details like a scab, digging so deep beneath you start seeing bone. When someone actually notices, you're not sure how to explain anything anymore.

I forced myself to take another deep breath. "So my family started reaching out again three months ago. Right after I skipped—" I was not about to say the words *Dad's funeral*. That was absolutely not going to happen. "They've um. They've been checking in on me. But they're getting... nastier? I guess? They've started wheeling out some new threats, and I just—here. Look." I handed Avram the letter. It was a single page stuffed full of ire and ink.

Anxious breaths knifed out from my throat while Avram read. It didn't take him long. Each character was smudged by the side of a hand or drowned in ink. Desmon had sent me something halfway to an inkblot test.

Avram looked up from the page and sighed. "Come inside. Tell me what you want to do about this. I'll make coffee."

HE USED the letter as a coaster. His coffee cup made a brown ring on the empty inch at the tail end of the paper.

Avram leaned his elbows on his thighs. He pored over the red ink, reading the words while I watched the bald spot on the crown of his head for signs of life. I sat in silence as my heart nailed its rhythm to my throat.

"Who sent this?" Avram asked when he was done rereading.

"One of my brothers. Desmon."

"Is he the older one or the younger?"

"They're both older. By two minutes. I was born fourth."

"Right," he frowned. "I can never remember the birth order."

"Anoïse is the oldest. Then Edgar. Then Desmon. Then me."

"And it's Desmon who's asking you to come home?"

"Telling," I amended. "It's an order. And I think all three of them agree on it. Desmon's only acting as their mouthpiece. Anoïse is getting crowned in seven days. They want me to be there for it."

Avram scanned the letter again. "I didn't see that in here."

I balled up my hands in the space between my knees. "My other brother reached out too. Edgar. He sent a missive earlier today. Said he was in the area to pick me up. I think he's taking me to Anoïse so I can swear fealty before they put a crown on her head."

"How come you're only freaking out now, then?" Avram asked.

I shrugged. "Easier to ignore when I thought it was just him." Last time I saw him we'd fought with singlesticks in Dad's feast hall over a series of scandals too inane to reiterate. I was not sure whether or not we'd be on good terms when he got here. "He said he'd arrive at Blackheath House tomorrow morning. Anoïse and Desmon fucking sent him after me."

"And that's why you need your injections?"

"Yeah. Because if Ed takes me back there's no way they'll let me go as easy as they did last time. There's no way they'll bring me back just to swear an oath so they can let me go again."

Avram frowned. "Are you going to head back with him?"

I took my coffee cup between two fingers. The mug was

lukewarm. And worse, it was black. Was Avram aware coffee still woke you up when it didn't taste like murdered dreams? I downed a mouthful as I worked his question over.

My primary concern was the life I'd built in Blackheath House the last five years. I didn't want to leave. "I was hoping you could tell me."

Avram dragged an exhausted hand down his face. I braced for scorn. Judgment. But he had the audacity to pause and consider his words before he spoke. "That's a tough one." He tilted his head. "How do you think Edgar will react if he gets here just to find out that you're staying?"

Have you ever really stewed over someone? Ever knifed to the core of every interaction you've had with them, searching the entrails for signs of who they are and what they believe? You can spend so long agonizing over that inexact astrology that you lose sight of what they're truly capable of.

That was how I felt when I answered, "With threats. Escalation. I...I think I have to go back. I mean don't get me wrong—I don't *want* to leave you guys. But I don't see how staying wouldn't set off a whole conflict." If there was one thing my family was good at, it was blowing everything out of proportion. "I still haven't heard anything from Anoïse either. I have no idea what she thinks about all this."

"Maybe she's still mad at you about the funeral?"

God. I still couldn't figure out why anyone was still upset about that. "Look, she told me to do what I wanted. And I didn't want to go."

Avram looked vaguely troubled. "It isn't that simple, Petre."

"But that's what she said," I insisted. "Why would she

say it if that wasn't what she meant?" If none of my siblings cared enough to tell me what the fuck to do what right did they have to get upset about what I chose?

"Maybe she wanted you to come without putting pressure on you. Petre. She's allowed to be upset."

"I'm not saying she can't be upset." There was something here I seriously was not understanding. I wasn't sure if I ought to press the issue. "But why wouldn't she have *told* me what she wanted if it was that important to her?"

"It's not always that easy, Petre. It's not always that simple," Avram said again.

"Well it should be." I knew I was being unreasonable. "But if it meant so much to her...maybe that's why I have to go back."

"Do you think the risk of being held there is worth it? You said you weren't sure they would let you leave again if you go."

I sighed. "I don't know."

"I just don't want you to walk into a trap, Petre. You've told me what your life was like back home. I wouldn't want you getting stuck there all over again. I'd miss you, kid."

I didn't doubt it. Avram used to work in the capital as one of Dad's resident mad scientists. Labcoats, I think, was the polite term. He was exiled around the time the four of us were old enough to start learning about factions, when we were beginning to test how much we could interfere in each others' businesses.

And that's where I was headed back to. Tomorrow.

Fear curdled in my stomach. Goddammit. I needed my injections already. "Maunders. I—I have to go. I don't know if it's worth it, but I don't want the rest of you to get in trouble."

"Trouble?" Avram lifted an eyebrow.

"I have to swear fealty to Anoïse when she takes the throne in about a week." Was it that soon already? Goddamn. The Three Months of Mourning for Dad were almost up. "If I don't then people might start talking about me. Wondering if I've *ever* been loyal to Anoïse or the rest of my family, if I won't swear a vow on it. And from there rumors can spiral. Maybe they start worrying that I might be planning something. Maybe the people around me are involved. Maybe Blackheath House has eyes on the throne, and suddenly—"

"Petre. You're getting worked up again."

"Oh, right." I took a breath. Easy and slow. In and out. "I don't want anyone here tangled up in any accusations."

"It also sounds like you don't want to see Anoïse."

Unwanted memories squirmed into my mind. Visuals of the day I left five years ago. I had already been threatening to leave for years. Anoïse had thought it was an empty threat. But she was the only one who walked into the stables when I made good on it.

I'd thought she would be mad. Instead there were only tears and red faces and clogged throats. I remembered the exhausted squeal wrapped around her words when she begged me not to leave, and the feeling in my stomach when I left anyway.

The last thing I ever heard from her was *don't go.*

God. Anoïse was going to strangle me if I went back home.

Avram's voice extracted me from my thoughts. "I just want to make sure you're thinking this through. You've got a good thing going here. Mercedes Blackheath has been treating you *very* well, from what I hear. And you're not having any trouble killing Gaunts for her, right?"

"I always have trouble killing Gaunts," I said. "They

never asked to be what they are." Nobody *tries* to breathe in ghostfog. To get infected with dead lives. But once it happens the results are rarely pretty. You have to put them down before they hurt someone. "But I do it cause I owe it to Mercedes."

"So have you talked to her about this? You two are friends."

More than that, of late. A couple benefits had come about recently. She was older. She knew what she wanted, and that I wanted to give that to her. It was fucking fantastic, really. *Except!* "Mercedes isn't here right now." She was on a business trip off in a town called Bullion, closing some kind of deal.

"Well, yes. But it sounds like this has been building for a while, right? Are you telling me you never talked this out with her?"

I became acquainted with how a corkscrew feels as it gets twisted. I swallowed the mousy noise building in my throat as I debated how best to answer him. Five years I'd been working for Mercedes Blackheath. I'd fought for her. Killed for her. I even fucked for her. Put on a kind of paramour show. So it wasn't like I didn't trust her, you know?

It was just— "I can't!"

"Why?" Avram asked.

"I don't know, I just shouldn't—"

"You're planning on talking to her before you leave, right?"

Hesitating there was probably a mistake.

In the absence of an answer his eyes went wide. "PETRE! She's your friend. You can't just leave without telling her anything."

I tightened my jaw, biting off my first instinctual reply. Who was he to tell me what I should do? I came to him for advice, sure, but not because I didn't know how to handle my relation—oh.

Okay. Maybe he had a point. At least in part. And yet? I wasn't sure he understood why I might not want to tell Mercedes. I did have to leave quickly, after all.

I realized I was not speaking aloud. I cleared my throat. "She—she's an only child. She wouldn't understand. She'd try to stop me."

"She might," Avram said, quite reasonably. He propped his ankle on the opposite thigh. "I won't deny that. But does it change anything?"

"I don't know."

His voice hitched up an octave as he adopted the dry, grainy old man rasp he used when he was doling out advice. "You seem very nervous about leaving. Do you want to know what I think?"

"Are we getting to that at last?" I sounded more annoyed than I'd meant to. "I'm sorry."

Avram waved the matter aside. "You're fine. I promise. I only think that you seem *very* scared to leave. I think you know you're making a mistake. You're worried Mercedes will give you a reason to stay here."

"Or!" I leaned forward, put up both index fingers. I was beginning to regret coming to him for advice. This was not going the way I'd pictured it. "Hear me out. Or! Maybe I *know* I need to go back. Maybe what I want doesn't exactly factor in. Maybe I'm worried she'll convince me to stay— because if I do that then everyone gets hurt."

Avram fidgeted. The chair creaked under his weight. "It doesn't sound like there's a way out of this without hurting."

"I just—" Exasperation filled me. "I don't know, Maunders. I just think it should be my mistake to make." I'd burned enough bridges with my family over the years. If I could just patch things up maybe they'd let me breathe. Maybe they'd let me come back to all this when I was done. Maybe.

Avram uncrossed his legs. He leaned forward and meshed up his fingers in between his thighs. He just looked at me for a while, smiling sadly. "Damn you," he said.

I blinked at him. "I wasn't aware I'd done anything."

"You're right," he sighed. "I can't in good conscience keep you here against your will. That sounds like something your family would do."

I felt the kind of guilty twinge you get in your stomach when you win an argument by taking things too far. "R-right."

"It *is* your mistake to make, you're right. And I do think it's a mistake. Let's be clear about that. But...if injections will keep you safe *while* you make this mistake, I figure I ought to juice you up before you go."

"So you'll help?"

He had to stop and think then. Hope floundered in my belly. "The last thing you need is withdrawals on the road. I've been hearing rumors there are more Gaunts out there than usual lately." Avram twisted his mouth like he was chewing on the thought. "I don't like it. And I don't like that you're making me complicit. I hope you understand that."

"Maunders—" It wasn't like that. Why couldn't he see?

He put his hand up. "I'm not saying I won't. I can't force you to do anything. I'm just telling you how I feel. Is that alright?"

"I...yeah. Keep going."

Avram blinked. "No, that was it. I dislike being dragged into this. But if you really think you should go, the last thing I want is for you to get hurt."

15

My stomach curdled in the anticipation of the pain about to come. "Thank you, Maunders. Seriously. It's—"

"Let's just get to the basement. Get you strapped down before I change my mind."

I wasn't sure if I could call this a victory.

CHAPTER

TWO

You ever retreat so far into your own terrified thoughts that reality itself seems to wither around you? Trawl the depths of your psyche thoroughly enough and remembered pain can nearly bleed through to your physical body. It's like there's an ambient unease nesting in the site of a recollected injury.

That's what happened on my way down to the basement under Blackheath House. That's what always happened. Once every three months, for the past seven years. Ugly anticipation churned in my guts. My skin felt tight, every sinew like a wire under stress.

But I had to do it. I had to. My siblings and I were used to the occasional brawl, and without Intramuscular Memory Injections I wasn't even able to achieve basic competency in anything involving fighting, riding, sword work, sneaking, or court etiquette.

The injections could code coordination into you for a little while. It was a warm gray sludge with patterns of programmed movement. The heat of the injections guided you. It told you where to go and how to move— though sometimes if your dose was high enough it could yank you around a little bit. It wouldn't make me a superhero or anything, but it would help me remember how to throw a punch or make sure I didn't start stimming in front of Edgar, if nothing else.

Avram fumbled with a ring of keys. "Can never remember which one it is." I swore he teased a grin when he looked down to check. Inserted one and took it out. "Nope. Not that one."

I felt like I was being chewed up. All I could think about were the straps waiting for me on the other side of the door. They weren't even the fun kind.

And Lord, the *needles*. I never got used to it. I just wanted it to be over with, and here was Avram taking his dear sweet time.

"You're doing this on purpose," I complained.

"I don't know what you're talking about," Avram said. "I'm just trying to find a key." He put one in and turned it, then shoved the door with his shoulder. It took a few tries to get the damn thing to budge. It always liked to get stuck in the stupid frame. It let out a screech like tires squealing as it swung open. "See? C'mon inside."

Avram switched on the floodlights. I shut my eyes for a few seconds and counted backwards from ten, just to get a grip on myself. It was a lot of sensory input all at once. Autism never handled the glare of bright lights well. It was like the visual equivalent of a noise that's loud enough to hurt your ears.

Basement mold had colonized the room. The stink of musk mingled with the bloody smell of the rusty pipes and sour sweat. I'd never grown accustomed to it.

"Make yourself at home, kid." Avram sat the coffee cup he'd brought with him down on the counter in front of a giant screen that made half the wall into a black void.

"Not a kid," I murmured, as I approached the chair in the center of the room. It was a reclined patient's chair made of cracked black leather, and it was shedding asymmetric scales, like some kind of decomposing sheath over a mattress of spongy, cake-colored foam.

"You're a kid to me." Avram took another sip of coffee before he switched on the screen, and it glowed blue. The blaring noise of all the brightness sapped my focus. I felt hollow.

Avram punched a code into the keyboard. I swallowed. It felt like there was pressure pushing on me from the inside out. He finished the input. The machine's guts wailed and groaned while his code made electric currents in the tangled pipelines. This was body language all reduced to ones and zeros.

I'd never learned much about how corpse technology functions. All I knew was that they were the scientific ruins left behind after the Second Annihilation. The same way the First Annihilation left behind magic landscapes that weren't supposed to exist.

I had no idea how it made viscous gray sludge respond to computer code. So I just listened, eyes forward, as the thin iron-colored fluid made its slow drip into the five syringes on the counter beside Avram.

"I'm old enough to know what I'm doing," I said, as Avram crossed the room to strap me in. He reached across my headrest for the buckle, one hand braced on my shoulder. It was cold. I shuddered.

"You're twenty-three, Petre." He buckled the first strap, pinning my forehead to the headrest.

"You say that like it's a contradiction or something." I

tried to pass off my nervous laughter as something closer to a genuine joke.

He grinned. "You'll understand when you make it to my age."

Making it to his age was not the kind of assumption I was prepared to make with Edgar coming in the morning. I'd be lucky if we didn't kill each other before we made it out of the courtyard.

My left wrist got buckled in next. Fuck. Why was I doing this? Was it too late to reschedule? Edgar wouldn't mind if I ducked out on him to get my dose tomorrow, right?

It took me a moment to realize I hadn't answered Avram. "You don't look a day over thirty-seven, Maunders," I said on impulse.

He strapped my thighs in tighter than I would've liked. "You're funny," he said, no humor in his voice. He stooped to bind my ankles to the chair.

"I'm serious!" I protested as he circled around to buckle my right wrist down. "I'll swear on any God you like, I really did not believe you the first time you told me your age."

He paused with the buckle, grinning. "Last chance to itch."

I groaned. "Well now that you *say* it—" I scratched a spot on the side of my nose that came to my attention, then he buckled me in. "Fuck. Maunders, man. I think I've still got a little thing in the corner of my eye. Is it too late to—"

"You're fine, Petre. Just relax."

I tried to steady my thoughts.

"You're okay." He squeezed my shoulder.

"I know," I lied. "I know." But I wasn't okay. Anything

involving being immobilized in order to receive a great deal of pain and heat was decidedly not okay.

Well. Not *anything*. But most things. Probably.

Certainly this, at least.

"I'd think you would be used to this by now," Avram said.

"You really would think that, wouldn't you? The only thing these last seven years have taught me is how to dread this more."

I was thankful he had strapped my head down so tight. I couldn't move to look at the needles.

"You're prepared though, yeah?"?" He took my trousers down. I felt his hands bunching up one of the legs of my boxers, exposing the upper portion of my thigh to basement air.

I took some deep breaths. I was not about to get hard while strapped down like this. I was not about to mortify myself like that. I swear to God. "Careful with your hands down there, old man."

"You're not my type," Avram said.

"I'm offended. Why not?"

He produced my mouthguard and stuffed it between my teeth. He was rudely direct about the whole thing. "Well, it's like you said." His antiseptic wipe made cold wet circles on the outside of my thigh. "I prefer my partners looking not a day younger than thirty-seven."

The needle pinched. The dry heat of gray fluid uncoiled into the space between skin and sinew. My teeth squeezed my mouthguard thin as molten muscle memory sluiced through me. My leg juddered; uncontrolled movements burned as the sludge crawled just beneath my skin. The leather on the constraints squealed as I jerked involuntarily.

The urge to run filled every corner of my body. The real world went away. There was just pain as my leg jolted against the restraints. The injections filled my body with heat and synthetic memories all at once. Sinews attempted to move like I was riding, feinting, or lunging with a sword. Programmed data stretched my muscles. I was breathing hard. My fingers strained to try and break free of the leather holding my wrists down.

Fuck fuck fuck. I had to get out of there. But I was pinned down. All I could do was grit my teeth as I shuddered through the information input. The muscles in the side of my neck went taut as the heat spiraled through me. A raw groan slid out of my throat as my fingernails made smirk-impressions in my palm.

He had to cut my leg off. That was the only way out of it, right? Lord, why had I agreed to let him do this?

I twisted against the straps holding me down as a feeling like melted wax slid underneath my skin. It was like there was a red-hot animal trapped within me, scuttling. I bucked my hips. Tried to twist away from what was already in me as short, frustrated breaths shot through my nose.

Then the heat cooled, like magma turning to stone. I blinked through the haze. The world felt very far away. There was only the sound of my breath and the rise and fall of my chest.

My senses expanded, and I felt sweat drip from my hair onto my nose. My chest itched. I wanted to put my nails on it. I reached instinctively to scratch before I remembered I was restrained. Distantly, I realized I'd started giggling.

I only remembered that Avram was still there when his hand brushed my cheek, he slid the rubber mouthguard out of my mouth. A line of gathered drool followed it out. A strand snapped, spilling down my chin and throat to pool in the space between my collarbones. I was a mess of sweat and spit. I coughed.

Avram shook excess saliva off the mouthguard while I sucked down grateful lungfuls of moldy basement air.

"How are you feeling, kid? Where are you at?"

"I've been better." I laughed. "Though you've got better bedside manners than Mom ever did. I ever tell you she was the one who gave me these shots back home?" Every breath rocked through me like it had tangible weight.

"I'm aware. I helped her perfect the technology while I was there. Before your dad tossed me out of the capital."

"Funny how that works," I said. "Mom used to have a strap on this kind of chair for my chest, you know."

"Used to?" Avram asked.

"Had to remove it after the time I broke my ribs."

"Good Lord. I'm surprised you kept with it."

"I couldn't stop bumping into door frames on my way around Mercy House. She thought it was embarrassing." And while Mom could never cure my autism, she could cure the imperfections in my body. So she got me on this shit. It was the best compromise she could come up with. Which was saying something, because Mom was probably one of the smartest people in the whole damn country.

She was the daughter of a couple minor bureaucrats in Dad's court. Her parents sent her to study with the labcoats when she was thirteen, in the hopes that an education could earn her an advantageous marriage.

And she *excelled*. She spent years working her way up to the top of her class, dissecting every shred of corpse technology she came across, earning top marks. She had a bright career ahead of her.

Then she met Dad. She was seventeen. He was forty-three. He pursued her for a while. The way Dad told it he'd never met a girl before who'd told him no. And when courtship didn't work, he decided it would be easier to go over her head with it. So he did some digging and showed up on her parent's doorstep.

Mom didn't want to marry Dad, but her parents just had *so* many business interests, you know? A few sinking companies, a couple of bad debts—and their creditors were getting angry. Why, a marriage to a King could make those problems simply disappear. And really, they'd been doing her so many favors, weren't they? They'd enrolled her in all those classes and paid for her education, so if she was *really* grateful for everything they'd done—well. You see where this is going, right?

She rolled with it. She did what she was told.

The whole affair took nine months in total. Mom's parents even provided fertility pills to make sure Mom produced an heir. In another few months she birthed the four of us in one go.

Nobody's quite sure why she threw that all away. Though there are several educated guesses. Anoïse figured she'd probably have done anything by that point to get an annulment. To get away from Dad. I wouldn't blame her, to be honest. Once a friend of Edgar suggested Dad had had plans to depose her, so she had to move first. And one time one of Dad's advisors guessed there was some kind of blackmail involved—maybe someone found some dirt on her. The same kind of shady shit that got Avram tossed out of the capital, maybe. I don't know.

What we *do* know is that at the time she betrayed Dad, Mom was Queen. She oversaw the labcoats, and knew more about technology than anyone else at court. And she used her position to convince a few vassals of Mercy House that *they* ought to be in charge instead of Dad. She told them she could make that happen.

Word got out, obviously. Dad had Mom's parents and his disloyal vassals hanged. He had considered putting Mom to death, too. The only problem was that she was too valuable as a labcoat. She knew too much about the ways that corpse technologies worked. In ways she hadn't shared with other labcoats. In ways no other labcoats could replicate. He needed her just to keep the damn place running. So he settled for locking her up, down in the basement.

She's been there ever since.

I was extracted from my musing as Avram stuffed my mouthguard back between my teeth.

I didn't realize how long I'd been lost in my head, pursuing the relief of unrelated thoughts, until my right thigh tightened around the needle Avram introduced.

Slowly, excruciatingly, we went through each injection. One for each limb. Sending preprogrammed motions in angry pathways through me with every dose. One by one we went through them. Until I was barely more than a stinging, sweaty red heap.

And then all that was left was the worst one. "Do you enjoy seeing me like this, Maunders?" I asked, to buy some time before the final shot. "You like tying me down like this?"

"I'm old enough to be your father, Petre."

A ragged laugh clawed its way out of my throat. "I dunno. Feels like you're having fun watching me squirm."

"I'm literally just giving you what you asked." He shook my mouthguard dry. "Though I won't pretend this isn't a little cathartic." He presented the last syringe. I sized up the needle. Dread made my stomach tight. I swallowed.

"You sure that's the last one? Nothing else left?"

"You can take a breather before we start on this one if you want."

I didn't even need to debate it. "Nah, man. Fuck it. Get it over and done with. I don't want to prolong this." I barely had a moment to gulp down air before Avram shoved the mouthguard back between my teeth. I had to work it into its proper place with my tongue. My teeth found their impressions in the rubber.

This shot went right below the navel. I couldn't see him deliver it. I just knew it started when the pinching did. A long, unending pinch sinking down, down, down. As if my skin was tightening around the needle. Collapsing in on it.

The sensation faded into the background once the injections came through. The gray sludge swirled like hot grease under my stomach. The heat drowned out the pain of the needle as it swam out from the injection. The heat rifled through my guts. For a long, horrible moment I couldn't even feel my heartbeat. I just strained against the straps. Twisted and screamed and wondered if I could chew my mouthguard into a tangled ball of rubber. Maybe I'd find a way to chew my tongue off next.

My chest became a forge bellow. Every breath only seemed to fuel the heat. I felt like it would burn through me and leave me a melted mess upon the table.

And then it started cooling. I felt weak. Exhausted. I wanted to sleep, but I was in too much pain. I wasn't sure if I could manage it. There was a reason I normally got these in the mornings.

Avram unstrapped me and I staggered down from my seat, skin peeling off the leather chair as I came free. The world was still hazy. I fumbled to get my trousers up and put my belt back on. "Fuck me, man. I never get used to this shit."

"I've noticed," Avram said. "But you're doing alright. Just—be careful. You got this dose twelve hours early. That means twelve hours of overlap with your last dose. It'll take a few hours for you to adjust. And there might be side effects."

"Yeah. Yeah. I just...just need a breath." I pinched the corners of my eyes. "A breather, I mean. I don't care about side effects. As long as it's done with in the morning. When Edgar gets here."

"Take your time," Avram said. "As long as you need. Weeks, even."

I straightened. "C'mon man. I told you I have to go!"

"I know, I know. I just—"

"You got siblings, Maunders?" I don't think I'd ever asked him that before. I wondered if I ought to feel guilty about that. I'd never found a reason to ask before. But what if he did? That's a while to go without learning that about someone.

"Used to. Cancer took her. I was fifteen."

I wasn't sure what to say. What do you say to something like that? I settled on, "How old was she?"

"Four."

I felt like my legs were going to give out—and not just from the soreness and the spasms. It was hard to explain to him why I needed to leave after that kind of statement. "You're not making this easy." I realized I'd said the wrong thing when he glowered at me. "God, I'm sorry."

He wrenched his gaze away from me. I was ashamed of how relieved I felt. "I should hope so, kid," he said.

"I just—" I performed a sort of noncommittal half gesture with my hands, then tightened them to fists and pressed my lips together. "You know?"

Avram just looked at me, confused.

"I don't know the details of what's going on back home. I mean—I know I have to attend the feast in seven days. But I don't want to risk that there might be something else driving their urgency. Something—you know—similar to... all that." The cancer and stuff.

Dad had been done in by a bout with lymphoma. Maybe someone else had it, and my siblings wanted me to make peace. That would explain the urgency in their letter. Why I had to go back. To make things right.

Though I did not like the panic that inspired.

"I know what you mean," Avram said. He spoke slowly. Like he was choosing his next words carefully. "But you're not going to talk me out of how I feel. I doubt I'll be able to do the same to you either, so—look. Right now we just have to focus on getting you to your chamber."

"What's going to be so difficult about—" I went to take my first step since he'd unstrapped me. I was numb, and really had to *think*. I had to actively remember how to move my leg.

Only when I tried, jolts of pain traveled in burning ribbons under my skin. My injections shot up through my right calf. They tried to help me along. But it felt like there was a simmering, bubbling feeling beneath my kneecap. The heat moved downward and clenched around my thigh. I felt the muscles there seizing up. As if skin was wrapping itself around that point.

I fell to one knee. "The hell was that?" I asked. "Did my center of gravity shift?"

"This was what I was trying to tell you about earlier," Avram said. "You were supposed to get your next dose in the morning. Your body still hasn't finished clearing out the last one."

"What, so now I can't even walk right?"

"Only for a few hours."

"You're *joking*."

"You asked me to juice you up, kid. Don't blame me for obliging."

"Why didn't you *tell* me?"

He shrugged. "Would it have stopped you?"

Fuck, he had me there. I frowned. "Doubtful."

"Then why waste time on the formality?" His hands were around me. One on my chest. The other tucked under one armpit and wrapped around my back.

"Feel free to dig your nails in if the spirit moves you," I said, without meaning to. My hand clamped tight over my mouth of its own accord. This also was a thing that happened without my permission. It took some effort to wrench it away. I actually had to peel my fingers off with my free hand.

Was I blushing? Could he see me turning red? "Avram." I looked at him out of the corner of my eye.

He kept his gaze forward. I was vaguely aware through the haze of fuzzy pain swimming through my mind that he was helping me through the door. "Petre."

"That was supposed to be an inside thought. Why did I say that aloud? Was that one of the side effects?"

"You ever hear the phrase *don't think about white elephants?*"

"I think I see where this is going."

"Should clear up in a few hours. Until then we'll tie you down."

I shut my eyes. I wasn't going to say anything. I wasn't going to let it win. I pressed my teeth together as my injections burned the sinews in my throat. I made a few choked gurgles as my lips turned white with pressure.

Then the IMI yanked my mouth open and stuffed new

words into it. "If this was all it took, I would've overdosed years ago—FUCK!" Breathing burned. My lungs felt sore. "The curse at the end was real," I admitted. "That one was me."

"Frankly I didn't notice a difference."

"Give me some credit. Usually I have *some* filter, Maunders. Goddamn. How come this shit is making me *say* things? I thought it only affected—"

"You've got muscles in your mouth, last I checked," Avram said. "And the IMI goes where your thoughts go."

I hated that. Because my thoughts were not something entirely within my control. "Ah shit. That's ridiculous. Come on, I—hey when did we get into the hallway?"

Raincloud gray walls boxed us in on either side. Every step felt like red hot knives sliding through my foot and up into my legs.

I collapsed. Heat stabbed through my knees and jolted through my palms. It was like burning needles sliding *just* beneath the surface of the skin. My throat felt tight and full in the way it often does before you vomit. My breaths were shallow, and I felt sweaty.

"Maunders," I said. "I dunno about this, old man."

"It's like any other dose, Petre." The fact that Avram was calm felt irritating. "It goes where your attention goes. It's just *more* this time."

"I know how my injections work, dammit. I just didn't know getting juiced up early would hurt like this." That would explain why it only hurt to walk when I was focused on walking. But usually the burn was not this bad. It was closer to the gentle heat on hands held out before a fireplace. I couldn't remember the last time it felt this intense.

Avram frowned. "Would you prefer to have *no* dose when Edgar gets here?" He reached down to help me up.

I focused on my breathing. Kept my mind blank. My injections couldn't hurt me if my thoughts could not activate it. Together we staggered through the hallway. "You certainly seemed to prefer it."

"I'd prefer your brother not come here at all. But I don't think it's my place to tell you what to do."

"That's why I love you, you know."

Avram laughed. "Was that one the IMI again?"

I indulged in a grin. "No," I said. "That one was me."

CHAPTER

THREE

M y memories of the next few hours were vague, insipid—like bruises in my mind. It was like trying to recall a dream of sleepwalking.

That's the trouble with agony, isn't it? The way it drowns you, eats up all your patience and attention. Even an itch can make it difficult to focus. Dial that up to the red heat that I dealt with from the dose crawling through my veins and at a certain point the pain drags you under, and it's like the whole world is intangible.

You know the feeling when your mind and the reality around you seem to trade places? When it feels as though that world behind your eyelids has more weight and is more real than anything that lingers right in front of you. That was the place my mind was stuck in as Avram guided me to my chamber. I remember his hands on me, and his breath in my ear. I tried not to linger on the arousal it inspired. I was worried my injections would force me to touch my cock in front of him if I focused on that too long. Or worse—touch *his*. That was a nightmare I didn't even want to begin to think about. Good Lord.

Fuck. Why hadn't he warned me this was a risk? Why the hell was he willing to brave all this just to get me to my chamber?

Everything was all a blur of heat and tightness and movement. I felt divorced from the world. Divorced from my body. My only companion was the constant pain.

Though I must have slept at some point. That was the only time no agony lived in me for the night. The only time I was allowed to feel nothing.

WHEN I AWOKE in the morning, it took a few tries to convince my eyelids to work with me. I peeled them open slowly, like the skin on a blister, and I winced.

The room was a silent riot. Too much stimuli. The way the sweat plastered the bedsheets to my back inspired revulsion, and the clammy heat still in my belly made me want to vomit. For a moment I considered just going back to sleep.

"Ah, you're awake." It was Avram's voice.

I blinked and shook my head to free my mind of the sleepy cobwebs housed within it. "I do anything in my sleep?"

"Don't worry, I've been making sure you don't stay asleep long enough to dream. I wouldn't want to risk it on this dose. Who knows what signals your injections would mistake for input?"

"Terrific." I managed to sit up of my own volition. That was progress. Though half the bed sheets joined me, clinging to the sweat on my back. "How long has it been?" I wondered why the IMI had not tightened a fist around me again yet. Had I leveled out on my dose?

"It's just barely six in the morning," Avram said.

"You get any sleep?" I asked. Even in the semidarkness I could see the bruise-colored smudges under his eyes.

Avram scratched the back of his neck. "You're a real handful, you know that?"

"I try," I said.

"At least Edgar is coming in a bit," Avram offered. "Your old dose will have cleared your system soon. Imagine if he had reached out days ago."

Something shriveled in my stomach. "I'd rather not."

"You were lucky, is all I'm saying. Hell, you're lucky Mercedes is off in Bullion. I don't know how I would've explained all this to her."

"Yeah." I shrugged. "Real fortunate." I wasn't sure if I sounded sarcastic, so I added, "No seriously. I don't want to take all your help for granted. I really do appreciate it."

Avram raised a coffee cup in a sort of toast. I wondered when he'd left to get more. Or had he used my coffee maker while I was asleep? "You don't need to tell me. I know you do."

"I don't suppose my brother has arrived yet?"

"Oh! A courier just informed me he was close. Said they'd come by when they had him in the courtyard."

Panic squeezed my heart. "Did you tell anyone about the injections?" Edgar couldn't know I'd marked him as a potential threat. I wanted to keep my suspicions private until I knew how he'd receive my misgivings.

Avram made his mouth a tight line. "Thought we'd best keep that one between us. I can handle rumors."

"Ah, man. I'm sorry you have to deal with that at all, though."

Avram shrugged and stared into his coffee cup. He

traced the lip of it with his thumb. "Hardly the worst rumor floating around about me."

That was true, at least. I'd heard a few myself. They usually involved human experimentation and reanimating old corpse technology.

I didn't want to ask Avram if those were the rumors he was referring to. It was a touchy subject, and I'd never quite found a comfortable way to broach it. And those weren't even the only ones. There were a couple involving him and my mom that I never really wanted to think about. Even a little bit.

The injection-burn that crept into the muscles of my jaw took me off guard. I had a moment to exhale a panicked little "Oh no," before my injections spat out, "And what rumors are those?" My attempt to close my jaw only wound up making my next words sound over-enunciated during the struggle. "Were you fucking my mom or something?"

As soon as the words were out I put my head in my hands and sank back on the bed. My back conformed to fit my sweat imprint. "God. I guess this hasn't worn off yet, huh?"

"Did you not mean to say that?" Avram asked. I was surprised he wasn't laughing at me.

"Maunders, why on earth would I ask that on purpose?" I wanted to blush myself to cinders.

Avram shrugged. "You've indicated that I'm your type, is all." His innocent tone was feigned. I'd bet money on it.

I felt my right hand rising. I was still trying to figure out what urge the injections were responding to when it crashed down on my cheek. My own palm filled my face with prickly heat. I slapped myself again. Again. I reached out to catch my own wrist, but the gray sludge kept pressing down, trying to hit my face.

Avram bolted from his chair. "HEY! *HEY!* HEYHEYHEY-HEHEY! PETRE! STOP IT!" He leapt onto the bed and held my arm down. My arm juddered, muscles spasming under skin. My injections rumbled in my chest, as though the force I would've put into the slap had to ripple through my shoulder.

"Breathe," Avram said. "Breathe, Petre."

The heat faded, leaving me sore in half my body. I took a breath as the shudders died down. "I can't meet Edgar like this. How long before this wears off?"

Avram slid off me and all but collapsed back into his chair. "Listen."

"Maunders, I need an answer."

"It's not an exact science."

"Then *estimate*," I said through clenched teeth.

Avram massaged his temples. "That was probably the last of it. You might have one or two more of these outbursts in you. We'll have to see. We won't know until it happens."

I rolled my eyes. "Encouraging."

"You're probably fine. There was only a twelve hour overlap between doses. Your previous dose has probably been bleached out of your system by now."

I groaned. "I'm gonna need you to change that metaphor for me before I get up and try to drink bleach."

Avram frowned. "Shit, Petre. Is that what you're thinking about?"

"I mean." I shrugged. "Not on purpose, but—"

"Do you...do you *want* to drink bleach?"

"What? Good Lord, no. You think I get a choice in what I fixate on? Things just pop in there whether I want them to or not, and I'm stuck thinking about it for a bit. I can't help it. Just change the subject already."

Avram frowned. "Well...it looks like you're not getting up to try it, right?"

"So far, yeah."

"So there's a chance these aftershocks are over with."

"They'd better be," I snapped. "Okay. Okay okay okay. Good. Good. We can do this. We've got this."

"What is it we've got?"

"I dunno. I'll figure it out when Edgar gets here."

Avram raised an eyebrow. "You do have a plan, yes? Beyond asking me to juice you up?"

I scoffed. "What? Yeah, man. Of course I have a plan. I mean. Haha. What kind of idiot doesn't plan for when his brother shows up to collect him after several urgent letters from his family while everyone's acting weird? You'd have to be a real dumbass to not have a plan, right?"

"Right..."

I rubbed the heels of my hands into my eyes. Pressed down on my eyelids until my vision went yellow.

"So...?" Avram asked.

"The plan," I said, "is that I'm going to play whatever bullshit game he and the other two are playing. And if he tries to keep me from coming back here after we're done and all the oaths are sworn I'll beat his ass. Then I'll tell him he and Desmon and Anoïse need to leave me alone."

A moment of held breath and anticipation hung in the air between us in the time it took Avram to consider his next words. "Um," he said. "Are you sure that's wise?"

"I can't exactly beat his ass while he's still acting friendly, can I? He'll give me a good reason eventually, I'm sure."

"I don't know how I feel about the idea of beating asses in the first place." I wasn't sure how he managed to keep his voice level.

"He's going to try to fuck with me in *some* way," I reasoned. He always did. All three of them did. "And when he does it will give me all the excuse I need to get away, you know? Does that make sense?"

"Mostly." Avram said. "The problem is you seem to want my seal of approval on this plan. And I don't think I can do that."

I found the courage to try sitting up again. "No, okay, that's fair. I mean—I just don't know of an alternative. But I appreciate that you're not crossing a line just because I drew it. I mean obviously I'd *prefer* you agree with me, but—"

"I don't think that's going to happen," he said, not unkindly.

"Yeah, I figured. So I appreciate the honesty. Lord. How much time have we—"

A knock sounded on the door. I jumped. "Hello?"

"Your Grace," a courier, a woman's voice, announced, behind the door. "I've been sent to inform you that the prince is waiting outside."

"Right. Tell him I'll be down in a second."

"He has requested no ceremonies or formalities," the courier added.

Avram and I exchanged a look. "Huh." I said. Then louder, to the courier, I added, "Understood. I'll still be a few minutes. Make sure he knows that."

The courier said she would. Avram and I waited for her footsteps to go silent before one of us spoke.

No ceremonies? That was odd. *Very* odd. A break with every regulation I was used to. I didn't think he was in any particular hurry, nor was there any reason to keep things covert. So why didn't he want formalities?

"Any ideas?" Avram asked.

"No clue," I admitted. "But it's interesting." Usually every step to prepare for a coronation was nothing *but* ceremonies. I always hated them. They were loud and obnoxious and involved too many primary colors, but I didn't dare to hope he was sparing me out of the goodness of his heart. There had to be a reason he benefited from picking me up covertly. I just wasn't sure what it was. "Guess I have to get ready, don't I?" Fuck. Where was my gas mask? There'd be ghostfog out there. And I'd need to get dressed.

"You think there's a trap?" Avram asked, as I hauled a trunk out from under my bed. "I can come with you if you want."

Oh, there was absolutely a trap. What *kind* was the only matter still up for debate. "I...I think I should see Edgar alone. At first, at least. Not that I don't think it'd be helpful to have you around. But like..." I scratched the back of my neck. "It's been five years, you know?"

Avram examined my room methodically. "Take your chameleon coat."

I looked at where it sat, lank, on a hanger in my closet. It was an old birthday present Mom made for me when I was sixteen. *To help with masking* she'd said when I'd unwrapped it. *Less pressure if there are fewer people looking at you.*

"But don't you think Ed's going to take this as a challenge?" Edgar was always closer to Mom than I was. He had the better position at court as the second oldest, and there were fewer things about him that she needed to fix. They got on far better than I ever could with her. Wearing this gift from her might make him think I was trying to signal something.

"Does it matter if he does?" Avram asked. "He can take

39

it however he likes. I think it'd help you to have it. Especially if you need to make any...getaways."

I trusted Avram's judgment. "That's smart," I conceded, and crossed the room to retrieve it. "No telling what's coming. It's smart. That's a good idea, Maunders. Thank you."

The chameleon coat took the form of a big gray greatcoat in the low light. I crossed the room in two strides, shrugged it on and patted it down. "Oh, I left a few cigarettes of Muse in here." Always helped to have some drugs on hand when dealing with family.

"That's good to hear," Avram said, as I made for the exit.

"Petre."

I jerked around to face him. "Huh?"

"Sword, too. And mask."

"Right." They were stashed in a trunk under my bed. The science-sword was an old gift Avram got me after I arrived in Blackheath House. He'd chosen the saber model, as sharp as cracked glass. It was slightly curved and came with a knuckle bow, a thumb ring, and a grip made of red leather. The handle was hollow and housed a battery made from an artificial human thyroid that Avram farmed himself. It pumped the hormones that regulate body temperature through some kind of wirework that translated it into heat conducted on the blade's edge with an intensity that could cut through most solid objects. Except, of course, other science-swords.

I took a caterwauler with me, too. Just to be safe—a small sonic handgun with a battery of artificial vocal cords. If you set it to kill you'd have one shot before it recharged. Lowering the setting to stun gave you two shots. I wasn't sure what I was in for, but I figured I might need it.

I plunged the barrel into the prongs waiting at the bottom of the holster and thumbed the lever to charge it up, then I strapped it on.

"Right. Am I forgetting anything else? Or am I all set?"

"I just—I'll miss you, you know. Even if you're only leaving for a little while."

"Don't worry," I said. "If anything happens, I'll be sure to ask myself what you'd do."

Avram actually laughed at that. He put one hand over his chest, as if he had to steady himself. "Oh man. You can't say things like that, kid. Now we're all in trouble. Lord help us. Promise me you'll be back soon, you hear me?"

"I will," I said. "I promise."

Avram grinned at me. "You're going to be great."

FOUR

R ight. So the only thing between me and my brother was a couple more Blackheath House hallways.

First time in five years.

No big deal, right?

Who was I kidding? I couldn't even pretend I was holding up well. I was home to too many thoughts, all at once. My skull was buzzing, swimming through the white noise of all the hidden meanings tucked inside conversations that I hadn't even conducted yet.

I still had to actually *meet* him, and on the way there all I could do was plant dialogue trees. I put my hands in my coat pockets. My old knife was waiting there for me. I toyed with the outline of its scabbard. Then I drew it from my pocket and the sheath and traced the blade's edge with my thumb without quite applying enough pressure to slice the skin.

It helped, holding that, to steady myself. It was an activity I could ground myself in.

I'd stolen the knife from Dad when I was eighteen. Any knife would've done the job, but this one was his. That was why I wanted it. My grandfather had given it to him as a reward for his heroism during The Bastards' Rebellion. It was a prized possession. His reward for successfully keeping my grandfather's throne.

And I stole it.

It happened right before I left, too.

I'd gotten in trouble for trying to take a small whale-bone ship out for a joyride. I'd been trying to impress a wainwright's daughter and her boyfriend. But The Mercy Guard had caught me in the act. Dad had hauled me into his office and thrown me down in a big chair on the other side of his huge coffin-sized desk. He'd been about to chew me out. It was going to be one of those big old fifty-minute rants. But as he took in that first breath—I think it was Lord Havilan Reacher who called him away.

I was alone. And the knife was just *sitting* there. So I took it. How could I not? You know? And do you want to know the funny part? I'm not even sure *why* I did it. All I knew was that the knife meant the world to him, and now it was mine.

You ever get *stuck* in one of the moods where you just can't stomach the idea that somebody else is out there having a nice day? Where your whole day is comprised of thoughts you'd never share with anyone? Where all you're capable of is being someone else's personal rain cloud? Well. When that's your *baseline*—when it's all you know—you learn to excuse a lot of ugly shit.

I'm not sure how long I centered myself, my thoughts, on that knife. I considered thumbing the gadget worked into the hilt to make the blade start spinning like a chain-saw. I decided against it. We wouldn't want to keep Edgar waiting, would we? I put the knife away.

The sunlight hemorrhaged through orange plasma

windows that shimmered in between the rib cage arch-ways. I was almost at the doors to the courtyard, so I retrieved my gas mask and tied it over my my mouth and nose. I'd picked the one with two big filters inset with jewels. "Alright." I took a deep breath. The microphone inside crackled with feedback. "Here we go."

I shoved the double doors open, exited out Blackheath House's fossilized lizard mouth and stepped into the courtyard.

You expect a bit of fanfare when you're meeting royalty. Or at least I'd learned to. You weren't allowed to travel anywhere alone. You were always traveling with a coterie of security guards, at least. If not a whole display of pageantry. Trumpets, banners, scutcheons, everything. Sometimes, if we were good, Dad would let one of us wear the old ancestral helmet. A big, enclosed pot of red steel with black mastodon tusks making semicircles on either side of your jawline. It was heavy as hell, and it made your neck and the space between your shoulder blades ache. But the looks you got when people saw you made that worth it.

I knew he said no ceremonies, but I'd figured Edgar was at *least* going to have a train of followers with him. Or maybe a few members of The Mercy Guard. Havilan Reacher, surely. He'd always been a mentor to Ed, on top of being in charge of the guard. He'd have to come, right?

But no. Instead, all I got in greeting was a dry ice smog of ghosts smearing the empty early morning air. It was dense today. More so than usual.

I mean, don't get me wrong—the world's been full of ghosts for some time now. Ever since we blew up half the planet, at least. But the morning air wasn't often *this* clouded with semiconscious fog. The specters shimmered out their capers through the yard, twitching like flames still cruelly bound to a wick.

I checked the strap that fixed the gas mask to my face. Didn't want to invite ghost air into my lungs. I wasn't about to chance infection and go Gaunt. I had to make sure it was secure.

I pushed through the early morning's graveyard mist, my boots knocking on the flagstones. I curled my hand around the curved red grip of my science-sword. Every nerve was alive while I looked for my brother, my heart making crazed judders in anticipation.

"Petre!" It was Edgar's voice. My injections yanked me in the direction of his shout. I could barely see him through the ghostfog, but his voice had come from the gardens of Blackheath House. A snaking lizard's tail of bone and greenhouses that curled from the rear of the fortress back around to the entrance.

Ed was leaning in the doorway, too far away to get a decent look. "What are you doing over there?" I asked. The courier had said to meet him in the courtyard. I hustled over, unsure how to identify the emotion building in my stomach.

Ed checked his fingernails. "You were late."

"It's been three minutes."

"Try five years." His words were wrapped around a smirk.

"If you can wait that long, three minutes should've been no trouble." I was close enough to get a decent look at him now, and when I did my breath slowed to a trickle in my throat.

Eye contact had always been difficult, but it was always noticeably *more* difficult for me to maintain when I was with Ed. He had eyes the color of scratched steel—a gray so vivid and light it was almost silver. They always looked like they harbored a veiled threat.

He had a beard now, too. Not a *good* one, mind. Not much had come in yet on his cheeks but he was making a valiant attempt with what he had. Though he *was* taller, which I resented. I always thought I'd win out on that front. He wore a science-sword at his hip. A backsword design, with a bit more metalwork around the grip than my saber model. A handgun I couldn't identify was holstered on his thigh, and his coat was absolutely immaculate considering all the days he must have spent riding.

Goddamn. The longer I scrutinized him the more my suspicion dissipated, without permission. I'd never thought of myself as particularly nostalgic, but seeing him for the first time in five years—it breathed new life into all the discarded memories and emotions I thought I'd tucked away forever.

I swallowed. "Ed, I..." What was I supposed to say? Where do you even start? After all that time? What kind of beginning could ever live up to five years apart?

Ed looked like he was asking himself the same question. He rubbed the back of his neck. "You got bigger."

I wasn't even sure what he'd meant by that. "Hadn't noticed," I said.

Edgar frowned, and we just stood there for a while. "Well, if you're not going to, I will."

His fist closed around my lapel as he dragged me into a clumsy hug that squeezed the breath from my lungs. I'm not sure how I got my arms around him, considering how tight he was holding me. But somehow I managed it.

He smelled like home. It was a smell of iron and saltwater and freshly printed paper. Goddammit. Why did that make me want to cry?

His arms trailed mine as he let me go. He gave my forearms a little handshake-squeeze as he stepped back. "God, Petre."

"What?"

"I didn't think I'd actually get to see you." He stepped inside the greenhouse as we talked. A flood of warmth and humidity smothered me as I followed after him.

I wondered if he was under the impression I had a choice. If I failed to come with him, he and Desmon and Anoïse wouldn't hesitate to blacklist The Blackheaths in every way they could. They'd undercut their business ventures, deny them loans, come after them with lawyers and fees and infractions. They might've tried to prosecute Avram. I dunno. It depended on how many of the rumors I'd heard were actually true. They might give it a shot if they thought it would hurt me for missing Anoïse's coronation.

Dad never cared enough to go through the trouble. And the customary three months of mourning his death had kept them from pursuing this for a time. But now Ed was on my doorstep. He was taking me back to Anoïse. How could he act like I had a choice in the matter? There was nothing I could've done to get out of this. Didn't he know that?

My only question was what we were still doing in this goddamn greenhouse. "Ed. Come on. Were you coming to collect me or not?" I wanted to get this over with.

Ed slowed his saunter through rows and rows of warped plant life. He looked over his shoulder. "We've got time. I want to see what Mercedes Blackheath has had Avram working on."

I wasn't sure I would have the temperament to move through this day if we lingered like this. It was always difficult to focus when I knew there was an event in the immediate future to prepare for.

Ed knew that about me. Sometimes he liked to take his time, just to see what would happen.

"Is this fun for you?"

"Oh absolutely." He slowed his pace theatrically. This felt like a test. Like he wanted to see what the last five years had done to me, or determine how much the time away had changed my disposition.

Well. If that was the game he wanted to play. Alright, asshole. I could play. "I would've thought I got at least a five-minute grace period before you started messing with me." I followed him through rows of plant life changed and misshapen by the magic from the First Annihilation.

Ed studied the observation panel on the far wall, where we could watch the labcoats at their work.

There were two areas of expertise for them. The first involved the study of magical artifacts and landscapes from before the First Annihilation—when warring empires whose names have long been lost got into a magical arms race that terraformed the world into impossible landscapes that weren't supposed to exist. They'd wiped out half the planet while they were at it.

Then there were the labcoats who specialized in corpse technology. After magic had fucked the world over so bad people didn't exactly trust it, we had to resort to other methods to get things going. After the First Annihilation, the survivors built strange tech on top of the arcane landscapes left behind. Until they got so good at it that they, too, blasted themselves back to the stone age, in the Second Annihilation. The tech they'd left behind died with all knowledge of how to use it. Labcoats were the only ones who knew how to reverse engineer some of it.

From behind the observation panel, they worked in teams. Using old tech on ancient magical artifacts. We could watch them use what they had to build new misshapen things.

Ed resumed his walk. I followed him between tables. Some were full of sunflowers with the crowns of teeth set inside each circle-center. Others displayed roses with curved serpent fangs spiking out from the stems.

And yet somehow Ed's presence was the most surreal thing in this room.

"You got a hug from me," Edgar said. It had been so long since I spoke that I had to retrace the steps of the conversation to remember what I'd said. "That's not enough?"

I'd been lost in thought so long it took a moment to recalibrate where we were in our conversation. In retrospect I should've expected him to mess with me. To take his time like this, to watch me squirm when all I wanted was to get this over with. That was the only way he ever knew how to interact with me—by treating me like an experiment. He was Mom's favorite for a reason. "Call me greedy," I said in a low voice. "Thought I could guilt a day or two of affection out of you."

Ed plucked a daisy with petals made of transparent fingernails and gave it an experimental flick. "Have I got something worth feeling guilty about, Petre?"

That provoked a stab of annoyance I hadn't been expecting. Last time I saw him was a few days before our birthday. We'd had a *very* public argument over a relationship of Anoïse's that Dad had interfered with at the time. I didn't think it was any of Dad's business. Ed disagreed. A couple blows were exchanged. I'd never bothered to make up. I figured Ed would understand one day that I'd been right about it.

I tried to look nonchalant as I twirled a flower made of shed snakeskin that made dual helix patterns. "You never thought you chased me away?"

Ed straightened. It almost looked like he was squaring up to me. "Every day." The words were cushioned in a rush of breath as he examined a pale blue rose trapped in hoarfrost soil.

"But..." I prompted.

"But." He put a pointed oomph into the echo. "I'm not sure what I could've done differently at the time."

I frowned. "I can think of a few things."

He raised an eyebrow at me. "You ever known me to back down?"

"I didn't say anything about backing down."

"You didn't have to. You were thinking it. Be honest." The words of challenge came out like casual banter, clipped down to as few words as Ed could manage. "You still think you're right. You think Dad shouldn't have stepped in when Anoïse found that lover, and you wish I'd tried to deescalate. You think it's all my fault. You put it all on me."

"You saying *I* escalated things at that dinner? I don't escalate."

He just looked at me for a long time. Silently. That was a tactic he inherited from Mom. Squeezing a moment of silence out as far as it could go. It helped to prompt your conversation partner to overthink. But I knew what he was trying to get out of keeping his mouth shut, so instead of filling the silence I just looked right back at him.

As I dragged my gaze up and down him I spotted something on his right wrist. It was barely visible between the end of his sleeve and where he'd stuffed his hand in his pocket, but there was a deep indentation there that was unmistakably a scar. "The hell happened here?" I indicated his injury and resisted the temptation to peel his coat back to see how far up his arm it went "You get into a duel after I left?"

"Oh, this?" Edgar extracted his hand from his pocket to show me the extent of the scar. It was half an inch wide and wrinkled at the edges. It went from his middle finger down the back of his wrist and vanished into his sleeve. "You wouldn't believe it. It happened at Anoïse's wedding."

I couldn't triage his tone. Was he joking? I tried to remember who Anoïse was even married to. The man was Havilan Reacher's nephew. I remembered that much. He was the heir to Reacher House. Fabrian? Was that his name? "Why the hell were you dueling at Anoïse's wedding?"

Ed laughed once. "I didn't *duel*. Not at a wedding. I'm not a moron. I just—" He frowned. "For future reference— in case it ever comes up—never play the knife game with Fabrian Reacher. Not after a few drinks."

"Good Lord."

"He did it on purpose," Ed insisted. "Never found out how to prove it. But I swear to God. He did it."

I raised an eyebrow. "How do you know?"

We'd reached the other end of the greenhouse and stopped at the observation window. "Sometimes you just intuit something. It's exactly the kind of thing he would do. Just to see what it felt like. The man's an idiot. Reckless. Stupid."

"Is he free sometime?"

Ed started to say something, but then his mouth just continued to hang open. He closed it and tilted his head to

51

one side. "You two would get along," he said. "You have a lot in common."

I wasn't sure if I could trust his assessment. I'd never met Fabrian Reacher, so it was difficult to tell.

I mean don't get me wrong, I'd been invited to the wedding. I probably should have gone, really. It was supposed to mark the end of generations of animosity between Mercy House and Reacher House. But I'd skipped it.

See, they held the wedding only a few months after I ran away, and I'd told myself it was too early to head back. I'd just get roped into living at court again with my luck.

And now here I was anyway. Doing exactly that. I felt a twinge of guilt and worry that Anoïse would have something to say about that when I got back. Fuck.

Edgar snapped his fingers under my nose. "Petre. Hey. Come on. Am I boring you already?"

I blinked, swatted his hand away. "Man, stop that. I'm not a fucking dog. Next you'll be trying to whistle at me to get my attention."

Ed's eyes lit up with interest. "Would it work?"

I shoved him. "Go fuck yourself." I chuckled.

Our conversation was interrupted by a fresh arrival of labcoats to the observation room on the other side of the glass. We watched as they sprayed down stalks of yellow grass with purple mist and dug up animal limbs from the red soil. They worked in teams. A pair were uprooting fresh sinew for repairs to Mercedes Blackheath's train. I'd been on it a few times before. It was a horned boxcar wearing black scales and buffalo fur. A half-living accordion of tissue and iron that seemed to pump and breathe on lurching wheels and shuddery legs. She had taken it to

Bullion. They'd want to prep for repairs by the time she got back.

"Remember the last time I came to Blackheath House?" Ed asked.

"It would've been *before* I left, right?"

"Yeah. Dad took me and Anoïse on a tour around the country. Had to check out the other two Great Houses. And their vassal-courts."

"This was when we were thirteen, right?" I asked, as I watched a labcoat in a gas mask uproot a strand of scaly sinew, glistening with fresh blood and black oil. Clumps of dirt still clung to the wetness.

"Yeah. Anoïse and I were gone for six months. He wanted us to know our subjects. Learn about the people we'd be ruling."

Another labcoat came in with a glowing knife and started sawing through strands that wouldn't come up clean from the ground. They started smoking when he put the knife to it. I watched them curl up and blacken.

"Oh shit," I said. "Yeah, you did do that." I was surprised to find that I did remember. The two of them were gone for three months. Dad wanted Anoïse and Edgar ready to take the country after he died. Edgar was the failsafe in case anything happened to Anoïse. Meanwhile they taught Desmon the work of ambassadors and administrators, and they taught me just enough to keep me out of their way.

"I'd never seen labcoats in action before," Ed went on. "There was always Mom, but—"

"—We were never allowed down there while she was working, yeah." I finished for him. Though that had never stopped Ed from trying to sneak down there on occasion. There was a rumor one time that Mom smuggled him in to watch a surgery. Desmon started that one, I think. But Ed swore up and down it was a lie to get back at Ed for something he'd done to Desmon.

"Blackheath House was the first time I witnessed what labcoats do. When we got here they were digging up a horse. They'd clawed a pink tub of unbreathing flesh and sheer white bone out from the ground. Stuffed it full of green fluid. It smelled like bile. Then there were these sacs. The thing started breathing as soon as they put them in. Then they opened up the skull. Worked the cogs in piecemeal. Rammed it through with wires. Panels. Circuitry. I wanted to look away. More than anything. But Dad was watching. And I didn't want to disappoint him."

I'd been enjoying the story up to that last sentence—because at that point I knew it for a filthy lie. Ed was as much Mom's creature as Anoïse was Dad's. The only approval he ever wanted from Dad was confined to the amount of power Dad could grant him. He wouldn't have studied the labcoat's operations out of a desire to impress Dad. If anything he would've wanted to bring what he'd seen back home to Mom.

But he knew the kind of relationship I had with Mom. I guessed that since Mom was still around he'd figured bringing her up would be a sore spot.

It didn't matter. His point was easy enough to decode—probably something about how going back to swear fealty might be ugly. Something I might not want to do. Something I dreaded but had to do anyway. He could have just said that, really. Something felt off about him. First he refused all rites and ceremonies. Now here he was talking in circles about duties and obligations and facing them even when you didn't want to. I couldn't see how that wasn't contradictory. Something was up with him. He was planning something.

"It's incredible," Ed went on. "How far we've come. Wasn't more than a few generations ago we were recycling old scraps. Used to take years to grow the biological components. We can do so much more now with what we've got."

He felt...wooden. Stiff. As if he'd put up guard rails on his personality. I squinted. "Have you been studying up on rhetoric, Ed?"

Ed rolled his eyes. "Can't I make an observation without implying something? I don't only speak in double-talk, you know." He smirked.

I indulged in a fantasy of smacking that look right off his face. I figured nothing would come of it if my dose had leveled out.

So you can imagine my shock when my injections decided they were going to kick in after all. My whole body lurched like you do when a hurtling vehicle comes to a sudden stop.

"Petre?" Edgar took a step forward, hands hovering in the air over me. "Goddamn. You alright? You're shaking."

I struggled against the burning sludge as it tried to drag my arm up into a fighting stance. The injections took hold slowly. They would pilot me once I tired out, I knew. "We're in trouble," I gurgled. "Fuck. You should probably run."

The injections shook me with a thrum of white pain and heat. Angry sludge followed vein-patterns under my skin.

"Petre, what?" Edgar blinked at me. "What's going on?"

My foot lurched forward of its own volition and wedged itself between his ankles.

"Edgar, I'm not joking!" I shouted.

He froze. Confusion teased out wrinkles on his face. God fucking dammit.

My whole body shook like struck steel. I didn't have much time. "Get away!"

Ed looked genuinely curious. Which surprised me. "Is this your drugs?"

"Lord Alive, Ed! Do you want to get hurt?"

"I was always telling you not to take that shit. It's dangerous."

"ED! GET OUT!" The burning sludge was wheeling my arm back. I didn't want him to get hurt.

Ed rolled his shoulders, then his neck. He cracked his knuckles. "I've got a better idea."

Sometimes you forget things when you spend some time away. Time bleaches out the details. Narratives and emotions and hindsight get in the way. You start to down-play the finer elements you've lived through. You'll never remember particularly vibrant pain the same way you did when you first experienced it. But sometimes something happens that snaps all the cracked edges of your back memory together.

All this to say: I was reminded in that instant just how hard Edgar could hit.

He twisted his hips, put his weight behind the punch. My whole body rocked with the momentum. Star spots flared bright and blotchy in my sightline. The world went fuzzy. Like I was hearing things underwater.

Sluggish heat filled up my forearms and my fingers as I fell. My injections yanked my hand around his wrist, dragged him down with me.

"Still struggling?" Ed cackled as he fell on top of me. "Brings back memories, doesn't it?"

There was the Edgar I knew. "I hope you're enjoying

yourself." I cursed. My injections gripped me hard and reeled my arm back. It was like a hand of heat just beneath the surface of my skin, peeling my arm backwards. I felt like a doll. A toy to be propped up in the right position.

"One of us has to." His words were wrapped around a smile as his knee came up between my legs. The heel of his hand slammed my temple hard enough to give me a headache.

I rolled to my side. Then Edgar's boots were right in front of me. When had he stood up?

"Can I move on my own now?" I'm not sure why I asked it aloud. But I tested it by trying to crab back, away from him.

I'd managed to roll over of my own volition when Edgar wedged his boot between two ribs. My side went red, and an instant later my shirt was bunched up in his big fists. He hauled me to my knees and slammed his knuckles into my jaw.

"Ed!" I sputtered. "You can stop now! I'm good!"

He jerked me roughly by my collar. "You sure?"

"I promise."

"Because I can hit you again if you want—"

I shoved him hard. "Get off me," I grunted. Lord, my side hurt. Goddamn that was a good kick. Holy shit.

Edgar swung his arms in circles, stretching. "That was fun." He grinned. "You ought to overdose more often."

There was a fullness behind my eyes. I pressed them shut. "Ed..."

"Why'd you take a dose high enough to do that to you?" Ed asked. I wondered if he'd been reading up on IMI. He didn't have a clue how it worked last time I spoke to him. He'd *hated* that I was on it. Wanted nothing to do with it. He thought it was cheating. When had that changed?

"I, um—" I didn't have time to think of a lie. "I didn't. I had to take them early."

Edgar's eyes narrowed. "Is that all? You could've waited. We have about a week to get back. Won't take more than a few days."

I shrugged. "Didn't sound like you minded back there."

"Don't get me wrong. I didn't. That was the most fun I've had this whole trip. But I'm not sure why you'd do that to yourself." He shrugged. That grin still hadn't died. "Seems risky."

"I had to," I insisted. There was no way he would've let me get my injections on time. I didn't care how much he insisted otherwise.

"Why, though?"

I couldn't tell him why. He didn't need to know I was worried he and Anoïse and Desmon would try to keep me in the capital. At Mercy House. Though that was the corner he was trying to box me into anyway. "It's not you," I lied. "I know what you're thinking. It's not because you came here, Ed. I promise."

For a long time he just looked at me. "It's only you and me here, Petre. What do you want me to think?"

"We're going back to meet Anoïse and Desmon. Maybe I wanted to be prepared to deal with them. I don't know. The road is dangerous!" Fuck. I should have led with that one. That would've been a better excuse.

To my surprise, it seemed to satisfy Ed. He blinked at me three times. "Right. Right. Anoïse and Desmon. Yeah."

That set alarm bells blaring. Did he just *forget* that I was on bad terms with all three of them? I wasn't sure what to make of that. "We are going back to them, yes?"

Ed coughed. "Of course. What? You think I came all this way just to cut and run like you did?"

I'd never known Ed to run away from much of anything, that was true. Maybe I was just overthinking things. Where else could we even *go*, you know?

Edgar stuffed his hands into his pockets. "Right. Where's Avram? I've got to yell at him."

Fear, shame, and confusion battled to be the first to register itself on my face. "I'm sorry?"

"What the fuck was he thinking? Putting you on that high of a dose? Have you been able to control yourself at all?"

"Not exactly." How was I going to explain this without letting him know I'd double dosed? "But I thought that it was over. I didn't—he told me—"

"He cleared you to come meet with me before you two were sure that this had passed?" He sounded more curious than angry. He was *supposed* to be mad at me.

This was getting strange. First he comes to me all incognito, then he blanks on the fact that we're going back to Anoïse, then he pretends he's not mad that I've classified him as a threat. To the point where he even refuses to yell at me? "Okay. Ed. What's going on? Come on. You have to tell me."

Ed laughed once. "I'm not sure what you mean."

"Come on. Don't tell me you're mad at Avram, man. Cut the shit."

"You want me to be mad at you?"

"Five years ago we would've had the knives out already!" I said.

"I'm not who I was five years ago. Are you?"

That gave me pause. Something was...*off*. About Ed. I just wasn't sure what. Not yet. But I decided it might be smarter to sort out how much of this was personal change and how much of that was something else, before I did anything rash. So I just said, "Fair enough."

"Fair enough?" Edgar must've been expecting a longer fight.

"Are we going to argue about this all morning or are you going to take me to the stables? Come on, man. Let's head out."

Two Annihilations can make animal life hard to sustain. Labcoats have spent generations manufacturing band aid solutions to this problem—figuring out how we can grow our meat. Or create ecosystems, or balance them when the previous species they'd concocted died away. The Outlying Islands provided us with the raw materials we needed, and the labcoats took their raw tech and found uses for it.

Cyborg horses were the solution to our transportation problem. I mean—don't get me wrong, they weren't alive. Not in the way you or I would be. They're just a cocktail of grown meat and machinery.

We kept them all in the stables. A concrete box full of horse stalls and yellow floodlights. I didn't like being there. When not in use the horses loomed over you like haunted taxidermy things. It always felt like they were watching me.

But at least it got me one step closer to getting this over with. Heading home to swear fealty.

I grabbed a wrench on my way in so I could armor up my horse. I'd never quite been sure why I had to do that. It was the kind of thing you never questioned. It was just what you did. You put the armor on when you went out, you took it off when you got back. String it through with wires and you're all set.

My horse was in its stall, plugged up with wavy coils

the color of brain matter. One of the floodlights in the cell winked when I entered.

"So." The armor was organized in a gigantic bin that was pinned to the wall. I retrieved the piece that bolted on over the left ribcage and lined the steel up with the bolt holes. "How are we doing this trip?"

Edgar retrieved his own horse from its stall in the stables. He hadn't taken the armor off, so all he had to do was unplug the circuitry he'd hooked it up to. "I dunno what you mean." He led his horse out by the bridle. It moved like a wind-up toy. "We're going back to Anoïse. She needs you to swear an oath at the coronation feast next week. It's not complicated."

"Well yeah, but—" I finished bolting the left breastplate on. The saddle came next. I plugged its prongs into receptacles that were lined up on either side of the horse's spine, and wired the circuitry into a socket couched in the base of the beast's neck. Saddle commands made riding easier. "—It'll take at least two days to get there if we hustle."

"I was thinking a bit more leisurely of a pace than that," Edgar said.

"How leisurely?"

"How's five days?"

"Cutting it close, huh?" I traced the mental map back home inside my head. If we took the fastest route we could make it home in three. "We stopping at Bullion?" That was on the way. And Mercedes Blackheath was there for a meeting she'd host in a few days. Might be cool to meet up with her, catch her up on what was going on.

Hell, if I could get some time alone she'd probably find another use for my mouth.

"We wouldn't get there until after dark," Ed said. "I packed us a tent, though. Might help. Best to avoid traveling at night. Hard to make repairs to the horses. And that's when Gaunts come out in force."

I felt a stab of annoyance at the fact that Ed was talking about riding and dealing with Gaunts as if that wasn't all I'd been working on for five years now. "No, I know," I said, "but if we set a good pace we can get to Bullion in decent time."

"The coronation feast is in six days. We've got time."

"I'd *like* to go quickly."

Ed's front two teeth came down on his burgeoning grin. "It'd be faster if we stopped arguing, you know."

"Then let's agree on Bullion," I insisted.

"We're *not* going to Bullion."

"We have to at *least* pass through," I said. "It's the fastest way."

"We're not going the fastest way," Ed insisted.

"That's what you said—but *why,* is my question."

Ed quirked an eyebrow. "I shouldn't say."

I shrugged. "You know I'll keep asking."

Ed stared at the ground. "The tabloids have been running a few shitty stories about me lately. I'm trying to keep a low profile. I don't want to get spotted."

Fuck. Well. When he put it like that I felt guilty. Was that why he didn't want any formal ceremonies, too? Maybe I'd been acting suspicious of him for no reason. Maybe I was the asshole here. "What kind of stories?"

Ed frowned. "Does it matter?"

I wondered if he'd deflected to buy time. I couldn't ascertain if he was being entirely honest. Five years ago Ed would've leapt at any chance to bitch at the stories the tabloids were running about him that week. "Well— usually. To you."

"I just want to keep a low profile, alright? The rest doesn't matter."

I debated whether or not to press the issue. There had to be *something* he wasn't telling me. I just wasn't sure what, but pushing him might make him shut down. How many choices did I have? I had to go back to Anoïse and that was ostensibly where he was taking me. All I could do in the meantime was roll with things and hope I was prepared for whatever he had up his sleeve.

So I finished securing the armor and put my foot in the stirrup. "Welp. I've always wanted to try camping."

CHAPTER
FIVE

Our progress out from Blackheath House was underpinned by the constant clink of a bicycle chain spiraling, and the thump of pig iron hoofs making prints on a sodden mulch of trampled leaves.

It's the weirdest thing in the world to ride cyborg horses, I swear. They're too stiff. Like taxidermy made mechanical. They're a mess of machinery and it always sounded like whatever was going on under their false flesh was going to fold under you like a cheap table and shred you to pieces.

That stiff in-and-out of synthesized breathing? The feeling of its mechanical stomach stretching out, rubbery skin pressing against the insides of your thighs? Absolutely horrid.

They were *almost* alive, but not quite. I mean—they breathed. But their reactions to things were all but nonexistent. They were warm, but only in the way hardware-in-use can be.

Every movement creaked, and they reeked of green

bronze and old leather. And of synth. That putridly perfect disinfectant stink that you might associate with hospitals.

"Petre." Ed and I traveled under the shade of yellowed bone trees that wept grainy black sap. "What were you focusing on earlier? What made your injections do that to you? When you tried to hit me." There was a smile brewing behind his eyes. Was he *amused?*

"I don't know," I lied. I wasn't about to tell him it was because he was being too pretentious with his speeches. Being too smug. I wouldn't have been so annoyed if he hadn't spent so much time testing me. Poking and prodding at my psyche in all the ways he knew I hated.

God. I didn't want to go back. This was all these people knew how to do. The only way they knew how to act. But they'd make it worse for me if I didn't.

I realized I hadn't answered Ed. "I dunno. Why were you mad at Maunders and not me?"

"I thought about it for more than a minute," Edgar shrugged. "Didn't seem right to blame you."

"I'm the one who overdosed. That makes it my fault." I didn't want him mad at Avram. Not even a little bit. He hadn't wanted to give me my injections. I made him do it.

"Avram gave you the dose. He's the labcoat. He's the one who's supposed to know how all this works."

"I talked him into it," I said, as the horses stomped through a scrub of dark blue foliage.

"Why'd you get the dose last night if you hadn't bottomed out on your current one?"

"I already told you."

He laughed. "Okay but tell me the truth this time."

I squeezed the sides of my horse and fidgeted with the pommel of my saddle. "I was scheduled to get it *today*," I admitted. "But I wanted to get it off my plate yesterday so I could spend more time with you."

"Oh, come on." He rolled his eyes. "I said the truth. That's even less convincing."

"Too saccharine?" I asked.

"Try telling at least a half truth. It helps the lie go down easier."

"I'll remember that," I said. "You are the expert, after all." I followed Ed down a bend in the road made of shiny black glass.

"Still," Ed added, "I guess it's not the first time Avram was supposed to know better, huh?"

I wanted to ask what he meant. Maybe he was talking about the rumors floating around the capital about Avram. But if Ed insulted him long enough I was going to hit him of my own volition. So I just said, "Guess so. I'm sorry about all that in the greenhouse, I guess." Maybe that would help to take the heat off Avram.

"It's fine, Petre."

"It's not. Don't lie to me."

"*I* had fun."

I wrung out the reins. I couldn't find anything else to do with all the restless anxiety rifling through me. God. What the fuck was I doing following him back home?

"Petre. Are you okay? It was just a joke. Calm down. Stop strangling the reins."

I reached into the inner pocket on my chameleon coat and had a moment of surprise when I registered that the color had shifted to dappled greens and dark browns. I retrieved the tin case of Muse I'd found in there this morning, when Avram insisted I should wear it. It was an anxiolytic, so I figured it couldn't hurt. I flipped the case open, dragged my mask down and stuffed a cigarette-sized roll into my mouth.

Dropping the mask was risky, sure. But I couldn't see any ghostfog nearby. I figured I had time to take a few hits without breathing anything in or getting infected.

"I'll be alright. I just need to calm down." I dove back inside my pocket. "If I can just find my damn lighter."

Ed leaned across the space between us to provide his own.

"You smoke?" I asked.

"Nah. Just helps to have a lighter for people who do. Desmon taught me that trick, you know. Said it had helped him out a few times when Dad had asked him to be his ambassador at Reacher House. Sometimes it's like a conversation starter. Or it builds rapport."

"Oh, shit." Ed thumbed the switch. A flame sprouted. "That's actually clever." I leaned the end of the cigarette onto the flame. Took a deep breath in. Muse tightened hazy gray fingers around my lungs, and the tension I'd been holding slid away. I spat out smoke the color of blued steel. My throat felt dry and grainy. "I'm okay," I said. "I'm okay."

He tossed the lighter to me. The IMI dragged my hand up on reflex. "Keep it," he said.

"You don't need it?"

"There are other lighters."

"We building rapport?" I asked.

"Could be. I *do* have a question."

"And here we were just starting to get along so well." I bit back my grin.

"Listen. I just wanna know—you ever try getting off the injections? Sounds like this really freaked you out, is all." I was surprised to find his concern seemed genuine. He was even picking at a stray scrap of fraying leather skin stretched over his horse's spine, between two plates of armor. Ed could never make eye contact when he was registering sincere emotion.

Which made the question hurt that much more. "Ed. You don't have to worry about me."

"I do though," he said, quietly. "I worry about you."

Worry was an interesting way to pronounce *get jealous*. He always hated that I could inject myself with the skills he'd worked for. As if pumping myself full of chemicals was anyone's idea of a fun time. But he always thought I had it easy. The IMI couldn't even match his skill, but because chemicals were involved he'd decided it was cheating.

I took another deep breath of Muse. I was going to need it. I felt it settle in my lungs and coughed it back out. "I'm not doing this with you," I said.

He had the audacity to blink at me, all innocence. "Do what?" I was less certain if he was acting, now.

But that didn't change my answer. I needed the injections. Especially if he or Desmon or Anoïse were going to try to keep me in Mercy House so that I couldn't cause trouble. They were always worried that I might be straining diplomatic relations with other houses.

I hadn't.

Not as far as I could tell, at least.

Okay. There was the one thing with Mercedes Blackheath a few years back. I heard through the grapevine Anoïse was furious about that one, but that was one time.

I would fight my way out if they tried to keep me there after I swore my oath. I'd do it if I had to. But that required the injections, just to reach basic competency. "We're not going to talk about this," I insisted again. It was an old conversation anyway. "I know the risks—"

"Didn't seem like it back there. Gotta be honest." He

flung it out so casually I wasn't sure if he knew how much it stung.

"That was different." I paused to suck down another lungful of Muse. My anger felt sludgy. Still there, but incompatible with the drugged haze.

"Petre. You didn't even know what the overdose risks *were*. How can you go making informed decisions about this stuff?"

"Certainly didn't keep you from having a fun time with it. Maybe I just want to entertain you with another overdose in the future. That's what you said I ought to do, right?"

Ed dragged a hand through his hair. "That was a joke, Petre. Calm down."

I squeezed the roll of Muse between two knuckles. I had to wait a bit before I took my next hit. Too much at once would make me go all dizzy. "I'm working on it. And in the meantime if you could drop the subject I'd really appreciate it."

"Are you just trying to protect Avram? Is that it?"

"It's not about Avram."

Ed waved that excuse away. "Of course it is. He gave them to you. What, you just want to avoid talking about him?"

"If you're going to talk shit about him then, yes, please."

"Shame." If it was possible to shake your head sarcastically Ed found a way. "I heard you liked him more than that."

"Oh? What has he told you?"

"You'd be surprised. I hear things."

"Try me."

"It's nothing you haven't said to him already." Edgar winked.

My face went warmer than it had any right to. "Listen."

"Go on. I'm listening."

Fuck. I didn't actually have a way to explain it. "I like him plenty. He's a smart man. Nice ass."

Edgar chuckled. "Is it true he's not the only ass you've been after?"

"Did Anoïse send spies down here or something? How the hell do you know that?" Damn rumors. They were going to get me killed one day. I knew it.

Edgar soured at the mention of Anoïse. I should've known better than to bring her up. She and Ed were the two eldest by about a minute. Dad always had them vying against each other, and there was always that bit of competition simmering between the two of them. "Come on," Ed groused. "I should be allowed to give you shit for this, after everything in the courtyard. At least roll with my punches."

I took another drag to numb the irritation coursing through me. "I don't like being punched."

"I hear Mercedes Blackheath has a different story."

"You heard about that one, huh?" I couldn't even look at him after that barb. It was not that I was embarrassed. I just—he was my brother. You're not supposed to broach that kind of subject with family, right?

"Heard about it? Anoïse wouldn't stop fuming over it for a full three months!"

I winced. If anything I'd done had given her an excuse to try and detain me in Mercy House where I couldn't cause trouble it would've been that incident. For the life of me I couldn't bring myself to regret it. "How does she tell it?"

Ed shook his head. "No. I want to hear it from you. Spill."

I debated the merits of telling him what had happened. "I'm not getting out of this, am I?"

"Not unless you want to go back to arguing about your injections."

Well. At least Mercedes was actually interesting to talk about. And unlike with my injections, I actually liked it when she hurt me. That was just part of the definition of a fun night. "I started hitting on her, like, *the day* I got to Blackheath House. After I ran away from you guys. I got caught in a blizzard shortly after I left home. And y'know? They say the best way to warm up is skin to skin contact. A bit of friction. Maybe it'd help to have my head between her thighs. They say your ears are one of the first things that succumb to frostbite."

Ed shook his head. "Did you actually say that?"

"I was eighteen. And I've never been subtle."

"Did she go for it?"

I snorted. "Fuck, no. Like I said, I was eighteen—and fresh out of a bad situation. She told me we'd revisit it in a few years."

Ed was back to picking at the leather fraying from his horse's skin as he led me single file down a narrow path with fossilized wheel tracks and a stretch of shoddy yellow grass shot down the center of the road. "I take it you'd talked things over by the time the incident with Anoïse's people came about?"

It had happened at a holiday gathering two years ago. I was twenty-one at the time. Anoïse had sent a small host of loyalists to Blackheath House. Never *did* find out if Dad knew that she sent them. "Anoïse timed it like that on purpose, didn't she?" I asked. "Sending people over the holidays when Mercedes couldn't refuse to host her guests?"

I'll give Ed credit. He feigned innocence convincingly, the way he raised his head to look at me, face blank, eyes curious. "I wouldn't know anything about it, I'm afraid," he said, in a tone that indicated otherwise. "Though I hear they tried to collect you."

"That was their plan. But Mercedes had other ideas. Since hospitality would not allow her to kick a guest out during the holidays without a scandal, she decided to provoke an argument with them. She suggested to me a few new religious festivals she thought Blackheath House ought to petition the crown to observe federally next year. Really leaned in on a few controversial readings of a couple sacred texts—until Anoïse's representatives felt obligated to step in."

"I don't see what this has to do with you and her," Edgar cut in.

"I'm getting there. So she started this huge fight, right? A big public dinner table argument. Until a couple of them chose some hasty words and she kicked them out. And since everyone there knew this incident was going to make the tabloids, maybe even a few newspapers—once the fight had settled down, she looked at me and in front of everyone told me to come to bed. She had to take out some frustrations, and she figured I could help." It was an optics game. Taking the Prince to bed. I was supposed to be a stand in for the crown.

And. Well. What's a man to do, y'know? I mean—I knew I'd get heat for it. Everyone all over the country would be chewing me out the next morning. But was I supposed to pass up an opportunity to do a little chewing of my own? I'd become something of an unofficial paramour for her since then. With semi-regularity. She kept a full stable.

I realized abruptly that Edgar hadn't spoken. "Is that how Anoïse tells it?" I asked, to fill the silence.

"Well." Ed chewed on his lower lip, and found an interesting stretch of yellow grass to stare at. "She found it a bit less...*amusing*."

"Right." I'd heard rumors that she thought I was straining a few political relationships with my presence there. If there was one thing all my siblings were good at, it was catastrophizing. "That's to be expected."

"She was concerned for you. She thought Mercedes was manipulating you."

That one was a surprise. "She didn't even have to talk me into it. Like listen—what was I supposed to do, say no? Have you seen her?"

"*I'm* not judging." Edgar put his palms up like he was imitating a surrender. "Just telling you what Anoïse said."

"And what do you think?"

Edgar developed a distant look in his eyes as he mulled it over. "I wouldn't have gone for her. Like. She's thirty-eight, Petre."

I bit back my grin. "Man. Ed. Listen to me. That ain't a bug it's a feature. I'm telling you."

"I'm just saying—"

"Is her age part of the problem? Cause seriously, I'm telling you—"

"Shut up," Edgar snapped.

"You haven't even tried it. Like what's the problem? Why are you so against it? Are you engaged or something?" I thought I'd heard some rumors about that. But I wasn't certain. Maybe he could enlighten me.

"I was," he grumbled. "Dad set something up with Havilan Reacher's daughter."

I tried to sketch the family trees in my mind. Okay. So there were two branches to Reacher House. There was the oldest, Orianna Reacher. Her son Fabrian was around our age. Fabrian was married to Anoïse. Then there was *Havilan*

Reacher, who was Orianna's younger brother. And *he* had a daughter, Guindolin.

The problem here was that Havilan Reacher had been our hostage for quite some time.

I mean. Okay. Nobody *called* him that. Technically he was given an in-name-only job as captain of The Mercy Guard, so that Dad didn't have to use the h-word. But like —Havilan Reacher had been caught planning to steal a few of our trading outposts in The Bay years back, so Dad couldn't have him roaming around, you know? The leadership position was closely monitored. He was surrounded by paperwork and enemies at all times.

"What happened?" I asked. "You said *was*. You used past tense."

Edgar crossed his arms. "I shouldn't say."

"Come on. Tell me."

Ed's gas mask shifted as he grinned. "Okay. Okay. But you didn't hear it from me."

I leaned over the cyborg horse. "What happened?"

"Havilan cut a deal with Dad. In exchange for a few more years of service, Havilan gets to marry his daughter to me."

I did the familial math. This was confusing. "So...Anoïse gets to rule with Fabrian and Orianna Reacher's branch becomes part of the family, while you get Guindolin and Havilan's side..."

"...becomes the new presumptive heirs to Reacher House. A secure transition of power for everyone," Edgar finished.

"Okay, I'm with you. So what happened?"

Ed's mood curdled instantly. "Dad called it off. Right before he died, if you can believe it. I swear to God, Anoïse was pressuring him to break it off."

Swearing to God was what Edgar often did to indicate he had strong feelings but no actual proof.

"She tried to set me up with one of The Blackheaths' vassals instead. Not even an heir to any significant titles. Thought it would be more...politically advantageous. That's what she called it. That's the phrase she always used."

"Incredible." I leaned back. If Anoïse had pressured Dad to end Ed's engagement then clearly there was enough influence in a match like that to make her feel threatened. But what leverage did Havilan's branch of the family have over her? Ed's match was made of second siblings all the way down.

"Incredible?" Ed echoed. "It's *bullshit*. That's what it is." He sighed. His whole composure slouched as if he was curling in on himself. "But we do what we must for Mercy House." He rolled his eyes.

"What are her plans for the coronation anyway?" I asked.

Edgar rolled his eyes. "How the hell should I know?"

I shrugged. "She didn't talk to you about it?"

"Do I look like an event planner to you?"

"Well—surely someone's talked to you about it. You think I've forgotten everything that goes into a family event? All the bartering everyone's got to do to keep all of the Three Great Houses satisfied?"

"I'm sure Desmon took great care of that," Edgar groused.

"Desmon always takes great care with everything." Desmon was always the one who gave everyone the least trouble. The best at blending in with expectation. Being the kind of person everyone expected a royal to be.

Dad raised him to be the one who would go in during negotiations. He was the family ambassador, who would flatter our businessmen and magnates before Dad came in to start negotiations. He always played by the rules. Planned events. Keeping things pristine.

"Do you even know what's on the menu, man?" I asked. "There's a lot of semiotics in a dinner plate. You've got a lot of symbolism to stuff down people's throats that way. Literally." I couldn't tell if he truly didn't know what was happening or if Anoïse was just *that* unprepared to become Queen.

"Frankly, I'm just impressed you know what semiotics means. You're not as dumb as you look."

"I had a better education than I prefer to let on, and sometimes it comes in—*hey wait a second!*"

Edgar laughed. "Might be I was wrong."

I decided to let him think that.

It was better than arguing.

WE ENCOUNTERED a Gaunt in the middle of the night. And just when I'd been thinking about how we'd been unusually fortunate up to that point.

We'd both climbed into bedrolls for the night on a bank of asphalt overlooking a concrete forest with chalcedony leaves. We'd been failing to fall asleep for hours. My thoughts were wandering through that three in the morning headspace when I asked him, on impulse, "How would you want to die? If you could choose?"

Edgar stared up at the stars. His mouth shifted behind his mask. "How would I want to die?" He made a low and unsatisfied noise of consideration with the back of his throat. "Is it too cliche to answer with old age?"

"Doesn't count."

"Fuck you too, then."

"Just answer the question."

You know how some people smile with their eyes? You ever see someone give you a *hollow* smile with only their eyes? Edgar was an expert at that. He spent a long time staring at the sky before he answered. "Lymphoma."

My stomach dropped. "Ed—what?"

"At least then I'll have inherited something from Dad, hey?"

"Ed—c'mon man. That's not funny."

"See? You got his sense of humor. I want something."

"What's your real answer?" I asked.

"Why'd you ask if you didn't want to know?"

I couldn't tell if he was joking. And I was too scared to check. Instead, I said, "No. But seriously. Come on. Do you really think I got anything from Dad?"

Ed chewed on my question. "Enough indifference to be an unsupervised asshole?"

He had a point. I was such a handful growing up that at some point Dad always had to pick his battles. Though I was not aware that privilege had been unique to me. "We were all assholes growing up, Ed."

"You were the only difficult one."

"That's because you and Desmon and Anoïse all had coteries of loyalists who got their hands dirty for you. You guys got taught politicking and how to build alliances and everything."

"Dad tried to teach you." Edgar stretched out on his bedroll. "It just didn't take. We learned. But that also meant we were stuck with rigid rules. You never had that."

I wasn't sure what to make of his recollection of home life. Ed and Anoïse never even fully conformed to Dad's rules either. But Dad would always look the other way any time they misbehaved while he was in a good mood. *Especially* if he was on bad terms with whoever they had targeted for their next fit of dramatics. "He never taught me in a way that I could understand. So I gave up."

"That's what *I'm* saying," Ed insisted. "You gave up. That's on you."

"And all I'm saying is he definitely gave you three way more than he ever gave me."

"Didn't get the lymphoma though," Ed deadpanned. "Not yet at least."

"Whatever." I rolled over, presented my back to him. "I'm done arguing about this, man."

"Who's arguing?" Ed asked with irritating composure. "We're just having a discussion."

He was so calm when he said it that I was debating the merits of strangling him right then and there.

Fortunately for him, a noise off in the concrete forest sliced through my concentration. It sounded like the crunch of boots on gravel. Then I heard a grunt. It was so faint I wondered if I imagined it.

Until Edgar said, "It's nothing, Petre. Just go to sleep."

Instead I dug up a flashlight. Trained it in the direction of the noise. "Right. I'm going to check it out."

Ed's bedroll stirred. "Petre, don't. You're being an idiot. You can't—"

"You just said it was nothing." I didn't believe him. There was *something* out there. And I couldn't just go back to bed. Not without knowing what it was. "So it shouldn't be any trouble, right?"

In all honesty, I just wanted a moment of space from him—or else we were going to start talking about Dad again. I didn't want to say something I would regret.

I grabbed the science-sword and shrugged on my chameleon coat.

"You're overthinking this," Ed insisted.

"You sound surprised." I scrambled down the bank of concrete. "If I'm not back in like two minutes, come after me."

I didn't actually expect that he would let me go without a fight. So when he didn't come after me, I felt a twinge of worry in my gut. What could possibly make someone like *Edgar* back down? It was just a noise, right? I wondered if there was something out there. Or some*one*, potentially, that Ed was worried about encountering on the road. Or maybe he was just waiting for me to get a little ways ahead so he could follow me without my noticing.

The forest of granite trees swallowed me. Occasionally a gemstone leaf fell with a harsh crack. I looked around for the source of the noise I had heard earlier. But there was no source apparent in the forest. Who the hell was out here at this time of night? Drunken revelers who had lost their way? How lost did you have to be to wind up here?

"Should've stopped at Bullion," I groused. "I swear to god if you people turn out to be teenagers looking for a place to fuck." It was an awfully long way to go to do something like that. A terraformed magic ruin from the First Annihilation was hardly even a decent place to do so.

Moonlight glinted through the chalcedony overhead, knifing through the gemstones in flat bands that glittered like a second set of stars. My chameleon coat was a shiny black. I was going to regret this, but I only needed a minute. Not long at all. Just enough time to collect myself.

The noise came again. This time it wasn't a grunt so much as a squeal.

I squeezed the grip of my saber. Pressed down on the

thumb ring. I hadn't strapped it onto my waist. I was just walking with it in my hand.

There were heavy breaths way out there in the dark. Sounds of impact I could only barely see.

"Help!" I heard a man's voice. "God—god—*please!*"

Fuck.

I whirled in the direction of the voice, faced twin granite trees branching out from the same trunk. A grizzled shape in the dark slinked between them. The guy looked like a damn mess. He moved in painful jerking motions like he'd been stabbed. He couldn't even breathe without grunting. He spilled through the two trees into the concrete clearing with me and dropped to his knees.

My injections nudged my feet forward before I could ascertain if that was a wise idea. I crouched in front of the figure, my hands under his armpits as he sprayed breath and spittle onto my face. "What happened?" I asked. "Who are you? Are you hurt?"

His hand flew to an injury on his shoulder. I trained the flashlight on it to get a better look, just in time to watch the dark blood gurgle out between his fingers.

It was a deep wound. It looked almost like a claw mark. And my stomach gave a lurch when I realized that the reddish brown of his shirt was not its natural color.

"You have to help me," he croaked, as he took both my hands in his.

"Fuck. Shit. Man. Okay. Hold on."

"You have to—"

Before I could puzzle out what I ought to do about the situation, another body slammed into the injured man from side on. The impact pried the science-sword from my grip. My injections yanked me away from the tangle of limbs as they fell. I scrambled backwards to get distance and shined my light on them. "Edgar?" *Fuck.* The sword was pinned beneath the injured man.

Our new arrival wasn't Edgar. It was a woman in a sackcloth. She straddled the injured man. She had something in her hands. A knife? A trowel? No—one of those handheld rakes with three prongs. What were they called? Cultivators?

Fuck. Was *that* what had fucked up his shoulder?

She was hissing obscenities, though I couldn't hear the details. Something about stealing, I think. By the time I managed to get over to where they were fighting, she'd brought the trowel down on the man's head. His body jerked, then shuddered when she wrenched it out. He didn't move again.

Sometimes a situation tilts on its axis and everything changes so quick you don't have time to figure out how you feel. Which is why I sat there wanting to cry, and unable to. I wished I could be horrified by what I'd just seen.

I should've moved. I should've done *something.* My injections were trying to shove me forward, pushing me to engage.

But she was just hunched there. Her whole body pulsed like a heartbeat as she breathed deep, in and out. Just staring at the man she'd made a corpse.

"The hell was that for?" I flexed the flashlight in my hand. I had to get to the damn sword, but there was no way she'd let me get close.

I watched as the woman rolled the body over, dumped the small of his back right over the middle of my scabbard. Goddammit. "Because." She unfastened his thin gray cloak and settled it around her shoulders. "He looked warm."

Warm? "And what did that mean?"

She did a double take when she saw me. A small,

alarmed grunt bolted out from her throat. "Oh. Hm." She looked me over. Didn't move. "Nice coat."

That sounded like something someone who'd gone Gaunt would say. There were enough context clues to indicate it. Enough that my heart was making a panicked hummingbird thrum inside my chest. "Let's not get any ideas here, lady."

She shifted around to face me, climbed off her knees and crouched on the balls of her feet. She tightened her grip on the cultivator.

I just had my flashlight, which I could not exactly wave around menacingly. So I just braced for her. "I'm not joking. Come on. You don't want a fight."

"You're right." She tilted her head. "I don't. I want the coat." There was an unsheathed eagerness in her voice. The kind of unrestrained desire that comes with obsessing over something for a while—to the point where it's all you can think about. Gaunts were driven by the obsessions of the ghost infecting them. The fog of the soul they'd breathed into their body. A long-dead life that took up residence in theirs.

"It was a gift." Mom made it for me. "It's not for sale."

She huddled deeper into the dead man's shitty cloak, wrapped it around herself like membrane wings. "Didn't say anything about selling." She was too obsessed with my coat. She was Gaunt alright. "Just give it to me." She scuffed at a rock lamely.

A trail of winter breath spilled from her mouth. Which was odd, seeing as it was nowhere near cold enough to see breath. I squinted at her. "I shouldn't ask this," I said, "but um. What were you like?"

She tilted her head. "What do you mean?"

"Before...you know?" I gestured vaguely at her. "All

this?" I wasn't sure if I could lure her away from the dead body, or my sword. But maybe if I could keep her talking some kind of opening would make itself available to me.

"Infection?" The woman spat the word out with a puff of winter air.

"Y-yeah," I said.

"Warm." She rubbed her arms.

"What changed?"

"What do you think?" The woman rocked from the balls of her feet to her heels. She was just staring, though she didn't seem to see what was in front of her. "I see his memories sometimes."

"I know."

"You asked."

"Sorry."

"He wasn't that old, you know? Maybe eleven. His dog got out during the winter. Ages ago. Centuries, maybe. Both of them froze to death. Together. Kid's ghost floated aimlessly for a while. Then he found me." A shiver shuddered through her. "You going to give me the coat?"

She still hadn't moved. There was no way I could scramble for it. Was I going to have to handle this with just a flashlight? I sighed. "I can't do that."

"Why not?"

"You've killed someone already," I said.

"For warmth."

"And how's that working out for you?" She wouldn't be warm again. We both knew it.

"Fuck you. You don't get it. I did you a favor anyway, alright? This man was Gaunt, too, you know. Had one of the Violent Dead in him. You know what *they're* like, yeah?"

"I do," I said. "Everyone does." It was in the name. It left little to the imagination.

83

"I did you a favor. So just give me the coat."

Should I have handed it over? It would've deescalated the situation, I think. But then she would have sought out warmth from someone else. And anyway—this was the one gift I had from Mom that actually *meant* something to me. "I can't. I'm sorry."

She flexed her jaw. Her grip around her still-bloody trowel tightened. Her fingernails were purple, I noticed.

Then she leapt for me. I kept my eye on the three wicked points on the end of her hand. My injections shot through my forearm and jerked my hand into the path of her rake. Sludgy heat wrapped my fingers around her wrist.

I was about to swing the flashlight down on the top of her head when she fed her knees into my stomach. I tightened my grip on her wrist when I doubled over, but she yanked it down. The three prongs were right in front of my face. And suddenly her other hand was in my hair.

I took a deep breath. Wrenched the arm that held her weapon to one side. Stepped into the space between her legs, and hooked the flashlight on the back of her ankle as I mashed my fingers into her shoulder. I pushed her onto her back, grabbed her ankle as it went into the air, dragged her under me and fell on top of her.

Warm heat and pain streaked across my chest. The damn cultivator. She'd fucking scratched me with it as I came down. I brought the flashlight down on her head once, twice. She jerked. Reached her arms up, groping blindly. She got a palm on my temple and two fingers from her other hand on the edge of my mask.

Then the world tilted around me and the concrete swam up to greet my head as she hauled me off of her. There were spots of light in my vision. The world was fuzzy. Sounds were muted. I made a dive for my sword and felt her hands snag the rim of my waistband. My stomach hit the concrete. I felt her kneecaps digging into my spine. I tried to twist my hips and turn around.

But then a shrill shriek split the air and hurt my ears. For a moment I thought it was the woman on top of me, but it was followed by the sound of impact and a breath of surprise. Her weight sloughed off me. Her lifeless head bounced once when her body hit the concrete.

Someone had shot a caterwauler. That must have been it. Someone had *shot* her.

She didn't breath out ghostfog with her final breath the way most people do when they die. When you're Gaunt, you and the ghost infecting you get to evaporate forever. I'd never been sure if that qualified as a downside.

I rolled over, tried to shine the flashlight in the direction of the caterwauler shriek. But the flashlight wasn't working. Must've broken when I hit her. "Tell me that's you, Ed."

Ed stepped into the clearing. "What did she tell you?" Through the moonlight I could vaguely see he hadn't lowered the handgun. "How much did you hear? How much do you know?"

I coughed. "That's a joke, right? She was Gaunt. She didn't tell me anything."

"Gaunt?" He lowered the caterwauler.

Why was he surprised? What the hell was going on? "Yeah, man. Who else is going to be out here? Especially at this time of night?"

"I—I thought it was…" He shoved the caterwauler into the waiting prongs at the bottom of his holster and thumbed the lever to juice it up again. "…Never mind. It's not important." He crossed the clearing. Held out his hand to me. "Need any help?"

I took his hand and Ed pulled me to my feet. "I dunno

what this is about." I was still shaking. I didn't like that—it felt too vulnerable. "But you three are really good at acting paranoid."

"Who? Me and these two?" He thumbed to the corpses in the clearing.

"You and Desmon and Anoïse, dipshit."

"I knew what you meant. That was sarcasm."

"No, but who the fuck did you think it was that you just killed?" I asked. Did he think someone was following him? Was *that* the reason he was trying to keep such a low profile that he couldn't even let us sleep in a damn bed overnight? But then who would be following Ed? I couldn't think of any rumors I'd heard about people he'd pissed off, lately. Goddammit. What was he hiding from me?

"I didn't know who I killed. I saw that you were in danger so I moved to protect you. Now do you want to head to Bullion?"

That took me by surprise. "What happened to keeping a low profile?"

Ed looked at the Gaunt woman's corpse. "Her. I don't want to risk running into another Gaunt tonight."

I wasn't sure whether or not to trust his answer. I wanted to keep arguing, because him asking *how much do you know* seemed to imply he was keeping something from me. Should I have pressed him for information? Probably. That might've saved us all some trouble later on. But I was out of sorts after that attack. And Ed's offer of relief, of city walls and a featherbed for the night? That was just too tempting to ignore.

～

"You shouldn't have left," Ed said, as we rode for Bullion.

"Oh come on, Ed. If you didn't want me to leave you would've stepped in before I was even out of your sight."

Ed's mask shifted. I could feel him smirking underneath it. "I *tried* to keep you in my sight. For whatever that's worth."

We rode down a steep bend, past trees with leaves that glowed pale green in the dark. "What's that supposed to mean?"

"I followed you. Before I even heard you cry out. You didn't think I was going to let you just *walk away*, did you? Only trouble was that stupid fucking coat. The one Mom gave you. I lost track of where you were for a short time. It was stupid. Letting you leave. We should have stayed in our bedrolls."

It was probably stupid. I wasn't about to deny that, but I was angrier now that I knew Ed hadn't even given me the two minutes I requested. "You're unbelievable, you know."

Ed shrugged. "You should listen to me next time."

"Or *what?*"

Edgar was silent for a long time. "Did you know our ancestors once used glass as a punishment for betrayal?"

I swallowed. What was the point of mentioning this? "Sounds familiar." I half remembered a tapestry depicting something like that back home, though I couldn't recall the details.

"This was right as we were emerging from the Second Annihilation. When the Three Great Houses were just beginning to take their shape."

I rolled my eyes as irritation uncoiled in me. "Ed. Where are you going with this?"

Ed went on as if I hadn't said anything. "Want to know how they did it?"

"Not particularly."

Ed's laugh was more breath than substance. "The justiciars would take shards of glass. Grind it up in a mortar and pestle. While chanting prayers to bless the occasion."

"Ed. Come on. Stop it."

"The traitor would be bound. His arms behind his back. And a small sieve would be fitted to the back of his throat." He sounded like he was reciting lines from a book he'd read some time ago.

My mind gave weight to the scene, unwillingly. Thoughts of cold metal clinging to the roof of my mouth leapt into my mind. I thought of the feeling of a net just beginning to dip beyond the back of my tongue. Revulsion squirmed through the hollow of my throat as a dull ghost of the imagined feeling was conjured back there. "Shut up," I muttered. "I don't want to hear this, Ed."

But Edgar looked like he was enjoying this. "From there, the contents of the bowl, sifted down as fine as sand, would be dumped into the traitor's mouth. And they would *chew*. And chew. And chew. And the only thing that could get through that sieve would be the blood filling their mouth. And once his tongue was shredded down to pulp they would allow him to spit the glass out. Well. Along with all the rest, that is."

The imagined feeling of grainy glass vexed the contours of my mind. I could not stop the thoughts, couldn't stop wondering how those sharp shards would feel sliding through the bed of my tongue. The idea of it quickened in my mind. I could all but feel the sting of severed muscle, the taste of iron and blood as tongue meat was churned into mulch. The crunch of glass glittering in the roof of the mouth. White teeth wearing a slip of bright red. I could imagine the ghastly pulped paste that had once been my tongue tumbling out of my mouth. A mushy puree of tongue and muscle and blood and glass all mashed to a slurry, a stain on the floor.

This was another one of Ed's experiments. He wanted to test how I'd react, I knew. Edgar was keenly aware that I was not entirely in control of where my thoughts went or how thoroughly they gave shape to what I thought of. He knew this would happen. He was fucking with me psychologically as some kind of sick revenge for wandering off.

Nausea rifled through my stomach. "Hey. Hey. Ed." It felt strange to talk, to use my tongue after experiencing something adjacent to hallucination. "Ed. Buddy. What the fuck, man? Are you doing okay?"

He seemed absolutely delighted. "I'm fine," he sneered. "How are you?"

"Why are you telling this to me?"

I could feel Edgar grinning beneath his mask like a man who up to this point had thought he was being very subtle. "No reason," he said, his voice too cheery. "Just listen to me next time."

CHAPTER
SIX

The sky was overcast with clouds the color of exhausted eyes by the time Bullion's black gates came into view from over a hill. There was no time to snag some saddle sleep at the pace we rode that night. It took us a few hours of riding just to get there—with a couple breaks between so the horses wouldn't overheat.

Bullion was in the shadow of the Forest Wall—a subcontinental wicker basket from the First Annihilation, filled with all the corpse technology of the Second.

Bullion itself was where labcoats harvested and reanimated the technology they found there. It was one of the places where they made the world work as it should; and manufactured all the environmental patches we needed to resuscitate a murdered ecosystem.

The sundown air was a cold compress on my skin as we approached the city gates. I spotted the sentries posted at watchtowers with rifles in their hands. Caterwauler brand long guns. I had to consciously remind myself they weren't for me, that they didn't view me as a threat.

I knew a brief instant of hope at the idea nobody would

try to check us at the gates. We would get in, find a place to bed down, and in the morning we'd head to Anoïse so I could get my oath of fealty over with.

We'd just got through the city walls, and I was in the middle of wondering where we were going to sleep for the night when I spotted two members of the city watch, horses cutting a swath down the lane to greet us.

One of them stood up in his stirrups and called for us to hold.

"Hey, Ed?" I whispered. "Are we in trouble?" My voice was rusty with disuse. I wasn't sure how much I wanted to talk to him after everything he did recounting that glass punishment. It was better to play things safe.

"We're not in trouble," Edgar said under his breath.

"How do you know?"

"I know."

"Well then why are we whispering?"

"You started whispering first. I'm just matching your tone."

The guards reined up in front of us. "Which one of you is Petre Mercy?" It was a formality. Everyone knew. Or at least—everyone could guess that guy beside me was Edgar. Dad kept me out of the public eye more than he did with the other three. Not everyone always knew who I was. They could've used process of elimination, though. I exchanged a troubled glance with Edgar.

"Petre...?" Edgar wrung out his reins. "Did something happen?"

Fuck. What the hell did they want *me* for? "Good question." I turned to the guards and frowned as I debated my options. It was possible that Mercedes Blackheath merely wished to contact me. She was in the city on business, after all. Maybe she'd heard that I was coming.

It was also possible that Desmon and Anoïse had put the word out that they wanted me, especially if they were worried I'd managed to evade Edgar. It couldn't have anything to do with Edgar, though. Or else they would be riding his ass, too.

"Your Grace?" One of the watchmen said. I realized just how long I had been silent.

"Hold on a minute," I said. "I'm thinking."

"Petre," Ed said quietly. "What is there to think about?"

I tried to puzzle out how best to handle my situation. I noticed Edgar close his hand around his science-sword. The guards across from us each had a hand over their guns. I realized they had radios plugged in on their pauldrons. It wouldn't be too difficult to call for backup.

"Your Grace!" The guard probed again.

"What is this about?" I asked, blind panic squeezing the words out from the center of my chest.

"We've been asked to prepare an audience for y—"

"By who?" Ed cut in. I was surprised to see him lending a hand here. All eyes fell on him for an instant.

"I'm sorry, Lord Mercy—Lord Edgar," one of the guards said. "I'm not at liberty to say."

I needed a way out. I remembered the letter. Desmon's letter. I still had it in my pocket.

A few things switched into place. "Hold on." I fished it out, unfolded it. Presented it to them. "I think there's been a misunderstanding. This should clear things up."

I waited for several horrifying seconds while the guards read the letter. They passed it back and forth between them.

"Petre," Edgar said slowly. "What is that?"

Hold up—

Hang on—

Just a minute—

He didn't know? He was coming here to bring me back to Anoïse and Desmon and Ed didn't even know I'd been *communicating* with them?

Something was wrong. Something was very, very wrong. Panic started throwing a tantrum in my stomach. "I'll explain later."

The guard folded it up and handed it back to me. "I see," he murmured. I saw his mask shift as he frowned. And then he laughed. "I mean, I suppose that covers things, doesn't it?" He turned to the guard beside him, like he was checking for some reassurance.

The other guard shrugged. "Worst case scenario is we have to find you again. But if you're on your way, we'll send word back."

My heart was hammering in the sides of my neck even as the guards made their retreat from Ed and me.

I felt like I had made a mistake. Like maybe I would've been better off letting Edgar draw his backsword and start swinging.

"Right." Edgar gave the reins a jerk. His horse shuddered and started moving into Bullion. "Terrific. Fantastic. This is *great.*"

"What?" I followed him. Maybe I could still play dumb. "What's going on?"

"He said you were on your way," Edgar repeated. "On your way *where*? Petre. What happened back there?"

"Ed, I—what?"

"Give me the letter." Edgar said. "I want to see what it said."

"What? Fuck you, no."

He lurched in his saddle, hand outstretched towards me.

93

I twisted away, and my injections kicked in. I didn't fight it as it sculpted my body, guided my fist into the side of Edgar's face. My first two knuckles caught his eye socket, but I maintained enough control to keep from hitting him hard enough to leave a mark.

I didn't move to intercept his return volley as his fist cracked my teeth together and made my ears ring.

We sat in our saddles, fuming at each other. I felt like a child. Like I was pouting. "It's *mine*," I said. Which didn't help.

"I just want to know what happened back there," Ed sighed. He rubbed his eye.

"Why did they stop you? Why did that letter you gave them get you out of trouble there? What does it say?"

"I don't know!" I probably said it louder than I should've, considering the crowd of people all around us. "None of you will tell me what's going on!" That was not, strictly speaking, true. But I was beginning to think Ed wasn't being honest with me. So I didn't see any reason to be honest with him.

Ed tilted his head. "What do you mean *none of you?*"

"The fuck do you think I mean? You and Anoïse and Desmon. None of you." This was the second time he'd forgotten about the two of them.

"Anoïse and Desmon reached out?"

I blinked at him, and realized it was possible that I had jumped to conclusions. Were the three of them not working together after all?

Ed must've read the confusion on my face, because he was quick to course correct. "I just meant," he amended, "—you know, they sent me out. I didn't know they sent you anything in advance. Is that what's in the letter?" He reached for it again.

I swatted his arm away. He was such a fucking liar. No *way* was he going to spin this. Anoïse hadn't sent him. That was clear by now. So why the fuck was he here, and where the fuck was he taking me?

I should never have gone with him. "I don't know why I thought this was a good idea, man. You should've left me back in Blackheath House. This was a mistake, okay?"

"Petre. You're not going back. You're not turning around." Ed insisted. "Just tell me what was in the letter."

How much do you know? He was asking it again. I wanted to cry. But I wasn't going to do that. Not in front of him. I wasn't going to give him that satisfaction. I raised my hands up, made a mock surrender, then took a breath. Then three more, or else I was going to say something stupid. I counted backwards from ten. "Listen. I'll share if you will. I'll tell you what's in the letter if you tell me where we're *really* going. What's it gonna be?"

"Petre. Don't be stupid. Use your brain. I'm taking you back to Mercy House. Where else would we go?"

I rolled my eyes. "I know I'm an idiot but I'm not stupid, Ed. Come on." My heart kicked things up a couple more notches. Which was wild because I was up until now laboring under the delusion that my heartbeat couldn't go any faster than where it was at.

"You're overthinking this," Edgar said. "We're going back to court. That's all. You're making a big deal out of nothing."

"This sure doesn't seem like nothing!" I shouted. "You're keeping such a low profile you'd rather risk tangling with a Gaunt than being spotted in Bullion—"

"We're here, aren't we?" Ed snapped.

"Yeah, *now*. You only caved after I nearly got hurt. If that hadn't happened we'd still be sleeping on the side of the road. You don't want any ceremonies, you're traveling without a coterie, you insist on staying away from crowded places, you won't let me out of your sight, and the *one* time I ran off you were scared I'd learned something. So what are you up to Ed? Come on. Spill."

"Nothing is *up*." Edgar sounded like he was trying to crush that last word inside his mouth. "It's nothing. Quiet down, will you?"

I felt overwhelmed. There was too much happening all at once. There was too much input going into my mainframe. This was too much. I needed an out.

I spotted businessmen and women in ermine-trimmed coats spill down a side street. Titans of industry wrapped in silk blouses inlaid with cloth of gold. They adorned their low necklines with broaches inlaid with pearls and wore gas masks inset with glittering jewelry.

Mercedes was holding a business meeting here.

I had to follow them. They could lead me straight to her. But I wasn't sure if I wanted Edgar following me.

"Fuck it." I dismounted my horse. Left it in the middle of the street. "If that's how you want to play things, fine. You can come get me when you're ready to tell me what's actually happening."

Edgar leaned out the saddle and tried to catch me, but I twisted out of his grip. "Get off me," I growled. "I'll see you around. If you want to be honest with me. For now, leave me the fuck alone. I need to cool off." I spun off.

Edgar stopped his own mount and hopped down after me. "No, *you* listen to *me*. I'm not done with you." He put his hand around my wrist.

I reacted automatically. Pivoted around and slammed my knuckles into his temple, hard enough to stagger him sideways.

He went to one knee. I stood over him with my fist reeled back, ready to go in case he got up. In case he tried to follow me. "I said I need to cool off!" I shouted.

Angry laughter ambushed him as he crouched in the dirt. "Was that your injections too?"

I should have left it there. But I was sick of him, so I drove my boot into his ribs and heard the breath oomph out of him. "I need some space. And don't follow me this time."

I left while I could. He'd struck a nerve. I hated him. I hated all of this. Coming here was a mistake. I should've avoided him. I should've hidden away and gotten my injections tonight.

I needed to find Mercedes. She was the only person in Bullion who I knew was here. I followed the road I'd seen the magnates ducking down and was soon swept along by the business quarter of the city. I was swallowed up in bright lights and the smell of sugar and saffron. I wormed my way between businessmen in fur coats and overpriced shoes and squeezed between the press of servants and magnates. I had to get away from Edgar.

I tried to remember where Mercedes had said she was staying. There was a hotel she owned nearby. Surely she'd have to be there, right?

"Petre!"

That was her.

I turned in the direction of my name, and only had only a split second to take in her one good green eye. She was missing about a quarter slice of her face. There was a jagged hole shaped like a puzzle piece around her left eye, shot through with clockwork machinery. Steel spiderwebs held her false skull together and sewed it to the rest of her. A glowing coal-red eye was inlaid into the epicenter of the mesh. I wondered, not for the first time, if it was difficult to sleep with a night light so close to your face.

Before those thoughts could linger she wrapped me in a hug that pressed me tight against her. I was so exhausted I could've melted into her. I molded my hands to fit between her shoulder blades. I could smell the scent of cinnamon in her hair.

"I've been looking all over for you. I thought my guards would've intercepted you by now." Her voice was muffled by a mouthful of my coat.

I took in a deep breath and tried to memorize the familiar feeling of her in my arms. I wasn't sure when I'd get to do this again.

"Petre," she said, carefully. "I don't believe a hug is supposed to last this long."

"Fuck. Sorry." Peeling apart from her felt like ripping off the safety of a bandage. "It's been a day." I wanted to drag her back against me, to wrap my arms around her. Press her body and her mouth real tight against mine, just so I could think about something else for a while.

But I guess I was supposed to be *responsible* here.

"So I've heard," Mercedes said.

My heartbeat jumped, startled. "You've heard?" I croaked. "What have you heard?" How much did she know?

"What are you doing here?" She hissed beneath her breath and looked askance at businessmen and women passing by. She led me through the crowd. To her hotel, I surmised. "What do you think you're doing? Are you insane?"

I blinked. "Wait. Back up. I asked what you've heard. I need to know." If someone around here finally had some fucking answers, I'd need her to share. "Edgar won't tell me what's going on. I don't know what's happening, and I just—"

"Were you seen? Did you come here with anyone? Have you been followed?"

I wondered if what was happening was perhaps more serious than I'd anticipated. "Mercedes. I—"

"Come inside. Quick." She seized me by the back of my coat and hauled me into an alleyway. I stumbled after her.

"This is not traditionally how you're supposed to make an entrance," I joked. Why the hell was she taking me into an alleyway—unless? "What kind of coming inside are you talking about here?"

She stopped for a moment to slap the back of my head. "Any other day," she said, chewing on her lip. "But now is not the time. I need you to focus, Mercy."

"If not that, then what—?"

"We can't use front entrances. I don't want you to be seen." Mercedes shouldered open a side door to the hotel and led me through.

I was thankful that she kept her back to me, so she couldn't see the bright red I was wearing on my face. "Ah." I said. "I suppose that does make more sense." I thought it over a bit more. "Hold on. No, it doesn't. Why can't we use front entrances?"

She shut the door more carefully than I thought was strictly necessary. "Because there's been a bit of a *crisis*."

My stomach dropped. "I don't suppose this has anything to do with Edgar?" What the fuck had he done? What the hell had he roped me into? Goddammit.

"Edgar? Petre, I was talking about the rumors."

I felt like I had choked on my own indrawn breath. "Rumors?" I coughed. I hadn't heard of any rumors. What the hell was she talking about? And since when did rumors count as a crisis? I felt like my lungs were crawling up my throat. "What rumors?"

"You really haven't heard?"

"I've been getting letters from one of my brothers, and the other one just picked me up. The hell is this about rumors?"

She gave me a wary sidelong look that made me feel a little dizzy. Maybe that showed up on my face because she looked around and whispered, "We should find somewhere more private to talk about this."

MORE PRIVATE DID NOT MEAN QUITE what I'd hoped for.

Mercedes harbored me in a room on the second floor that smelled like freshly printed paper and vacuumed carpet. I sat down on the end of the only bed provided. "How'd you know I was here?"

"Avram told me you'd be coming," she explained as she locked the door. "My sentries spotted you at the gate. I tried to bring you here so I could explain things. But I think they misunderstood why I needed you here. They've been reporting on your movement since you first entered the city."

"You really wanted to update me on all this, huh?" I asked. "So what's all this about rumors?" I wasn't sure if there was anything Mercedes could share that I'd find shocking. There was one time where Edgar had borne the brunt of a couple incest rumors when we were teenagers. The tabloids *loved* those. Every couple years they tried to snag one of us in an incest story. Something about the four of us being the same age gave it some weird, unique appeal.

That "one soul, four bodies" flavor of annoying bullshit that's usually reserved for twins.

When the four of us were fifteen Edgar had been caught with an arm around me after I'd had something of a meltdown in public. He'd been trying to calm me down. *You're going to be okay. You're okay. Please be okay. Come on, Petre. You can't embarrass Dad like this. Just breathe with me. Deep breath. You'll be okay.*

It had worked, but the tabloids ran with the rumors for a few weeks. He ambushed me with knives in my personal chamber a few weeks later, a few hours after we'd got into an argument about sorting out who was to blame.

All this to say—I was prepared for anything.

"First things first," Mercedes said. "Can you remove your head?"

Except that. "Mercedes, I—what? No. Of course not. How could I remove my head? I mean sometimes I wish I could, but—" Not permanently, mind. But it often felt like I needed a break from my brain.

"It's one of the rumors." She shrugged.

I sat down on the end of the bed. Gathered my hands in my lap. "Does anyone actually believe it?"

Mercedes frowned. "Depends on who you ask. I've got some superstitious cousins who swear it's true."

"You've got to be kidding."

Mercedes rifled through the bureaus. Checking for bugs, most likely. Sometimes she was prone to bouts of paranoia. Usually when she was already stressed about something else. Growing up in court environments will do that. "Others think it's an exaggerated metaphor." She elaborated without eye contact.

I stared at the space between my legs. "A metaphor for *what* exactly?"

"Well, we all know you didn't skip your own father's funeral for nothing," Mercedes joked. "Clearly your refusal to set foot in a place of God means you're a demon."

"Right," I said. "Clearly."

A handheld radio on her hip blared out a soft whine. A high-pitched squall of a voice garbled something that was probably in code. She retrieved it and pressed the button. "Say that again."

The same warped static voice repeated the report.

"Shit. Alright. Thank you."

She tossed it to me. My injections yanked my hands up. Put them right in the radio's path. "Keep it," she said, without answering the question. "I'll grab another from one of my guards when I leave. I'll use this to let you know if something's happened."

"Wait, but what was that report?" I asked her.

"Oh! Edgar is looking for you. He knows you're with me. One of his people must've spotted you. We're still sorting out how many here he's got on his side."

"Great." His people? Who the fuck were his people? What the fuck was going on? I threw myself backwards on the bed. I spread my arms out, prepared to let the comforter envelop me. But it was springier than I'd expected, and I almost bounced right back upright. "Phenomenal. Just fantastic. Is all of this related to the rumors?"

"Well." Mercedes bit her lip in a way I attempted not to get aroused by. I looked away. Time and place. Time and place.

"What is it?" I asked.

"Most of the rumors revolve around you conspiring against your sister. There's some attempt to take her throne in most versions."

"Mercedes—" I swear to god. She could've just started

there. Cut to the meat of it. Like what the fuck? I wasn't conspiring against Anoïse. I didn't want anything to do with her. I just wanted to be left alone. "Do people think I've started some kind of civil war?" Maybe I was asking the wrong questions. But I had so many, and how do you even begin to prioritize them? Like—what was I doing here in some hotel of all places when Anoïse might be out there thinking I was planning some kind of coup?

"One of them involved an escape you did, from what I hear."

"Where did I escape *from?*" This felt too surreal.

"Mercy House."

"But—but that's ridiculous. I haven't even been there for five years."

"That's what I thought, too. I've been hearing these rumors for days now. I didn't think much of them. Until I learned your brother, *allegedly,* had sent people to my meeting here. Then Avram told me Edgar was coming to see you. And I started wondering if maybe there wasn't some merit to the rumors after all. Maybe someone *was* planning to overthrow Anoïse. Maybe the rumors just ensnared the wrong sibling."

My stomach dropped. "Mercedes. What are you saying? Is Ed planning something he thinks I'd be sympathetic to?"

Mercedes pressed her lips together. "Well. I don't see any other reason he'd send people here to interfere in my deal regarding the crown's munitions contracts, unless he was planning to—"

"What the fuck? *Munitions?* That's what you're in Bullion for?" I felt dizzy, like I was choking. What the hell was Ed trying to do in Bullion that involved interfering with fucking *munitions contracts?* Fuck.

I tried to go over her theory. Ed had been imprisoned,

and escaped, from Mercy House. He sent supporters to interfere with munitions contracts. And he picked me up because he thought I would support him, but he'd been trying to play it safe by keeping me in the dark about why he'd come.

That was why he'd been so keen on keeping a low profile. *That* was why he was worried about how much I knew after everything with the Gaunt. Maybe he thought the Gaunt was an agent Anoïse sent after him. I don't know. I don't know. All I knew was suddenly it made sense why he'd been so paranoid since picking me up.

Good Lord. He was trying to rope me into a goddamn coup. A civil fucking war.

He had been trained to rule, just like Anoïse. Her coronation would've felt like the denial of his birthright. Everything Dad had raised him for, but he didn't know what to do with his life if he wasn't the one on top.

Anoïse's interference in his potential marriage-alliance must've been the last bit of salt in that wound. The thing that pushed him over the edge, if it had happened just around the time Dad died. Now he just wanted to have it all, any way he could get it. God. Fuck. What the hell was *wrong* with him?

I was retroactively thankful we hadn't stopped at any inns. Now there would be fewer chances of new rumors running wild across the countryside. Though I was certain enough people had already seen me with him.

"There are also rumors," Mercedes's voice retrieved me from my thoughts, "that his supporters are searching Bullion for some kind of helmet."

I blinked at her. "A helmet."

"Something wrong?"

"You can't be serious."

"Why not?"

I didn't fucking know. "Are they looking for bubble wrap as well? That sounds ridiculous."

She snorted. "I'm just telling you what I know. I'm not saying I buy it. Unless you think I expect you can take off your head, too?"

That was fair. "Why couldn't you keep him out of Bullion?"

"Petre." Her tone flatlined.

"Well?" Was she annoyed? Had I annoyed her?

"He's a Prince. I have suspicions about him, yes, but if I try to keep him out it could become the catalyst for a conflict bigger than I could anticipate. I don't have all the information. It's all just rumors. And your sister isn't answering any of my communications. We've only just put these pieces together in the last few hours, and it's the middle of the night. I don't know how fast we can get word to her that your brother is here."

"But we have to do *something*." I wasn't sure what, but there had to be some action we could take.

"I've got my eye on him. I can tell you that much. If he tries to interfere, I'll take care of it. This place is crawling with The Blackheath Guard. I'm getting reports about his whereabouts and who we think are loyal to him. And it's good to know that you're not working with him."

"God, no. I don't want anything to do with any of them."

"I never doubted you for a second."

"I don't suppose you've tried to tell Anoïse that?" I asked.

"I don't suppose you'd believe me if I told you I haven't been able to reach her?"

"That does *feel* like a fucking joke." Or at the very least I certainly felt like a punchline.

"Nobody's been able to get a hold of anyone at the capital. I'm worried something's happened. Something they're trying to keep under wraps. I can't prove anything, but—"

I'm not sure when my hands found my skull. I gripped it tight. I had a headache, and some part of me was trying to push the pressure that was pulsing out back *in*. "The hell do I even do, Mercedes?"

"Well," she said, "here's what I'm going to do. I'm going to see if I can't locate your brother. Keep him occupied. And I think you need to find a way to reach your sister."

"You said you couldn't make contact."

"Not through radio or letters. But you *were* summoned home, yes?"

So Avram told her about the letter too. That was helpful. I wasn't sure I liked the idea of going home, though. "Yeah. Desmon gave me an inn to meet him at and everything."

"So you'll need to get out quickly."

"Edgar will try to stop me. Can you help me get out?"

She frowned. "I don't know. If you take any of the main roads, Edgar or someone loyal to him might find you. You'd have to sneak out. Take the back roads. And even then, you'd have to do it quickly."

"How?"

Mercedes' jaw tightened. "I'm trying to think. All the rooms on the ground floor are occupied for the munitions meeting. And it'd take too long to explain things to any occupants. Not to mention we still need to sort out how many of them are on Ed's side. We don't want to alert anyone to the fact that we're onto him. That we're ferrying you out of his reach. So I—hm."

She offered me her hand. I took it. She hauled me to my feet and led me to the window, which was glowing orange from the shimmershield outside. "Follow my finger. See the back streets? The alleyways—?"

"To the outer exit," I said. "To the Forest Wall."

"If you can sneak out of here quickly it should be a straight shot back to your sister."

"Is there a catch?" I asked.

Mercedes frowned. "I don't know if we can get out the way we came in. Someone might intercept you. Take you to Edgar."

I calculated all her unspoken implications. "...So you're going to sneak me out a different exit, right?" I barely dared to hope the situation was not too dire.

She frowned. My stomach dropped. "It might be a bit more dire than that."

"In what way?"

"I don't know yet!" Mercedes shot back, matching my tone. "We don't have all the information. All we know is that Edgar is currently looking for you. Which means someone knows you're with me. Which means someone on his side has access to our radios. I don't know how many eyes and ears he's got in this place. So you need to make your exit quickly, and we can't use the radios to coordinate with anyone. So—" She indicated to the shimmershield behind me.

"Are you suggesting I jump out the window?" I asked.

"Well." She shrugged. "You'll have to turn the shimmer-shield off first. Unless you have a better idea?"

I opened my mouth to speak.

Before I could she added, "One that does not lead to you potentially being spotted or captured on your way out of here."

I closed my mouth.

"Edgar could catch up with us every second we spend arguing about this," she added.

Civil fucking war. You had to be kidding me. "Right," I said. "Right. Go distract them. I'll be fine."

"I know you will." I think she tried to sound reassuring. "Oh, and there's one more thing—"

In an instant she had her arms around the back of my neck and her mouth opened against mine. She pressed herself against me. I didn't want to break contact. My hands found her hips. A small groan burbled out from the back of my throat.

She pulled away. I felt dizzy. The world was swimmy all around me.

"For luck," she explained.

I indulged in a grin. "These are *long* odds."

"And you'll have to make it work. I believe in you."

I GOT REACQUAINTED with my fears after she left. Terror was a living thing scuttling inside my belly, trapped and panicked. It quickly colonized the contours of every thought. I shut off the shimmershield.

The windowpane opened sideways. I stuck my head out. Nighttime had eaten up the skyline while I wasn't looking. The crisp outside air tasted like apple skins.

I strapped the gas mask on over my mouth and nose, looked down and considered the drop. Right. Just jump out the window. Simple really. How hard could it be?

There was a dumpster down there and everything. That would probably cushion things. I just had to hope there was nothing very pointy in there.

But before I could even consider the drop I heard a commotion on the ground floor, down on the asphalt. There were sounds of impact and yelling from around the corner, out on the street, where I couldn't see.

I was suddenly grateful I hadn't convinced Mercedes to sneak me out on the ground floor. We would've walked straight into Ed. If that *was* Ed. God. Fuck.

I climbed back inside. Pushed the bed out from the corner, until I had enough space to wriggle behind it and keep pushing.

I'd have to build a barricade, just to be safe. It might take some time to work up the courage to get through the window, and I didn't want anyone walking in on me before I could.

The bedposts made a long and anguished screech, like how I felt on the inside. I wished I could've made a noise like that.

I told myself I had time. He still had to figure out which room I was in. I had time. I could do this.

Then the radio Mercedes had offered me switched on. I knew an instant of hope. Maybe she'd gotten Edgar detained.

"Petre." Nope. Fuck. That was Edgar's voice. "We need to talk."

SEVEN

I slammed the bed against the door. Wedged it up as snug as it would fit.

The radio switched on again and Edgar's voice fizzled out. "Petre. Come on. How much have you heard? We can work this out."

I moved to the bureau. Toppled it over with a clamor loud enough to make me wince. I grabbed it by the hind legs and started pushing into the space the bed had left behind.

"Petre." Ed used the same admonishing tone of voice Dad did. "Talk to me."

How the hell did he even get a radio? I thought Mercedes said she'd staffed this place with members of The Blackheath Guard. Had Ed incapacitated one of them? Was that the emergency that had dragged her away? What was going on?

I switched my radio on. I was out of breath. "I hear you sent people here, Ed. What's up with that?"

"I didn't plan to be here," Ed admitted. "This is why I didn't want to stop in Bullion. I know what this looks like, but Anoïse just asked me to send some people to take care of—"

"No, go *fuck* yourself, Ed." I shouted, "Don't lie to me!" I ripped a few of the bottom drawers out and crammed them into the remaining space. Built up a giant wedge to keep the door shut.

"Petre. I know you're upset." He was infuriatingly calm.

I felt dizzy. Like something in me was crawling out of my skin. But I wasn't going to get drawn into this. I was too frustrated. He'd tricked me. Lied to me. Almost made me a traitor.

I had to get to Anoïse.

I assessed my handiwork. I wasn't sure if my haphazard pile was the proper way to build a barricade. I'd never had to do this before. Might've been more helpful to stack the bureau on the bed. But I didn't have much time to over-think this. It would work fine for a first try.

"I know I could've been more forthright with you—" Edgar's voice crackled over the radio.

That settled it. I switched on. "Oh, you *think?* You noticed that, did you? You're planning an entire fucking civil war to overthrow our sister and the subject just kind of slipped your mind, did it?"

"I, um." Edgar laughed. He actually laughed. I was going to stab him if he got through that door. Good Lord. "I'm trying to own up to it." I'll give him some credit. He managed to only sound a little bit frustrated. "You know? That thing you're always saying we never do. Just tell me what room you're in. Open the door. You don't have to go back to Anoïse."

That gave me the courage to get one leg through the window. Though my dangling leg made the length between me and the trash heap below all the more apparent. How well could I expect that to cushion my fall? Fuck. My stomach attempted to somersault out the window.

Instead I switched the radio on. "A bit of advice, Ed. When you're owning up to something don't immediately weaponize it for a couple of extra points in a stupid argument. That's not the same as owning it."

In response I heard a caterwauler scream. The top corner of the door was reduced to hairy splinters. There was not enough open space to see Edgar.

The radio on my hip switched on, though I could hear his real voice on the other side of the door. He was closing in. "Look, I'm doing my best here. Just come with me!"

I listed to one side and tried to work up the courage to get my other leg through. Where was Mercedes? She was supposed to hold him off.

I turned the radio back on. "Fuck off, Ed. Seriously. I'm not going to help you overthrow our sister."

Edgar pounded on the door. I watched it shudder on its hinges. The whole structure jumped every time he kicked it. Then chunks of the door frame went flying, as Edgar's science-sword sliced into the door.

"Right!" Edgar called through the slowly widened opening. "Because you've just been dying to see her these last few years, haven't you?" He made a couple more hacks in the door with his sword. Slowly he worked enough room to wriggle through.

All I could do was sit there and try and work up the nerve to jump out. My injections kept trying to push me, but I pushed back. I wasn't ready. Not quite yet. It was a long drop, and it was going to hurt no matter how I did it.

"It's not like I've been back to see you either, Ed. I don't want anything to do with the two of you, but I can't have

Anoïse thinking I support whatever stupid fucking rebellion you're trying to put together."

Edgar had enough room to crawl. So I started inching out the window while he slithered through the opening like a snake. "If you go back to Mercy House she'll never let you out again!" He held out his hand.

For an instant. And *only* for an instant. I considered it.

Then my resolve hardened.

"I'm sorry, Ed. I can't." He was all the way through now, so I had to wrap this up. I offered him a salute. "See you around, man." I squeezed my eyelids shut and hauled my other leg over the ledge.

Immediately a flare of pain went up in my hip. But I hadn't hit the ground. Not yet. What the fuck? I kicked my legs out, testing. And I opened my eyes to find I was suspended in the air.

My science-sword was stuck crosswise against the window. I was hanging by my belt.

I could feel the pressure building. The leather straining. I fumbled with the swordbelt as I dangled, but I couldn't get the leverage I needed to get it off. I could feel my heartbeat in my neck as my breath went thin and I braced one foot on the outside wall. "Fuck fuck fuck fuck." Red leather squealed under the weight and stress I put on it.

I didn't want to drop. I didn't want to drop. Even if I made it down safe I would be helpless without a sword. Especially since Ed already had a visual on me.

Edgar's head came out from the window. "No fucking way." Even he didn't seem to believe it.

I felt my face growing red. And then I felt a little bit hysterical. "A little help?"

Edgar sent me a wicked grin I wasn't sure if I liked. "I

dunno, Petre. Sounded like you were pretty keen on getting away."

"Ed." I couldn't help the note of panic that infected my voice. "Ed. I swear to God."

"God's not the one you need help from right now."

"Lord Alive, Ed. Just get me back up."

"And you'll behave?"

I couldn't help it. "Go fuck yourself."

"That doesn't sound like behaving to me."

"Fuck you. Let me up and we'll talk about this."

To my surprise he stretched his hand out. Mine was sweaty, so I had to really dig my nails in to get a good grip.

"Careful," Ed cautioned. "Dig in too hard and I'm going to drop you."

"Don't you fucking dare."

"Calm down. It's not a threat. That's just what happens when your hand hurts."

I used the outer wall as a brace as Ed hauled me up by hand and hip. A couple times we had to switch hands, and holds, as I wormed my way up the hotel wall.

Eventually I was half in the window, braced on my stomach. My hands were around the back of Edgar's head. And he was holding me under my armpits. From this angle, he was the only thing keeping me from the twenty-four feet to the tarmac.

And then he stopped.

"Ed," I said, breathless. "Ed. What are you doing?"

He bunched up my shirt in his fist. "A little bit of insurance before you get your feet under you." His words were wrapped around a smile as he undid my sword belt, and I heard it clatter to the floor.

I started thrashing. Trying to hit him. But before I could land a blow he just stepped forward, and I was dangling out the window, legs kicking, completely in his grip and at his mercy. "Tell me you'll behave," Edgar said. "And I'll let you through." He wore a crooked taunting sibling grin.

"I already *told* you that you can go fuck yourself, asshat!" I kicked, uselessly.

Edgar looked down to the street below. My heels knocked together as I dangled, chest barely touching the window frame. Then he looked back at me. "It's a long drop."

I'd had a long day. I wasn't thinking straight. And I wasn't sure what else I had to do at that point. I think my injections might've taken over.

I braced my hands on the inside wall and pushed my shoulder into his chest. Got the leverage I needed to somersault into the room. My heel met something solid on the way in. Edgar grunted. I sprang for my sword.

Before I could I felt Ed's knuckles on the back of my head. His other hand closed around my heel, and my ribs met hardwood. I was one fingernail away from my science-sword. I tried to grab it, but he hauled me back before I made contact.

He fell on top of me. My injections dragged my elbow around as I twisted. I felt it hit his jaw.

I sat up and grabbed him by the back of his neck. Yanked him down to my level as my back embraced the floor. I twisted with my hips and we switched places.

I didn't give him any time to recover. I got my knees on top of his arms and I just started hitting him. Slamming my knuckles into his face. My ears felt full and the room was spinning. I pinned Edgar's head between my knuckles and the floorboards two times. "I WILL *KILL* YOU!" I roared.

"You think you can just—" His knees slammed into the small of my back. I braced on all fours and rocked my weight back before he could climb out from under me. I hit him again. "I swear to god!" I screamed. "You can't always get your fucking way, Ed! I ran away because I want to be left alone! You think you can just show up and make me a part of your stupid fucking—" I couldn't think of the right word, so I abandoned that sentence altogether. "I will fucking kill you! Do you understand me?" I wasn't even sure he could hear me.

Ed managed to get one arm free while I was screaming. I only realized when I felt his hand in my hair. He twisted his hips and hurled me to the floor.

I rolled with the momentum. Came up clutching the science-sword. My injections burned in me. I spun at the same time I extracted the saber from the sheath. Pressed a button in the thumb ring to pump it full of thyroid hormones. Heat up the blade's edge. I brought it around and—

—motherfucker had his science-sword in the way while I was trying to kill him. How fucking dare he. Our swords coughed sparks when they met.

I moved against his bind, turned the curve of my saber upside down to get around his backsword model. He stepped back before I could reach him and swatted my sword out of the way. I brought it back around when his science-sword was headed for me. Tried to move off his attack line and come in from the side at the same time.

But something else hit me first. It wasn't Ed. Wrong direction. It was a concussive blast that punched the breath from my body with enough momentum to take me off my feet. The world flashed white when the back of my head hit the far wall. I couldn't organize my limbs fast enough before I hit the floor. I dragged my gaze up to see a young man in the doorway, a caterwauler in hand. I noticed there was a small crowd of rich people standing around the man in the doorway.

Then Edgar stepped between me and the young man and hovered the point of his blade against the hollow of my throat. I could feel the heat crackling around the double edges. It prickled. "You think I came all this way without a plan? You think I hadn't anticipated someone might find me out? That I wouldn't have backup? And supporters? And I'm supposed to be the one who doesn't know anything about *you?*" He doused the science-sword in his sheath with a jet of steam and crouched over where I sat slumped against the wall, too stunned to speak. Or to remind him Mercedes had already told me about his supporters.

"So," he picked up my sword. He inspected it, then turned his attention back to me. "Here's how this is going to go."

∼

ALRIGHT. Here's what I know.

Three months ago, Dad died. I skipped the funeral. It was held without me. Anoïse stood vigil for a week, and then life was put on hold to begin the customary three months of mourning.

Business as usual, right?

Except that during that vigil, Anoïse received word that Edgar was planning to take the throne for himself. His legal case, as he explained it to me, possessed *just* enough gray areas to frighten Anoïse.

Edgar's theory was dependent on the fact that the physicians who ripped us out of Mom's womb were not ordained by God, and there was no clear divine vision of what the line of succession could look like. That meant clearly he was supposed to sit on the throne.

The argument was more compelling than I wanted to admit. Edgar was better liked. Reared for rule, just in case anything was to happen to Anoïse. He figured he could bring more important politicians in for a cabinet, to advise on policy. He had a better head for negotiation and math and economics—all according to him, mind. This was the same man who liked to tell Anoïse that she'd be too emotional and temperamental if she made it to the throne, so take it with a grain of salt. At the end of the day he argued to his supporters that all his success meant that God truly favored *him* to be the next King.

So—with that in mind—you can understand why Anoïse might panic.

"She made a plan with Havilan Reacher," Edgar told me.

"He wasn't on your side?" Wasn't he Guindolin Reacher's dad? Wouldn't he want his daughter on the throne instead of his nephew? Or did he just not care? Was that even a part of Ed's plan? It had to be, right? But how could that be possible if he didn't even have Havilan Reacher on his side?

Ed didn't answer directly. Which was probably smart of him. "I don't know. Somehow I wound up under house arrest," he said. "So—"

"Hold up. Anoïse put you under house arrest?"

He shrugged. "Maybe Havilan suggested it. Or Desmon. I don't know how Anoïse learned about my plans."

I felt like there was a gunshot wound in the center of my stomach. "I take it the house arrest didn't go well?"

"Actually, it went fine at first."

"How long is *at first*?" I asked.

"She confined me to my chambers about a month into

Mourning. I minded my business for a while. Kept a low profile while Anoïse tried to find a paper trail to my plans. I only walked out last week."

He'd said it so nonchalantly that for a minute I was sure I hadn't heard him right. "Walked out?" I repeated. "What do you mean you *walked out*?"

"I mean what I said. Nobody's found out how I managed it. No deaths. No sign of struggle. Me and all my supporters left without a scratch on us."

I wasn't sure what to make of any of this. This was civil fucking war he was talking about. Like the kind that Dad had fought when he was our age. The Bastard's Rebellion.

My jaw tightened, molars pressing together. History lessons filled my mind, not in words so much as dream-like images. Memories of yellow pages and mildew and old, blotted ink. Our great-grandfather sired seven bastards who chose to wage war, fighting for my grandfather's throne.

How many men and women were made ghosts? How many soldiers became apparitions? Mist and memories of who they once were.

The war choked off our access to The Outlying Islands. We didn't have the resources to make masks. Our people breathed in specter storms made during pitched battles— hundreds of Gaunts. Hundreds with the *Violent* Dead in them.

Those living in the countryside were infected without a way to keep themselves safe. Some fled, swarming the roads, killing, making more people into ghosts. Into more Violent Dead. It grew and grew. The nation soon pitched on the precipice between the wholesale slaughter of The Bastard's Rebellion, and the chaos of a Gaunt plague.

It could have doomed the nation. It was a once-in-a-generation kind of disaster.

And here we were all over again.

"So what are you doing here of all places?" I asked. "You've got a lot on your plate, it sounds like. Did you just swing by to see me for the fun of it?"

Ed shrugged. "I thought you'd be on my side."

"You're not the only one who seems to think so, from what I hear."

"I wouldn't doubt it. I heard some rumors on the road. Did you know you can remove your head and pitch it like a bowling ball?"

"That's what Mercedes said." I folded my arms and glowered at the floorboards while I tried to process this. No real line of succession. That was how he was excusing this? I mean—I felt I really ought to be more surprised. Edgar had *for years* complained about doing all this work to rule only for Anoïse to inherit. *Always felt like I was training to be a failsafe.* Those were his words.

Anoïse and Edgar were always simmering with the tension of...Well. *This.* The oldest two being trained for the job only one would take.

"So, what are you doing in Bullion, then? Trying to get munitions?"

"God, no," Edgar said. "I have supporters here to handle this deal. I didn't want to come here. I'm trying to lie low. I wouldn't have, if the Gaunt hadn't compromised your safety."

I noticed he made no mention of the helmet that Mercedes told me about. Maybe it *was* made up. That was too ridiculous.

Goddammit. What the fuck had I stumbled into? "I dunno, man. I just—if you've got everything under control then why did you need me? And don't tell me it's just because you thought I'd be on your side. If you didn't think I could give you something you wouldn't have come here. I know you."

He seemed a little shocked that I even had to ask. But he got over it quicker than I expected. It almost hurt my feelings. "Apparently not. The most important is the fact that we all love you. The three of us, I mean. Me, Anoïse, and Desmon. We trust you. In our own way. You're the only one who never had ambitions. So I know I can count on you to be honest."

That made no sense. Nothing made sense. I still needed more answers. And I was still debating what to do. I still didn't even know where Edgar was even taking me.

"Alright." His voice snapped me out of my chaotic reveries. "So. Will you head out with us in the morning?"

I tried not to pay attention to the way my sword dangled in his grip. The red leather was cracked in places. Was that from my fall out the window? Yellow cracks that made veins through the red. I wanted to reach for it, but my ribs still hurt from the stun shot. "Will I go with you?" I repeated, to buy myself some time.

I mean. What kind of a question *was* that? Would I go with him? Like fuck! How could he even think I had a choice? "I just jumped out the window to avoid this."

Ed frowned. "Well. You don't *technically* have a choice in the matter. But I was trying to be polite."

Goddammit. He couldn't even talk to me straight right now. He had me completely at his mercy and he was still trying to gift wrap his betrayal in decorum. Unbelievable. "I don't suppose you'll at least tell me where we're going?"

Edgar pressed his lips together. He held his breath. "Somewhere close." His voice was clipped, impatient.

"Once I find what I'm looking for. We'll be out of here tomorrow. We can be where we want to be by nightfall."

I fought to keep my mind blank. I wanted to follow a mental map in my mind's eye. How many places were one nightfall away?

I shook my mind clear of those cobwebs. There would be time for that later. I didn't want to get hung up on that issue. "Is Mercedes on your side, too? You *did* get past her security fairly quickly." I doubted it, but it might help just to check. Even if he wouldn't say it straight, maybe he'd give some indication as to the reality of that situation.

Edgar scowled. "God, no. Honestly. I'm surprised Anoïse didn't say anything to her. I thought she'd tell her nobles all about this. I didn't think keeping a lid on it was important."

I wasn't sure what to say. A sibling rebelling right before a coronation was not the way to make sure vassals stayed on your side. She would probably go public with this by the end of the week. Once the Months of Mourning were up. She'd have to wait until she had a crown on her head to let everyone know.

Though I'd be lying if I said I wasn't surprised that she hadn't even given Mercedes some kind of quiet little heads up. Was Anoïse more paranoid than I'd suspected? Did the incident with Mercedes at that dinner years ago set Anoïse on edge? She could trust Mercedes. Couldn't she?

Unless. "Is that why you brought supporters here though? To get her on your side?"

Edgar sighed. "I wouldn't even dare to try, really."

"You? Not try?"

"Fuck off." Edgar gave me a greasy smear of a smile. "You know how close Mercedes was with Dad. Of course she's siding with Anoïse. Anoïse was Dad's favorite. Asking anything else is tantamount to spitting on Dad's ghost. It'd be a waste of energy, anyway. It won't happen."

I wondered if he knew you can't spit on ghosts. They're fog, it'd go right through—you know what? Never mind. "Heaven forbid." I rolled my eyes. "No, you'll just turn her own munitions corporations against her. Like the sweet, benevolent soul you really are."

Edgar actually laughed at me. He put his back against the wall and slumped down it. The hand that held my sword faced away from me. "We're preparing for war. I can't play fair. Come on. Use your brain. Would you prefer I let things lead to bloodshed?"

"I would prefer it if you didn't do any of this in the first place." I wondered if that was perhaps too honest. "You should have told me all of this from the start, Ed."

"Could've saved us a lot of trouble, huh?" I expected him to say more. But he just grinned, his lips thin as a wire coat hanger. "I could've just taken you all the way back under my guard. Like I'm doing now."

"I notice you don't have any actual guards," I observed, indicating the door. I would've thought he'd have people stationed in front of this door just in case I tried to escape again.

Ed laughed. I couldn't tell if he was nervous or not. "We've got a lot to do here, I'll admit. And there are only so many of us in Bullion. But don't worry, Petre. You won't get anywhere. Trust me."

I didn't like his confidence that he could wrangle me if I made another go at an escape. Then again, he'd managed to keep me in his grip so far. And I'd botched the last escape attempt horrifically enough that I could understand why he thought he had this situation under control.

Ed stuffed his hand into the inner trim of his coat and

dug a flask wrapped in brown leather out from his pocket. He downed a mouthful and proffered it to me. "Whisky?"

"I shouldn't." I snatched it out of his hand anyway and swallowed a quick indignant mouthful. It tasted like tarmac in the sun and friction burn. The slug was warm on its way down my throat. I could feel it spreading in the center of my chest.

I asked my next question on impulse. I didn't want to give myself time to second guess. "So who is it that you're planning to make Queen?" I asked. "Once you have your throne, I mean." I doubted he would tell me. But it was worth a shot, right?

Edgar took longer than I expected to answer. Even the thought of it gave him the inspiration he needed to toss another mouthful of his drink right down his throat. "I don't know yet," he answered. "I'm still waiting to see how the sides will be divided. And even if I *did,* I doubt I'd tell you. Just know that I have allies."

"Havilan?" I guessed.

"The guy who helped put me under house arrest?" Edgar said. "What do you think?"

I noticed that was not explicitly a *no.* I wasn't sure if I should trust him when he said that wasn't true. The Mercys and The Reachers had been fighting over trading outposts in The Bay for generations, and we needed access to The Bay in order to keep our supply chains functioning. Taking The Bay would be foundational to any successful war against Anoïse.

Anoïse had her marriage to Fabrian. But Ed could just as easily promise supporters more territory in The Bay. I wasn't sure how that would go over with our vassals, though. Unless he'd only obtained the loyalty of vassals without any assets near their holdings.

Though Anoïse might use that against him. Promise the vassals who stayed with her ownership of the traitor-territories. A fief or two. She could probably flip a couple vassals to her side that way. The Bay was one of the biggest trading areas on the continent. Even one port could raise a family's assets significantly.

"Sounds like you've stacked up well against Anoïse," I said.

"I'm working on it," Edgar said bitterly.

My injections made insistent heat in my hand. They tried to tug me in the direction of my gun. But it didn't bring the same overdose potency it had this morning. It could only make subtle suggestions. Ones I ignored. Though the thought of shooting him was tempting. God, he made me so mad. Couldn't I at least hit him?

No. That wasn't going to help. I let my frustration out with all the air in my lungs. I performed the mental math of social alliances and economic marriages. I'd never been good at math, but hopefully my calculations were serviceable here. "All things considered, with all the muddy rules around succession, it sounds like you've got good odds."

"I'd still like more support. Though I dunno what I can fairly promise."

"If only someone else had twins our age you could marry to build an alliance," I joked. "That'd even the odds."

"It would be nice," Ed admitted. "Having someone else who gets all the...the stuff." He gesticulated vaguely. "That comes with this."

"You mean how none of this wombmates shit is actually that important?" I asked.

"And how everyone thinks it is. The way they think you're tied at the hip."

"A fraction of a whole human."

"Two souls, one body," Edgar said.

I did the math. "Well, technically—"

"I know," he said.

"Twins times two," I said.

"Twins squared," Edgar amended.

"The square root of octuplets?" I suggested.

"Four is the square root of sixteen, Petre. Not eight."

"I was never good at math."

"There is that."

Fuck. I was going to miss him when I got out of here, wasn't I?

CHAPTER
EIGHT

I didn't sleep. And not for lack of wanting to. Sleep would have been a welcome relief from the deranged spirals making themselves at home behind my eyes every moment I had an instant to think.

But I needed to leave this place. And there was no way I could do that while Ed was awake.

So even after my brother went to bed, I stood up. Just for the chance to stay awake. I crept along the floorboards until one squealed. I considered jumping out the window a few more times, but I wasn't leaving here without my sword.

As the night progressed, I realized this was the first time in my life I was actually thankful that Edgar snored like a garbage disposal in a sink drain.

I was surprised when Edgar started sleeping, to be honest. That was a fucking bold move if I'd ever seen it. I'd *just* tried to escape, and he thought he could nod off in front of me? Though I supposed when the first escape attempt goes *that* badly I might fall victim to a touch of hubris, too.

Hell, knowing him he wouldn't post guards in any spot

as obvious as right beside the door. He wasn't about to give me that clear of a target to get by. If anything, he'd have his people orbiting the hotel to keep an eye out for me, while others did whatever work was required in Bullion. I would have to keep that in mind when I got out of here.

In the meantime, I managed to steal a few precious seconds of sleep. We'd had a long few days and we both needed as much we could get. But I was too on edge for unconsciousness to last, no matter how exhausted I was. It was still a pinch of sand out of an hourglass. I could sleep for moments at a time, resting upright against the wall, as the vague visuals living underneath my eyelids wore absurdist semi-clarity every time sleep tried to claim a foothold on my mind.

But every time my head fell forward the waking world dunked me back into the cold reality of my situation. I slowly eased out a breath through clenched teeth and tried again to plan the route of my escape. I'd do it just as soon as I could see my hand in front of my face. I wasn't about to fumble for my sword and climb over a barricade in the pitch black.

The daylight snuck up on me, in between those little ounces of sleep. Every time I wrenched my eyelids apart the sky had bleached a little brighter. The black faded to the dull gray, then slowly brightened until I could actually see the room.

My saber's red sheath was apparent even in the dull semidarkness that washed out the color from the world. It was flat against the floor. The saber's grip was pinned under Ed's ass.

I crouched, one foot between Edgar's outstretched legs, between his ankles. My own legs were stuck in an awkward lunge. I grabbed the end of my science-sword. Tried to pull it out in an arc. But all I succeeded in was prying the sheath off of three inches of curved science-steel. The metal plating on the end of the scabbard scraped against the wooden floor and I froze. Knotted with stress. If my molars pressed together any tighter my jaw was likely to spring some kind of rupture.

But he kept sleeping. I inched closer and didn't breathe as I settled into a low crouch. I pinched the end of the knuckle bow that I could actually reach. I inched it out from under him, slowly, slowly, tongue protruding in concentration. I barely made a noise. Though small noises I *did* produce berated my senses like the cacophony you would find in an active war zone.

I'd just managed to get it out from under him when Ed's hand fell on top of mine. He squeezed my hand. My gaze flew up to his face. But his eyes were shut and he still was snoring softly. I wondered if he could feel the tremors of fear that spiraled out from my knuckles? I wet my lips. Slowly slid out from under the palm of his hand and eased out of his grip. God, my legs were sore. I wanted to stand up. To stretch them. Instead, I waddled backwards on tiptoes and gave myself some room before I stood.

Getting up and over my own barricade felt like the hardest part of all. I wasn't sure if the bed was squealing anywhere near as loudly as it felt. And every few minutes Edgar's snoring was interrupted by a snorting indrawn gasp for breath.

I moved slowly. Carefully. Braced against every surface available to me. It felt like I was oozing out the cracks between the doors. And I did as best I could to be quiet.

As soon as I was out, I took soft steps down the carpeted hallway.

I put on my mask. Just in case.

I thumbed the elevator button. Waited. Waited. Buckled on my sword belt. I jammed my finger into the button again. And again. "Come on, come on."

I should've just taken the stairs. I was about to make a move for them when I spotted Edgar at the end of the hall. His caterwauler was already trained on me. "Fuck."

He sped across the hall towards me. "Show me your hands," he said. His hair was a messy tangle, floating like a black halo around his head.

Panic cinched inside my belly. I put my hands up "I was wondering how I hadn't woken you up. I thought I'd made more noise than that when I left."

"You'd been moving all through the night without leaving. I thought it was nothing at first."

I tried to keep my tone more friendly than he did his. Which was a wee bit difficult. The same way it's hard to keep your hands up for long before your arms start getting tired.

"Now," Edgar said, "You're going to tell me where you're headed."

The elevator light vanished. The door dinged, and the hatch slid upward toward the roof with a hiss of steam. I motioned to it with my head as it slid open. "Down," I said with a shrug. I wondered if I should lunge for it. But I doubted that the door would close in time. Hell. I doubt I could even get to the first floor before Ed could hustle down a flight of stairs.

Fuck. Why did I wait for the elevators? Stupid. Fucking idiot. What the hell was wrong with me? I had to get to the stables.

I realized Edgar was speaking. I think he had just finished cursing me out.

"Petre. Take something seriously. For once."

I put my hands on top of my head. "You think I don't take things seriously?"

"You have a funny way of showing it."

"I'm not avoiding anything." I still wasn't sure how to get away. But I figured if I kept talking a plan might materialize eventually.

"Of course you are! That's all you know how to do! That's what you're best at! Avoiding things. Running away."

I squeezed my eyes shut and counted down from five. "You know why I had to do that."

"The same way you *had* to jump out the window last night? That didn't work. So you're trying again now. It's what you always do, Petre. I know you."

I chuckled. "You *think* you do, I'm sure."

"Anoïse told me about what happened. Did you know that? She told me all about the night in the stables. The night you left."

I rolled my eyes, because it was easier to do that than it was to tell him how infuriating this was. She had no right to dictate the narrative of what had happened that night. It was *mine*. She wasn't *allowed* to twist it. And I knew she had. Otherwise he wouldn't have brought it up. I was going to hit him. "What's your point, Ed?"

"I'm just saying. Avoiding things, running away—it's what you do best."

"You don't know anything about me. Or Anoïse. Or anything about what happened that night. Fuck you."

Ed straightened his elbow. Closed the distance between the barrel of his gun and me. I took a step back and watched his scrutinizing gaze crawl up and down me. "I think I can guess. Can't be that different can it? How many ways can you run away?"

I wanted him to drop the gun for just one second so that I could knock his teeth in. That was all I needed. Just a split second. "When Anoïse told you about that night, what did she say? Did she *tell* you that she had two other chances to stop me before she found me in the stables? Did she *tell* you how every time I said I wanted to run, she'd fight me on it? Tell me nothing was wrong? That she made me squash every issue I had with her. With Dad? With that place? With what it did to us? The way it put us at everyone's throats all the time. The constant paranoia it inspired. Even after Dad ripped the woman she loved out of her arms, after he publicly humiliated her—she *refused* to even hear a word against him. Not *once*. Did she tell you she defended Dad twice the day I left? When I was upset at him? She wouldn't even let me say anything in *her support*! Did she tell you that, Ed? Or did she skip to the part where she cornered me in the stables? How she cried at me like a fucking baby and had a breakdown once she'd figured out it was already too late."

Fuck. Oh man. That felt good to get off my chest.

I wondered if I'd let myself get carried away.

Edgar didn't say anything for a long time. He didn't blink. He didn't move.

So I kept pushing. "You know what? Maybe you're right. Maybe it *is* similar. Maybe you *do* know it's too late to stop me from leaving. Just like she did. You're using a gun instead of tears, but it's mostly the same."

"I'm trying to stop you from making a mistake," Edgar said.

"Ask me where I've heard that one before."

"You don't understand—"

"The hell I don't!" I had to hiss to keep myself from shouting. I wondered if provocation was a better tactic to take here. "Stop saying that. I mean Good Lord, Ed. Do you even *want* me to go back with you?"

Ed rolled his eyes. "I've got a gun trained on you for a reason, Petre."

"I just—"

"You just *what?*"

This felt like getting halfway through a bullshit essay before I realized that I was onto something. "I'm just not sure you know what you want. But I don't think you're going to shoot me." I put my hands down. Turned to leave. Let my right hand hover over my holster in a way I hoped was not too noticeable.

"Petre!" Ed shouted. "Stay *right there.*"

"If you wanted me back there you would've shot me by now," I called back. "Dragged me to wherever it is you have to go."

"You just got shot last night. Do you really want to try this again?"

I kept going for the stairwell. "It's not last night anymore, man. So just let me go in peace and I'll leave you to your idiotic little rebellion." I flipped him off over my shoulder.

I heard the soft whine of his handgun when he slammed the trigger home and turned around in a panic as a screech blasted from the barrel. A vibration in the air like summer humidity rocked towards me broke the glass on the entrance to the stairwell.

I turned my back to the door. The world held its breath.

"That was a warning shot," Edgar growled. "The next one won't be."

I dialed back the hammer on my gun. Couldn't haul it back far enough to knock him out without the whine of the caterwauler alerting him to what I was doing. But I could at least momentarily stun him. "A warning shot, huh? Well. You're a better person than I am." I pivoted and drew my gun at the same time. I was already squeezing the trigger as I brought the barrel up.

He realized what was happening right in time for my sonic shot to slug him in the chest. He folded at the waist and the impact kicked him off his feet.

I took off running before he even hit the ground. The whole second floor would have heard our exchange. This hotel was about to come alive with Ed's supporters.

I slammed the stairway door open with my shoulder and burst through. The door swung shut behind me, choking off Edgar as he was in the middle of shouting my name.

I hurtled down the stairs. I could taste copper in the back of my throat. I tried not to think about my knees giving out. Avram had told me once that knee pain was a part of getting older. That one day they'd stop cooperating for no reason. Was I old enough yet for that to be a concern? I wasn't sure but that was an easier thing to think about than anything to do with why I was running.

When I hit the bottom steps I heard the stairwell door open above, floors above me. I made for the first-floor door, tossed a plastic trash can into the entrance on my way out.

I was suddenly engulfed in the music of violas and violins. Businessmen and CEOs had woken up for breakfast. Heads turned to look at me just in time to watch me stumble into a serving man, smushing a tray of breakfast food and white wine all down his shirt front.

I looked back and saw Edgar about to emerge from the stairwell.

I peeled the tray out of the serving man's hands while he gaped at me. I spun the damn thing at Edgar as he came through. I didn't watch it fly long enough to see if I hit my target. I just turned and ran. Hurled myself over a table to the nearest back exit. I kicked the table over behind me, lobbed wine glasses and plates at Edgar. I toppled chairs, threw everything I could into Ed's way. I had to get to the stables.

One of Edgar's supporters was already moving to intercept me. The blond guy who had shot me yesterday. I wriggled under his outstretched arms, ducked behind him, put my boot against his back and shoved. He sprawled onto a fancy table, scattering plates and silverware.

I fell on top of him. Snatched a glass vase and pitched it down on top of his head. I grabbed his hair while he was dazed and slammed his head into the table.

I heard a caterwauler keen somewhere in the dining room. I had no idea if it was The Blackheath Guard or Ed's supporters. A stray shot struck the shimmershield in the front window, and the orange plasma winked out.

Edgar was busy fighting it out with Mercedes' security. His supporters and her forces were clashing all around me, as munitions dealers stood by and watched the chaos.

I had to get out while Edgar was distracted. I made it a few more steps before one of Ed's supporters lunged for my legs. She squeezed my knees together, put her weight behind the lunge. The world tilted and suddenly I had to eat a mouthful of the carpet.

I wriggled one leg free. Slammed my boot in her face. She scrambled to keep her hold on me. I kicked again and her grip loosened enough for me to wriggle free.

She found a hold on my ankle on the way up, so I stomped on her wrist with my free boot, then kept running.

Edgar was getting closer, but he was still mired in the press of bodies. There was fighting all around us. Some combatants had drawn science-swords. Sabers models, backswords designs, a couple rapiers with orange plasma shimmershields covering the empty spaces in swept hilts. The force fields sang as swords moved through the air.

Another of Ed's supporters climbed atop a table and jumped down at me, fist drawn back. He wore a set of brass knuckles that crackled with an electric current.

That was bad news.

My injections burned under the surface of my skin. I surrendered to its suggestions as it dragged me out of the way of the man's blow. The two of us swapped places. "Don't," I tried to warn him. I was out of breath. Couldn't tell him how he was making a mistake. "Injections. You can't. You're going to get—"

But the next blow tagged my shoulder, shot electric currents through muscle fibers and the drugs inside them. My injections went haywire.

I'm not sure I even know *what* happened. My injections squeezed my eyes shut. I knew I was moving. I couldn't see but I was moving. I felt the give of flesh under my hands. Felt sweat, and a warm wetness that was not sweat. My knuckles met resistance and a deep ache set into my fist. Someone lurched beneath me. My knees hit the floor. I'd landed on top of a body. He shuddered under me.

Then the current died, and I opened my eyes, and the man was on the floor, a bloody mess. No ghostbreath, though, which meant he wasn't dead.

I ached. My shoulder had probably been burned. How many bruises had I acquired? New pains introduced themselves to me as I clambered to my feet.

Edgar had managed to dispatch the security forces holding him back. But he looked exhausted. Bedraggled and bleeding. "PETRE!" He reached for his gun. Would he have set that to stun or kill? Frankly, I wasn't interested in finding out.

I turned heel, tried to run, and immediately tripped over the man whose face I had just demolished.

I heard the wail of Edgar's handgun. The electric current shimmered over my shoulder. My ears were ringing as the shot turned the gigantic glass hotel display window into a pile of transparent knives on the floor.

I vaulted over that new opening. Tinnitus was making chaos in my eardrums. Shouts came at me muted. Distant. The Blackheath Guard were swarming the middle of the road. Screaming things I couldn't hear.

I took off running, trampling broken glass. I felt a stitch blossoming in my side. Which was only worsened by the pain in my right hip, the bruising from my short stop out the window last night. But I kept on, and all but had to windmill my legs to keep myself going. It wasn't so much stamina as it was inertia.

I could see the stables at the end of the road. I was nearly there. I was getting closer. Fights raged all around me. Swords sliced through the air, making that whooping, surprised breath sound as they cut through space.

I shook my head. No time to take that in. I had to ignore it. Had to stay ahead of Edgar.

Which became difficult when I felt his fingers closing on the back of my coat. I could feel the toes of his boots nipping at my heels. Some of my hearing was returning by that point. "Petre." I could feel his breath on the back of my neck. "Leave it to you...to choose the most...dramatic... option."

"LET GO!" I shouted.

He jerked on the chameleon coat. I had my elbow ready to go for the sudden stop. Our collision cracked it right into his face at high speed, and he went down. I shrugged my coat back on.

He was getting, unsteadily, to his feet, so I kicked him back to the ground before he could and made for the stables again. Hustled faster, until I tasted copper in the back of my throat. I burst through the doors like a thrown spear.

I booted the door shut behind me, slammed the bolt into the catch. It was an old, old building. Earthen floor. Still made of wood. I wasn't sure if it would hold. I paused, to catch my breath, as the confused chaos-noises outside continued to rage. I just had to breathe. Just for a second. I was in so much pain, I just needed a short break.

That break was soon interrupted when Edgar slammed against the door. Apparently he'd recovered. He made the door buck in its frame—once, twice, thrice.

I pressed my back against the door and held it shut. Dug furrows in the dirt with my heels to keep it closed.

And then the slamming stopped. "Petre," Edgar breathed. "You there?"

I tensed. Did not stop bracing against the door. I could see him through the slats in the wooden boards. "You taking a breather?" I asked.

"It's just some mess we've got ourselves into, is all."

I was surprised to find that I did too. "Sometimes I think that's what this family does best."

"Sometimes I'm inclined to agree with you. So, come on. It's not too late to mend this. Unbolt the door. Come with me. Come on."

I really chewed it over for a minute. I swear. I really did. If only because I figured that might put a stop to the fighting. "Are you still planning on dethroning Anoïse?"

His silence told me everything I needed to know. "Listen," he said.

"Ed..."

"No, listen. Petre. This is the thing nobody else understands. The thing I *get*. The thing we need, now more than ever, is to understand what it means to hold the kind of power that we do."

I was still tense at the door, and I could hear the fights outside. "Uh huh," I said. If only to keep him talking. Once I refused, he would return to his violence. There was no doubt about that. But I wanted one final moment like this before it came.

"And we..." His throat betrayed him, closed up on the words. I heard him swallow. "We have to be careful with how we use it. Our daily trivialities have consequences. Our grudges can shape nations, Petre. Don't you get it?" He pounded on the door insistently. "*Look* what our little fight has turned into outside these stables. Look what's become of you trying to get out. You come with me and this whole thing grinds to a halt. All that, and it's just on *you*. It's all on your head. Two seconds and a word, and all this violence stops. Think about that for a minute. Think about what it means to shape the world that easily."

Well. He certainly knew how to make it feel tempting.

"Anoïse never got it like I do. It's not about the laws, decrees, the policies of an administration. It's about the people who are put in charge of *making* things the way that they are. I know more people than her, and I get on with them better, too. I can work with them better. I can organize a state better than she can, because unlike her I get how people *work*."

"Yeah. I've certainly noticed that." I was getting tired of his preaching. "Cut the shit, man. Being charming and well-liked isn't the same thing as knowing how people work. That's not the same as running a government. It's a cute speech and all, but I'm thinking even if you *weren't* better liked, you'd still be here."

"I'm telling you—I wouldn't."

It was my turn to pound on the door. "Ed. Don't fucking lie to me right now. Or I'm cutting this short and getting on a horse." I wasn't sure why I didn't just do that already.

"Petre. You can't. You're making a mistake."

"I'm not," I intoned, slowly. "You don't trust me. That's clear by now."

"Petre—"

"You wouldn't even tell me you were planning a rebellion until last night! Stop trying to bullshit me. I know you don't trust me. I'm just a trophy for you to collect. Go on! Admit it!"

"I do trust you," Edgar said. "I needed to make sure that *you* trusted me."

"That's what not trusting someone *means*, Ed!" I frowned. Felt pouty. "Fine. You really think you trust me? Prove it then. Answer me just one fucking thing."

"Anything."

"How'd you do it, Ed? Anoïse had you under house arrest. How did you manage to escape from Mercy House?

Edgar was silent for a long time. "When we get to where we're going—"

"Ohhhhhh, I feel *real* trustworthy now, Ed! Won't even tell me where you're headed. Alright. This has been nice, but I'm headed out. Don't come after me. And don't send anyone after me, either."

"Petre, you're being—"

"Because if you send anyone after me, I'll kill them. And you can have their severed head as a present. My treat. Got it?"

"*Petre!*" Ed pounded on the door.

"Tell me I'm joking, Ed. I dare you."

I didn't wait for him to do it. I just left. Really dug the balls of my feet into the hustle. Edgar was pounding on the door. Next time I checked I saw his science-sword chopping through the flaky wood.

The dirt was uneven and hazardous, but I found my way into one of the horse stalls. It was unarmored and had no saddle. It was plugged into a coil of wires. I ripped the plugs free, scrambled up onto the horse's back.

I hated that it had no saddle. No armor. No protection. I could see the way its reins fed into the skin. The way the bridle climbed inside the horse's throat. It was easier to imagine it was only a bridle when the horses were wearing armor.

I heard the scream of Edgar's caterwauler going off. The wooden door turned to dust and splinters, and he was through.

I jerked the rein like the starter cord on a lawnmower, and the cyborg horse churned out synthetic movement. I squirmed at the machinery beneath me. I could feel it moving, just beneath the taut tarpaulin of false flesh. Without the saddle it felt like I was stuck in some kind of horrible massage chair. You know the ones I mean? The real cheap kind that sometimes makes you more stressed than when you sat down.

Or maybe that's just me.

I had to grip the damn thing with my legs and really *lean* to get it to turn the way I wanted. It was easier with the saddle. It plugged into the machinery beneath. Gave you easy ways to input your commands. Did the work for you. I needed to threaten to fall off this damn thing every time I wanted to turn, to kick in this machine's failsafe drives and keep me secured on its back.

Iron hooves slammed down in the dirt. Blazed right towards Edgar as I clung to the sides of the horse's neck. Edgar leapt out of my path, and I sped past him.

The streets of Bullion were hives of violence. Armed forces scrambled to relieve Mercedes' security. I steered my way through Bullion with my knees. The world slid by me. Between the speed of the wind and the tinnitus, my ears were thrumming.

I hurtled out of Bullion. On my way towards the Forest Wall, off in the distance. Just like Mercedes had shown me.

The Forest wall had swallowed me up by the time the sun had finished rising.

And once the sky had bleached to pale blue, enough time had passed that I figured I was safe enough to slow down. Anyone who wanted to catch up with me would've done so by now.

And even if they hadn't, I was going to die if I didn't get a chance to catch my breath. Physically, I mean. And mentally. Emotionally, too. Come to think of it.

I followed a snaking trail of churny red soil shot through the forestry. Mom used to tell us the forest was man-made. By a sorcerer, before the First Annihilation, when magic burnt itself out. There were attempts to colonize it as science and technology took off. But the Second Annihilation wiped those out, too. All that was left were corroded factories and warped trees attempting to emulate every element on the periodic table.

I don't know how Mom knew all that, though. I doubt Dad ever let Mom come here. No matter how much she may have wanted to. Dad had her locked up in the basement since the day he found out about the coup she had been planning.

Maybe that was why she loved *hearing* about the ruins

in this place so much. The signs of life that grew on top of this corpse of a city.

Dad, or a representative he'd elected, used to take the four of us on camping trips here. And we'd come back and tell Mom all about the things we saw here. Trees with black veins. Stripped bark revealing inner rings of smoky quartz.

We'd tell her about the ruins that the foliage was teased through. How it shredded ancient buildings into scattered fragments. How the trees sounded like witches cackling when the wind blew.

At its height, the damn things braided themselves in tangled clusters. One great big mass twining together. Housing old stone towers that leaned together like exhausted brawlers. We'd tell her about the spires of machinery. Soil salted with broken glass. Big iron plates with blisters of rust.

Although.

Listen—

I *say* "we".

Mom was more interested in hearing this from the others. But I wasn't about to think about that right now.

Because for a while everything was just...peaceful. Here in the shade. Surrounded by the ruins of the First and the Second Annihilation.

Of course—someone had to come and ruin it.

You'll never guess who.

I heard the sound of his horse before he even came around a bend in the trail. I wasn't sure what had taken him so long. Or why he hadn't thought to armor up his horse before he came after me. What could he have been doing that would cause this kind of delay that *wasn't* armoring his horse?

Those questions were soon swamped by the fury I felt

when I realized that this one instant of relief had been stolen from me. I booted my horse into high gear. It churned clumps of trail behind me as Edgar gained on my path.

I leaned forward, as if that would help me become more aerodynamic. I gripped the horse with my calves. When I dared to check over my shoulder, I was staring down the barrel of Edgar's handgun.

I lurched to one side as Edgar squeezed off his shot, and almost steered the horse right into a gigantic tree. I managed to correct my course and kept speeding on. Did he have another shot left? I wasn't sure. It would depend on if he'd set the damn thing to stun.

The fact that he was still aiming indicated he probably had enough juice for a second shot. I had to twist to my other side to avoid it. Really leaned into that lurch too, because we were coming down on a steep bend in the trail. The bruise where my sword belt had snagged my side was flagging ribbons of pain.

Edgar had gained ground during the steep turn. He was right on my fucking ass. My jaw was tight enough to give me a headache. I could've sworn Dad had taught him not to tailgate. Like God fucking dammit. This was how accidents—

Oh.

I had an idea. One that made my stomach shrivel up, like fingers forming into a fist. But it was better than nothing.

I braced myself. This was probably going to hurt.

But I couldn't think of another way to shake Edgar off my trail. And he was right on top of me now, so if his gun had enough time to recharge. Well. He'd have to be a truly abysmal shot to miss at point blank range, wouldn't he?

So I tightened my jaw, and as I came around another turn in the trail, I shifted to one side to steer my horse, and then I held my breath, and I gave the reins a sharp tug.

The cyborg horse lurched to a halt, and I dropped to the ground.

CHAPTER
NINE

Nothing ever really goes exactly how you planned it, does it? That's the problem with schemes. Life is never the perfect story you make of it inside your head.

I did not expect the crash would be that bad. I had no idea that cyborg horses could explode.

Edgar didn't see what hit him. He was riding too close behind me. There was no time to react. No time to move out of the way. I don't think I'll ever forget the fear in his pie-eyed face when he realized what was happening.

And when the horses collided, it was my turn to be shocked. Something had triggered deep in the guts of their machinery. I wasn't completely sure how it had happened. Not at the time. For all the years I spent riding I had no idea how these horses worked.

When they crashed, I wondered if someone had smuggled a pipe bomb into my horse, because the creatures were shredding themselves apart. Steel and iron screeched like dying animals. The horses uncoiled into a mess of stretched-out shapes and steel machinery. A tangle of synthetic flesh and iron, wrapped in a viscera of oil and blood.

I staggered to my feet once it was done. I was exhausted and dehydrated. My blood was pumping. I was going to shit myself. I thought Ed had died. I hurtled toward the wreck.

Nothing moved. Fuck. *Was* he dead? I wasn't sure. Something sick and twisted crawled through the depth of my stomach.

Then Edgar *screamed.*

I had to do a circuit of the mess to find him. To get around to the other side of the wreck. He wasn't dead. It looked like he'd tried to dive off during the crash.

His stomach was going up and down rapidly, and he was breathing hard; making grunting noises in the back of his throat.

"E-Ed?" I dared to get closer, and realized something had happened when he'd attempted to abandon his mount. His left arm was still tangled in the wreck. I felt dizzy looking at it. It didn't feel real. He was lying face up, but his elbow was the wrong way around.

Or rather—I couldn't tell which of those bloody angles *was* his elbow.

The whole mess of machinery shot through his arm at all angles. The seething mess was salivating blood.

"What did you do?" Edgar squeezed the words out all in the same breathless wheeze. It sounded like he was crying. "What happened Good Lord God it hurts so much."

"I don't know what I did!" Bile boiled its way into my throat. "What happened?"

His voice was strained. "It hurts oh god oh fuck make it stop hurting do something!"

"I don't know what to do!" I shouted. Through the

white noise of my panic I realized something about Ed's speech was somewhat...different. I was so accustomed to him talking with authority. All the clipped, controlled sentences had bled away. Had that all been artifice?

Fuck. Now wasn't the time to dwell on this.

"Fuck fuck it hurts god fuck make it stop hurting Petre I can't I can't I can't!"

I wasn't sure what to say. What I could do. The world was blurry. When had I started crying? I tried to speak but my throat wasn't working with me.

Was I crying? How could I be crying and still feel so calm? Was I calm or numb? I wasn't sure if I could ascertain the difference. I certainly felt panicky. I realized that I had put my hands on my head. "Ah fuck oh jeez oh god shit, man. Uhhhh uhhhh uhhh don't worry, man don't panic we'll figure this out." I tugged down my mask, retrieved my case of Muse, and stuffed a roll in my mouth.

"Are you fucking smoking at a time like this?" Edgar screeched.

"Would you prefer I help you while I'm panicky?" I lit the end of it and dragged in a breath. Two breaths.

"*You're* panicky?" Edgar tried to shift his weight, and his whole body shuddered, spasmed. Like an animal caught in a bear trap, processing its pain. The big stupid pile of machinery lurched sideway, subtly. Lamely. Edgar let out an afraid moan.

There was no getting him out of that. He'd been skewered from too many fucking directions. He was pinned in there too deep to untangle.

I couldn't breathe. I couldn't think. But I had to brainstorm *something*, right? I dragged in another breath of Muse. "Stop it. Fucking shut up. I'm trying to think. Fuck! God, I'm sorry. I shouldn't tell you to shut up."

"*Just fucking do something! Please!* Do something or fucking kill me one of the two." Edgar wrinkled his eyes shut.

My hands, back in my hair, tightened into fists. I was trying to figure out if this was actually real life. Real life wasn't supposed to shift this suddenly. So catastrophically, at once. It was disorienting.

Edgar pounded his head against the ground as he wailed.

"Ed fucking stop do you want to give yourself a concussion on top of—" I gestured vaguely at his injury. "All that?"

Fuck. He was still crying. "As long as I'm unconscious!"

"Lord," I swore. I paced back and forth, surveyed the wreck. "I—I think I can get the first aid kits."

"I just want it to stop make it stop Petre I can't—"

"I'm trying," I said through a clenched jaw. I could *see* the med kit that came with our horses. It was buried under a foot of twisted steel, but I could see it. "It's right there." I leaned, careful not to touch the wreck. It was too much of an awkward tangle, and I didn't want it to twist through Edgar's arm more than it already had.

I eased my hand through twining helixes of bloody steel, dripping with oil and decorated with horse guts. "I can see it," I said. "I got it."

"Get it out GET IT OUT!"

I tried to ease it free of the wreck. I couldn't angle it in a way where I could get it free without pushing against the mess, and when the heap threatened to topple, I had to let it go. "Fuck. Shit. I can't. I can't get it back out."

"GET IT OUT GET IT OUT GET IT OUT!" He thrashed more than I thought was probably wise. I made a wide parabola around Edgar as I tried to figure out what to do. He was breathing rapidly, and I felt guilty that I wasn't more injured. Like merely existing next to him was a kind of insult. I felt a stupid paranoia that if I got too close he might try to bite me.

"Ed." I wasn't sure how to break this to him. "I think we're going to have to cut it off."

"Fucking hell man do you think?"

"Yeah," I said. "God. Fuck. I don't know how to do this." I dragged in the last of my Muse. Fat good it did me for something this intense. I tossed it away.

"Those injections don't even come with some fucking surgery programmed in there?"

"Well, why the fuck would I need to know surgery, man?"

His eyes lolled back in his skull. "You've got to be kidding me." He sounded like he was going to start crying again. His head lurched towards his trapped arm. He looked pale. "Ah shit. Aw, God. Oh man. Fuck!"

"Don't look at it." I crouched beside him and considered swatting his face. But I didn't want him to flinch or try and move that arm. "Look at me. *Look* at me, Ed."

He did. I retrieved Dad's old knife. And he must've been in a real fugue because he didn't say anything about it. "I'm going to make you a tourniquet. Hold still."

"Goddamn. Goddamn. Fuck me. Fuck. Fuck." He kept swearing, but he didn't move, which I took as permission.

"Let it out." I cut up his shirt. Had to stop halfway through, because I figured there was no way to roll him over to get the wrap underneath him. I had to be strategic about this. I managed to cut up his shirt so that I could twist what was already there into a tight enough tourniquet.

Edgar was looking at his wound again. "Petre god it hurts fuck man I—"

"I know," I said through a clenched jaw. "Stop looking at it. Don't let your mind go elsewhere. Stay with me, man. Talk to me." I stripped away Edgar's shirt, exposed his bicep. When did he get a tattoo? Was that a ram's skull? I'd have to carve it in half. I wasn't sure how he was going to feel about that. "Do any of your supporters know you're here?"

"T-told them I was headed after you. Yeah."

Small mercies. "I'm sure they'll be out here to pick you up in no time. Till then." I poised Dad's knife to the middle of the ram's skull. Goosebumps came out to play on the surface of Ed's skin. I fiddled with the switch on the grip. But before I could get the blade spinning, Edgar spoke.

"H-hold on now," he said.

"Ed. We've got to get on with this."

"I know. I just. There's a bit of whisky in the inner pocket of my coat." He blinked rapidly and looked at my knife. My stomach was hot and tight. "I could use some."

I nodded. Grunted my annoyance, as I peeled back his lapel and dug it out. Then I pulled his mask down and dumped what was left in it into his mouth.

"Okay," he wheezed. "Okay. I'm ready. Go."

I thumbed the switch. The fine double edges shifted, went serrated, and started spinning. "You gonna stay with me?" I asked.

He tilted his head. He seemed a bit delirious. Was he looking at the knife? "Wasn't that Dad's?"

"I don't know what you're talking about."

"That looks like Dad's old knife."

I kept my voice flat. "The pain is getting to you, Ed. You're delusional."

"Dad was looking for that thing for five years. That has to be h—"

I pressed the knife into his bicep while he was talking. "I don't know what you're talking about, Ed. You're delusional."

Ed shuddered under me and screamed.

I looked away, focused on my task, as I choked down stomach bile. I wasn't going to puke. I *wasn't*. It was just that my face felt green and sick, that was all. I was going to be fine.

I blinked and felt lightheaded as the blade chewed through Ed's bicep.

Fuck. Cutting up limbs was so much easier when you were only killing people. I wasn't supposed to be this squeamish. But it was Edgar—not a body, not a Gaunt, not faceless meat. This was my *brother*.

His blood spilled through my fingers as I sawed into him, all warm and red and sticky. The world smelled like copper. I planted his head in the dirt with my off hand. Pressed my teeth together. Shoved my knee down on his free shoulder. I tried to pin him, hold him down so he couldn't writhe.

My blade gnawed through bright red bone. I winced. Why was I wincing? This was nothing I hadn't seen before. Though never this intimately, I suppose. Usually it was just a quick slash with the saber and I was done. This slow and horrid trawl through bone and muscle was new, and I could barely see what I was doing through the blood that drooled from tongues of sinew.

The knife made a high-pitched grinding noise as it caught on bone. Edgar made a sound like he was trying to imitate it. He cursed at full volume.

"*I don't wanna I don't wanna I don't wanna.*"

I ignored him. Kept sawing through his arm. Blood

gouted from the wound, squirting from stringy sinew that shrunk back to hug his flesh.

I winced. Was I crying? I couldn't tell. I just sawed through him as he writhed and choked and screamed. I could feel him kicking as I sliced through bone. He tried to buck me off, but I was sitting too high on his chest.

"I can't I can't I can't I can't I can't."

I finished sawing through his arm, and all but sloughed off him. We were both soaked in his blood. We laid beside each other for a long time.

It was almost a relief when he started whimpering. When he broke down crying, I felt like I could breathe.

"I'm not here," he whispered to himself. "I'm not here. I'm not here."

I'm not sure how long I laid there. At some point I sat up and hugged my knees to my chest while Edgar stared at the morning sky. The birdsong seemed perverse. Too calm. Too quiet, underpinned by the faucet drip of my brother's blood.

At some point I stood up, and without a word I sat Edgar up, and propped him up against a tree. I dunno why. I suppose I just thought that might help. And I wasn't sure what else to do.

"Ed," I hated myself for what I was about to say. "I don't know if you can hear me right now. But I need you to know that I still have to leave. I can't go with you."

He didn't look at me. His face and voice were hollow. Completely blank. "Why not?"

Dammit. I wanted to cry. I just couldn't figure out how to. "Do you want to know what was in the letter, Ed?"

If you were feeling generous you could call what shifted beneath his mask a smile. "I think I have a decent guess."

"Yeah," I said. "Yeah." I breathed out slowly.

"She got to you first, huh?"

"Desmon, actually," I muttered. "On her behalf."

"Figures."

"Is anyone coming for you? Do you think?" I asked.

"Yeah" he said. "Soon."

"So are you just going to stay here? Or?" I was not sure how to help him get back to his supporters while still getting free of him.

He looked like he was debating whether or not he ought to shrug. "I'd prefer not to move until help arrives."

"What if Mercedes arrested your supporters?"

"She didn't."

"But what if she did? We don't know if help *will* arrive, Ed. Come on. We have to get you out. You can't stay in that tourniquet forever."

"Help *is* coming," Edgar insisted.

I rolled my eyes and slogged my way through my doubts. "Ed. It's been hours." Had it been hours? How long were we laying there? Time was such a fuzzy concept in the midst of all this. It was hard to tell. "We didn't get that far out from Bullion, and there's still no one." Why couldn't he see that? I couldn't just pick him up and carry him. I needed his cooperation if I was going to get him out of this alive.

"Help is coming," Edgar said again. His voice was completely monotone, and I hated it. "It's just going to take them a bit."

I rolled my eyes. "Fuck this."

"I can wait," Edgar said through a clenched jaw.

"Well, *I* can't. So you're coming back with me."

"And how exactly do you plan to do that, Petre?" Ed asked. "What? You think I'm in no shape to be left here but you think you can fucking drag me back to Anoïse?"

"Ed, I—" I took a step closer.

"Just go."

I combed my hands through my hair. The gesture made me feel strangely guilty. As if there was something wrong with still having, still using, both of my arms. "Ed. Come on. I can't just *leave* you."

"That's what you were just trying to do, wasn't it?"

"Well, not like this!"

"Yeah. Well." He fidgeted, slightly, and found a bit more of an upright position. He shifted his remaining arm, like he was preparing to cross it. Then he winced. Looked to the ribboned mess of steel and oil and blood tangled in yarn ball patterns on the road. "It's not like you don't have a history of leaving. I've come to expect it. You can go. It's fine. Really."

The urge to help was fleeing quicker than I would've liked. Killing him with kindness wasn't looking nearly so appealing as the other kind. "And what's *that* supposed to mean?"

"You always leave. It's just what happens." He slouched again, and stared at the stretch of soil between his legs. "I thought it might go differently this time, you know. I really did. I thought if I got there first you'd understand why I had to do what I'm doing. I guess I was wrong."

"Ed," I groaned. "Come on. You're being ridiculous. It's not like that, I swear to G—"

"Just get the fuck out of here, man. I'm done with you."

I took a step closer. "You can't—"

Ed dragged his caterwauler out from its holster and trained it on me. He dialed the hammer back with his thumb. The gun's whine changed pitch as he drew the hammer towards him, changing its settings. "What did I say?"

"Goddammit, Ed. The hell do you think you're doing?" I was trying to help. Lord. What was wrong with him?

"Leave," he said. "I'm not going to tell you again."

I wanted to deescalate the situation. Really, I did. But it had been a long day, and I was feeling petty. So I took a step back and asked, "Is that an order, Your Grace?"

He squeezed the trigger. I felt the air thrum near my ear as the sonic blast shrieked. I was breathing hard. My heart made quick time like a crazed bird in a small cage.

"Were you actually trying to *hit* me?"

"Depends. You planning on leaving yet?"

"The hell was your setting on that gun, Ed?"

"Dunno. Didn't check. Would you like to try again?"

"Ed. Come on."

"By all means, stick around if you like." He slammed the gun into the holster. Thumbed the switch to juice it up. "For a little while. You've earned yourself a minute while I recharge. Unless you want to say something stupid in the meantime. Make me stand up and stab you."

"Ed. You haven't even had stitches yet. No medical treatment whatsoever. You can't move too much or that tourniquet will come undone."

"Better fucking leave then, shouldn't you?"

"Ed, you—"

He shifted. A lurch that kicked my panic up a notch. I took a step back, not entirely of my own volition. "Alright alright alright. Fuck. I'm going. I hope you have fun out here. Don't let that stump get infected."

"Go fuck yourself!" He shouted at my back.

"I hope someone picks you up before your arm turns gangrenous!"

"They will!" Edgar shouted.

"Good! Fucking phenomenal." I realized I meant that

sincerely. "Don't send anyone after me again. Or I'll take your other arm, too, asshole."

I heard his caterwauler scream. This one never had a chance of coming anywhere near me. He didn't even bother aiming. *"I fucking won't,"* he shouted. "Just get the fuck out of my face, Petre. Fuck off!"

"I will!"

I wasn't sure when I'd started crying.

PART TWO

CHAPTER

TEN

I made it to the capital the next day.

I don't quite remember much of it. I think my mind had to sort of...go away for a little while.

After all that.

I got pretty far that first day before I bothered to stop. I needed to put distance between Edgar and me, in case he changed his mind about sending someone to catch me.

I stayed in a small trading village called Salttown overnight, and hit The Rill sometime the next morning— the river that makes Mercy House's territories somewhat of an island.

I paid a ferryman to get me across. He seemed confused, and I didn't realize until later that it must've been because I was still all bloody. So I walked downstream and had the most cathartic bath of my life. Scrubbed my clothes and left them to dry overnight.

But they didn't dry. Not completely, anyway. They were still a little damp by the time I shrugged them on and made the last leg of my journey. Which was a surprise, since I had slept till noon. But I got to the capital quickly, all things considered.

I hugged the edge of the shoreline, parallel to The Bay the whole way home. My feet hurt like you'd never believe.

I'd been planning to reveal my identity to the sentries posted at the front gate and catch a ride to Mercy House, in the inner ring of the city. But by the time I got there I learned that was not the best idea.

The road had picked up travelers the closer I got to the capital—and the closer I got to court, the more I learned about those rumors Mercedes had told me about.

The merchants clogging the road were, for example, insisting I'd had sex with a cyborg horse. Which had, somehow, influenced my decision to run away at eighteen.

A couple kids a few miles farther on soon contradicted them. They were gossiping about the fact that my *real* secret was something involving snake women and demonic pacts.

As I neared the capital itself, I overheard a couple of labcoats drinking coffee and attempting to puzzle out how I had escaped Mercy House without any sign of injury to anyone.

It was unbelievable. They'd mixed me up with Edgar.

So I figured maybe I shouldn't reveal who I was to the guards at the gate. I didn't want to get in trouble, if they had picked up the wrong details from passers-by. Desmon had given me an inn to wait at. The Dripping Bucket. I could stay there.

In hindsight, maybe I should've introduced myself to the guards—because the inn turned out to be home to the worst rumor yet.

THE DRIPPING BUCKET was a grimy place that blared too much heavy guitar music. The kind that drowned out everything else.

The lights were all hazy, like someone had smeared petroleum jelly on all the bulbs. You could probably see better by the glow of neon signs than any lighting in a place like this. It didn't help that last week's uncleaned beer stains were establishing colonies across the floor that made your shoes sticky for the next few hours. Couldn't even see your way around the spills.

All this to say—yeah. Sure. The Dripping Bucket was a decent place to go when you wanted to find rumors. People talk. It happens. I was braced for it.

But when I *got* there, what I actually heard—well. I didn't think even The Dripping Bucket could come up with something *that* horrid.

Turns out, not only did I make pacts with demons, not only did I fuck horses, not only did I escape the home I hadn't seen in years—I was also fucking my brother, Edgar.

Just when you think you've heard the most depraved shit. Somebody brings up incest. Typical.

It's fine though. I wasn't planning on meeting Desmon sober anyway. I needed something to wash the thought of *that* out of my mind.

Along with everything else that had happened the last few days.

I sat in a booth that was wrapped in cracked black leather. Residue from old spills still lingered on the table.

I was still a little shocked that Desmon had agreed to meet me in a place like this. He and I used to come down here as kids when we had no wish to be recognized. Desmon always had to wear a disguise. I never had that problem. Not the same way the other three did. A few too many family embarrassments growing up ensured that Dad took...certain measures, to keep me out of the public eye.

Tabloids had caught pictures of me here and there, obviously, but they were much rarer than they were with the other three. Last time it had happened was during that incident with Edgar, and even then, Dad had stepped in to make a few threats to make sure everything got suppressed.

I wondered if Desmon still came down here when he wanted to get away. I would've thought he had outgrown this place by now. You would have expected two princes to have a more formal reunion.

I watched two men playing pool while I waited. An old man wore a frock coat made of leather, paired with a cheap shirt with strings and lace down the front, mostly undone. He played against a young man who looked like a marble sculpture who had wished to be a real boy. His hair was so yellow it was almost white. He was snuggled into a coat of coyote fur, the hem of which unfortunately hid his ass from me.

I wanted an eyeful, because those jeans looked tight. Left little of his thighs to the imagination, at least. I chewed on my lip.

The young man bent over the far side of the pool table. I could have sworn he was looking right at me.

The older man coughed. "Come on, kid. I've been trying to tell you how to line these shots up. Haven't you been listening? I'm going to feel guilty when I win. Like taking money from a baby."

I examined the table. The older man must've been playing stripes—because there were none left on the table. Only solid colors. And the eight ball. It looked like the young man hadn't even made one shot so far, and he didn't seem to heed the older man, either. He was too busy. His head lolled to one side, and I thought he'd winked at me for a moment.

But I realized he was just lining his shot up. He'd thrown one leg up on the table, half-lazed across it. "I'll get there eventually," the young man drawled. He snapped the stick forward, and for a second the table turned into a game of pinball, until the cue ball cracked against the purple four ball, which clinked into the pocket.

I held my breath and waited to see if the cue ball would follow it in. It seemed to tilt on the slimmest edge, and then was still. It didn't fall in.

I exhaled my relief.

"Huh." The young man swept stray strands of hair out of his sightline. "I think I'm getting the hang of this."

My next three minutes were spent watching this man sink every last ball in with military precision.

He had a good eye. Sharp aim. Good use of geometry. I'd never been great at this game myself. I often took more of a *try any swing and see what happens* approach, which rarely netted victory.

But *this* man? He was precise. Calculated. And by the time he was done the older man was red in the face.

"You cheated," the older man said.

"I'd never. Your instructions were very helpful, is all." He smiled, and knocked his cue into the eight ball.

I realized at the same time he did that the young man hadn't taken enough time to line up that shot properly. He didn't take the care he had with all the others. The cue ball knocked sideways into the eight ball, bounced it off the wall. The two virtually swapped places.

The young man paled. The older man sneered, and

snatched the cue stick out of the young man's hands. "Very kind of you."

"No—now—now listen. Listen. Listen. Maybe I was playing down what I could do a little bit. That's a fair critique. I'm open to it. Let's give this fairer odds, hey? Rack them back up, play it straight. It's like you were saying. You wouldn't want to take money from a baby, you know what I—?"

In the time it took the kid to protest, the older man sunk the eight ball in the far right corner, then turned to glower at the young man. "We're done here." He held out his hand expectantly.

The young man made a show of giving himself a pat down. "I could have sworn I had it with me somewhere."

Something warm and tense tightened in my stomach. By the time I swung my legs out from under the table, the older man had the kid by the lapels of his fur coat.

"I've got it on me!" The young man shouted. "I do! I've got it. Must've left it back at my table, with my friend there." He gestured at me.

For a moment I nearly registered surprise. I was curious now. I wanted to know where this was going.

The older man let him go, crossed his arms. He watched the younger man scamper over to me and slide into my booth.

As he did, he dragged his breath in audibly. For a moment I was scared he recognized me. His eyes lit up with intrigue, or what passed for it. I watched the slow rise and fall of his chest, the way it strained the confines of his shirt, and I realized I had been forgetting to breathe.

He cleared his throat. "I don't suppose you've got any money?"

Ah. So he didn't know who I was. Perfect. "I don't even know your name, man."

"My name's not important." The young man laughed. "I just need money."

I looked him up and down. The fur coat and the thread work on his shirt did not exactly scream broke. "You haven't got any?"

The man's eyes widened as if he'd had a realization. "Hang on. Lemme check." He rifled through his pockets, turning each of them inside out as he went through them. "Huh. Well. Would you look at that?"

"What?"

"Still nothing."

I took a sip of the beer I'd been neglecting this whole time. Wiped my mouth with the back of my hand. "Better hurry," I said. "Wouldn't want a man like that getting impatient."

"That's why I'm asking you."

I chewed on the thought of offering him some help. He was cute. Though a little on edge, and I was on the lookout for any hidden knives. But still—he was cute. I could certainly afford to buy him a drink. But he didn't need to know that. Not quite yet. I wanted him to work for it. "You forgot your money?"

He leaned across the table. "Did you want me to check again? Or would you prefer to do the searching?"

I nearly choked on my drink. I leaned in close enough to smell him. "It's just quite a thing to forget, is all. How'd you afford the drinks without any money?"

"Who says I've had anything to drink?"

I just looked at him.

"Right." He cleared his throat as a flush crawled up his face. "Might've had a few beers before I came here. Maybe more than that. I lost count." His teeth snagged a smile before it could finish forming. His laughter was more breath than substance. "Anyway. I left home in a hurry."

"Clearly." I chewed it over. The man was lucky. He was exactly the kind of distraction I needed right now. Probably a few years younger than me. Nineteen? Twenty? "How much did you have to drink before you got here?"

"Hang on," he said. "Let me think." He frowned. Stared at the ceiling, counting things off on his fingers while murmuring to himself. "Hm. Alright." He shrugged. "Nowhere near enough."

Laughter bolted from me before I could swallow it. "That kind of night, huh?" I counted out a couple coins. Slid them across the counter to him, then tossed in a couple bank notes for good measure. "Is that enough to help you out? Or will you need more?"

"Oh, that's more than enough. You won't regret this," he said, and slid out of my booth. I expected him to head over to the older man, but instead he made for the counter.

The older man was watching me, and looking over to the younger man. Maybe he thought he was looking to make change.

He sauntered over to me, pool cue gripped in white knuckles. This place was too crowded to draw my science-sword if it came to that. I still had Dad's knife on me, but I didn't want to think about that right now. It put me in mind of Edgar.

Still. It was there if I needed it, and that was good to know.

"You with him?" The older man asked.

"Seems that way," I said. "Dunno what he's doing though. Did you catch his name?" It was worth a shot.

The man eyed the counter. "Here he comes."

THE FALL IS ALL THERE IS

Fuck.

The young man approached; a beer bottle wrapped in one hand. He tossed the change onto the table. "Seriously, though, I cannot thank you enough," he said, without acknowledging the older man.

I looked at the spare coins scattered across the table. My heartbeat quickened. I swallowed. "Um. Are you sure that was wise?"

The kid didn't seem to hear me. His eyes were intent on the drink. He took three gulps, his throat working. "Hm? Oh! No, not remotely." He raised his half empty bottle to the man he owed. "Sorry, friend—I haven't got any money."

The big man let go of the cue. His hand knotted into a fist.

I tried to lurch to my feet, to intervene, but before I had the space to stand the older man was swinging.

The kid brought his forearm out in a semicircle, pushing against the crook of the older man's elbow—but not far enough. The blow tagged him in the temple.

My teeth tightened as the kid staggered. He tossed his beer bottle into the air, caught it by the neck, and came in high, swinging it into the big man's head so hard he broke it.

I realized what was happening, grabbed my beer and sprung out from under the table as the force of the blow knocked the man's head into it. He clung to it, half-conscious. The table tipped, both hit the floor, and then the big man let go.

The kid's hair was in disarray. His clothes were more askew than they were before. He was shiny with sweat; still looking at the hand that held the stump of the beer bottle. "A waste," he said. "And here I was hoping I wouldn't get noticed." He turned his attention back to me. "I really hate to cause a scene. You won't tell anyone about this will you?"

I was sitting atop the high back of my chair, beer still in my hands. I held my breath, watching him. "Not a soul."

The young man tilted his head. "What did you say you were here for again?"

I shrugged. "I didn't."

"Oh." He pointed to my beer. "Are you going to finish that?"

"Help yourself." I passed the drink to him.

"You're a good man. Thank you. I'm going to need this. That guy's friends will be looking for me pretty soon."

I wasn't aware he'd had friends here. I wondered how long till they realized he was missing.

"Are you sure that beer was a good idea, then?" I asked.

The man examined the glass, looking into it like he could see his reflection staring back. "Hey. I'm curious."

"Yeah?"

"Help me puzzle something out."

"Hit me."

"What have I done so far tonight that makes you think I'm the kind of man who has good ideas?"

I snorted. "There is that."

He downed half the drink in one go. Grimaced. "God. I hate this shit. It's awful." He finished the rest. "Anyway. Even so. What's the worst these guys can do? Kill me? That'll be one for the history books." He set the glass down beside the older man's head. "Thanks for the drink. This has been fun and all. And I really *was* planning to stay a bit longer. But I should get out fast. There's going to be a fight soon, and I'd rather throw down outdoors, you know what I mean?"

"Are you sure?" This was the closest thing to a pleasant interaction I'd had the whole trip home.

"I wouldn't want to fight in a venue like this," the man chuckled, stuffing his hands into his coat pockets. "Might get in trouble, you know?"

"Oh *now* that's a concern."

"The *concern*," the man said, pointedly, "is being even passively responsible for any damage to that face of yours."

I wasn't sure if I wanted to hit him or kiss him. Maybe both. "Are you going to be okay?"

The man's mouth twisted into a cracked glass grin. It was like he'd never even thought of it before I brought it up. "Hm. I mean—here's hoping, am I right?" He rapped his knuckles twice on the upturned table. "Knock on wood." He turned to leave.

"Hey, hold on a second." My hand closed around his. I jumped down from my seat, dug my heels into the floor. "What makes you think my face hasn't seen any action before?"

He looked me up and down, then looked over to the opposite corner of The Bucket. I followed his sightline and spotted the man's friends eyeing the two of us from across the room. It looked like they were having a debate amongst themselves.

He went back to scrutinizing me. He bit his lip. God. Even his teeth were immaculate. "Hm." His mouth quirked up on one side.

"Hm?" I asked.

"I'm thinking." The older man's buddies were headed towards us, wearing outrage.

"About?" I realized I still held his hand. I debated whether or not I ought to let go.

"Purple seems to suit you. Might be you'd look cuter with a couple bruises."

I took a few deep breaths. Tightened my grip on his hand, really dug into his skin, pressed my nails into his palm. Hard enough that he even winced a little bit. I liked that more than I had a right to. "I don't mind taking a few."

"You mind taking anything else?"

"I take all kinds of things."

It was his turn to squeeze my hand. "Nice grip, too," he added.

When I looked up, we were surrounded. Pinned into our booth by a semicircle of adversaries.

But the young man only looked at me. "That'll come in handy."

"I bet." Fear felt delicious in my belly for the first time in a while, a warm inviting pressure that churned my guts to heavy cream. "Shall we get this started?"

I took stock of the half dozen bodies squeezing us into confined space. The man nearest me slipped on a set of brass knuckles. At least *his* didn't crackle with electricity.

I looked back to my companion. He combed his hand through his hair. "I was actually wondering if we could ignore these boys a little longer."

"You do seem to be enjoying yourself here."

"Me? Oh no, I'm terrified." His words came with a nervous chuckle and a rictus grin. "I just wanna see how long we can keep this going before one of them—"

The man with the brass knuckles hit things off. He came in on my left. I clocked him stepping into my space and the world snapped into focus. The geometry of combat made all its angles known to me as my injections yanked me out of the way of his haymaker.

He staggered into my path, and I followed the warm

programmed suggestions spiraling through my hands and seized a fistful of his shoulder. Held him down while I fed him my knees. Then wrenched him upright and kicked his ankle with my heel. He went down hard.

Another man was on me before I could do anything else, a nameless body slamming into me. Two hundred and fifty pounds of mass wearing a black beard.

The table braced the small of my back. My weight pushed it back upright, and I felt its edge pressing against my spine. I was dimly aware the music had died away. There were shouts. Screams, behind the broad back of my new attacker. He was too close. I couldn't see the world beyond him.

Panic swallowed up my thoughts as the front of my shirt tightened in his fist. I tried to get up, but his knuckles slammed me back down.

Fuck. Was this how Edgar felt a few nights ago? God *damn*. Spots of yellow light bleached the world out of my vision. I had to do something before his fist came back for round two. My head pounded. I kicked but couldn't wedge a toe between his legs. Couldn't reach his stomach with my back flat on the table.

So when his fist came down again, I ate the punch. In a fit of panic, I took a firm hold on his wrist. Held his knuckles where they'd landed in my eye socket. Pinned him there long enough to get a hold on the side of his face, spin him sideways as I twisted my hips. The hand pinning me sprang free of my shirt when his weight shifted.

My injections took it from there. I got my hand on the back of his stupid fucking head and twisted onto my side.

He took some blind shots at my kidneys in the instant it took to introduce his forehead to the table. I dragged him back up by the roots of his hair. Blood was making tributary patterns on his face. I slammed him down again.

Fuck. I'd just got these clothes washed last night. I wasn't planning to get them bloody again so soon.

He slumped to the floor, and I climbed to my feet, dizzy. Realized The Dripping Bucket had descended into chaos. Tables had been upturned. Everyone was fighting. Grunting. I spotted a couple knives that glinted pink in the neon lights.

A couple of the men who had surrounded us were bleeding on the floor. And the young man in the fur coat was still close by. I spotted him as he finished introducing his broken bottle to someone's inner thigh. He kicked the man onto his back then turned to me. "Ah! You're still conscious! Wonderful!" He shouted so I could hear him over the riot of sound and fury. "You were a great help. Taking care of that one guy."

I held up two fingers.

"Only two?" The young man smiled. "I thought you said you'd done this kind of thing before."

I laughed. A loud, mad cackle. "Recently."

"How recent?"

"It's been a long few days."

The young man seemed to stiffen slightly. I wasn't sure if I should ask why. "No kidding."

"Are you okay?" I asked.

Someone found the back of my shirt before he could answer. I staggered blindly, my injections making haywire suggestions. Wasn't even sure if this was one of the old man's friends or just someone looking for another guy to punch.

I twisted around with the momentum of my backwards stagger, threw a blind elbow that hit a jaw. But as I turned around my balance failed me, and I slipped into an awkward sort of hug with my attacker—some wiry man in a white shirt a size too small—and we both fell to the floor. I wound up straddling his torso.

I wasn't sure who this man was, but he had a knife. My injections determined that the weapon took priority. Which was very helpful considering the blade was on a course for my belly.

The injections curled my hand around his wrist. Jerked his arm up over his head. I put my knee on his shoulder and started pressing on the back of his elbow as far as it would go.

The injections wanted a compound fracture more than I did, so I eased in. Went slow and built up pressure. "DROP IT!"

I was surprised when he obeyed. I snatched it by the hilt and tossed it under a table. Didn't want to keep it. It was too risky in this kind of chaos. Odds were too good someone could get it off me. Or I'd be tempted to use it as an easy out when it wasn't warranted. I had to finish this man off quickly.

Apparently he had other ideas about me making him unconscious. And by *other ideas* I do in fact mean *a fantastic right hook.*

I slumped off him, braced on my hands and knees. Blood welled into my mouth. Had I bit my tongue? My cheek? My lip?

Fuck. I'd given him time to stand. I was at eye level with his hands. He was wearing rings. Was that why I tasted blood?

His hand got around my throat. I was on my knees. I tried to make the world stop tilting. Spinning. But the world refused to work with me. I shut my eyes and hoped that might make it better, though I didn't have much luck.

I was debating my next course of action when I heard the young man scream. I twisted, in time to see a speeding mass wrapped in coyote fur hurtling over me.

He threw a wild punch as he came down on top of my assailant, whose body jerked once and went slack.

Fuck. Who taught that kid to fight like that? Hot damn.

He helped me to my feet. "Are you *sure* you're good at this?"

"You caught me on an off day. I promise."

He pinched my chin between two fingers, tilted my face to one side while the chaos raged around us. "Huh. Looks like I was right."

"About?"

He touched a bruise that had formed under my eye with two fingers. Lightly, because that was all he had to do to make it ache.

I wanted him to press down harder. I wanted to kiss him.

"You do look better with a couple bruises." His hands found my waistband. He dragged me forward by it. "Come with me."

ELEVEN

I crashed through the bathroom door with his hand down my trousers. He jerked me once, twice, three times, then put both hands on either side of my face and pressed my mouth against his.

He left me no room to breathe. He kissed angry. Like he was trying to bite *through* me.

"Eager, are w—" was all I had time to get out, before he tightened his grip on the back of my head and crushed my mouth against him.

I learned as I kissed him that I had acquired a split lip. Each kiss left an imprint of my blood. It looked like he was wearing smeared lipstick.

He dragged me, walking backwards, not breaking his kiss as the grimy bathroom wall met his back.

"Right next to the urinals?" I asked.

"You know it's cute that you expect me to believe this is the worst place you've had your cock touched." He stole a couple greedy kisses. Teased the injury to my lower lip with his tongue. Each kiss sent flares of pain out from my mouth.

I tasted blood. I let out something halfway between a surprised yelp and a groan.

He wrapped his teeth around my split lip. Squeezed a fresh bead of blood out from the injury and licked it off my lip slowly. The wound housed an angry heat that I adored. A grainy groan worked its way out of my throat, and I worked the buttons on his trousers while we kissed.

He caught my wrists. Peeled them off his trousers. He put my hands on his hips without taking his mouth off mine. I moved in closer and grabbed a handful of his ass.

Fuck. I still didn't even have his name. And now didn't seem like the correct time to ask what it was.

He bunched up the lapels of my chameleon coat, and suddenly the room was spinning. The bathroom walls slammed into my shoulder blades. He teased me over my trousers, and I moaned into his mouth.

His other hand put pressure on my bruises. I wasn't sure if he'd already determined where they were or if the last few days had banged me up *that* badly.

He pushed my head to one side, put his mouth on my neck. He undid my belt while his tongue worked on my throat. I felt as though my knees were going to buckle. He'd got my trousers undone by the time he took his mouth off me. "I thought you'd like that," he said in a low voice, as I shimmied my trousers down. To fill the silence he put his free hand in front of my face. "Lick."

I dragged my tongue up from the heel of his hand. And he wrapped it around me. Started working me, pumping with his wrist. I bucked my hips.

I eased down the wall slowly, till I was sitting. He knelt with me. I dragged him closer by the sides of his face and kissed him as he jerked. His other hand was squeezing my throat. "Fuck, fuck."

He eased back slowly. I was about to complain before I realized he was looking at my cock. He made eye contact as he drooled a strand of saliva onto it while he worked the head.

At some point he put his hand back around my throat.

"Is that the best you can do?" He could play harder than this, surely.

He tightened his grip. "Not remotely." He dragged me forward, kissed me again as he picked up the pace. I bucked my hips to his rhythm.

"Fuck," I heard myself murmur. "Fuck. Fuck. Don't slow down don't slow down don't slow down I'm gonna—"

He stopped.

I panicked. "What—why—why did you—?"

He leaned into the space between us. Teased my split lip with his tongue again. He smiled when my cock twitched. "Ask me nicely."

"You motherfucker—"

He let go completely. "That's not how you pronounce please is it?"

"Oh, fuck you."

"I'll bet you'd like that."

"I hate you."

"Should I stop then? I thought you wanted me to do something with this?" He gave some slim attention to my head.

My mouth opened and he mirrored it. "Ahhhh—y-yes. Yes," I rasped,

He pulled away again.

I groaned. "You're gonna make me cry."

"Aww. Promise?"

"Please. God. Fuck. Please you have to—I have to finish.

179

Come on. After all that you can't just—please. Fuck. You have to let me. Please."

"Please what? Use your words. Tell me what you want me to do."

"Oh God." I closed my eyes. Tried to squeeze the words out. It took a mental push, and I wasn't sure if I had the mental energy to make it sound sexy. "Please fuck me. Come on. I need you to put your mouth on my fucking cock. Is that what you're looking to hear?"

"You're sure?" He actually giggled. "You sound upset."

I glared at him. "You're pushing your luck," I said, flatly.

He shrugged. "Worth a shot." He managed two pumps, the most delicious relief I'd ever felt flooded me. He started to duck his head down, and then he brought it back up. "What was that?"

"You're joking, right?" I was angry now. I had to drag in a few deep breaths before I spoke. "What's going on? What are you doing? Why'd you—?"

"Stop it." He was on his feet, tucking his shirt into his trousers and buckling his belt. He was still hard. I tried to memorize the outline of his cock.

"No, come on, what the fuck was that about?" I asked. "You can at least give me some kind of explanation, right?" I scrambled to my feet, tried to make myself presentable. It seemed like he was backing out. So I had to get dressed.

He slapped me. It seemed mostly playful. Mostly. "It's *not* that I don't want to," he snapped. "Don't jump to conclusions. I just—" he indicated the door with his eyes. "I *hear* something. Now keep your voice down."

I held my breath and listened. "Oh." I realized the problem. It wasn't that he heard something as much as it was that there wasn't much of anything to hear in the first place.

And considering we'd exited a chaotic brawl a few minutes ago—the fact that there was only muffled groaning was...troubling. To say the least.

"The hell is going on out there?" I peeked out the bathroom door.

All my fears and hopes trainwrecked together at once.

Desmon was in the doorway to The Bucket, watching a contingent of The Mercy Guard, as they rounded up the last of the unruly stragglers. "Fuck. What the hell is Desmon doing here?"

The noise the young man made sounded like he was choking on something. I whirled. He was wild eyed, and looked panicky. "Fuck me! Are you serious? Desmon's here?"

My heartbeat kicked things up a notch. I raised an eyebrow. "You know Desmon?"

He scoffed. "Yeah, of course I know him, why wouldn't I —hang on. How do *you* know Desmon?"

I pressed my lips together. I couldn't actually *tell* him. Especially when I had no idea who I was dealing with, or what flavor of rumors he'd heard about me since Edgar escaped. "I asked first."

He scowled. "So what?"

Fuck. This wasn't getting me anywhere. I debated if I ought to just step out. I couldn't let Desmon leave without me. I looked out the door again. I wasn't sure what to make of any of this.

I heard a squeal. When I looked back, the young man was opening the bathroom window. "Where are you going?" I hissed.

He looked confused, and thumbed to the window. "Out?"

"Clearly. But like—why?"

"You said you *know* Desmon," the young man said. "Why would I stay here?"

He had me there.

"This has been fun and all." He bent and climbed out of the window. I wondered if I should feel guilty for trying to memorize that last eyeful of his ass. "But it sounds like you'll have to handle this one without me. For what it's worth, I wish you luck." He wormed his way out faster than I would've expected anyone could get through, and turned to offer me a salute. "Maybe we'll see each other around. Finish up what we started here. Hell if I know."

He turned to leave. I was about to make my exit, to go see Desmon, when the young man doubled back. "Oh! And one last thing! If you could shut the window behind me I'd be much obliged. I really *would* prefer it if nobody found out that I was here. You can do that, can't you?"

I stepped over to the window, and dragged his face through for one last kiss. "I'll think about it," I said, and gave his face two playful slaps before I pushed him back out and shut the window without another word.

And then I was alone. And I wasn't sure what to do. What to say. I didn't want to go out there yet. I was too tweaked out. Like I was coming apart at the seams.

I needed a chance to breathe. I felt like I was going to puke. I had to center myself. I took out a case of Muse and stuffed a roll in my mouth. I wanted to cry when I used the lighter Ed had given me.

I dragged the rancid smoke down to my lungs. The worry didn't vanish. But Muse had wrapped the world in a gray haze. It felt as though my thoughts were voices coming through a windowpane.

I took out Dad's old knife. Got to my feet. Traced the outline. Assured myself I had control. Even if it was just control over my body. I took a few deep breaths. Still holding onto the roll of Muse with my front teeth. I walked, aimlessly. Back and forth. My hands steadied themselves as they traced the outline of the blade. I sat down under the urinals. There was nothing to fear. Nothing to fear.

Until the door flew open.

TWELVE

T sliced my thumb on the edge of the blade. The Muse fell from my mouth as my injections yelped to life and helped me up. I dragged my feet under me as a man in armor came through. Was he a member of Desmon's security detail? When did The Mercy Guard get new armor?

I saw his eyes widen from under his half-helm. I followed the direction of his gaze to Dad's old knife and tried to muster up a shred of panic from under the drug haze. "Oh, shit," I heard myself say.

"Knife!" The Mercy Guard lunged for me. The injections yanked me out of the way of his gauntleted fist. The warm gray sludge wrapped itself around my knee, dragged it into his breastplate. White pain flared up in me, and I staggered back.

"This is a misunderstanding," I said, doubled over. I braced my hands around the vambraces on his forearms. Also, I had to control his arms, or he'd put me on the ground. "I was putting it away."

He put the pressure on me, tried to back me up. So I

obliged—pulled down on his arms and spilled out of his way.

He lurched forward as I dragged the heel of my hand down onto the back of his helmet. I steered his armored forehead right into the little clamshell urinal cake. The mouth of porcelain erupted into splinters, and the guard groaned.

I made sure the knife was in my pocket by the time he dredged himself to his feet. Though I have to say I was surprised he managed to get back up in the first place.

I raised an eyebrow when he turned around. How the fuck was he still conscious? I know he was wearing a helmet, but *damn*. The steel had a dent in the temple, and he was still getting up. He barely even looked phased. Shit.

I raised my hands. "I told you. I was putting it away." I showed him the M's of my palms. "See? Empty!"

He reached out without a word. His gauntleted fist was cold around my throat. I reached for the crook of his elbow, but he hurled me in a semicircle before I could make contact. The world reeled around me, and suddenly a bathroom stall blocked me in on both sides. I pinballed between them as I slowed my momentum and staggered back. I braced my hands on the sides of the stall. I was *not* going to hit the ground.

But he was standing in front of my only way out.

"Man, the brawl is over. I was just in here pissing. What the hell?" I didn't want to jump to conclusions about what was happening here. All I knew was that I was very keen on not drowning in a toilet.

He still didn't say anything. He just stepped forward. I didn't have room. I was panicking. There was no room to maneuver. I couldn't stop his fist from slamming into my chest. All the breath rushed out my body in a spray of air and spittle, and I folded.

I clutched my stomach, as if he'd stabbed me and I had to hold my guts in. My knees hit the tiles, and I felt cold worms of metal fingers in my hair. He hauled my face up. I was staring up at bathroom lights, and his raised fist.

"You gotta be kidding me." I would've rolled my eyes if I'd had time.

"JERIM!" A voice barked. The Mercy Guard jumped. His hand unknotted from my hair.

I was so out of sorts that I didn't recognize the voice until its owner hauled my new friend Jerim out from the stall and took his place, bent over to check on me. "Lord. Petre. I'm sorry about Jerim. Did he hurt you?"

For the first time in five years, I looked Desmon in the face. He'd gained some weight since I last saw him. But then he'd always been the biggest of the four of us. He carried it well. He was half as wide as the bathroom stall, and when I looked into his eyes it was hard to breathe. "I missed you too, shithead," I said.

"Come on." He dug his hands under my armpits. "Let's get you up."

I let him think that whatever he was doing was actually helping, as I climbed to my feet.

"Lord," he said. "That's a lot of bruises. Jerim really roughed you up, huh?"

"Something like that." He didn't need to know about my involvement in the brawl he had disrupted. Or the man who had just snuck out the bathroom window.

"What happened to your thumb?" Desmon asked. "You need anything for that?"

"Oh." I had forgotten it was bleeding. In the process of

checking I gave Desmon a very red thumbs up. Which he must've mistaken for confirmation, because he had a brown bandage around the wound an instant later.

I flexed my thumb. "You just travel with those?"

"I-It builds a rapport, at times. When necessary." He shrugged.

Yeah. That sounded like something Desmon would do. "You should know your friend did sort of um. *Interrupt* me." I motioned with my head to the toilet behind me.

Desmon looked to Jerim, who only shrugged. "He had a knife."

Desmon frowned. "Right. I'll save you a table while you um." His mouth quirked down, and he made a vague gesticulation at the toilet. "I'll order food for us while I wait. You still like the bison here?"

Lord Alive, I didn't think that he'd remember. This place made sandwiches from trees made of fur and bison meat, farmed in The Forest Wall and The Outlying Islands. It was my favorite meal here. "I need that immediately. Please. Yes. I'll be out in a second. I promise."

"I should've waited out there," Desmon said, on the way out.

"Oh no, I'd prefer this kind of awkward interaction to another hit from *Jerim* over there. Thank you for intervening. I'll be out in a sec."

Desmon left me to my business. I took a minute just to collect myself. God. Fuck.

I stood over the stalls, spread my legs, one hand braced on the wall over the toilet. Pulled my cock out and took care of the problem that the man who'd fled out the window had left me with. After all, if I was dealing with Desmon, I'd want to do it with a clear head.

HE HAD two bison sandwiches in a basket waiting for me in one of the booths, while he chewed on a few deep fried tongues harvested from a tall plant out west.

"Shit," I said, "I didn't think you were actually going to get it."

Desmon took a bite of his meal. "Why wouldn't I?"

"Guess I'm used to people foregoing promises lately." I ate half of the first sandwich in one bite. I forgot how good they made them here. Pink juice dribbled down my chin. It was still steaming when I bit in. Curls of clear vapor rose from the red meat. I had to pocket it in the side of my mouth to give it time to cool off. "Lord. I never realized how bad I missed this."

"I thought you might." Desmon covered his mouth with his fist, like he was coughing. "There's a reason I figured we would meet here, you know? Old time's sake and everything." He took another big bite. "I'll bet you're wondering why we sent for you."

By now I was pretty sure I had an inkling. But I wanted to see what kind of story Desmon told me if he didn't know what I knew. "God, yes. I'd been wondering."

Desmon leaned back in his chair. "You're not going to like it."

I shoved what was left of my first sandwich in my mouth, choked down my instinctual reply. I was about to say something shitty about Edgar. The urge to do so felt nearly physical.

Instead I cleaned the grease from my fingers with a napkin and did my best to look disinterested as I retrieved the second sandwich. I wished Desmon had bought a drink. He'd probably refused to on purpose. He would've said *you didn't ask for one* if I brought it up. "Listen. I know I won't like it. If I was going to like it, you wouldn't have kept it secret in all the letters. So whatever you've got going on, I can take it. Just tell me what's happened and I'll clear things up with you as best I can."

Desmon tilted his head. "Clear things up?"

I blinked. Maybe I was letting on a bit too much. "Desmon, don't get hung up on that. Just tell me—"

Desmon grinned, leaned forward, elbows on the table. "No, now I'd like to know. What is it that you think is going on? What do you think you need to clear up?"

"Desmon, I—"

"Petre. You can tell me."

I took a bite of my sandwich. Just to give myself some time, and an excuse for why my face was turning so red. I had to find a way to underplay what I knew. "Have you heard some of the things they're saying about me? Around the country, I mean? There were some rumors I overheard—"

Desmon looked concerned, though I couldn't ascertain if it was genuine. "I haven't, I'm afraid. What sort of rumors?"

I sighed. Scratched the back of my neck. Finished off my meal. "Oh boy. Where do I even start? People think I'm possessed by some demon. They think I fuck horses, or snakes—or—or—or Edgar, even! I've heard all sorts of things." Feeling somewhat confident, I added, "They—they're even saying I'm planning some sort of rebellion against you guys. Haha."

Desmon just stared at me, food in his mouth, not chewing. "Oh dear. Well that *is* unfortunate. I told Anoïse that this would happen."

Frustration built in me. "Told her what would happen?"

I leaned across the table. "Desmon. Please just fucking talk to me. What the fuck is going..." I trailed off when I realized Desmon was *amused*.

He covered his mouth with his hand. At least he put on a show of hiding laughter. "It's nothing, don't fret. I only —" Held laughter almost had him coughing up his own food. He cleared his throat. "Sorry. Went down the wrong way. No, but—I told Anoïse that people would talk if you skipped Dad's funeral. I advised her—she should have ordered you to come home. But for some reason she insisted we ought to downplay the vital urgency of the situation we find ourselves in. She didn't want to guilt you into coming. And now look what's happened." He giggled. "Everyone is mixing up their rumors. Petre. This is *delicious*."

I wondered if that was bait. He was trying to see if I would agree and give away that I knew something about what had happened with Edgar. But he couldn't bait me that easily. "Desmon, what on earth are you talking about?"

"The rumors, Petre! That's what's so funny about all this." Laughter made a ragged edge of his voice. "Don't you see? It's not *you* who's planning some risky, stupid gamble to move against us. It's not you that we have concerns about. No. Not at all."

"I—what?" My heart jackhammered in my chest. I hoped I sounded convincing in my disbelief. "What? What on earth do you mean? What?" I was not entirely certain if I was responding the way normal people talk.

Desmon wiped his mouth with his napkin. "It's the rumors, you see—they 've got the wrong brother. It's not you we're concerned about. It's Edgar."

Sometimes when you put on a performance you start to

overthink how many times you're allowed to do something before it seems a bit inauthentic. I responded with, "Desmon, what?" But all I could think about was like—how many times and how many ways can you say *what* or *what do you mean* before it got suspicious?

Desmon seemed too involved in his own amusement to notice. He just chuckled to himself, and cleared his throat. "Alright. Alright. I think that's out of my system. Allow me to start from the beginning."

At last, he elaborated. And I sat there, listening to him explain the situation. I wondered if he was leaving things out on purpose, or if he genuinely had never considered some of the details Edgar gave me to be relevant.

Because at least with Edgar all I had was his version of events to go on. But now that Desmon was in the picture. Well. It was easy to see how both of them had left out key details.

Desmon's account of things, for example, completely left out anything pertaining to a match with Guindolin Reacher, and the fact that Anoïse had ruined it. He skipped right to the part where Dad died, and Anoïse was hearing complaints about Edgar.

Edgar's version had called this paranoia, but the way Desmon told it, she had every right to think of Edgar as a threat. They'd both been raised to rule, but she was the only one getting rewarded for all that hard work. *Immediately* after wrecking Ed's prospects for the best marriage he could've hoped for as a younger sibling.

But what had to be the most glaring omission was that Desmon never once mentioned the house arrest. I don't know how he expected me to overlook that part. Because even if I *didn't* know Edgar's side of the story, it would have been funny that Desmon expected me to be amazed at our brother's miraculous escape, when he gave no indication he was being *held* to begin with.

I sat back when Desmon finished, and debated what the best course of action would be. I wasn't sure what to do. You know? Like, if Desmon couldn't be honest with me—maybe Edgar was right. Maybe there was no place at court for me.

Then again. Maybe Edgar was lying, too. Maybe they'd both left some stuff out.

This kind of shit was why I'd run away. Nobody could ever tell me anything straight. You always had to secure *leverage* out of someone. It was so...transactional. I didn't want to get involved.

"So." Desmon leaned forward and waited for me to fill the silence.

I kept my face blank. It wasn't difficult, as I was very tired. My eyelids wanted to droop like molten metal. "So what?"

"Do you have any thoughts on all this?" He didn't sheath the anticipation in his voice.

God. I wasn't sure if I wanted to do this. But I figured it would be better if he heard it from me. He'd be more suspicious of me if I started keeping secrets. "I like the version Ed told me a little better, I have to say."

Desmon nearly choked on his food. He thumped his chest a few times like there was something in there he needed badly to dislodge. "Ex*cuse* me?"

I tried to keep my tone more casual than I felt. "I mean, well yeah. What do you expect, man? He set himself up for me as a kind of slighted underdog, fighting back. It's more difficult to pitch the status quo, so it's not like I hold it against you, but—"

Desmon pressed his fingers into the corners of his eyes. "God. Petre. No. *No.* I meant what do you mean about talking to Edgar in the first place?"

I shrugged. "He showed up on the same day I got your letter. Said he wanted to catch up for a few days." I didn't think Desmon needed to know about Bullion, or about what had happened to Edgar's arm. I wasn't sure if I could trust him with that information. I'd save that for later, once I got a better layout of everyone's goals and loyalties. "He tried to abduct me. But I ran away."

I could practically see Desmon calculating the social math. Quantifying the theoretical integers of every possible interaction I'd had with Ed. The gears were spiraling behind his eyes. "Why did you come back to us?"

That question took me off guard. "What do you mean?"

Desmon shrugged. "We've asked before," he said, by way of explanation. "You didn't come. What's changed, Petre? Why now?"

I wished I hadn't eaten all my food so quickly, or that I'd had a chance to sleep, before I'd been asked that question. My head was too full of white noise. "Oh. Y'know?" I made some vague gesticulations into empty air.

"I don't," he said. "It's why I'm asking."

Desmon was a damn genius at making me feel like an idiot while saying almost nothing.

I wondered if a touch of sincerity would help. Just a pinch, mind. Wouldn't want to overcommit if I didn't know how it would go over. "Ed couldn't be honest with me. He couldn't tell me the truth about why he came to fetch me. And when he couldn't persuade me he tried to abduct me." I winced. Why couldn't Desmon just have a goddamn expression. Be a human. Fuck. "I know I haven't always had the best relationship with you or Anoïse, but my back was against a wall. I wasn't sure what else to do." That last part felt like stretching the truth just a tad. The *reason* it was the only thing I could think to do was because I was fucking terrified of what Desmon or Anoïse might do to me, or people I cared about, if I didn't come home. But I wasn't about to admit all that to him.

Desmon blinked at me. "Compelling," he said, flatly.

I felt like my stomach was making balloon animals out of my guts. Goddamn. How did he steer the conversation like this with only a few words? "I wouldn't call it compelling—" I started to say. And then I stopped. Why was I allowing Desmon to dictate the rules of our engagement?

I took a breath and tried to remain calm and think of something to say that would put a spotlight back on him. "I can't tell if you're being sarcastic."

He paused for just a little bit too long. I indulged in a fleeting satisfaction that I forced him to *think* for a little bit. Though I was quickly robbed of it when I realized how easily I was becoming reacquainted with the way things were done here. I wasn't sure I liked how fast I'd rediscovered the art of telling half-truths.

"I'm only saying—" Desmon shrugged. "You've got a lot of reasons to side with Edgar. That's why we weren't completely honest to you about him upfront. We had assumed that degree of honesty was too risky. We had to make sure you thought all we needed was an oath of fealty. And, if Edgar reached out to you, we wanted to see what you'd do."

Well. That was interesting. That was a cute little spin he was trying to put on things. "You're saying the only reason you didn't tell me what was going on was as a test?"

"I'm saying Anoïse and I talked it out, and we figured

that if Ed reached out, he was unlikely to be honest with you about why he'd come. He'd try to keep it under wraps. And we figured it wasn't our job to explain things to him, if he ever tried to talk to you."

He didn't expect me to believe that, did he? If they didn't trust Ed to be honest with me, then why would they assume I'd run from him? If they knew Ed was gunning for me they would have intercepted me.

But Desmon didn't need to know that I saw through him. Not just yet. "Truthfully, I'm not sure what Ed really saw in me."

"Probably the same thing Anoïse did." Desmon grinned. "I doubt the two of them wanted you for different reasons. Whatever he said to you, I'd bet he was onto *something*."

"Careful now, Desmon. I could make up any reason I wanted to if I felt so inclined. What if I said he wanted me back because he missed my cooking?"

Desmon laughed. I was annoyed to find that I was smiling too. "Well. Issary *has* missed you, too. You've been gone a while. She's wanted your help in the kitchens."

Oh. I hadn't expected that to hurt as much as it did. And frankly I was astounded Issary was still alive. Wasn't she like ninety when I left? "Fuck, man. I miss her, too."

"*Is* that why Ed wanted you around?"

"Oh!" I snorted. "Fuck no. He had some spiel about how I was the only one of the three of us he could be honest with. The only one without ambition or something."

"Yes!" Desmon pounded the table. The silverware and I jumped. I had to fight down the panicked spirals when my injections attempted to program a reaction into me. "See, I *told* you. I knew he and Anoïse came to similar conclusions. That's exactly why we need your help. We have to avert a war, and there are too many demagogues out there trying to cloud our judgment. The ambition of powerful men is a dangerous thing, and we need you to balance that scale."

How much of my life had been an attempt to balance scales? And when had I ever been good at it? "I don't know about that." I couldn't think clearly. Nothing made sense. And I was not sure I wanted to be back home.

Desmon tilted his head. "What do you mean?"

"I..." I didn't answer at first. Not to gain any kind of leverage, it was just—I didn't know how to. I needed a minute just to organize my thoughts.

I had to level with him, didn't I? That was the only way I'd know if coming back was the right decision. "I just. I dunno man. Why should I trust your view of me if you've proven you can't give me all the information? How is that any different from what Ed did? If you need me so badly why can't you be honest with me?"

Desmon blinked. "I can't say I follow."

"Lord Alive, can you stop treating me like I'm an idiot?" I tossed my napkins at him. He flinched. "Come *on,* man. You know Edgar gave me his side of the story. What are you stupid? You're smarter than that. I expected better of you."

"I—" Desmon blinked rapidly. Was I about to make him cry? I wasn't sure whether or not I wanted to see that. "I don't—"

I leaned across the table. "You never told me about the marriage brokering before Dad died. How Dad had promised Guindolin Reacher to Edgar. But Anoïse scared Dad off the deal with Havilan that would make it happen."

He gawped. "I—I hardly see what that's got to do with—"

"And you skipped the fucking house arrest, Desmon! That's a pretty big piece of it, no? No, don't look at me like that. Why am I supposed to be impressed with his escape if he wasn't locked up in some capacity in the first place? How the hell is it an *escape* if he wasn't imprisoned to begin with?"

"I—okay. Alright." He showed me his hands. "It's possible I haven't been completely honest with you."

"Oh, it's *possible*, huh?" I wanted to hit him now. But I couldn't. Not with Jerim and the rest of The Mercy Guard crawling all over this place.

"Yes. It's *possible*." I wasn't sure if he failed to notice my concern, or if he'd ignored it. "But you have to understand. It's been five years, Petre. There are...concerns. We can't be sure who you would side with. For the sake of our security, we can't—"

I'd had enough. "Desmon. No. Stop it. That's exactly what Edgar was doing. The second I ask for more information, you guys shut down! Don't you get it?" I scraped my chair back and stood up. "Alright, man. Thanks for the meal. I appreciate it. Really, I do. But I can't do this."

I made for the door. There were some stables at the end of this block. *Someone* must have had a horse in there that I could use. I wasn't actually sure if I was going to leave. I was still scared of what Anoïse would do if I didn't report to her. Walking away was my attempt to discern which of my options would be worse.

Desmon followed me out the door. "Petre, wait! Come on! Stop it! Let me explain."

"You've explained plenty, man." He grabbed my shoulder, but I shrugged him off. "Trust me. You don't have to say any more than you already have. You made your thoughts on all this *very* clear."

"Petre—stop—Anoïse needs you here."

"Find a way to tell her what happened then." I didn't want to hear her *don't go* again. I shouldered the stable doors open and looked around for a horse. I didn't have one. I remembered what had happened to Edgar. The visual of all the blood and screaming as I sawed through his arm jumped into my mind's eye.

I wanted to puke. I wanted to go back to Blackheath House. I didn't need my own horse. I'd take any. It didn't matter which. Desmon probably had his own ready to go.

"Petre!" Desmon's voice echoed on the stable walls.

"You got a horse around here?" I scoped the place out and spotted a sleek and shiny black horse. It looked expensive. That was probably how he'd got here. "Ah, here we go."

"Petre, stop—!"

"Unless you have something new to say in your next breath, I'm not interested—"

"*Listen* to me, jackass!" Desmon's voice was loud enough to make me flinch.

I had one hand on his horse when he said it. "Alright. I admire the backbone." I turned slowly. "So I'm going to give you one more chance. But!" I held up a finger to stifle him. "Pick your next words very carefully. Because if they don't start off right, I walk. Before you get to the end of your sentence. Is that clear?"

"I—" Desmon swallowed. Shut his eyes. "I am...*sorry*." He sounded like he had to choke the words out.

I have to admit, that one took me by surprise.

"I'm sorry that I wasn't entirely honest. That I withheld information. But we really *do* need you. In fact—if you can come home, give your account of what happened with Edgar, I think Anoïse would be willing to award you your own fief. Land of your own. We would acquire it from some of our vassals who have rebelled. You help us out, you tell us what happened with Edgar, and it's yours. It's yours and you can settle down and do whatever the fuck you want with it. Host whoever you want, do whatever you want—we'll leave you alone. This whole thing won't take more than a couple days, just to fully get your story down in writing. Take your advice on what to do next. And then you can get out of here before Anoïse even has her coronation feast. And nobody needs to ever contact you again. Without permission."

That certainly gave me pause. "I—I need a minute." I had to think. There was no assurance that he had not just invented this on the spot just to get me inside Mercy House's walls. "Why do you care so much about what happened with Ed?"

Desmon shrugged. "We don't know how accurate our reports on Edgar have been. We didn't know he was coming to see you. Truthfully. We hadn't a clue he was even traveling in your direction. So clearly we're not receiving the most reliable information. Your account could paint a clearer picture on how things stand with him, and if anything has...*escalated*." He chose that word very carefully. "We only need to talk to you for a few days. Get an account. Clear things up. That's a pretty good exchange when you get a fief in return, right?"

One would argue that was a little *too* good. But I wasn't sure if I wanted to let the chance slip. Especially when running away could mean Anoïse mistook my *apathy* for *sympathy with Edgar*. So. "Do you have it in writing?"

"You want it in writing?" Desmon stuffed his hands into his pockets. "Come with me and I'll get it for you."

I chewed on that. "Come back to me when you have it in writing."

"No, that's not how this works, Petre! There's a give and take to all of this. How can you ask me if I trust you if you won't trust *me* in turn? Isn't that why you were saying you left Edgar?"

"Desmon, I—you literally lied to me." It was by omission, but I was sure it counted.

"Yeah. I know. I'm sorry. But *you* were dishonest about Edgar at first, too. Dishonesty is what we do. You're not some passive put-upon agent, here. Spare me the misery tour you're trying to take me on and take some responsibility, Petre. We're trying to undermine Edgar before he sets off something catastrophic, and you think *now* is the time to be petty about it? Give me a break! Lord Alive, I don't know what more you want from me."

"I just—" I tried to cut in.

"Did Edgar give you this kind of back and forth we've got going on here? I'm telling you if you come back with us I can get Anoïse to draft a proposal to give you a fief where you can do whatever you want. Get high. Farm. Fuck goats. Whatever you want. Just come with me and I'll make it happen. And if I can't you can waltz right out of there."

I mean, what I *wanted* to do was get on a horse and ride away. Maybe knock some of his teeth in first. Steal his horse while I was at it. But mostly I just wanted to get out of there.

The only problem was he had a fucking point. And I couldn't stand that.

While I considered everything, Desmon added, "You walk away and the offer's off the table. You're not getting a deal this good again, you hear? You have your chance. Here. Now. Take it or leave it. What's it going to be?"

❦

Mercy House was couched behind a gigantic turtle shell. Three stories tall, and twice as many centuries old. It was filled with wires and old circuitry. As I neared it a hexagon-door spiraled open, and the horse hauled me through for the first time in five years.

As I came through, I spotted the old, abandoned guard tower where Anoïse and I used to hide when we wanted to talk, assured that we would not be observed—until the night we stayed too long, and they had to send a search party to find us.

There was the abandoned church that looked more like a god's cracked rib cage, which Edgar and I used to explore. Until Edgar found ancient explosives squirreled away inside its walls.

Desmon was often fond of the stone garden. Brickwork made beneath irradiated soil. Gemstone spirals branching up from out of the dirt, granite flowers the size of night-stand tables, and a fire pit in the center of it all.

The cyborg horse's hoofs knocked across the door bridge—a wooden tongue protruding from a skeletal mouth. Mercy House was built around the frame of a massive mastodon. I rode into its jaws, flanked by massive tusks on either side.

The fortress's foundations were made of bone and cinder bricks. Spires of steel and fossils and concrete, all gift-wrapped in razor wire. The mastodon's bones used to sometimes shed dust like dead skin. It came down in a gray rain on days when the wind was fast and heavy, and when the real rain came that dust thickened to finger paint.

I wasn't sure if I had made the right decision.

I'VE HEARD it said that sometimes you find your home in other people.

And if that's true, mine must've been that person with the annoying voice that grates on your patience for no identifiable reason. Like, there's nothing *wrong* with them—it's just that there's something so goddamn frustrating about them that you can't stand, so you're just looking around asking yourself "doesn't anybody else *hear* this?" But no one else is saying anything so you just have to swallow your ire and pretend there's not that *something* about them that just makes your eye twitch.

I'd forgotten what this place smelled like when you weren't nose blind to it. The whole fortress wore a stale cologne of smoke and iron.

My old chamber was mostly untouched. The bed was made. I'd left it in disarray five years ago. The place was quiet and dark and cold. The desk in the corner had gathered dust.

That first night back in my chamber was filled with reminders of why I had left. There was a crack in the foot of the door from where Dad had once kicked it too hard. I had run away during an argument and locked myself in my room to catch my breath and calm down. He had followed me. When I wouldn't unbolt the door, he kicked it so hard, so many times, that the damn wood splintered. Slats of light still bled through it every morning.

There was a hole in the plaster on the far wall where my fist had gone through one time. In my defense I had been very angry. How was I supposed to know whatever I was angry about wouldn't be worth remembering all these years later?

There were bloodstains I'd never bothered to wash out of the rug, from the time Edgar brought two knives to my room one night and ordered me to defend myself. I think that was the time he was mad about the incest allegations in the tabloids.

He'd sliced the side of my throat when he tried to pin me down on that rug. I think he'd been trying to grab me, forgot which hand held the knife? Maybe? I don't know *how* he planned for that to go.

The fight was a blur, but I remember the wound bled more than any wound had a right to bleed. Too much, I thought, but Mom had patched me up and told me I was lucky Edgar missed the vein and didn't cut too deep. She said she'd have to add some coding on how to deal with knives to my injections.

Fuck. I was beginning to remember why I hated this place so much.

In my desk I found the letters Anoïse and I had sent back and forth as kids. We'd leave them for each other when we were mad and wanted to get our feelings out without an actual conversation. I was glad I couldn't read my own illegible EKG lines that passed for cursive when I found them.

From what little I could decode, I realized the things I would get angry with her about were often petty trivialities. Had I always been such a disastrous little gremlin at that age? Fuck. It was beginning to make sense why Mom had tried to sew my mouth shut. It was like I'd been *looking* for things to be mad at. At least I couldn't read the whole thing.

The fact that my letters to her were grouped in with her letters to me, though—I didn't think we'd left all of them in one place. Anoïse would've had to bring them here and leave them for me in case I came back. I wondered if this was a recent addition. Was she trying to send a message to me? Something hidden between these lines of old text? Or had she put them here shortly after I had gone?

It was a shame she couldn't be bothered to waste her ink on an explanation.

It dawned on me I was perhaps overthinking it. I stuffed it back inside the drawer I had retrieved it from and went to sleep in my old bed for the first time in five years

CHAPTER

THIRTEEN

W hen I woke up on that first day back, too sore to move, I realized this might not be as simple as I'd anticipated.

It wasn't that I was completely immobilized. It was more that the pain of moving awakened all the aches and injuries I'd sustained over the last four days. It rocked my mind back through the memory of what I had endured.

All I could do during that first day was relive the last few that had brought me here. Obsessively scrubbing through every detail until my mind was raw, then I kept going.

The world around me hurt the way it does when you poke an injury. But that was all I could do. Prod away.

I don't think I moved much that first day at all. I woke to food some servants had left me, but otherwise I barely climbed out from under the security of my covers. And even that was an awkward safety—a reminder of the years it had been since I was home. And that now I *was* home.

But I didn't have to be for long. If I could just convince my body to work with me.

It took until my second day to figure out how to finally peel myself off the bed. To leave my chamber.

I wandered the old familiar hallways I'd left behind. I knew the pathways better than I thought I would. I'm not sure why, but once I came back, the often-overlooked nuances of this place developed a new vibrancy.

The whole fortress was a hive of activity, getting ready for Anoïse's coronation feast. It was only a few days from now, and the courtyard was a panorama of wagons and noise and color and people ferrying crates and wagons to their rightful places. There were supply lines going in and out of the fortress. Synthetic security pugs, each with one misshapen camera lens for an eye, ranged between legs, giving off the same eerie discomfort the horses did.

Folks with banners were arrayed in islands of social activity. Color-coded into clusters of family loyalties by their liveries and raiments. A couple of our vassals lingered in the far corners of the courtyard. Orianna Reacher had sent a few of her own vassals to serve as her ambassadors, by the look of things.

I had no time to participate in the swarm of people preparing things. I just needed an excuse to move. To think.

I kept checking Desmon's chamber. His room was the center of the gravitational pull that shaped my orbit through the fortress. I couldn't stray far, just in case he came back, but as I kept checking in at his room to find him not there—it provoked a few suspicions in me, after some time. It wasn't just that I kept *missing* him. It was that he was never there in the first place.

I was going to slit my fucking throat if I had to keep waiting for Desmon. It was insane to keep trying his chamber again and again.

Had he been assigned a new room after Dad died? Was

he part of the new administration and needed to be closer to Anoïse's room? I wasn't sure.

Hell, where was Anoïse's room anyway? The chamber she'd had when we were kids was locked. Though that was no surprise. It was hardly fit for a queen.

But Desmon had said they needed me here to avert a *war,* so clearly he and Anoïse had needed me here for something, right? Where were they?

I wondered if I was just being impatient. Averting a war had to be a time-consuming business, didn't it?

I passed time in the training rooms, a floor above the basement. I'm not sure why. Maybe it was just because this was where we kept training swords and singlesticks. They hung on wall racks across from rows of pells for when you had to run drills. Adjacent to the weight rooms with kettle-bells and barbells and stationary bikes.

Exercise would clear my head. It would make sure I could think.

It was while I was running through a set with dumb-bells that I realized it would be a little under two months before I needed my injections again. And I wondered what would happen if I was still *here* when I needed them.

I would have to see Mom, wouldn't I?

I tried to put that out of my mind. Desmon assured me I would only be here a few days.

It wasn't that I didn't think I could handle seeing Mom. That wasn't the difficult part. I could've seen her at any point since coming back. I knew where she was—she wasn't allowed to leave the basement, after all. I *knew* she was one floor below me. All I had to do was talk to her.

She could probably get me an audience with Anoïse without issue. I could tell Anoïse about how I'd cut Edgar's arm off, and how I'd left him to rot in the woods—how long ago? Had it only been a few days since then?

That couldn't be right. Could it? Fuck. I'd spent a whole day combing over those details, and now I couldn't even remember how long ago it was.

This was why I needed to recount it to Anoïse. To get it off my chest—and get a fief, while I was at it. I could resolve all this any time I wanted. All it would take was an afternoon with Mom.

The only problem was that—well—This was *Mom*. This was the woman who had threatened to sew my mouth shut. If there was even a sliver of a chance you could resolve a problem without her help, you'd take it, too. Trust me.

I was performing dumbbell presses, thinking all this through, when one of The Mercy Guard walked in on me.

I set the weights down and realized it was the same man from the bathrooms two nights ago. "Jerim, right?" I asked. He was still in armor. "I like the new—" I didn't have the breath to finish my sentence. I'd just noticed his helmet wasn't dented anymore. I touched two fingers to my temple and hoped that that would illustrate my point.

He peeled the helmet off, revealing a tangled mop of sweaty black hair. "Right," he said. "Jerim." He looked at his helmet like he was confused. Then shook his head and looked at me. "You need a spotter?" He indicated with his head to the dumbbells.

"Just finishing up, actually." I got to my feet. and hauled them across the gym to a rack of weights. "Why do you ask? Do *you* need a spotter?"

Jerim was busy unbuckling his breastplate. He tented his armor in the corner of the room. "Teya will be here soon," he answered.

Just who the hell was Teya? I didn't remember anyone

with that name here. Was it short for something? "Another Mercy Guard?" I asked.

He nodded once. "Something like that."

Irritation provoked a fit of deranged laughter. I strangled it quickly. "You being cryptic like that on purpose, man? I'm just trying to make small talk. Tell me about your friend."

He moved to load up a barbell. "I don't have to tell you anything, Your Grace."

Your Grace. That had to be my least favorite nickname. Too formal. It reminded me I was a Prince. There was no way Jerim could have known how much I hated that, but somehow it still felt like spite. This guy seemed cagey, and I wasn't sure why. "Suit yourself." I chewed on my lower lip. "Have you seen Desmon, by the way?"

"Not since we got home the other night," Jerim said

I tried to decipher his tone. Was he being short with me? I wasn't certain. But it reminded me of Edgar. And suddenly my mind was full of images of his arm coming off, freed from the wreckage of our downed horses.

I couldn't even get away from those thoughts when I was keeping myself busy. I felt like I had to follow two conversations at the same time, or keep track of different visuals on two screens. There was the world immediately before me, with the smell of sour sweat and the clank of black weights. Then there was the world in my mind's eye, haunting me with images of Edgar and cyborg horses, the Forest Wall, and all I'd endured since then at The Dripping Bucket.

Jerim's hand closed on my shoulder. The cold of his palm bit through the layers I was wearing. "Your Grace? Are you okay?"

I forced myself to get up slowly. I didn't want to startle

him with my own startling. "I-I should go. You and—and—Teya, was it? You have your fun down here. I have to leave."

He let me go, which surprised me. "If you insist." He shrugged and wandered back to his weights. I had been worried he might stop me, like somehow he'd know the kind of thoughts I had buzzing like fruit flies around my head.

Briefly, I considered heading to the basement. Mom almost certainly knew what Anoïse and Desmon were dealing with. And I was mostly sure I could get her to tell me.

But like I said—this was Mom. If it took me longer to figure this out another way, it would almost certainly be worth it.

So I decided to try the administrative offices.

They were deep in the mastodon's heart of Mercy House. A few floors up, a few hallways down, zigzagging through stone and skeletal architecture wrapped in a skin of steel and concrete.

I tried to arrange a meeting, but no one had time for me. There were documents to examine, meetings to be held.

The rest of my second day was spent held up in waiting rooms that reeked of freshly printed paper. I wanted to contribute to the effort to avert war. The sooner I did my part, the sooner I could get the fuck out of here.

I had promised Avram I wouldn't be long. I had said that I'd come back soon. I just wanted to get this wrapped up. I had to speak to my sister and tell her about Edgar.

She'd get it in a way nobody else would.

But I couldn't even find out what her schedule was, much less *when* she was prepared to speak with me. Nobody, it seemed, was prepared to speak to me. Nobody even seemed to recognize me. Like, oh sure, there were a few familiar faces in those offices. But if they registered the fact that I'd been gone for five years, they didn't express it. Everyone in there seemed to regard me as the same nuisance I had been before I left, with little regard for the fact that I was only here again because I had been summoned by my own sister. My presence was clearly necessary, but they had no time for it.

Every administrator met my requests for help with rolled eyes and shuffled papers. By the time I realized they were trying to stall me out until the offices closed, I resigned myself to spending the rest of the day making circuits of the halls. Weaving through the preparation for the coronation feast. Maybe I would check Desmon's chamber again.

But every time his door was locked and nobody would answer. No matter how many times I slammed my fist into the door and screamed.

They had eaten up my whole day. By the time I got back to my room, I was so exhausted, drained and empty from all the meaningless conversation and idle noise I'd been surrounded with.

Have you ever been subject to a slow buildup of frustration? Grievances mounting over the course of days? But sometimes you don't have an outlet for it, do you? So it just kind of *sits* there. Seething. Dead weight burning in the back of your mind.

Sometimes it lingers there while you're doing other stuff, almost like holding two thoughts in your head at the same time. You have to keep shaking it loose, but it gets its hooks back in you quickly, while you're thinking about something else, rerouting your thoughts back to it.

What's the longest you've ever been stuck in that head-space? A day? Two days? A week?

Eventually you do something stupid, right? You always do.

~

I was up by early morning on the third day, trying to unjam the door to Anoïse's old chamber before the rest of the fortress woke up.

Sure, there was no way she was actually inside, but there was always the possibility that whatever or whoever *was* in there might give me some idea where I could find her, right?

Alright, look. I'd run out of options, nobody would speak to me, and I just wanted to try something. Anything. I know it doesn't make much sense in retrospect, but I was desperate. Sue me.

I tried to focus in those early morning hours. But my mind kept wandering off on me, trying to remember where I had first learned to pick a lock.

I was *pretty* sure it was something Mom had taught me? She generally enjoyed anything that could make life harder for Dad.

I think she'd caught me trying to break into one of her labs. I'd needed another hit of Muse after an especially trying day. I was out and Mom had been in a bad mood, so I hadn't wanted to try asking for more. I had figured it would be easier to just break in.

But she'd caught me. Slapped me a few times. I thought she was furious about the break in. But suddenly she went all *you're doing it wrong.*

She started walking me through it. Wouldn't let me leave, not even for food, until I'd opened the lock a few times. That was all I was allowed to do for the day.

Never even got the damn Muse for my trouble.

I think I wound up teaching it to Anoïse in exchange for her allowance money for the week.

Fuck. I was supposed to be focusing on the lock in front of me.

I wished I'd been more honest about it with Desmon when I'd had a chance. Bottling it up felt like a physical force building pressure under my skin. I needed to tell *someone* about this, just to tease the pressure out.

After all, I'd agreed to come back so that I could help. What would they have me do, sit on my hands and wait for someone to come fetch me? How many days was I supposed to wait around for that to happen?

I needed to find a way to give Anoïse my account of what had happened over the last few days, or I was going to go insane and—

"Oh, it's you."

The voice behind me startled me to my feet. My injections jerked me around. I swung the lock pick in a downward grip in my fist as I spun.

I felt a hand on my forearm before I'd even finished turning around, as my arm was yanked over my head. My surprise guest closed the distance between us, chest to chest.

It was the young man from The Dripping Bucket. And he was very close.

I could feel him against me every time he exhaled. I could smell his breath. Was that whisky? Hardly breakfast food. Did he have more on him? "The hell are you doing here?" I asked.

"You were bent over. I wanted an eyeful."

"Only an eyeful?" I frowned. Wrenched my arm free, shoved him back.

He staggered, cackling. "Something wrong with that?"

"Not at all. Just disappointing, really. One eyeful? Is that all?"

A servant came down the hallway then. I checked my nails, and the man found an interesting bit of thread to toy with on his coat, while the servant glared at us out of the side of her eye.

As soon as she was gone, he stepped forward.

"Do you even know what chamber you're breaking into, kid? This is quite a way to prepare for tomorrow's feast."

Kid? He was calling me kid? I could all but guarantee I had at least three years on him. Where the hell did this guy get off calling me kid? And how honestly was I supposed to answer his question? It didn't seem like he had figured out who I was.

Although the fact that the coronation feast was *tomorrow* gave me a jolt of surprise. I thought there were still a few days left. Where had all my time gone?

I realized I still hadn't answered. "A locked one?" I hedged.

He rolled his eyes. "Do you know who it *belonged* to?

Past tense. Interesting. At least that was confirmation that it was currently unoccupied. I wondered again where she was now. Maybe Dad's old chamber? That would be under lock and key, and there was no way anyone would even let me close enough to check.

It dawned on me that I hadn't answered him yet. I panicked, blurted out a hasty, "Um. Depends."

The man blinked at me. "How on earth does it depend?"

"It depends—" I really drawled the words out, tried to buy myself some time to find an answer. But nothing good made itself available to me. "On—uhh. Whether or not you'd like an honest answer."

The man raised an eyebrow and tucked his hands behind his back. "Would you prefer if I asked The Queen?"

Oh, so not only did he know that this used to be Anoïse's chamber, but he also had a way to contact her? He wasn't just some household staff, or an administrator.

So who *was* he? Which of the Three Great Houses did he belong to? And how far up the pecking order did he reside? Had he just arrived here for the feast, or did he live here regularly?

There were too many questions. And while I was pondering them, he took another big step into my space, backed me into the door. "I asked a question," he said.

I swallowed saliva. "And I'm thinking of an answer."

"There are only two."

He was so close. I could feel his stomach strain against his shirt. That slim movement almost brought us close enough to touch. I shut my eyes. "Do you really have access to The Queen?"

He leaned away from me. I could see the calculations behind his eyes.

"I, um." He coughed. "I know people."

"People who would like to know what we've been up to?" I blinked at him, all innocent eyelashes.

"Does that mean you haven't told anyone what happened the other day, then?"

"No one's come to talk to you about it so far, have they? Shall I change that?"

He backed up into the middle of the hallway. Gave me a sour smile. "I'm a little shocked you didn't tell Desmon, if I'm honest."

"How and why would I even broach that conversation?" I almost added, *he's my brother, that's disgusting,* and only just bit off the end of that sentence at the last second. I cleared my throat. "*Shall* I broach the conversation? I can if I want. Though I don't have to. If you do me a favor." He didn't need to know I had no way of contacting Desmon. There was no way he'd know that, without knowing who I was.

He dragged his eyes up and down me. Bit his lip. "I can do you a favor alright. The Queen doesn't need to know what you were doing in her old chamber. I can keep that to myself. Did you need something else?"

Without thinking, I reached out to straighten his lapels. "Tell her whatever you like." Maybe that would convince her to talk to me, so that I could get this fucking shit over with already. "You can be as honest as your heart desires." I punctuated this point with a slap that turned his head sideways. I watched him go red.

He had nothing on me. No name, no motive. At best he had a handful of hunches. Maybe he *suspected* who I was. But what was he going to tell Anoïse? It'd be dangerous to throw around accusations about a Prince without even having a shred of certainty that that was who he was dealing with.

"I'd *like* an audience with An—with The Queen, actually," I said. "If you can get me that you can be sure our secret will remain unlearned."

"The Queen is. Um." He cleared his throat. "She's busy. With everything. Feast's tomorrow, you know. Lots to prepare for."

"It's very important I speak with her," I tried not to sound too desperate. "What? You can use her as a threat but not to help me?" I had not cut off my own brother's arm just to sit idly by and *wait* to tell her who was on what side, and what had happened in Bullion.

"I'm not sure if she's accepting new appointments. Have you tried the administration offices?"

A stab of old annoyance twitched in my eyelids. "I've been," I said. "They couldn't do much for me."

He shrugged. Pushed his hand through his hair. "I dunno, man. Sometimes you really have to pester them."

"I don't suppose you can put a good word in for me?"

The young man tilted his head. "And how would I do that without your name?"

I pressed my lips together. "Well, there goes that plan, I suppose."

"You won't tell me your name?"

There were too many variables. I couldn't risk it. Fuck. I should have seen this coming. What was I thinking? Trying to get an audience with someone who didn't even know my name?

It was his turn to advance. "Listen." He put one palm flat on the door, pinned me against it. "I'm *willing* to help you. All I need is your name. Can't do you any favors if I don't know who I'm doing favors for."

I was sorely tempted. I needed someone in here on my side. Anyone. But I was also well acquainted with what this place did to people. How it reduced them down to the favors they could do for you.

He and I had a good time at The Dripping Bucket. Outside of court, when we didn't know we'd see each other again. It was easy to get along when we both assumed there would be no strings attached. But I would be an idiot to assume this man would be on my side when he learned who I was all because he'd drooled over my cock.

"I..." I couldn't find the right words. "Fuck, man. I..."

I wasn't sure I liked the way heartbreak teased out the wrinkles on his face. I knew that look. I'd seen it before, too many times. It stung to see. Especially when he eased away from where he'd pinned me.

"No, it's alright."

I ate up the empty space he'd left behind. "No, wait. Come on, I—"

"Stop." He shoved hard into my chest. "You clearly don't want to tell me anything. You think I don't know when a man's not into it?"

Ouch. That felt a step too far. "It's not that I'm—"

"Tell me your name."

"I—" I faltered. Fuck.

"SEE?"

"That's not what I—"

"I don't need excuses." He waved me away. "If you want help just ask for it. But don't try to talk to me out of both sides of your mouth like this and expect I'll have the time of day to entertain it. Have fun breaking into The Queen's old bedroom, alright? I'm out."

I wrapped my fingers around his forearm. Tried to haul him around.

But all at once the man was behind me, and I was trying to figure out where my hand had gone—until I felt it pressed against the small of my back.

Shit. This guy was fast. Hot damn. His fingers pressed into the bones of my wrist and dug into my opposite shoulder. His breath was warm in my ears, and I tried not to get hard.

"I have been used enough to know when people see me as a resource."

"Oh?" I snapped. "And what makes you think I don't know what that feels like, too?" I tried to shrug out of it, but he only tightened his grip. He twisted my hand and lifted my arm up my back. "Ow, fuck!"

He shook me. "Because if you knew how it felt even half as well as you *think* you do, the two of us wouldn't be here right now."

I was trying not to get turned on. That felt inappropriate at a time like this. Even I had limits. I wanted to spit out my name, to tell him who I was. But I—I couldn't, okay? I didn't even know this guy, so how could I just trust him on a whim? Not here. Not at court. That was fucking dangerous. That's the shit that gets you killed.

"Fine. You want me to do it myself so bad, I'll figure something out."

The man let me go. I thought that was going to be the end of it. But before I could walk away, he'd closed his fingers around my face. Alarm yelped through me as he shoved me against the wall. White pain reared in the back of my skull. "Man, what the fuck—"

His grip tightened. "Don't—put—it—on—*me*. Got that?"

My hand went for his wrist, and I wrenched his fingers off my face. "Fuck off," I grunted.

"Good." He stormed off with a swirl of his coat. "Oh," he called over his shoulder. "And for what it's worth, I wish you luck."

I wanted to yell. To scream. I was annoyed that I'd been tricked into coming back here. Into trusting Desmon. I didn't even have a way to determine the veracity of his promise to give me a fief.

What options were left to me? What could I do? I *had* to talk to one of my siblings.

They were the only ones who would get it.

I could feel the speed of my brain turning things up. There was probably a meltdown in my immediate future. It was like pressure building in me, pressing out.

Which meant I either needed to find a release valve to take some of the pressure off, or I was going to have to find a place to explode.

~

I ARRIVED at the administrative office as gouts of irritation made ugly patterns in the heat of my belly.

It wasn't fucking fair. I *had* to speak with someone. How long was I supposed to go just failing to mention that I'd cut Edgar's arm off? That he'd shot at me. I needed someone to hear it. Someone who *understood* what the violence in this family was like.

I couldn't just talk to anybody. They had to *get* it. And so few people truly got it, the way Desmon did. The way Anoïse did.

Like, there's this concept out there—and this always bugs me, man—everyone seems to think that love is this inherent force for good. Like it's this thing that sits in you pleasantly, and it feels warm and soft and beautiful and just peachy. That it's the kind of thing that arrives with string accompaniment and a chorus of lilting angels. And when you do something and it feels good, then that's love, right? And when you do something, or someone else does something—and—and it *doesn't* make you feel good, that's *not* love, right?

But I don't think that's true. I think love's a lot more neutral than all that. There are some languages that have dozens of words for love for exactly this reason.

Because that's the thing, isn't it? Love isn't some delicate flower blooming in a quiet grove. It's fucking *napalm*. It's an indiscriminate mess of chemicals that gets dropped on you from on high, and you don't *get* a say in the matter, because suddenly you're on fire, and everything's burning, and the whole world has tilted on its axis, and the flames have reduced everything to smoke and heat and nobody knows how to deal with it, to contain the blaze, to keep it all under control. Everything hurts and your throat is raw and you're choking and you're crying and you can't tell up from down anymore because all there is is incandescence everywhere you look.

That's love.

Anyway, all this to say—*yes,* Edgar and I fought. *Yes,* we beat the shit out of each other. *Yes,* I cut off his arm—and *yes,* I would bet my life he was prepared to find some way to get back at me, after all that.

But don't for a *minute* think we didn't love each other, alright?

Not for a second.

That's why I needed to talk to Desmon or Anoïse about this. I wasn't about to unpack all this only to hear another well intentioned, wrongheaded speech about what love is, or about what I should have done or should have felt.

Which isn't to say I showed up in the administrative offices that afternoon with any hope I'd be successful in finding an audience. But if I was going to blow up at some-one, that seemed like the best place. It was so boring there, I figured it could use some new gossip to spice things up.

The woman at the front desk was dark-haired, with red glasses. She sat wrapped in a short skirt and a doublet that were both slashed in rows that exposed the black lining underneath. She was making notes in a gigantic book. I was not sure how she could've possibly tuned out the noise coming from the hive of cubicles that seethed behind her. The constant drone of busywork and low-voiced chatter. The screech of radio-speech, and the heavy sound of occupied typewriters. The sound was so exhausting that for a moment I'd forgotten what I arrived for.

"Lord Mercy?" The woman at the front desk blinked at me. "Your Grace?"

I hadn't been called *Lord Mercy* in a long time either. Those words snatched me out from the hazy murk brought on by sensory overload. I drummed my fingers on the desk. Just so I had something to center myself. "Yes?" I cleared my throat. "I'm sorry, I was looking to make an appointment."

I already knew the answer would be no. Yet somehow I still held my breath for a few seconds while I waited for an answer.

"Lord Mercy, you were here just yesterday."

"I insist," I said through clenched teeth.

She rolled her eyes and opened a gigantic book, full of tabs and old brown ink. "Schedules haven't changed since the last time you came in. Who would you like me to look up for you?

I cycled through the list of names in my head. People I could talk to about Bullion, who might be able to uncover where Edgar was likely to be hiding. Maybe that would make the idea of an appointment with me more appealing to Anoïse. "Lord Havilan Reacher?" I asked. "Is he free?"

"He's out right now. But he should return sometime this evening. Maybe I can schedule a meeting for you and him sometime tomorrow?"

That was interesting. What did *out* mean? Where had he gone? I supposed talking to Havilan Reacher was better than talking to nobody. I might not be able to talk as in-depth or be as upfront, but it was better than nothing. So I said, "Sure, yeah."

She finished making notes, flipped to a tab in her big

book, and scrawled something else down. "Right. You can meet with Lord Havilan tomorrow. I've put that down for you. Is there anything else I can assist you with today, sir?"

I wasn't sure what to say. I wasn't opposed to a meeting with Lord Havilan. He was better than nothing, but even a meeting with him was less than useless if I couldn't relay anything to Anoïse or Desmon. I didn't *need* Lord Havilan. "I'm sorry. I still have to speak with one of my siblings."

The woman sighed. "Lord Mercy, what do you expect has changed in the day since you were last here?"

"I don't have time to wait for something to change," I groaned. "I need to—"

"I can take a note for you to give to one of your siblings next time I see them."

I tried to tamp down on the fury at the fact that she couldn't be bothered to muster up one shred of an emotion. It sounded like she was simply reciting lines. Well-practiced droning that only further irritated me.

She didn't even wait for an answer before she opened up a drawer. Placed a yellow legal pad beside her giant book. She looked at me expectantly, quill poised. "Whenever you're ready."

What I was ready to do was walk out. Or throw something. I was still trying to decide between the two. I could entertain good arguments for each.

I forced myself to take a breath. To settle down. That's what Avram would've wanted me to do, right?

I attempted counting backwards from ten to one. But I only made it to three before I said, "I need you to take me to my sister. *Now.*"

The woman remained infuriatingly placid. "I'm afraid that's not possible, Your Grace. As I've already stated the last time you were here, The Queen is very busy, and—"

I wanted to pound my fist on her desk. But my injections held me back and wrapped me in a skein of polite decorum. "Okay. What about Desmon?"

"Your brother is not involved in any proceedings."

Like *hell* he wasn't! But what the fuck could I say to that? I had no proof what he was or wasn't talking about. I had no clue what he'd told administrators to keep me from contacting him.

Have you ever reached a point of such unbelievable frustration that *better than nothing* remains wildly unsatisfying?

Like.

I needed to speak with someone *today*. Now. I knew what had happened in Bullion. I knew Edgar only had one arm. That he was probably still recovering. It had only been three days. With a little help I'd bet we could've narrowed down where he was hiding. We could end this all here if someone would just fucking *talk* to me.

And instead here I was failing to make an appointment with some lady who refused to register an emotion, as if we weren't teetering on the precipice of a war, and I was just supposed to sit on my ass and hold in all this useful information because everyone was busy with other meetings? Like what the fuck?

"Is there anything else I can assist you with today, sir?"

I cracked my knuckles. Just so my hands had something they could actually do. I could've sworn she'd said those exact words already. Was she reciting from a script? "I'd like to speak with someone *today* please." I tried to wrangle my voice into approximating calm. But it probably came out low and threatening.

"I'm sorry, but as I've already explained to you, sir, there are no openings today. If you'd like to come back tomorrow you can speak with Lord Reacher, so long as he has no new obligations when he gets here, but—"

Oh, there was even an asterisk on my appointment with Havilan, then? Great. Just fucking great. I wanted to cry. "I need to speak with somebody *today*. I was told to come back today to work something out."

"I'm not aware of anyone in these offices who has made such an assurance, Your Grace. But I apologize if one of our representatives misspoke to you."

My stomach shriveled into a ball of heat when I realized I might have to speak with Mom. If no one here would work with me, that was quickly narrowing to the only option on the table.

I shook my mind clear of those thoughts. That wasn't important right now. There was still a chance I could find a way to pull this off, right? "Look, is there *anything* I can do to speak with someone today? Anything at all?"

"If you'd like to take a radio, we have a frequency where we broadcast openings. It's on a first come first serve basis, though, since we're backed up. So you'd have to get back down here quickly if someone's schedule opens up. Although if you'd prefer to take a seat, that's also an option."

"I DON'T HAVE TIME TO WAIT!" I needed to make sure Desmon and Anoïse actually required my help. Plus, Desmon had still not gotten back to me about his promise about the fief.

Why had I taken it? Why hadn't I walked away? Why did I keep falling for the seductive line of reasoning that perhaps these people had *changed?*

I had an impulse. And I needed to follow it. My injections didn't want me to, as it did not fit into programming it had for an environment like this. So when I lurched forward, it tried to shove me back. Throw me into one of the seats beside the door.

My knees trembled, working against the heat inside me, I pitched the radio against a far wall, where it shattered with a crack that sounded like a gunshot.

The woman at the front desk jerked up, looked at me. "Your Grace!"

I wanted to crawl over the desk that stood between us. I felt like an animal. Unhinged inside my body. Like something in me was trying to crawl out of my own skin. "Someone in this place needs to take me to my sister *now!*" I shouted. Every word was louder than the last.

I was distantly aware someone had called security.

"Y-Your Grace, a-as I keep saying, that—that's not—"

"I have information that could stop this fucking war before it happens, but I can only do that if she talks to me *now!*" I spat. "Someone in here needs to fucking tell me where she is!"

"Sir." The woman was shaking. I really wanted to feel more guilty than I did. But I couldn't quite manage it. "I—um—if you take a seat someone will be able to assist you momentarily—"

"I'm not a fucking idiot!" I shouted. "I'm not just going to patiently wait for The Mercy Guard to ferry me away and make me someone else's problem. Take me to my fucking sister or find me someone competent enough to do that for me or I swear to God—"

A cold hand closed around my shoulder. Metal. Lobstered mail. It pinched me through my clothes. Had they called The Mercy Guard?

I turned around, tried to throw an elbow. But the one who they'd called in caught it. Shocks of pain spasmed up my forearm, as he grabbed hold and twisted my arm behind my back. "I don't suppose you're taking me to Havilan?" I asked. "I hear I have an appointment."

"Havilan's not here." A male voice said. Jerim's.

"You again?" I asked. "Are you the only guard they keep around here or what?" I wondered why it always had to be this guy, because that was easier than debating how much dignity I had lost in there, and how much I was about to lose being marched through the hall with my arm twisted behind my back.

I turned back to the front desk workers. "You have to listen to me," I yelled. "I have to speak with my sister." White pain flared in my shoulder as Jerim dragged me back. *"I have to talk to her, goddammit! Listen to me!"*

Jerim wrenched me through the threshold before they could say anything.

HE DROPPED me off in my chamber, and slammed the door shut. I paused for a minute, and I took a few deep breaths.

Why was I always running into this guard, Jerim? This felt like too much of a coincidence.

I opened my chamber door. Slowly. Slowly. I saw the back of his breastplate vanishing down the hall.

Who was this guy, anyway? I wanted to know more. And I was betting I could sneak after him quietly enough that he wouldn't notice if I followed.

I only paused for a minute to put on my chameleon coat.

I wasn't completely sure why I was doing it, to be honest. I think part of it was because there was nothing else to do, and I wasn't just going to sit here and wait for someone to come to me. I had to get out there and make sure something happened.

But I think the other part, the more insidious line of reasoning, the one that sneaks up on you, that you're scared to even justify to yourself—is that I was well acquainted with feelings of uselessness. Most of my life involved feeling incompetent. So to know the second someone said they needed me for something, they just dropped off the face of the earth? Even for a few days?

It makes you question things, you know? You wonder if any of what you heard was true to begin with.

So I had to follow him. I had to grab a caterwauler and see where he was going. Because maybe if I could do this— even if it was stupid—maybe I could do *something* right. Even if there was a strong possibility that none of it led anywhere. And if it *did* lead somewhere, it would probably take me right into a whole lot of trouble.

You're told you're needed. You're told you're useful. And when you hear that you don't want to go back to having nothing. Not being good at anything.

It's just. I don't know—sometimes when you've had nothing for long enough, you'll take a fistful of thorns just so you can remember what it feels like to have your hands full.

FOURTEEN

O ver the next—I want to say twenty minutes—I became well-acquainted with the back of The Mercy Guard's breastplates.

I followed Jerim from the other end of hallways. Past windows reinforced with shimmershields that sang a chorus when the wind pressed against them. I barely dared to breathe as I tailed him.

If anything, it felt like things were going too easy. There remained a steady stream of travelers headed into town or retiring to their chambers after working that day.

All I had to do was keep a decent pace behind him and look like I had a destination in mind.

This became more difficult when he took a secluded stairway in one of the back halls, in the less traveled corridors.

I watched him enter it from my vantage point on the other side of the hallway. Debated heading after him. I tried to remember where the stairwell led.

I hurtled to the door. I didn't have time to debate it. I had to catch it before it closed. I put some oomph into the balls of my feet, and slipped through sideways just as it swung shut.

I hustled down the steps. They took me all the way to the basement. The entrance reeked of mildew, so it couldn't be close to the basement corridors that held Mom.

This space was a grimy, long abandoned corridor. A neglected area in Mercy House. Closed off for reasons I'd never asked about. I felt like a skulking storybook monster as I followed Jerim down the dark intestine-tunnels.

At one point I was home to the horrifying realization that only the dim yellow of his torchlight ahead lit my way. The silhouette of his back was all I had to go on.

I had to step carefully. The last thing I needed was for him to turn that flashlight around. Bathe me in a pale glow while he remained a vague shadow. That wasn't a fight I was confident I could win.

Jerim turned a corner, and I watched as he reached an end to the dark maze. The eye of his flashlight roamed over abandoned workshop tools, swallowed up in an exoskeleton of gathered rust on corpse technology that had been left long ago to decompose.

"Jerim," a female voice sprang from the dark. "You're late."

"Got held up," Jerim said. "I was just about to clock out when the secretaries called me in to deal with the new prince."

New prince? What did that mean? I was born in Mercy House. I mean—sure, I'd arrived *back* here fairly recently. But that didn't mean an awful lot, did it?

"What about the others? Are they late too, Teya? Or is it just the two of us again?"

"Do you have to ask?" I could almost hear this new woman, Teya, rolling her eyes.

"Hm," Jerim murmured. "I figured." He crept into the dismally dark space. I spotted the flashlight moving and held back. I tucked myself behind a corner, and listened

"So," Jerim said. "Where's—"

I heard a door on the other side of the room. It opened once, and swung shut. Like someone was having trouble coming through. It opened again. Then it happened a third time. I wondered if there was something in the way, barring entrance. But it sprang open wide enough on the fourth try that I heard the doorknob smash the concrete wall behind it.

There were footsteps. Grunting. Someone's voice. A new arrival. "Lord *Alive*." He sounded pained. It was a man's voice—a gravelly bass I was familiar with.

"Lord Reacher!" Teya said. More footsteps. "Are you hurt?"

"Only a little," Havilan said,

I wondered where he had been. And how he got hurt. Was it related to everything with Edgar? I wasn't sure.

"Do you have the helmet?" Jerim asked.

Holy shit. Was Mercedes actually *right* about the rumor regarding why Ed had gone to Bullion?

"Jerim!" Teya barked.

"We don't have time to waste on formalities!"

I felt dizzy. How much was there that I didn't know? And why the fuck was everyone obsessed with helmets, lately?

"It's fine, Teya." Havilan's voice sounded strained. "He has a right to know."

"Where is it?" Jerim barked.

Havilan let his breath out slowly. Audibly. "I...failed to procure it."

"You *what?*" Jerim sounded incensed.

"Mercedes Blackheath stopped all shipments in or out of Bullion days ago. My agents tell me there was a scuffle there. Can't get reliable information on what the details are, though. The whole place is on lockdown, I'm afraid."

I felt my guts shift. My stomach tied itself in jagged knots. I had been the cause of that scuffle. I was the reason Havilan Reacher was in—was in—*whatever* kind of trouble he was in now.

"I don't know the details. But I managed to acquire the layout of the place. I know where they're holding it. If you give me a few days, I can probably—"

"Lord Reacher," Teya said, "Forgive my friend, but we need it soon, and we are running out of options" There was an edge of a threat that I detected in her voice.

"I'm well aware of that, Teya," Havilan said. "I will do my utmost—"

"There is no *utmost*," Jerim said. "We need it now."

"I don't have the damn thing now!" Havilan said. "I can't give you what I don't have!"

I heard a noise in the dark. It could have been anything. From a footstep to a knife escaping its sheath. An awful, seething uncertainty squirreled itself inside the contours of my thought and made a home there.

It had *almost* sounded dangerous—or it could have been a boot scraping the stone floor. Or the brush of some-one's clothes. Anything, really. In that brief instant, that fluttering moment of fear I nearly cried out, and caught myself in time to reduce it to a guttural squawk.

"What was that?" It was Havilan's voice.

Fuck.

I'd fucked up.

I'd almost interceded when nothing was actually wrong in the first place. Fuck. *Fuck.* This had been my chance to figure out whose side Havilan was on, and here I was unable to actually keep my damn mouth shut. To get some information and get out.

"I'll check it out." It was Jerim's voice.

What the hell was wrong with me?

I heard metallic footsteps coming closer. Sabatons gaining ground on the cement floor. The flashlight beam was coming closer as I pinned myself flat to the wall.

The second I saw the tip of the flashlight, I grabbed it. Switched the light off, and jerked Jerim into my adjacent tunnel.

Jerim let out a surprise yelp. I didn't have much time. Had to get out of there. I pried the flashlight from his fingers, cracked the handle over his helmet. It made a clang so loud I swear *my* teeth vibrated.

"Jerim!" Havilan Reacher called through the dark.

I should've expected he wouldn't go down. If he could shrug off going face first through a urinal, a flashlight to the head would be a goddamn gnat to him.

But I only put those pieces together when Jerim's gauntleted fist smashed into my mouth. I went down to one knee. Sprang back up.

I couldn't stay here. Not if Jerim had backup. Who probably had flashlights. I'd get caught.

So I kicked him, heard the clatter of armor as he was dumped on his ass. That gave me the space I needed to turn on my heel.

I switched the flashlight on and started running, feet clapping the ground like enthusiastic applause.

The grimy tunnels slid past me as I moved through them. I took every turn that made itself available to me. The world was wrapped in shadow and pale light. I wasn't sure if I was going in the right direction. The only thought in my head was that there was noise behind me, and I had to get away.

I took every turn that made the noise of my pursuers more distant as I sucked down exhausted breaths that tasted like mildew.

By the time the noise of Havilan and Jerim and Teya had vanished altogether, I realized I had no goddamn clue where I was.

AS THE HOURS PROGRESSED, the white of the flashlight became my only companion. The air smelled like what you get when white dust and cobwebs have generations to pile into every crevice. I was boxed in on all sides by slabs of granite.

"Alright. Alright. Alright. *Think.* All you have to do is retrace your steps."

I tried not to think about how each labyrinth turn looked just like the last one. How every sweep of the flashlight prompted shuffling in the small places I couldn't see.

Anxiety took up residence in the corners of my eyes. I tried not to think about the way I flinched at everything.

I'm not sure how long it was before I decided I was lost. Before I bridged the gap between not *currently* having any clue where I was and realizing I wouldn't *be able to* reacquaint myself with more familiar surroundings. I'd been thinking some iteration on *surely I should've found the right turn by now. It's just ahead, maybe* for quite some time before *a turn or two ahead* became *never.*

At times I wondered if I went in circles. The semidarkness was a fertile playground for my worst paranoias. The dusty air tasted like gray film on my tongue every time I gulped down worried breaths. Each basement hallway looked the same, save a few that housed uneven triangles of glass scattered in the shape of fractured teeth. Or dark stains on the stone floor that could have been rat urine or a man's blood. Either option was a possibility that I did not wish to entertain.

But as I cycled through the same few passageways I began to memorize the patterns smeared across the stone floor.

What if I never got out of here? What if I was trapped down here forever? My death would be wrapped in unexplained darkness and dust and layers of sediment a mile thick. What if no one ever found me? Would they even bother to look?

I'd promised Avram I'd be back soon. If I was going to die at court I'd want a knife between my ribs. Eyes to stare into when I saw a blade slam home. A face to look into, and a moment to realize what was happening so I could use my attacker's eye as a receptacle for saliva, right before I died. In an ideal world that was the kind of death that God would grant me.

But I was not a stubborn man. I could bargain. I'd accept a different kind of death. Poison, maybe. Shitting my brains out till dehydration did me in. There were worse ways to go, right? There had to be. And at least if that was how I went out I could give future generations a bit of a chuckle if nothing else.

But this? Lost down here to abandoned tunnels, the same few right turns, and the anxious dry-marker-on-a-whiteboard squeal of rats? It felt undignified to make these forgotten tunnels into my crypt.

Time down here was an unknown sluggish thing. Crawling at a slow and inexorable molasses drip. I was tired. I'd walked long enough that my feet were sore, at least. And I wasn't sure how much I had left in me. Had it been hours? It had to have been. At least one. Definitely. Probably a few. But maybe more than that.

When the flashlight flickered my heart started to pick up the tempo. I reached out, made sure the bulb was secure. It was a little loose. That could've been it.

It was probably nothing. But the fears that had up to this point been vague paranoia began to crystallize when a potential road map to my doom reared its head. There was *no* way I could find my way out by touch alone.

I hurried along. I'd been down these passageways before, sometime earlier. I was spiraling. Literally. I paid no attention to the echoes my boots made on dust and stone. Or the crunch as they trampled through broken glass. I just had to find a way out. That was all that mattered. It was the only thing that—

Hold up.

Broken glass.

I stopped. Spun on my heel. Trained the flashlight on the shattered shards. "Now how did *that* get there?" I crouched. Examined the splinters. They weren't dusty. They didn't even look that old. It didn't seem like someone had dropped anything down here recently.

I mean, who would? Y'know?

I performed the geometric calculations in my head. Tried to extrapolate from the way the glass had fallen, where it had come from. Was there a hidden window in the wall somewhere? A one-way mirror?

I tucked the flashlight under my armpit. Switched it off. This seemed like the kind of thing I could do by touch anyway. If I could ignore the sound of rats and scuffling. Agitation filled me with dry itchy heat as I ran my hands over the walls. I followed the leylines laid out in the mortar between bricks. I pressed into the grainy spaces, looking for a sign of where it had come from.

I was about to give up when something shifted. One of the bricks slid sideways. I wasn't sure how. I couldn't tell in darkness. Was the one beside it hollow? It slid sideways perfectly into the receiving brick. And it was only after I finished that I realized the thumb I'd injured on Dad's knife a few days ago was engulfed in new red pain and wetness and heat.

I recoiled. Dropped the flashlight into my free hand and put my thumb to my mouth, to suck the blood off, accidentally pried a glass splinter free of where it was lodged in Desmon's bandage. I spit it out and shook my hand. Goddamn. This was the second time in the last few days I'd hurt that thumb. I retrieved the flashlight and switched it on with my free hand.

I was right. The brick had slid sideways into another, beside it, that had been hollowed out. You could only tell by viewing it from side-on.

In the empty space was a small rectangle of shattered glass, arrayed like sharpened teeth. That must have been what I had cut my thumb on.

Was it some kind of window? With—was that a latch? On the other side?

I spent more time than I would've liked to admit debating which hand I should use to reach through.

I settled on the right hand—the one whose thumb I'd sliced open. If it was already injured there'd be no big loss there.

Getting my hand through was easy enough. Maneuvering the latch was the tricky part. It was already poised up, like a reared horse. I couldn't pull it up any more than it was without prying it off, and it did not seem to move from side to side.

It took some time to figure out how to move the latch without skewering my wrist on the sharpened teeth of broken glass. It involved a lot of pressing with my injured thumb. Awkward angles. Inching it down.

I pressed it down as far as it would go. Held my breath and waited.

Nothing happened.

"You're shitting me," I groaned. "Is this some kind of joke?"

I thumbed the lever down again, really squeezed down until the blood was sluicing out from under my thumb, down either side of the cold brass lever. The wound was warm with pain.

Then I heard something click. And the whole wall lurched sideways. I only just extracted my hand quick enough that I didn't lose it entirely. Though a moment later I realized I'd sliced my palm, too. A bloody gash going sideways through the heel of my hand.

But I was not worried about the stinging blood and pain. It barely registered, when faced with the new environment around me.

Sometimes, when overwhelmed, pain becomes all you can focus on. But I think the reverse is also true. In a new environment, certain kinds of pain become a sort of background noise—an accent to the scenery. That was what happened here.

I was so surprised when the wall actually slid away that the pain of my bloody hand became a minute sting. I wiped it clean on my trousers, as I marveled at the hidden room that had unveiled itself.

I had to cross a rotten wooden ramp to get down into it.

The whole place, as far as the flashlight could make clear to me, was tied up in ribbons of spiderweb and dripping wires. Both hung from black grate banisters, on a walkway high above me. They were hazy shapes in the near-dark, and I couldn't see a way up. Though half the room was boarded up with rotten wood that reeked of mold and mildew.

I trained my flashlight on some kind of power generator in the center of the room. Or what had once been one. It was an ancient iron beehive with liver spots of black rust.

I'd seen this kind of power generator before. Every fortress worth its salt had at least one. Though this one looked like some sort of simplistic prototype. And there was supposed to be a gigantic, ribbed canister in the center. An energy source. I wasn't quite sure how it worked. But at some point it had been deseeded.

Idly, I smeared more blood off on my trousers. Then I moved to get a better look. Shined my flashlight through a gap in the black rust on the hive and peered through.

Oh. It wasn't that the power source had been removed. It had been *replaced*. Whatever the original generator looked like, it must have been massive. Three times the size of a man, judging by the steel crater it had left behind. Steel inner rings made race tracks in the empty bowl meant for the generator.

The replacement barely looked big enough to fit even the smallest, innermost ring. It looked like some kind of ruby. A big red dome, like a bloody blister. It glittered in the glow of my flashlight.

When had this been replaced? It was clearly not in use right now. But how long ago had this thing been abandoned? Had the generator been swapped out because the ruby was a better power source, or had its owners simply needed less power? How much power did a ruby even have?

I traced the circumference of the machine, until I found a wire that was thick as a horsetail braid. I followed it across the stone floor and traced its path to a pill-shaped tank of dirty glass, with patterns on it that looked like dried...was that water? No. There was a greenish tint to it. The color of diseased mucus. It had been shattered, or withered naturally, over time. And the metal space around the broken glass was scabbed in—well—what I *hoped* was rust, at least.

I wondered if I ought to keep looking around. How much time did the batteries in this flashlight have? The only way out I could see was atop the banister, from a little door in the corner. Was there a way to get up there? I couldn't see one.

Before I could strategize, I heard hinges release a murdered wail as someone pushed a door open, and a rectangle of light bled into the room. My heartbeat made itself known in my injured hand.

I couldn't see who had entered. They were a silhouette in the light, casting a person-shaped shadow over the scientific wreck. I trained my caterwauler on the target. "Who's there?"

The figure standing in the doorway scoffed at me. "What in *hell* do you think you're doing? Put that thing away before you hurt yourself."

Oh.

Shit.

Mom.

CHAPTER

FIFTEEN

I put the gun away without hesitation and shined the flashlight, just to make sure it was her. "Mom?"

She had on a white button down and gray trousers, and she wore a labcoat two sizes too big. Most lab coats were, on her. She was barely five foot two. I think she preferred having the room to getting it resized.

But if she was wearing it that meant that she'd been working. And it was awfully late at night for work. Or at least I assumed it was. Was there something she'd been doing that had to be done away from other labcoats? Hidden from prying eyes? I wondered what wing of Mercy House she and I were in.

Mom put up a hand to shield herself from my flashlight. "Turn that thing off, dammit!" She dragged her hand through curls of mouse-brown hair. "And who else were you expecting?"

I winced and hurried to the observation balcony. Tried to do a circuit of the space below. "I wasn't expecting anybody, frankly. What are you doing up?"

I didn't need to put the flashlight on her to feel her frowning. "Working."

"At this hour?" I realized I was not aware what hour it was.

"If you'd prefer, I can go to sleep, dear. I can always come back for you in the morning."

Frustration and panic conspired in my mind. "Wait—stop—I just—" I put the flashlight on her in time to watch her hands strangle the rail.

"Stop?" She raised an eyebrow. "I haven't done anything dear. I'm not sure what I should stop."

I had to ignore that. I *had* to. If I said anything she'd suck me down into one of those nitpicky arguments over the definitions of words. We'd be shouting at each other, and I wouldn't be out of here for another few hours. And that was if she didn't decide to abandon me down here to teach me a lesson.

I couldn't take her bait. She was obviously frustrated at my intrusion into her basement. "Is that door up there the only way out of here? I don't see a ladder."

She frowned down at me, looking as if she were testing a theory on how long she could stretch a single silence.

I set my teeth and stared back. I always blinked first. I wasn't going to blink first. I was not the same man who'd left five years ago.

She was waiting for me to ask for clarification. She wanted me to double check if she'd heard. But I knew she had. I was not about to give her the satisfaction of my uncertainty.

"I'm thinking," she said.

"About?"

Mom rolled her eyes. "Five years, and already you've

been so disrespectful. I'm not sure if I can remember where the ladder is."

"What? Mom, I didn't even *do* anything!" Outrage provoked the response before I could bite it back.

"Don't pretend you don't understand."

"What the fuck are you—?"

"Language." She sounded bored. Like she was reciting lines. She loosened her grip on the banister. "Do you want out of here or not?"

"Of course I—"

"Then start acting like it."

I winced and balled up my fists. I wasn't even entirely sure what I had done. I was beginning to remember why I dreaded this so much. But I dreaded being trapped down here even more.

"I...I'm sorry for the disrespect, Mom. Now will you help me get up there so that I can get out?"

"Is that how we ask politely, my dear?"

"Please," I said, immediately. I just wanted to get it over with, to get the words out. To get out. I had to get out. "Mom, please. I just want to get up there. It's dark down here, and I don't know how long it's been. I don't know if there's another way out." I knew this was not the best thing to admit to her, given my situation. Bluffing could have helped me down the line. But I was tired and exhausted, and I had no patience or energy for any game of strategy.

Mom rolled her eyes. "Alright already. No need to make it into a whole show. There's a ladder in the other room. Let me go get it."

"Mom, wait, can you—"

The door swung shut with a nightmarish wail from the hinges again, and the dark consumed me. She never even gave me a chance to ask if she could leave the door open.

I didn't move. I didn't blink. Or maybe I did. The whole world was the color of eyelids anyway, so how would I know?

There were rats in the dark. I could hear them moving. I could feel my hand, still stinging, crusted in dry blood.

I tried not to think of old myths. Legends of cannibal rat queens who ate their young, who were drawn to blood and bleeding. They weren't real. Just old stories Mom would tell to frighten the four of us when we were kids.

And I wasn't a kid anymore. So there was no reason to be scared.

I had to pee. How much longer was she going to leave me down here? I wondered if she had forgotten me. Did I have time to go pee in the corner? If she caught me in the act, she'd definitely leave me to figure this one out on my own.

At some point she returned though. I wasn't sure how long. My thoughts were all white noise and panic by that point.

She set the ladder down on a grate without lowering it. "Now," she said. "Petre. Honey. I was thinking."

I chewed on my lip, biting back my *oh no* as well as a couple insults, and managed to murmur, "About?"

"You got back a few days ago, didn't you?"

I squinted. "What about it?"

She drummed her fingers on the railing. I hated the sound of her nails on the hollow metal. It set my teeth on edge and made me think of how it felt to do it. A sensory nightmare. She knew I hated it, which I think was why she did it.

"You haven't been to see me," she said.

"I was told you were busy." I shocked myself with how

quickly and easily the lie came to me. "Hell. You're up working at this hour, so I assume—"

"And you're up, too," Mom interrupted. "Though I'm told you've not been particularly busy."

You ever hear something and feel your thoughts go into a lurch? "Hang on. Who told you that?" Was someone trying to force me to go meet with Mom?

Mom scowled and spared a glance at the ladder. She still hadn't offered it to me. "Stop *prying*."

"YOU'RE ASKING ME QUESTIONS!" I shouted.

"I'm the one holding the ladder." Mom shrugged. "And if you want out you ought to tell me what you were doing down there. Without yelling."

The first thing I did was shut my mouth. I needed time to think. I couldn't exactly tell her *everything*, now could I?

"I can leave you down here with the rats for a few hours if you need some time to think of an answer," Mom offered.

"I—I'm trying to find the right words," I managed.

"Truthful ones, too, I should hope."

"I—I'm just looking to get in contact with Anoïse. Or I *was*. This afternoon. But I threw a fit."

"Oh, *God*." I wanted to die when I heard all the scorn she laced into those two words. She pinched the corners of her eyes.

I stopped. Didn't want to interrupt if she had more to say.

"Well, go on." Mom crossed her arms "I'm sure it gets worse."

I stared at the ground. Fidgeted with the flashlight. "I had to get escorted out of the administrative offices. Under guard."

"Petre. You didn't."

"And then I followed one of the guards down here. I

don't know his name." I sewed that lie in quickly. I wasn't sure what kinds of connections Mom had made over the years. If she knew who Jerim and Teya were then she could tell them it was me down in these tunnels. Hell, she could tell *Havilan*. If they were on the same side. Would Mom look to overthrow Anoïse? She couldn't be. Anoïse would be too paranoid to let her anywhere near a scientific journal if she even *suspected* Mom was planning something like that.

"Is that it?" Mom asked.

I shrugged. "I...I got turned around. I just...I wanted to talk to Anoïse. Or Desmon. I needed someone to talk to, Mom. Someone who gets it. Gets this. What this place is like. Who understands what it's—what we're like."

"Petre." Oh god. She sounded like she wanted to cry. "I've been here this whole time."

"I know. But I wasn't sure what to—"

"You think I don't understand how this family operates?"

I was sick of interruptions. "WOULD YOU LIKE TO TRY CUTTING OFF EDGAR'S ARM AND SEE HOW FUCKING WELL YOU'RE THINKING A FEW DAYS LATER—" She opened her mouth to interrupt again, so I added, "*NO I KNOW ABOUT MY LANGUAGE.* DON'T EVEN SAY IT. Please. I'm begging you. I don't fucking care anymore." When had I started crying? Fuck. That was the last thing I needed right now. Especially in front of Mom.

I dragged in one of those breaths that makes a *ph* sound. I tried to speak. Somehow I managed, "You can leave me down here if you want. I'll be okay on my own. If you don't want to help me, you don't need to. But don't keep stringing me a—"

"Shut up."

Oh. I had given her a reason to feel useful, hadn't I? I

wanted to ask what she was going to do, as the silence stretched. I heard movement on the grate above me. Mom grunted, and the ladder pitched down.

"Come on up," Mom said. She held the ladder for me, and I climbed.

I got up to the grate, and realized Mom was much shorter than I remembered. It took some time to adjust to even the dim light spilling in from the doorway. But when I did, she'd reached up to cup her hand around my cheek. "Oh, Petre. Look at you."

"I know."

"You're a mess."

"I know."

"Have you been sleeping? Icing those bruises? What happened to your hand? Come with me. Let's get you cleaned up."

"Yeah," I lied. "Sounds nice." I had to play her dollhouse games. Tell her what she wanted to hear. Or else she'd get scornful and start talking about the autism. The way she wished that she could cure it, the way it was hurting everyone around me. I would pick a fight. And then she would never help me.

Mom would have to dictate the terms here. I would have to follow the path of the conversation she laid out. Make her feel useful, for as long as she kept me down here. And if I could just play along, I knew she would tell me where I could find Desmon, or Anoïse. Things were always so *transactional* at court.

I could have my audience with them. And then I'd be out.

MOM'S WORKSHOP was a palace of fluorescent lights.

I didn't complain as she led me through the dull granite halls. I shivered. The whole fortress was cold, but the rest of this place had nothing on the basements. The creeping chill infected even stone walls.

The basement was shot through with age old wires. Machinery ate up dead space. Mostly abandoned workbenches made the ugly hall into a labyrinth of makeshift spaces. Labcoats embroidered in yellow thread as dark as dehydrated piss sagged on hooks in every corner of the room.

She led me to her workbench, where she rolled up a schematic before I could get a decent look at it.

"The hell is that?"

Mom blinked at me and bunched up the schematic in her hand. "This? Oh, nothing. Did you want coffee, dear?"

I wasn't sure if she wanted me to say yes or no. For all I knew she was extending me a poisoned apple. Or was she merely trying to redirect the conversation. Trying to create some trust before she steered us back to everything with Edgar. "I'll take it black." That would taste disgusting, but it would keep me on edge. It would remind me of Avram. "What corpse technology were you looking at?" I asked, again.

"Just something I learned about during that coup I attempted when the four of you were little, dear."

"That sounds incredible." It took some effort to avoid deadpanning feigned interest. "What does it do?"

Mom thumbed a coffee maker. Drummed her fingers as she waited. "We don't know *who* made the tech. Its purpose was initially for the storage, preservation, and archiving of memories."

That sounded familiar. I'd heard a couple reports of

people who had scavenged items like that over the years. Rare scraps of corpse technology that could upload the memories of a user and stored them in binary code, fitted to a flash drive.

Avram had looked into similar devices when he and Mom were creating my injections. They'd never managed to find a less painful alternative though, but tech like that was a high value find on an archeological dig. There were historians that would pay through the nose to get their hands on something like that. "So you're looking to preserve some history?"

"Oh, goodness, no. I need to find the technology that can do that and have it rewired."

"Rewired?"

"Oh, you don't want to hear about that, do you?" Coffee was ready. Mom poured it into two mugs. She brought it over to her workbench and slid one across the table to me, with two analgesic tablets.

I swallowed them, though I barely noticed a difference. "You got anything stronger?"

"Nothing that will keep you tethered to this earth. Though my chemists have been working on new tablets for use in med kits after combat, which—" Mom's mouth twisted. She waved the matter away and leaned across the workbench. "Give me your hand."

I stretched my injured hand across the table as Mom unclasped a box full of first aid supplies. She triaged my wounds. "Is this from Edgar?" Her voice carried a note of approval, of potential admiration if it turned out to be her favorite son's handiwork. Frankly, I was surprised she'd taken this long to bring him up. That wasn't like her.

"No." I left it there. If she wanted to know more, she

could ask me. I was betting she'd prefer to know about Ed. I didn't want to overshare. She had to ask me.

"Tell me what happened," she said, not looking up from the injuries to my hand. "About Ed, specifically. Is he okay? Make sure you tell me everything. And I'll be sure to get the information to your sister." She peeled open an antiseptic wipe. "This will sting," she added, as if I didn't know. I set my teeth and braced for it.

I always felt guilty when things took this kind of turn with Mom. When I gave her an excuse to feel useful. When suddenly the two of us reached an uneasy peace. It was difficult to enjoy because I knew it wouldn't last.

Mom had thoughts on everything that had happened between me and Edgar. Critiques on how I could have handled things better. She treated it like I was in possession of as many facts about the situation as I had now.

And every time, I had to sit there quietly and listen. Not just absently, I couldn't smile and nod. Mom needed me to take this in fully. I needed to demonstrate that I had heard her in how I responded.

I couldn't contradict her unless I had an interest in provoking her ire, and she was the only lifeline I had here. The only way to get an audience, and then get out. The last thing I needed was Mom flipping her attitude on me. I couldn't let her switch back to antagonism. So I swallowed every criticism with a smile, and I told her all about taking off Edgar's arm.

She finished dressing my wounded hand around the same time I had finished my account of things. I wondered if she timed it that way. It wouldn't have surprised me.

What did surprise me was when she asked, "Do you think you did the right thing?"

I wasn't sure how to answer. The question was so broad

that it felt like a trap. Slowly, I said, "I think I did the best I could do at the time." And offered her an apologetic shrug. "Time will tell, though."

"Yes. I suppose it will." Mom sipped her coffee. "No wonder you're back at court. I suppose you never could allow one of your siblings to have the last word."

I wanted to tell her she was wrong. That I came back out of the goodness of my heart, or love for this family, love of this place.

Any other reason than spite would work, really.

But nothing came. There were no excuses. There was only a truth she laid out too coldly and flatly to be denied. Any attempt to deny it would look ludicrous. "They were... they were very persuasive." My hands searched for the solace of my pockets. I didn't want to be scolded for fidgeting. Not at my age. "Or rather—very good at misunderstanding everything I said persuasively."

"The exact right way to rope you in, I know." She leaned across the table to regard me. "You always need the other three to *understand* you."

She didn't have to say it with such contempt. "You're right."

"Don't look at me like that," Mom said.

"Like what?" I tried to bar a note of panic from infecting my voice.

"Like I've taken the wrong tone with you. I'll speak to you how I like." She laughed in a way that I'd always suspected was manufactured specifically to slice away her internal tension—to cut herself free from the cancer of empathy, and the worry that what she'd said had made me feel bad. "I'm not sure why your brother wanted you so badly."

"He said it was because he loved me." I said it automatically.

I realized I may have made a mistake when Mom's face went blank. She'd always liked Edgar more. I watched her carefully as the cogs turned behind her eyes. As she tried to fit this new information into her narrative. "He's very good at making people feel wanted, isn't he?"

I wondered if Mom was implying insincerity. On the other hand, I wasn't wholly sure that I disagreed. "He is," I said. "Did he make you feel that way?"

Mom stared down at her workbench and frowned contemplatively. "He did," she said, quietly.

"I'm sorry he left you." My heartbeat shuddered. There was a good chance what I was about to do would blow up in my face. "But there's still time to make the most of the people you have here."

She stared at me, flatly, and my bowels turned to ice.

"Mom. I need your help." No use backing out now, I supposed.

Mom blinked at me. "I'm not sure what you mean. What do you need my help with?"

"If Edgar's drawing support, then we're in danger. I need to speak with Desmon. Or Anoïse. Desmon said when I came back that they needed my help to—"

Mom clutched a hand to her chest and cackled, big and loud.

"What?" There was a sinking feeling in my chest as her laughter went on. "Mom, what? What is it?"

"Your—your *help?*" She asked, between breaths. "Is that what he called it?" She giggled. "Oh, dear, that's too funny."

I kept my face blank. "I don't know if I get the joke."

"Then let me tell you a secret."

"I'm listening."

Mom leaned across the workbench conspiratorially. She looked around to make sure nobody was there. Which was ridiculous. It must have been the early AM hours. Everyone was asleep. She just wanted to draw this out for no reason.

"Petre. Listen to me. Nobody needed your help. You don't need to have a hero complex about this. You're not here to save anyone."

"I'm not trying to have a—"

"Spare me," she rolled her eyes. "I'm not trying to indict you. I'm just saying—your siblings know how much Edgar loves you. And they thought bringing you here might curtail his plans. That's it. That's all. That's the only reason you're here."

Disorientation reeled inside my skull. The room spun around me. "I—Mom—what?"

"You're not here because someone needs your help."

"But—Bullion?"

"You think your sister couldn't piece together what happened? Lord Havilan got back hours ago to give his report."

She was bluffing about that part. She had to be, right? Havilan had said himself he only knew scattered fragments. She was exaggerating. Trying to make me feel useless. That had to be it, right?

"She's had eyes in the area for weeks now."

"But—that wasn't—that isn't—" If she had people scouting the area wouldn't one of them have picked me up when Edgar caught me? Though I supposed Anoïse did not know I was there. I wondered how much more of this Mom was making up. There was so little here that I knew with certainty. And the doubts she provoked lingered in the spirals of my mind.

"All I'm saying is that you were merely another calculation your sister wanted under control. You're not here to help. Unless you count inaction as *helping*. But no one needs you to do anything, Petre. You're only here as a hostage."

I wasn't sure what to say. What to do. I tried to find a reason Mom would have to lie about this, but the thing that scared me most was that it fit. It all fit. "I—no, I—" I couldn't have gone through all this just to be a hostage. Did Anoïse put me through all this just so she could be the one to say she had possession of me? She and Edgar didn't even have a *use* for me, was that it? All they wanted to do was keep me from the other? Have me under watch? Under control? That was all there was to it? "You can't be serious."

Mom blinked at me. "Why do you think I was so surprised to find you in the basement? I was worried someone had given you something to do!" She laughed again.

By some miracle I managed to keep my voice level. "Mom," I said. "Where's Desmon?" New plans were threading together into an intent. I couldn't get near Anoïse without some suspicion. But Desmon? He was the one who had lured me home. Who had promised me a fief in exchange for a few days of helping.

He'd asked me to fucking trust him. Unbelievable.

Mom wiped at a tear in the corner of her eye. I wasn't certain it was actually there. "I'm not sure if I should say."

"You're not exactly under orders not to tell me."

"I might be." Mom checked her fingernails theatrically.

"I've never known you to listen to your children's orders."

"It doesn't often work that way around, does it?"

I leaned forward. "So why now?"

"Would you like to know? Really?"

"Very much so."

"It's because you have yet to make this interesting for me."

That gave me an idea. If she wanted interesting, I could certainly provide. I still had Dad's knife in my pocket, after all. I slid it out and deposited it on the table, between us. "Is this interesting enough?"

Mom was not often shocked. I relished the sight of it. I wasn't sure when I'd see it again. She picked it up and looked it over to make sure it was the knife she thought it was. "Where did you get this?"

I was certain Mom would use the fact that I had the knife as ammo to get me in trouble the exact second it suited her needs. She didn't need to know how I got it on top of that. This was enough blackmail material on the face of it. She made a decent shot at getting more though. "Doesn't matter where I got it, does it?" I pried it gently out of her stunned fingers. "What matters is what I'd like to use it for."

"Oh? And what use is that?"

I downed the last of my coffee. "I'm thinking of showing it to Desmon."

"And by that you mean...?" Mom smirked.

"Well." I rolled my eyes. "I should hope it doesn't come to this." I removed the knife from its sheath. Gave it an experimental twirl. He had fucking lied to me. He'd brought me back here just to brick me in. It was exactly the scenario I dreaded most. The exact thing I had been hoping to avoid. "But in a worst-case scenario I think it might fit between his ribs."

I thumbed the switch on the hilt.

The double edges went serrated and started spinning.

SIXTEEN

I t was the early AM hours when I went to find Desmon. I wasn't about to get even a little bit of sleep beforehand, so neither could he.

Mom had told me where to go. I made for the chamber quick as I could, frustration building in me as I went.

When you walk the same paths long enough, every landmark will just bleed into the background. Things that once grabbed your attention become ancillary data through the alchemy of repetition. You know what I mean? It's incredible how quickly a tapestry depicting some form of torture involving glass and a not insignificant amount of red thread can go from *shocking* to an empty symbol saying *turn left here.*

But then sometimes? That repetition ends. You spend a while away, and when you come back, you see that tapestry, and you just have to stop and look at it for the first time in a while. You realize it leaves you with some things to think about.

Things like, *who the hell invented tapestries?* I just want to talk. I promise. Who decided that the best way to convey your family history was via blanket fort?

And perhaps more importantly, why was *that* the agreed upon best way if the goddamn medium couldn't even convey a decent picture? Who the fuck invented these things, you know? Was it Josiah M. Tapestry? Was that his name?

And not only are these thoughts doing a bit of a huddle-up in your mind, but then underpinning all that is that sort of soul-crushing loneliness that can only be brought on by a brother and sister who have called you back home in the hopes that they can keep a sibling they don't even like in line. And you're mulling over how in the hell you let them drag you back, let them convince you that coming home was a good idea, despite everything you know about this place.

You know? The general feeling we all go through from time to time? That bleeding, incandescent anger you can't help but stew in?

So you take it out on tapestries and all the old antiques and decorations. You want to tear down everything on the way. You wonder if punching a hole through the canvas paintings of your ancestors could be linked back to you. Your fists can't be *that* identifiable, surely?

We've all been there.

I tried to adjust my focus on the walk there. But no matter what I did, I kept circling back to thoughts like these. In my defense, it's only because I was extremely bitter. My ire infected every thought that dared to cross the periphery of my attention.

I'm not even sure what I wanted out of the interaction if I'm honest. I planned to march in there, confront him and...

and then what? I wasn't sure if I had thought that far ahead. I wasn't sure I wanted to.

Though stopping to crouch at Desmon's door and pick the lock made me feel ludicrous. I was boiling-angry, my thoughts mired in a seething sort of fury. So stopping to fill up my time with that kind of minutiae did feel a bit ridiculous.

I had tried to trust him. I'd chosen to believe it was possible he had changed, or Anoïse had changed. That anything about this place had changed. All because he'd learned to say the words *I'm sorry*. Fuck me. All he'd done was gotten better about hiding who he was.

I eased the door open. The hinges groaned, and I stepped into a room that smelled like stale perfume.

I spotted Desmon's wide silhouette in the low light as he stirred behind the net of lace that shrouded his bed. I wondered if he could smell me coming. I must've reeked of sweat and mildew. Dust and cobwebs. Probably a bit of blood.

"Who's there?" His words were runny with exhaustion.

I shoved his curtains aside, knelt on his bed.

He clawed up a dagger from under his pillow. "Don't!" He squawked.

I seized his wrist, pushed him back down. I slammed his hand on the bedside table once, twice, then the knife sprang from his grip.

"Please," he squealed. "Wait please—you can't—I can pay—"

I wrapped my hand around his throat, which shut him up. I felt it wriggle under my palm when he swallowed.

"Can you?" I growled. "You've already promised me a fief."

His eyes widened when he realized it was me. "Petre—ack!" I tightened my grip around his throat and slammed my knuckles into his jaw. "Give me a reason to trust you right now or I will kill you and go straight to Ed, Desmon." Even *I* wasn't sure if I was bluffing or not.

His hand flew up to the one I had around his throat. He scratched thin white lines down the back of mine. He gave me a nervous grin. "Listen—"

I slapped him. "Go on. I'm listening."

"It—it's a little difficult to think with your hand right—"

I placed my dagger against his belly. That shut him up. "You're a smart man, Desmon. Why don't you think a little harder? Go on. I'm waiting. Give me a reason."

"I—you—you'll *get* a fief," he winced. "Just as soon as this conflict is done. Just like I promised. I never technically broke my—"

"Desmon."

He blinked at me. Innocently. "Petre?"

"Mom tells me that I'm a hostage. Is that true?"

He raised a finger. I fought down the urge to hit him again. "You talked to her, huh?"

I wondered if I was perhaps being too gentle with him.

"I will admit I may have. Um." He swallowed. Licked his lips. "Taken some liberties with the...angle...of my approach. When I informed you why we asked you to come back here."

The way he parsed it was astounding. "Desmon. Hey. You feel this knife in my hand, right?"

He closed his eyes. Sounded utterly exhausted. "Yes, Petre. I feel it."

"I'm poking you with it right now. You feel—?"

"Yes. I get it. I feel it. What's your point?"

"Do you want me to gut you? It's been a while since one of us has stabbed the other. We've got a fantastic streak going, you and me. But if you'd like to break it by coming at this the way you are right now then please be my guest."

Desmon sighed through his nose. "A pen. That was a pen. It doesn't count."

I wasn't sure at first what he was talking about. Then I remembered the time we were seventeen. And a family friend, Henry Ring, stabbed me in the back of my shoulder with the nib of a quill. Really drove it in there. I was surprised he managed it. The tip broke off too. It took a while to dig it out. "That was on *your* orders? Fuck. I forgot about that. I thought Ed was the one who sicced him on me."

Desmon shrugged. "I didn't have the luxury to get caught the way you three did."

"Oh, huh. I forgot about that. I thought the last time was when I—fuck. Goddammit. Shut up." I shook him. "That's not what I'm here to talk about. Fuck you." I shoved him back and scooted off the bed. I needed to move. To think.

Desmon rubbed at his throat and sucked down a grateful breath. "Okay. Great. Terrific. So you're not going to stab me?"

I frowned, then put the knife away. "I'm reconsidering it," I hedged. I didn't want to go join Edgar if I didn't have to, and if Desmon could still hook me up with a plot of land and a place to mind my own business, I was going to walk out of here with that. I didn't want to be a part of this.

But that meant getting Anoïse involved and getting this in writing. I needed clarity on what was expected of me if I was going to get my part of our bargain.

"Right," Desmon said. "So where are you at right now, then? How are you feeling?"

"I'm feeling like you should fetch a courier."

He rubbed his eyes. "Petre. God. It's the middle of the night. Can't it wait till morning?"

I blinked at him. Drew the knife an inch out from the sheath again.

"Okay. Okay. Okay. God. I'm up. I'm up. Calm down. Good Lord." He climbed out of bed, tied a silk robe over his chest and sat down to write a missive. When he was done he opened a desk drawer and pulled out a tiny mechanical bird.

"It's programmed," he told me. "Mom invented them." A little pin dangled from a copper crow's foot. "You just put the pin in the correct slot, right here on its belly, so it knows which door to go to. And the beak knocks." He attached his missive to the other leg.

"And they bring that to Anoïse?" I asked.

"And she sends one back," Desmon nodded. "Mom's trying to find a way to build some capable of long-range travel." He pet this one with the backs of two fingers. "These ones don't handle strong wind well. Pretty unreliable. Can't let them travel very far. So they stay indoors."

I wanted to be impressed by it, but I was too angry at everyone and everything. Giving anyone props for the things they did well felt like ceding ground to emotions that were not anger. Which was just about the only thing that I was willing to indulge in at that point.

He slotted the pin into one of the waiting holes and the whole clockwork mass flew up, wings fluttering like a hummingbird. He tossed it into the air and it took off in a swoop, sweeping out the door and down the hall, towards the mastodon's ribcage.

We sat in silence. I collapsed into his bed. It was soft enough to make me want to lie down and go to sleep, but I couldn't allow that. Desmon had his elbow propped up on the desk and held his head up with his palm. "You weren't supposed to find out, you know," he croaked.

"How long did you think you could keep it a secret?"

"Long enough to tell Ed that we have you. Anoïse thought she could convince him to surrender that way."

I wasn't sure if what came out of me was laughter or crying.

"What?" Desmon asked.

"Man. You *really* should've told me. He's not about to take peace terms on my account. Not after I cut off his arm."

Desmon straightened, leaned forward. "Petre, I—you *what?*"

"You should've told me that was the plan. I would've said this sooner."

"Why *didn't* you?"

I just looked at him. For a long time.

Desmon frowned. "What?"

"I can't tell if you really don't get it or if you're just being obtuse."

He raised an eyebrow. "You want to talk to *me* about obtuse?"

I rolled my eyes. "You want to talk to me about withholding information?"

He snorted. "There is that."

"I just wish you could've been honest with me," I said.

"We're trying to avoid a war. How much value do you put in honesty right now?"

"Right. Sorry. You're usually so good at being honest. I must've forgotten about the fact that our fucking brother rebelling has changed everything. You're like a different person now. I hardly even recognize you."

"How funny do you think you are when you say this shit?" He blinked slowly, like he was nodding off. Fatigue blotched purple smudges under his eyes.

"Do you want my honest answer?" I asked, "or the one you're hoping to hear?"

The clockwork bird came drifting in through Desmon's door while he was debating how to address what I'd said to him. It settled down on his desk, new parchment wrapped around its foot. Desmon took it and unfurled it. "It's Anoïse."

Took her long enough. "What does it say?"

"She wants us to head to her room," Desmon said. "She demands a private audience with us."

THE MOONLIGHT MADE striped patterns on the ribbed hallways. Turns out Anoïse's room was at the base of the mastodon's spine.

On the way there, we kept arguing.

"We *care* about you, jackass," Desmon said. "Anoïse wasn't going to move against Edgar until she knew that you were safe. We were trying to be proactive. We were helping."

My fingernails carved irritated red trenches into my palm. "You've certainly got some way of showing that. I'm really feeling the love right about now."

"What would you have us do? Would you prefer it if we went right to war while he still had you? We figured keeping you here would slow him down. He *likes* you. It's more complicated than you're making it. We're trying to avert a war."

I wasn't sure what I ought to say to that. The prospect of war haunted every current of my thoughts. "How do *you* feel about it? About Edgar's claim, I mean?"

Desmon sighed and led me down an adjacent hallway, through concrete halls between the ribcage and the knobs of the spine. "You know, Petre. When you're trying to pry information out of someone, you're usually supposed to talk *around* a subject."

"Quit being pretentious and answer the question, jackass," I said, realizing I was not quite as calm as I had hoped.

"I'm worried, Petre. Okay?" Desmon said. "Are you happy now? Is that what you want to hear?"

"Not remotely." I wondered if I ought to say more, but I couldn't think of anything. Not right now. "Look. I'm not sure why I asked, okay? Maybe we should drop it. Just head to Anoïse in silence. Or I'm going to say something I regret."

We approached a pair of double doors that were flanked by two members of The Mercy Guard. Desmon thumbed to me. "He's with me." He handed the guards Anoïse's missive, and they opened the doors for us.

We were through, into a hall of finery. Silk banners draped from fossilized bone and steel rafters. There was a red and black door at the end of the hallway with banners embroidered in the mastodon herald of Mercy House.

Desmon picked up our argument where he'd left it. "Since when has saying something you regret ever been a concern for you? Have you ever really cared that much about me, Petre?"

I laughed. Mostly to break the nervous tension. "I mean. Come on. Look where it's got me." I moved past him. "Is Anoïse in here?" I moved to knock on the door.

He caught my wrist. The pads of his fingers pressed down on my veins. He could probably feel my heartbeat. He squeezed and when he spoke his voice was low and raw. "That was not an easy question. And I demand a better answer."

My whole arm tightened when I made a fist. "You... *demand?* Do you? Is that what you do?"

"Petre." I could see the muscles in Desmon's throat move when he swallowed. "Please?"

Slowly, I peeled my wrist out from his fingers. This was unlike him. He was probably just tired. I didn't want to make any sudden movements. I didn't want to spook him. "I don't know if I've got one. Not tonight, at least." I flexed my hand and turned to the door. "Tonight we have more important things we need to—"

The door flew open before I could close my hand around the knob, and I was looking down at Anoïse.

She was as tall as my chest. Which was an improvement since the last time I had seen her. She had Mom's hair, and big eyes that always seemed to register surprise.

Anoïse received this moment with the same shocked disbelief that I did. Mouth open, moving without making a single sound. But that was over in the time it took her to dig her nails through her hair, parting it to one side without breaking eye contact.

"O-oh," she stammered. "Petre. You...you made it home safe. Good. I didn't think you'd—" I was wondering if she was going to treat this whole thing like any other formal meeting when she rolled her eyes and murmured, "Oh, to hell with it."

Her arms were around me so quick and forcefully I staggered. She wrung all the breath from my body, as she fit the crown of her head neatly under my jaw. "Shit. Anoïse. I—" I couldn't figure out what to say.

"I've missed you. Fucking idiot." Her voice was muffled against my chest. "Don't let anyone tell you otherwise."

"I—I've missed you too." I meant it.

I mean—I still wanted to get out of this place, but *now* I felt guilty about it. I couldn't ask her. Not here. Not now. Not after this. I was going to be here for a while, and that made it difficult to breathe.

I couldn't let her catch on to that though. "I didn't think you could get taller. But you managed it. I'm proud of you."

"Shut up."

"I'm serious."

"Shut up!" She pushed gently away from me, holding my arms. "Tell me everything, Petre. God, how have you been?"

How do you begin after such a prolonged silence? Five years without a word to someone you love—and then— and then—and then you're *there*. With them. Again. In the same room. When you never thought you'd have that chance again.

But what do you say?

Until mere days ago I thought I'd long since finished my clumsy exit from her life. I'd made a new one. Living at Blackheath House for a few years. How do you reduce the last five years down to a hello?

"Oh, y'know?" I rubbed the back of my neck. "Around, I guess. What can I say? You invited me home. I wish you could have made some time to see me. Even a little bit. I'm not greedy. Anything would've been nice, before now." I wondered if my tone edged too close to annoyance. Had I made my true feelings on the subject too obvious? Too easy for her to detect?

She frowned, mouth drawn down like a war bow, wrinkles coming out for the occasion. "You've picked an interesting way to get my attention."

"I still have Desmon's letter," I forced my voice to stay calm. "Would you like to compare notes? See whose methods are more interesting?"

"I hate to interrupt this reunion but can we hurry this up?" Desmon groaned. "I want to sit down."

Anoïse glowered at him, but she motioned us inside with just her head. Our footsteps made dark patterns on her carpet, and when I saw how many pillows she had on her bed I felt an instant of envy.

"I hear Mom told you some things she shouldn't have," Anoïse said.

"That's part of it." I took a seat across from Desmon. An unused chess board filled the space between us.

Anoïse made her bed into a makeshift throne. "And what else?"

"I just—" Hatred spun away from me, though not for lack of trying to retain it. "I had concerns."

Anoïse steepled her fingers, eyebrows going up like an arrow volley. "I don't doubt it." She just looked at me. I wished I could detect what was going on behind her eyes.

Desmon seemed to melt away. It was just her and me and all the years of silence knotted in between us.

The last thing she'd ever said to me was *don't go.*

The longer I stared the harder it was to remember why I had.

It took five years to listen. Five years to come back. But looking at her there—I felt eighteen and out of my depth all over again. Renewed fears squirreled their way inside my thoughts.

Then I looked away.

"Where should we start?" I'd wanted to start with what I'd learned about Edgar. But now that she'd asked I wasn't sure how to introduce the subject.

"He cut off Ed's arm," Desmon offered.

Anoïse and I both looked at him.

"Desmon!" I snapped.

"What?"

"Petre," Anoïse cut in. "Good Lord, I—what the hell? You did—Desmon. Tell me you're joking."

"No," I said, before Desmon could respond for me. "He's not. It happened. He tried to get me on his side in Bullion days ago. I tried to leave. He wouldn't let me. Our horses crashed." That made it sound a bit more passive than it was. But fuck it. Now was not the time for nitpicky details. "His arm got injured. I had to do something about it."

Anoïse blinked at me. "So you're the reason Bullion is shut down? Why everything is in lockdown and no one will talk to me? You're the reason Mercedes Blackheath refuses to speak with me?"

"Yeah," I muttered. "Yeah, that was all me, I did all—wait, what? Say that last thing again."

She paused. I watched her retrace the conversational steps. "Mercedes Blackheath won't speak with me."

I squirmed. I was too exhausted to unknot all *those* implications. "...That one wasn't my doing."

Anoïse rolled her eyes. "Oh. As long as that's the only one. I was almost upset with you!" She brayed out manic laughter.

I wasn't sure at first if she was joking. "I just feel," I said, carefully, "that given everything that's gone on the last few days, I have more reason to be upset with you than you do with me."

Now listen—the look she gave me? I have no way of

verifying that what she was thinking was anything along the lines of *off with his head*. But like. Come on. You ever see someone's face and you just *know?* This was like that.

Just. Fury.

Desmon decided he'd be the one to break the tension. "How mad can you possibly be? You haven't even taken her arm off yet."

I kicked him under the table. He kicked me back. I let it end there.

"You and Desmon tricked me into coming back here," I protested. "Lured me in just to keep me here. Not even for any particular reason. You just didn't want Ed to get to me. Is that correct?"

She pinched her mouth into a pale pink line. "It was more complicated than that."

"How?" I shouted. "You're trying to keep me like a stockpile. Hoarding me. Like kids who don't know how to share your toys."

"That's not what I was doing at all! You're just assuming things! Fucking stop it!"

I rolled my eyes. "God, it's good to see you too, Anoïse. Good to know that after all this time you and Desmon can still tell me I keep making a big deal about nothing. I can't believe I actually came back here. Five years to get right back to where I started." I clung to that sentiment. I had to remember that. I couldn't let her make me feel guilty for leaving. I couldn't let that happen.

"Oh, fuck you. God, I forget why I even asked you to come back."

"You didn't," I shot back. "You didn't have the balls to do it yourself! You made Desmon here do it for you!"

Desmon paled. He looked like he wanted to vanish completely. "Don't drag me into this, I beg you."

"I was trying to get your attention," Anoïse shot back, "and I figured if I reached out—"

"—That I wouldn't answer. I wouldn't come back, right? That I'd think of it as an attempt to toy with my emotions. That's my *point*, Anoïse! You tried to hide what you were doing! What your goal was! You kept trying to obfuscate why you wanted me back!"

"What was *I* doing? You're the one who just said Desmon—"

"Stop," I said, but she kept trying to press the issue. I had to speak over her. "Stopstopstopstopstopstopstop*stop!*" I held up a hand and kept going until she was done trying to interrupt me. "Stop." I said one last time, when she was silent. "I'm just frustrated is all. I shouldn't be taking it out on you. I'm sorry. I really have changed. I promise. I'm not going to get dragged into this."

"I'm not trying to drag you into anything—" she protested.

"I know!" I screamed, wincing at the way the words filled the room, the way they screeched like overextended support beams. "I know," I said again. "I'm not trying to accuse you of anything." God, but I hated how many people jumped to conclusions about the things they thought I was saying. Maybe that made me a hypocrite. I don't know. "I'm just annoyed, I guess. It's like..." I forced myself to breathe, to think, before I said what was on my mind. "Dad *just* died and you're already—"

"Petre, stop."

She paused. I think she was expecting I would interrupt. But I swallowed the irritation. I forced myself to sit there, face as red and warm as diseased skin while I heard her out.

"You don't understand. We didn't have time to do anything other than this. Edgar is—"

"I'm up to date with Edgar, thank you. I'd like to know what else I'm missing. Are there any other hostages I ought to know about? Any plans that are in motion to deal with Edgar? And what is Havilan fucking Reacher still doing here? I thought you would've dismissed him by now. I'd love to know that."

I mean, what I actually wanted to do is leave and come back five minutes later and try again. But I didn't have the time to simmer down. I wanted answers.

She took a breath. Slowly. Deliberately. Like she was trying to summon up a shred of patience. "Are you implying —" Anoïse began.

"I'm not implying anything!" I roared, rising to my feet. "I don't imply. Shut up. If I have something to say, I will *tell* you. And right now I'm kind of angry that it took this long just to tell you I cut Edgar's arm off. And that's not even half of what I've been through. He was off in Bullion looking for a helmet! He had supporters ready to cut in on a munitions deal! Just think of all the planning you could've done the last three days! Think of everything that could have happened here. But no. You two already decided I had nothing to offer. You just wanted me here to say that you had me here. That's it! That's all, and it's not—"

The door flew open and the man from The Dripping Bucket waltzed right in. "Anoïse, we're out of—oh." He saw me and I watched him go bright red. "Um. Is now a bad time? I wasn't aware that you were seeing paramours." He noticed Desmon next. "Wait. Hold up—" It was almost amusing watching him do the math in his head. "Why is your brother here, if—"

"Settle down, Fabrian," Anoïse sighed. "They're both my brothers."

It was my turn to blanche. "Fabrian?" I echoed. "Fabrian *Reacher?* You mean this—?" I gestured to him. Holy shit. I was going to die. "Anoïse, this—this is your *husband?*"

Anoïse blinked at me. "Is there something wrong?"

I was not sure immediately how to respond. The only places my mind admitted me were full of white noise. It was impossible to think.

Fabrian Reacher.

The King.

Oh, *man,* that title was going to take some getting used to.

Fabrian turned the brightest crimson I think I'd ever seen. "Anoïse. What do you mean this is your brother?"

Desmon looked from me to Fabrian. "She has three."

I wanted to laugh. I wanted to die. I kind of wanted to kiss him, if I'm honest.

"Is something wrong?" Anoïse asked.

I wasn't sure if my voice sounded as strained as I felt. I turned to her. "Did you want your...your husband...to hear everything I have to say?"

"And what is it you have to say, Petre?" Fabrian asked. He all but shouted it. I was going to punch him if he was going to make what had happened between the two of us so obvious so quickly. At least that would shut him up.

But I was worried he might actually enjoy that.

Desmon raised an eyebrow. "Have you two met before?"

"Once," I said.

"Twice," Fabrian said.

"Twice." I glowered at him. "Briefly. Both times."

"Right." Fabrian stared at the floor. "What he said. Listen to him."

Anoïse rubbed at her temples. "I plan to," she said. "The rest of you—get out."

Fabrian tilted his head and blinked at her. "I just got back," he said.

"Leave," Anoïse said. "Both of you. Or I'll get The Mercy Guard and you will be escorted out."

Oh. I still had to tell her what I'd overheard involving Havilan and Jerim and Teya. I filed that away for when we were alone.

Desmon was the first to get up. "Well," he said, "if this means at least a little sleep before your coronation feast tomorrow, you can count me in. Or out. Of this room, I mean. I hope you guys can work this out. I'll see you in the morning. Let me know how it went." He seemed in a bit of a hurry when he left.

"Right then." Fabrian turned to watch him leave. "You're sure about this?"

Anoïse's knuckles flashed white around the edge of her bed. "Jasriel's been waiting for you to join her for a few days now."

"Jasriel?" I asked.

"She's not important," Fabrian spat.

"Isn't she?" Anoïse's eyebrows went up.

"*Right now*," he added. "Not important right now."

"I'll let her know that."

"Anoïse." Fabrian palmed his face. "I swear to God."

"Church is that way." Anoïse pointed out the door.

Fabrian pinched the corners of his eyes. "Adreon wouldn't give me this kind of trouble."

"I'm not Adreon," Anoïse said.

"Who's *Adreon?*" I asked. This was too many names.

Fabrian shrugged. "Someone I'm about to go see, I suppose." He left in a huff. It took me three tries to remember I had to stop staring at his ass on the way out. He was my sister's husband. And here I was, thinking about digging my fingers through that hair. Entertaining idea of pulling his head back, of having access to that throat. Fuck.

"Is there a problem?" Anoïse asked.

I jumped. Startled. Worried she could hear my thoughts. "I'm just...I'm processing the fact that you got married."

"Go on. Say it." She crossed her arms and rolled her eyes. "Everyone does. I know you want to, too. Get it out of your system"

I wasn't sure what she thought I wanted to say. Because once I shelved the, uh, everything else about the situation, the only question that came to mind was, "Are you happy?"

Anoïse didn't respond right away. She started blinking very fast. "We, um." I heard the slick sound of her swallowing saliva. Greasing her voice free of all the squeals. "We make it work."

That gave me less to work with than I hoped for. "I...I don't." I managed. "I just—" I shrugged. "I wanted to be sure, cause um. I just. I thought you weren't...well. *You know.*"

She made her mouth a tightrope, walked her response carefully along that narrow line. "What is it that I know? Enlighten me."

"I just—" When did it get so hot? I clutched my head, and tried not to think about Fabrian Reacher. Staring at the ground I said, "I thought you preferred the curtains to the sword." I winced.

Anoïse scoffed. "You think I *wanted* the arrangement?

Dad made it. Fabrian was fourteen when we got married. It was awful."

"Yeah. That...that's what Edgar said. He was supposed to marry into Havilan Reacher's side of the family. Marry his daughter, Guindolin. While you got Orianna Reacher's heir. I know. I know. I just. I don't know. Hm. Have you two...?" I let my thoughts drift off before I said something stupid.

Anoïse lifted one eyebrow. "Do you think about that often?"

"No, what the fuck?"

"I'm just saying you seem awfully hung up on—"

"Don't," I said. "Don't you dare finish that sentence, Anoïse. You know me. You know if you put that thought in my head I don't get to decide how long it haunts me. You're my fucking sister, why would I do that? Unless you want me to struggle to *stop* thinking about it, specifically because I would hate it, then don't finish that sentence. Alright?"

She sighed. "I've never understood how that shit works. How do you think of something you don't want to be thinking about? Just don't. Move on. It doesn't have to haunt you."

"Yeah. Well." I shrugged. "If it's hard to hear about, imagine living with it. Moving on isn't as simple. Not for me."

She rolled her eyes. "Could've fooled me."

I let that barb slide. "All I meant was like—*politically*—" I wished I was more certain she'd take my meaning if I left it hanging. "Don't you two need to....y'know?"

Thankfully, she did. "I don't have to do anything," she mutters. "Much less *tell* you what I did or didn't do."

I wanted to hide, to crawl in a hole. To be out of sight, be anywhere but here. In the silence, I figured now was the right time to shift back to the more pressing matters at hand. "Havilan Reacher got back tonight, too. Met with a couple guards in secret, in an abandoned stretch of basement tunnel. Anyone tell you about that?"

"Not yet, no."

"A couple of The Mercy Guard went with him. There was something about a helmet he was looking for in Bullion, same as Ed was. But he couldn't find it. Said Mercedes Blackheath shut the city down after the conflict between me and Ed, and he couldn't get in. But he got the uh...the layout of the place."

Anoïse looked up. "He couldn't get the helmet?"

I blinked. "You know about it?"

"I sent him."

"Then why was he so secretive about it?" There was something about this that didn't fully track, but I couldn't determine what that was without a full picture.

"Probably because I asked him to keep it secret." Anoïse sat down across from me. "This is your problem. You assume things."

What was she trying to imply when she said that? "You don't trust me," I said.

"I never said that," she said. "See? This is exactly what I mean!"

I winced. I'd never been as good at navigating this world of double meanings as my siblings. They'd all found ways to adapt to it, and while I could manage it with the people I didn't like much, I hated being so indirect with people I cared about. "You trust Havilan," I guessed. "Is that what this is about?"

She winced. "I don't doubt his loyalty right now if that's what you mean. I don't know what you want me to say. I'm sorry, Petre. He's had every chance to defect, and he's done everything I've asked of him to avert this war."

"I think his daughter, who Ed gets on with, who was promised to marry him, might like to start one. I think it's possible he's promised Havilan can have The Bay. And don't you think his daughter would want to be Queen?"

Anoïse sighed. "And how could Ed do that without ruining his alliances with all our vassals who he left with?"

I shrugged. "Covertly."

"He's smarter than that," Anoïse shot back.

"I think we'll have to disagree about that."

"Shut up," she groaned. "No really. Stop it. Come on. I know things didn't end well with him back there, but if he wasn't smart we wouldn't *be* here. We would've caught him by now. Now you're just being obtuse."

"Obtuse? How am I being obtuse?"

"Are you going to actually listen to my answer, or are you going to argue with what you think I said?"

All the little pinprick aches I could make in her psyche reintroduced themselves to me. "I just want you to admit you don't trust my read on this situation."

Anoïse's fingers shriveled into fists. "Alright. Listen. Do we have to make this about politics?" She asked in a small voice. "I'm so tired of it, Petre. You keep telling me that I brought you back to thwart Edgar. You keep assuming the only reason I'd want you back is a political one. And I just—I really hate that you think that about me, you know? Didn't it ever occur to you that maybe—maybe I need someone I can just *talk* to?"

I swallowed, and felt guilty about my earlier accusations. "Is there something you want to talk to me about?" And if there was, why the fuck hadn't she reached out sooner?

"I just want to speak to you as my brother, not a prince. Can't we have that? At least for a little while? Before we get into everything else? We've only just started—"

"No, but—" I wasn't sure I was getting my meaning across. I was so fucking tired. "*What* is it you're so keen to talk about?" It was late. She was getting a crown on her head *tomorrow*. And there was a war brewing. What else would she have preferred talking about?

"Anything." The word sounded chewed up on its way out of her throat. "God. It's not like we've got a shortage of things to catch up on. Give me anything that isn't politics to talk about with you."

I realized the problem I was having when I couldn't think of anything. "Anoïse. We're royalty. How do we escape it? Everything we do is politics."

"Does it have to be? Even right now?"

I wasn't sure how to let her down easy. I drummed my fingers on the table. Just so that I had something to do. "Unfortunately."

"Fuck you." There was no venom in it. She didn't have her heart in this at all.

I closed my eyes. I wasn't sure what to say. "Listen. I'm not trying to reroute us back to politics, I promise."

She rolled her eyes. "But...?"

"But. Desmon promised me a fief if I helped you. And I need to make sure that's true."

"Do we have to talk about this tonight?"

"That's the whole reason I came here." I was not certain when I would have an opportunity like this again. "We made a bargain. He was able to give ground to me. Literally. I don't know if I want to be here if that bargain can't be respected."

"Are you threatening to switch sides?"

"Now who's assuming?" I tried to keep my voice, my tone, gentle. I wasn't going to get anywhere if we started screaming again. "I just want to make sure Desmon made his promise in good faith."

Anoïse was silent for a long while. "Desmon didn't know the mess you made in Bullion when he promised it to you, did he?"

I took a deep breath. "Alright, now because I don't want to *assume*, I will ask you. What are you saying?"

"You helped to make this messier. Whatever happened there, Mercedes Blackheath won't talk to me. I don't know if that means she's joined with Ed, or there's something else going on. Or what. But I need you to find a way to figure out what happened there before I make good on this promise."

I was furious at how fair her request sounded to me. I didn't want to have to be doing any of this. But fuck me. She really *had* to go and have a point. The audacity. "So if I can tell you which families are on who's side, you'll get it in writing that you've promised me a fief where I can fuck off to when all of this is over?"

"When all of this is over, yes. I will."

It seemed a very strategic form of phrasing, to put it mildly. *When all of this is over.* But I could see the sense it made, even if I despised it. What use was it doling out new fiefs during a war? Handing out power when alliances and disputes were constantly shifting? I didn't like it, but I couldn't find an angle to attack her logic from.

All I had to do was figure out what side The Reachers and The Blackheaths had both joined and let Anoïse know as soon as I'd discovered. And the coronation feast was tomorrow. Which—it was possible that would help to elucidate matters. No one loyal to Edgar would offer up a hostage willingly, would they?

Then again, if none of us could prove anything anyway, what would a double agent have to fear in coming to her coronation? If we locked them up we'd jumpstart the war we were hoping to avoid. I was uncertain of whose side Havilan was on, but here he was in the damn capital anyway. And here we were questioning his loyalties anyway.

I recalled I'd scheduled an appointment with him tomorrow as well. That was something, see? I was on the right track already.

How hard could it really be to avert a war?

CHAPTER
SEVENTEEN

I dreaded visiting the administrators in the morning, but Anoïse had let me go last night with a letter. So I dared to go in hopeful.

The front desk woman scowled when I stepped through the door. "Your Grace, I thought we told you to—"

"I have a letter this time." I waved it. It was my ticket out of here. I was red faced, sleep deprived and out of breath. Business as usual. "And an appointment. Queen's orders."

"We—we're very busy, Your Grace. The feast is *today*."

I did not attempt to make my pretend shock all that convincing. "Better hurry then. I believe I made an appointment with Havilan Reacher?"

"Right. Yes." She retrieved the gigantic book she'd paged through days ago and found the familiar page. She traced it with her thumb. "I—I'm sorry. Lord Reacher seems to have canceled this appointment."

My heart leapt into my throat and made a racket. I was going to puke. "Canceled? What part of *Queen's orders* wasn't clear?"

The receptionist closed her eyes and recited from memory. "All officials are permitted twelve hours to cancel meetings in advance, Your Grace. And Lord Reacher's horse took some damage on his way home. He requested time last night to repair it in an operation."

I leaned over the front desk. "And where is this operation?" I asked.

"I—" She looked in either direction. Put her hands up. I supposed I should feel guilty for the attempt at intimidation. "I can't s—"

Guilt had fled me long ago, and I was sick of being here. I wanted out as soon as possible, so I reached over the desk, grabbed her by the lapels and hauled her close. Her hands closed uselessly around my wrists. I ignored it. "You seem to be under the mistaken belief that I'm making *requests*. I am not. You're going to tell me now. I am talking to Havilan Reacher. Here or wherever he's doing his operation."

The answer spilled from her mouth in a panicked breath of air. "I—he's in the stables. The stables. The stables. He wanted to do it on his own. Please, Your Grace, I—"

I let her go. She staggered back and fell into her chair.

"Thank you." I was lightheaded. "For your cooperation. And understanding," I said through a clenched jaw.

I had to hurry. Had to talk to Havilan. Now. I was getting the fuck out of here, and soon.

My fourth fucking day here and already I was thinking about what Avram would say if he could see what I'd done. Or what this place had done to me? I wasn't sure which. Blaming Mercy House felt like an excuse.

But it would work for now. Just so long as I didn't have to think too hard. I had more important things to worry about.

I HAD to weave between the guests and new arrivals to get to the stables. Distant second or third cousins and vassals and family friends were arriving in all their pageantry. They wore glittering masks paired with the most outrageous doublets, helmets, and headdresses I'd ever seen. A few splinter branches of Mercy House wore iron helms with mastodon tusks, or armor designed to look like its skeleton. There was not a single wrinkle in the colonies of gathered guests making scattered circles throughout Mercy House's hallways. Most of them looked like they belonged to our house. Or The Reachers'. They all wore the most immaculate smiles I'd ever seen.

Like most family gatherings, they began by separating into small clusters, color coded by family banners and general familiarity. At this stage of the morning most of them were probably answering the same general questions you navigate from extended family at this kind of occasion. I overheard a few *what have you got going on these days* from a couple awkward older men as I passed. A few times I almost bowled over servants carrying trays of food to the kitchens.

I thought it was odd that I hadn't spotted any of The Blackheaths yet. I would've thought Mercedes would be here by now. Missing this was the most suspicious thing she could possibly do.

She'd been quiet the last few days, but I figured she'd arrive for the feast. Or at least send a few ambassadors. I don't know. *Something.*

She was usually early to arrive for this kind of thing, but she didn't even have a delegation here that I could see. No banners clustered in the courtyard with all the family branches.

I shelved those thoughts. There would be time to figure this out after Havilan.

I had to hurry.

∽

THE STABLES HAD cement floors and floodlights that flaked on you. There was a stink of oil and new machinery, salted with the smell of sour sweat. It was a cocktail that voided my ability to focus.

Rows of synthetic horses were lined up on either side of me, plugged up with wavy coils the color of brain matter. Golden threads of copper wire were shot through synthetic flesh like embroidery. They were barely breathing—in stasis. Panes of glass separated me from row after row of unblinking eyes. Only the one on the farthest end was open.

I heard the sound of bolts and wrenches being used. Havilan was grunting in there. During those final steps to close the distance between us, I wondered what form of address I ought to use.

I *wanted* to call him Havilan, but he'd doubtless see that as a sign of disrespect. I could pretend I didn't know that— that my cognitive dysfunction made it difficult to determine what the rules were. But I did not want to make that move too early.

We were still in the preamble, he and I. And I didn't want him to know how I'd be playing this game. Not just yet. This was not just a conversation. We were getting the measure of each other. Verbal sparring is still a form of combat. The moves you make during your introduction will set the tone of the fight.

"Lord Reacher?" There. That would settle him in—make him confident I would be deferent to him. I needed him to be comfortable for this exchange. I needed him to think I was on his side.

"Ah, Petre," Havilan said without turning around. His barrel of a back was facing me. He hunched over his horse. I wondered how he'd injured it. Last night he'd indicated that this had happened near Bullion. Did he know what happened there? Between Ed and me? "I was hoping you'd show up," he added, still without looking. His cyborg horse was down on its side, and Havilan's arms were half submerged in gears and gyros and synthetic tube-intestines.

"I'm here for an appointment?" I said it like a question. It wasn't. "I hope you don't mind."

Havilan turned only his neck at first, then the rest of him came with it, wearing sleeves of oil and viscera. He was missing the middle two fingers on his right hand. I almost gasped. I'd forgotten about that. He'd lost them in The Bastard's Rebellion when he and Dad were teenagers. Usually he had robotic ones that clamped on over the stumps, with a little flash drive that plugged into a scrap of corpse technology at the base of his spine.

He wiped his forehead with his left hand, clearing the sweat and making a smear of black grease. "Yes, yes. Of course. Come over here, would you?"

"I—what?" I debated if I ought to obey. I needed to make him comfortable. But *that* comfortable? What if he tried to knife me?

I had to remind myself that I was being unreasonable.

Then again, I needed to establish I had some fight at

least. But then again *again*—disobeying so soon would just ring petty.

"Did you hear me?" Havilan's voice sliced through my thoughts. He held up his maimed hand. Crooked a finger. "Come here," he said again.

He thumbed to the horse with the opened belly. "I'm curious. Look in there, boy. Tell me what you see."

I forced my legs to move, one step at a time, until I stood beside him. I peered inside from a distance. "Lord Reacher, what is this about?"

"Just look."

I crouched for a better vantage point, ignoring that he'd called me boy. I braced my hands on the carpet of oily straw and peered inside.

The horse still breathed—just barely. It was not quite alive enough to feel pain. There was a cartilage of accordion shapes where its lungs should have been. The whole thing was a mess of steel sheets and wires squirreled through ligaments and viscera. Its innards were shot through with wires, gyros spinning, making it move. I heard the trickle of the horse's breath, saw the oil greases running down the spiderweb's twine of industrial steel.

I could have told him all that. That's what I saw, wasn't it? But was that what he wanted to hear? There was clearly some lesson he wanted to convey. I just had to figure out what it was.

"What do you see?" Havilan asked again.

"I'm thinking." How dumb could I pretend to be without him catching on? Dad'd had him in charge of the guard since he took the throne when I was three. He'd been around as long as I could remember. I imagined he'd have some insight into how well I could function, so I had to be careful.

But it had been five years, so I had some room to maneuver. "Uhhh...there are some guts here. They look squishy. I see some cogs. Iron rods, steel...stuff? I think. I don't know. Grease and gyros and oil, yeah? There's a lot in here, Lord Reacher. Am I—um—uhh—am I on the right track?"

Havilan only frowned. I wished I could gauge the meaning behind that downward quirk. "Would you like to know what *I* see?"

I nodded once. "That would be helpful."

He leaned forward, forearm on his thigh. "I see pistons. Machinery. Cyborg organs in need of operation. A machine requiring the teamwork of every facet built into it. Everything in its place. Filling its role. These beasts are a complex web, Petre. Damage to one piece can corrupt the whole thing, in time. Everything needs to be precise. Perfect. There is no room for error. Even too much stress on the joints can wear down the stability of the whole structure."

I kept silent, maintained a vacant face, and did my best to look like I was still staring at this horse. Like I wasn't paying attention. I wanted him to wonder if his metaphor was obvious enough.

"This thing has been with me since I was fourteen." He leaned forward to pet the thing. "When I had all my fingers." He gestured to two clockwork ones sitting with his wrench and various bolts. "This was back when I worked with your father and grandfather to end The Bastards' Rebellion."

Now here we were again with a new rebellion brewing, and here Havilan was, sitting across from me, as I realized how many years he'd had to plan for the next time this happened.

"I know the fashion these days when your horse breaks

down is to get a new one. But I grew up in a time when you fixed what you broke, instead of just buying something else. I damn near lost my horse in that first battle. Had to wait days to go back for it. Couldn't stand the screams. Had to wait for all of them to die. Had to wait till the carnage ended. But I wanted to go back for it. Build it back up."

"That sounds awful." I was vaguely familiar with the feeling from my time killing Gaunts, but I'd not been in a real pitched battle—the kind with armies. Not just yet.

Havilan cleared his throat. "It got damaged when I killed the youngest bastard. Josceran, I think his name was. Your grand-uncle I believe. Knocked him off the saddle with my axe. I was strong back then. Most would've needed two hands to lift that thing. Not me. I put him on the ground, and my damn horse kicked his stomach inside out. But not before he slipped his sword through its exposed underbelly, and the damn horse folded on top of him."

"Funny how that works out," I said. "What happened to your hand?"

"Oh, this?" He held up his maimed hand. "When he stabbed the horse he hit the mainspring. Damn good aim, too. These things wear armor for a reason." He sighed. "When you've been fighting as long as I have, eventually you lose something. You can only roll those dice and get lucky so many times."

"I didn't know that." For once I was not lying. I had to take some deep breaths slowly. Was that how Ed had lost his arm? Had our collision hit the mainspring? Two cyborg clockwork horses shredding themselves apart, with Ed trapped in the middle.

Fuck. I wished I'd known that sooner. Hot damn. Why did I want to cry?

"I'm not surprised you're unaware," Havilan said. And I

wasn't sure if he was insulting me. "It wouldn't look good in advertisements. Hitting the spring is rare but it happens."

Had he inflected that with a sort of *knowing* tone? Or was I perhaps reading into it too much?

"Especially from the underside," Havilan added. "My damn horse exploded. I only just got off the thing in time. Threw up a hand to shield my face as I ran. Better my fingers than the rest of my head. Wouldn't want to look like our dear Mercedes Blackheath, eh?"

I swallowed what ire that comment inspired and tried not to think about it. I hoped Mercedes arrived soon. If we didn't hear from her at all it might have troubling implications as to her loyalty. "It exploded and you put it back together?"

"I've had to repair this damn thing fairly often. Probably doesn't have an original piece in it. Except for me. I guess I'm the one constant."

"Where else have you used it? Any other battles?" I knew the answer, same as he did. Leading his attempt to take The Bay from us. That was what had landed him as a hostage here, away from his older sister and his daughter. His only company here was his nephew. Fabrian.

I knew it. So did he. But I wanted him to tell me himself.

Havilan chewed on that for a moment. Stared off into space. As if we weren't both thinking the same thing. "There have been a couple incidents involving that silly little bay, as I'm sure you recall." He slapped the horse's rump. You ever hear the smack of flesh containing something mostly hollow underneath? It makes you shudder. Like if you patted a friend on the back and were rewarded with the sound of a dropped bicycle.

"This thing sustained some damage in petty conflicts,

to be certain," Havilan said. "And not all of them have been wise. I'll admit that."

I noticed he said that part pointedly.

"I've repaired it every time. It's good to know how to fix things. Comes in handy to get that practice in, yeah? To know how something works. Inside and out. To understand all the work you put into something that looks so clean and precise. Far too often I think we take such things for granted."

"I agree."

Havilan grinned. "Do you know how to repair horses, Petre?"

I knew I shouldn't let that question get to me. It was stupid. He *wanted* me to feel useless. Why would I let that get to me? He just wanted to get under my skin. I just—I couldn't help it. I already felt useless enough. I wondered just how dumb I could pretend to be to avoid a direct answer. "I—I'm not sure—" I rifled through my options. Tried to find a way to spin this in my favor. He could end this here and walk away thinking I was an idiot. He probably wouldn't even be wrong. "I'm afraid I don't. Do you know anyone who can teach me? What about your daughter? Guindolin? Will she be coming for the coronation feast?"

I hoped the insinuation I was making about his daughter, and his loyalty, was at least a little subtle.

Judging by the look on his face I had my doubts. "She's...held up. Though a few of our vassals will be joining us for the feast."

"And your nephew," I added. "The King. He'll be there too, right? Or at least I'd hope so." I laughed.

He didn't. "A couple splinter branches of Reacher House will be here. Though if you're interested in learning from my daughter, I can put a word in with The Queen. See if I have leave to send you to her. If you'd *like* to see her, that is?" Havilan offered me a grin shaped like cracked glass.

Stupid. Stupid stupid stupid. I should have seen that coming. We both knew the answer to that question. Anoïse would never let me go, but I *also* could not challenge Havilan. Not directly. Not without risking his ire, giving him things to gossip about.

"I...I'd like to see her here. I've heard a lot about her, you know. Ed talked to me about her a few years back. But I wouldn't want you to sacrifice anything on my account. It'd be such a hassle to get you over to Reacher House. I wouldn't want to trouble you. Not after all you've done in service to the crown. And you deserve to see Guindolin too, you know?"

Havilan leaned over, staring into the downed horse. He stroked his chin. I wondered how seriously he was considering what he was about to say.

I kept my eyes utterly vacant. I knew too many people who mistook that for the absence of all thought. Good. I could let them think that. I could live with that. They'd only understand their mistake once they'd overstepped.

See, Havilan Reacher's mistake that afternoon was thinking that we had both started our scheming by that point. And nothing could be further from the truth. Our game had not *begun*. I was setting up the board.

When he was done thinking, all he said was, "My daughter has her own learning to do, Your Grace."

"We all have learning to do," I told him.

Havilan chuckled. "You're telling me."

I heard a crash before I could figure out how to reply. It sounded like struck sheet metal. There was no echo. And the silence that followed was like an exclamation point.

Havilan craned his neck to try and see around the corner, but he did not get up. He turned to me. "Check on that, would you? I'd like to know who or what made that sound."

I wondered if this was a trick. A trap. Maybe there was someone with a knife waiting for me. "Of course," I said. "Oh, and in case I get distracted, would you mind very much if we picked this conversation up again during the feast tonight?"

Havilan chuckled, though it seemed like he suppressed a sour glare. "By all means," he said, tonelessly. "Just go make sure nobody's spying on us, if you please."

The sound of his work resumed as soon as I rounded the corner, to the far side of the stables. An oil drum lay on its side, undamaged. That would have felt like good news, if it weren't for the fact that the door was ajar. I was reasonably sure it had not been earlier.

Which meant either someone was spying on Havilan, or someone was spying on *me*. For all I knew, beyond that door, someone with a blade was waiting to house it in my throat.

I made for the door without so much as a backwards glance or a word of goodbye. It seemed fitting.

Nighttime was just beginning to eke itself out on the world as I stepped outside, but it was still light enough that I could see somebody in the distance. Somebody *running*.

I took off after them.

I DIDN'T EVEN BOTHER PUTTING on my mask. Which wasn't the smartest idea, yeah, but if someone was spying on me, I wanted to know what they heard, and which face I had to watch out for at the feast tonight.

It was still stupid, I know. But sometimes you zero in on an issue without regard for your own safety.

Hell, sometimes you do that so often you forget what caring for your safety looks like—you learn a practiced apathy, to the point where it's easy to default to what you're good at.

It helped that the runner was slow. We'd barely even made it halfway through the courtyard before I started gaining ground on them. Sharp breaths knifed from the pinkness of my throat. I tasted that back-of-the-tongue kind of copper you get when you're sprinting for the first time in a while. My legs were made of jelly, but I was a hand's span away from the back of this guy's coat. I wanted to shout. To say something. But I didn't have the breath to conjure up words, so I threw myself forward and squeezed my forearms around their knees as the uneven terrain became a welcome mat for my ribs, and we went down together.

I'm not sure if I pulled myself on top of them or dragged them under me. Who was moving and in what direction was not something I had the time to puzzle out. I was panicky. I needed to see who it was. My fingers sank into the thick wool on the shoulder of their coat, hauled them around and—

—before I could get a good look at them, I felt a knee squirming through the space between us. Their boot pressed against my crotch, then I was tilting through the air. The ground and the sky did a coin flip, and I landed on my back. I still felt the boot-print on my cock. The asshole had flipped me upside down.

As I was catching my breath, the other guy stood up, and I saw it was The King. Standing over me.

That guy from the inn.

Fabrian Reacher

The *King*.

How the hell was I able to catch up to a guy like him? I'd never seen anyone move as fast as he did a few nights ago. What was slowing him down *now*?

"You really should be wearing a mask."

I struggled to my feet, retrieved my gas mask from my coat pocket and shrugged it on.

Fabrian reached into his inner breast coat pocket, retrieved a flask, tugged his own mask down ungracefully and downed a mouthful of its contents.

"Um," I said. "What are you doing?"

He scowled. "Does it matter?"

I put my hands up. "Only curious."

If it was possible to swallow angrily, he found a way. "I'm trying to hurt my liver. The hell is it to you?"

"The hell do you mean 'the hell is it to me'? You're pregaming before your coronation?" Fuck. I didn't have time for this. I had to get back to Havilan Reacher.

He rolled his eyes. "Oh sure, you hurt my ribs and I'm supposed to roll with it like everything's fine, but when I try to hurt my liver suddenly I'm the asshole. Give me a break." He downed another mouthful. Gasped. "That *said*, would you like to hurt my ribs again?" He tugged his mask back on.

I didn't want to hurt his ribs. I had to get back to interrogating his fucking uncle. "What were you doing back there? At the stables? Were you invited?" He was Havilan's nephew, wasn't he? Was he trying to lure me away from Havilan? Why would he do that?

I moved to turn around, head back to the stables.

Fabrian wrapped his hand around my elbow and spun me around to face him. "I came to apologize, if you must know," he said, forcefully.

"What? For what reason?" I wracked my brain for something worth apologizing for. We'd only had that moment in The Dripping Bucket—and a brief moment in Anoïse's bedroom. And the hallway. I supposed the hallway could have used apologizing over. But now? While I was busy talking to his uncle?

I saw a blush claim territory on his face. He coughed. "No—I—I just—I didn't know if you'd seen something like what happened at the tavern before, so—"

Did he think I was unaccustomed to violence? "Listen —you're young." I winced. So was I, I guess. "I don't expect you to put all the pieces together here. I'm not sure how much you've been briefed on who I am or where I've been since you came into the picture. But if you think that's the worst I've seen—I mean—" I had an idea of how I wanted to finish that ramble. But I couldn't quite find the right words. What would Avram say? "You're fine, I promise."

Fabrian blinked. Once, twice, three times in a second. "Oh. I know that," he said plainly.

"Well, then what's the apology for—"

"It—it's what I hurt them over, okay?" He stomped his foot. I almost expected a pouty lip. "It's the fact that if I hadn't forgotten my coin purse none of this would have happened. It's the fact that I could've just told them who I was and ended it. I owed you a better introduction." He shrugged. "I've been meaning to apologize for a while now. Then I saw you in the hallway earlier today. Figured I'd get that out of the way. By the time I realized you were headed for the stables it felt like it was too late to back out. So I followed."

I felt like I was letting him distract me. I wasn't supposed to let him distract me. I had to figure out where his uncle's loyalties were. "Man," I rolled my eyes. "I don't have time for this."

"Listen, I'm trying to apologize—"

I cut him off. "And I'm trying to accept it. That wasn't sarcastic. I mean it."

He didn't actually respond to that. He just stood there, looking at me. I became aware of potential eyes and ears all around me. I needed something new to say, some way out of this, before people started gossiping. We'd already been rolling around on the grass. If anyone saw that. Well. The rumors would certainly be fun to navigate. For now I needed to get out of here, get back to the stables. "Shouldn't you be getting ready for the feast? Are you feeling okay?"

Fabrian looked himself over, hands trailing down a grass stain on his leg. "I'm feeling like I'll probably need a change of clothes. That's all well and good though. I need any excuse to avoid it that I can find."

It struck me that I was talking to The King. Why did he have so many moments alone, unwatched and untracked? Did Anoïse not give him a security detail? Or was he good at avoiding them? "Avoid the coronation? Why? The train of followers isn't doing it for you?" I asked.

"Any time they're sicced on me I try to ditch them. I can't breathe around these people." He produced a cigarette from his breast pocket, went to fit it to his mouth, then realized he was wearing his mask. I saw it shift as he frowned. He tucked it back in his pocket. "Sometimes I need a moment to myself."

I was too young to feel this old. Twenty-three was not the right age to be having *kids these days* sort of thoughts, y'know? But *my* dad would've murdered me if I'd been in such a monumentally important position and ditched the people who were there to make sure I was not murdered. Hell—some of my earlier memories involved my grandfather telling stories about all the whipping boys he tore to pieces to make sure Dad did not do this exact thing.

I realized Fabrian was still looking at me. "Though I guess you're right. I should be heading back. If you don't mind," he said, pointedly.

He shouldered past me on his way inside.

Havilan was gone by the time I got back to the stables. Which left me in something of a sour mood. I'd obtained a few hunches that he might be up to something, but there was nothing he had said that I could use as evidence of anything, which I would need if I was going to have any chance of getting out of Mercy House.

I smothered my frustration. Buried my emotions in an inaccessible place, subterranean-deep.

EIGHTEEN

I joined the revelry.

Or rather, I skirted around it. I'd never quite been good at these gatherings—to the extent that a family gathering is something you can be good at.

The day progressed with field games for the younger children, while distant relatives I had no memory of assured me of their relationship to me, as they clung awkwardly to the safety of beer bottles still dripping with ice water. They all had stories about how they'd met me when they were little, and had some kind of exclamation regarding how much I'd grown.

The day decayed to the gray of an overcast afternoon, as I interloped from group to group and slowly scripted out the same few awkward conversations when they came wearing new faces.

What do you do for a living?

What are you up to now?

Have you been promised to anyone yet? Are you seeing anyone now?

Sometimes there was an embarrassing story or two when they really wanted to spice things up.

Thrilling.

Each island of guests performed a gradual ascent up the hill and into the skeletal mouth of Mercy House's mastodon, preparing to attend the feast hall. Though I swear they moved on a geologic timescale.

I had no reliable way to gather more information on Havilan or The Reachers. Not right away. So I focused on The Blackheaths instead. I asked every group I interloped on if they'd seen them, where they'd been, and had anyone spotted Mercedes Blackheath just yet?

There were the usual rumors about Bullion, and what had happened there. Repetition on what Anoïse had said had happened last night, about how Mercedes had put the city under lockdown and wasn't answering any attempt to contact her.

Rumors varied about Mercedes. There were the usual hyper sexualized rumors. The gossip about who she was sleeping with now, and why.

There was one more pattern I noticed, as I inquired after her. A few of the guests had the same kind of stock response. "Oh, I'd heard Lady Blackheath was busy in Bullion. I hear there was an incident down there. Though I'm not quite sure about the details."

Almost exactly. Like. We're talking nearly word for word, every time. I wasn't sure what it meant, but it felt as if they were—

Oh.

Reciting the same lines.

Huh.

I searched my memory for the names and faces of the people who had said that. Only a select few of our guests had used that pattern. How many? And which family did they belong to? I filed names and faces in my mind's eye.

And when I thought I had a pattern, I went to Desmon with it. He'd been in the middle of entertaining a distant second cousin when I peeled him away.

"The hell are you doing?" He hissed at me. "This better be good." He downed a big mouthful of his champagne. "We have to head into the feast hall in a few minutes. So make it fast."

"I've been talking to The Reachers," I looked around to make sure no one was listening in on me.

"Yeah, they're crawling all over this place. I'd be surprised if you weren't."

"Why did Anoïse invite so many of them?" I asked.

Desmon sheathed his free hand in his pocket. "I told her she should've been stingier with the invites if you must know. But she wanted to cast a broad net. Figured anyone who was on Ed's side would want to avoid this."

"The only way we could *do* anything about someone on Ed's side is if we could prove it," I groused.

"That's what *I* said. But Anoïse was saying if we don't invite the people we suspect, it gets suspicious. And they can claim outrage. Especially if we're wrong. We'd lose key supporters."

I was surprised to find that it made its own kind of sense. "Damned if she does, damned if she doesn't, huh?"

"I guess. Was this all you wanted to talk to me about?"

I remembered why I'd brought him out into the hallway. "What? Oh! No. I've been asking The Reachers about The Blackheaths. And I thought you should know their answers were...interesting."

Desmon nodded along with me. "And you remember what I said about making this fast, yes?"

"Right. Okay. So some of The Reachers, when I asked about The Blackheaths, their answers seemed somewhat... rehearsed? They all used the same language, you know what I mean? But only some of them. And when I tried to figure out who was giving me what information. I think—" I frowned. How to say it? "I don't think we're the only ones with internal tensions in our house, Desmon."

Desmon stared at me without blinking. It set me on edge. "Those are some serious allegations."

"Listen. I think there's a reason Guindolin Reacher isn't here. I think there's a reason some of The Reachers have rehearsed answers to everything in Bullion, and some of them don't. I think there might be a split in loyalty between Havilan and Orianna Reacher. Between the people who want Fabrian to stay on the throne with Anoïse, and the people who want Ed to take the throne with Havilan's daughter."

Desmon rubbed at his eyes. And then his temples. "But we—fuck. We can't do anything without proof, can we? And why would Havilan do all this work for us if he was planning to move against us?"

"Maybe he's trying to play both sides for the time being?" I suggested.

Desmon rolled his eyes. "Makes it difficult to prove we're not just being paranoid, hey?"

"That's exactly the problem."

Desmon finished the last of his champagne in one go. "I wish Dad was here. He'd know what to do."

I bit my lip. I didn't think I would have anything helpful to say, as far as the subject of Dad was concerned. Around the time I was wondering what I *should* say, an alarm of trumpets blasted noise out into the halls.

"Right." Desmon clapped me on the shoulder. "I'll let

Anoïse know what you've noticed. See if there's anything to be done. In the meantime, let's get inside. I don't want to miss dinner."

I fell in line, joined everyone else in the feast hall. Small signs in the center of each table denoted which family was supposed to be clustered around them. I scanned the room for Blackheaths. There was still some hope Mercedes had sent a representative to speak on her behalf.

But when I scanned the crowd. I couldn't find anyone. I wondered if my eyes were glazing over. I had to be missing something, surely.

I spotted Anoïse at a table in the center of the room, entertaining a host of guests. I kept my eyes on her as I walked in. A side effect of the setup for feasts like this meant that guests from other houses were constantly visiting other tables. It was house politics in microcosm, with small courts the other families were streaming in and out of. The spaces between the tables were occupied by cooks and couriers and family representatives ferrying messages between tables.

My mind wheeled with thoughts of potential maneuvers all these representatives and politicians might make. Things that were almost impossibilities seemed more likely due to the fact that I'd thought of them.

I reached Anoïse's table just in time for a servant to step into my path. Anoïse looked up as the servant spun away from me. The woman's tray of drinks tipped through the air, towards someone coming in sideways down an adjacent path, between two seats.

Fabrian.

He realized what was happening an instant too late. I shut my eyes, heard the sound of glass crashing.

When I opened them, he was still spotless. I wasn't sure

how he'd been quick enough to evade them. He didn't even have anything spilled on his shoes.

The servant was stumbling through her apologies. Without a word he took the tray from her hands. She didn't even seem to notice. He said something quietly to her and she hustled off, and he crouched to retrieve the broken bottles. Laid them out on the empty tray.

I bent to help him. "You're looking well," I whispered with my head down. These words were just for him. Unobserved remarks.

He plucked a shattered sliver of brown glass, still dripping, and examined it. For a second I thought he was going to lick it clean. But instead, he just frowned. "A waste," he said, and dumped it on the empty platter.

He bit his lip.

I wanted to do that, too.

"I'm surprised you managed to avoid that," I murmured.

"You really want to get me out of these clothes, don't you Petre?" He grinned. "This is the second time today. I've been thinking about the first time. I owe you an apology."

"Again?" Thoughts of undoing that shirt squirmed into my mind. They were easier things to think about than the uncertainties around me. I considered taking him by that coat, pulling him to me. "I thought you already did that."

"No. That one was trying to distract you. I had to make sure my uncle could finish repairs to his horse."

Ah, shit. I knew there was a reason I'd been able to catch up to him. Fuck. Were they on the same side? That made no sense. Why would they be? I felt a sinking ball of heat inside my guts. "And what is this apology for? How do I know that this one is more sincere? Are you distracting me now?"

He grinned. "Depends. Are you looking to speak with my uncle again?"

"Something like that." I looked around for Havilan. "Is he here yet?"

Fabrian's mouth made a downhill slant. "He's been seated next to Anoïse for the occasion," he said. "I don't have much time before he notices I got up."

I had not been expecting that. I paused in the middle of reaching for the last sliver of glass. He looked...unsettled. His brows came down to a point at the bridge of his nose, wrinkles forming ridges of creased skin.

Fabrian smoothed it all out in an instant, snatched up the last sliver of glass before I could. Then he grabbed my wrist. "I can take you to him. If you want. Just say the word."

"Um..." I swallowed the coming crack in my voice and cleared my throat. "Yes. I'd like that. It would help."

He looked at me. I held that eye contact. "I was hoping you'd say that. For what it's worth I'm sorry your hand got hurt."

"What? No, I hurt this hand last night."

"Someone should really see to that cut on the back of your hand."

"What? Fabrian, I don't have a cut on the back of my—ow!" He knifed the glass straight through the gauze. Mom's bandages soaked up fresh blood. "Fabrian. What the hell?"

"We should really get that looked at." His eyes shifted to the exit. "In fact, I insist."

"Oh." I thought I was beginning to understand a little better now. "But—Havilan's right—"

"Don't point." He helped me to my feet and wrapped his hand around my wrist. "Just trust me."

I did. I trusted him. It might have been stupid, might

have been the dumbest thing I could do. But I did. "Where are we going?" I didn't want to get my hopes up. My sister was about to get a crown on her head, and I figured I was probably supposed to be there for it. And I imagined an oath of fealty would certainly still be expected of me.

Fabrian had to fight against a tide of tightly packed bodies to drag me through the press of pageantry, out the double doors.

The sound of trumpets was muted as we spilled into the courtyard. "Fabrian. What's happening? We're missing the coronation. Your absence will be noted."

"I'm counting on it. Put on your mask."

I did as I was told. God. If anyone caught me with him Anoïse was going to have my head for putting her through all this embarrassment. "Aren't you supposed to get a crown with her?" The crowd had thinned out now that most of them were inside. He led me through a field of yellow grass, shiny and wet with vitreous fluid.

"Oh, I've made certain that is decidedly not the case," Fabrian said. "I told every bureaucrat I could that this day ought to be about *her*. It's her father who died, she's the one who's inherited and who's doing the actual ruling. I wouldn't want to take away from that."

"Right," I said. "So what's the real reason?"

He snickered. "Would you believe me if I told you it was stage fright?"

We walked across black brickwork parallel to the mastodon's femur. I thought I might have an idea where we were going. "Are you taking me to the stone garden?" Why would we go there?

"Might be," he said.

"You're...aware that that's an awful hiding spot, right?"

"Who said anything about hiding?" Fabrian asked.

I wasn't sure I could think of another reason we'd be out here in the middle of the night, while my sister was undergoing the most important ceremony of her life. "They'll send out search parties, you know. Surely this isn't a surprise to you?"

"They won't," Fabrian said, as he dragged me through a cobblestone pathway to the gardens. Discarded beer cans and the shredded remains of the evening's festivities littered the walkway. But the iron gates were open, flanked by black trees with branches crowned in fangs and ivory horns.

The gardens were full of marble and gemstones. Flowers and foliage and statues that came out uneven, spiraling in patterns stone was not supposed to. "How do you know?" I asked.

"My uncle will make sure of it. He'll hold them off. For as long as he can." Fabrian led me past a purple amethyst dianthus, big as a desk, and gray agate trees squeezing out petals of spinel. "He'll want to find me first. Trust me."

We stopped at a fire pit in the center of the garden, where the blaze was low and orange in the ashes.

"Fabrian. Come on. What the hell are we *doing* here?" I asked him, out of breath.

He looked around. As if he were checking to make sure the two of us were alone. As if anyone in this whole skeletal fortress had eyes on anyone who wasn't Anoïse right now. "Is this fire going to make it difficult for you to concentrate?"

"The smoke would drain my attention more than anything else. Why?"

"Fair enough." He looked more than a little panicky. I didn't think I ought to like that as much as I did. He ran his hands through his hair. "Uhhh. Ummm. Fuck. Right. Cool."

He gathered up my coat in his hands. Dragged me towards him. "I hear this is called a chameleon coat. Can it help you hide?"

"That's why they call it that," I said.

"Right. Fantastic. I'm going to take a piss."

"What?"

"Privacy, please—" He spun me around, planted his boot on the small of my back and pushed.

I staggered forward, and the flagstones embraced my chest. The world was ringing. "What the fuck are you—"

"Quiet." I heard his stream going. "Face down, quickly. Uncle's coming!"

There was a lot of angry panic packed into his voice, so I decided not to question it and put my head down. My chameleon coat changed colors. I hoped the darkness hid me.

I heard the distant blare of trumpets and revelry inside. Fuck. I couldn't believe I was missing this. I mean, my God.

I heard Fabrian wink his stream out. The smoke had subsided. He shoved himself back in his trousers as boots started knocking on flagstones, coming closer. "Uncle," he said. "What can I do for y—"

I heard a smack. Fabrian grunted. I heard the scuff of boots on stone and skin on skin. "I should kill you," Havilan Reacher growled. "I should plant this knife between your ribs. You idiot. You had one job."

Fabrian brayed out nervous laughter. "It's harder than you might expect to ditch an entourage. Even when you'd like to."

Another smack. I heard Fabrian stagger and take a few deep breaths. He chuckled.

I tried not to move.

"All you had to do was distract the prince," Havilan

barked. "*Before* he came to question me. You've been telling me for five years you don't want to be King!"

"And I've been telling you for months now that it's better me than Guindolin!"

Havilan smacked him again. Twice. Fabrian took it without a word for some time, and then he sniffed, audibly.

"I didn't mean that as an insult," he said, quietly. "This is hell. I hate it here. You don't want to bring your daughter into this. You don't know what you're doing to her."

So Havilan *was* working with Edgar? Had Anoïse breaking off Edgar's engagement been the catalyst for the civil war we were headed towards? I swear to God. If my fucking instincts had been right this whole time—

"I'm her father. I think I'd understand better than you do."

"How long has it been since Daddy's been around to see her, then?"

Whatever Havilan did next drove the breath from Fabrian. I heard his knees hit the stones and the absence of his breath made me want to stand up and intervene. How was I supposed to just lay here?

Slowly, Fabrian regained his breath, and he used it to laugh. Which turned into a whoop of surprise when Havilan dredged him to his feet.

"You think I haven't *wanted* to see her? How many years have the Mercys kept me here? You think I chose to leave her behind? Do you have the faintest clue what would happen if I left? I thought Orianna raised you better than this, boy. You're smarter than that."

"All I'm saying is you don't *know* her," Fabrian spat. "I'm not saying that's your fault. And don't call me boy. I'm old enough to know what it's like to be kept here for a while. You said it yourself. I never wanted to marry in."

"Then why aren't you working with me? You were supposed to distract the prince."

"I did my best," Fabrian protested. "But I'd rather not see him and his siblings put on pikes. Forgive me if I find myself a bit conflicted."

"Do you really think Guindolin would resort to that when she takes the throne?"

When. The confidence was a bit alarming. Then again, he was one of the best generals in the country.

"It's not Guindolin I'm worried about," Fabrian said.

"You think Edgar would do that to his own siblings?"

"Or worse if he thought he could get away with it. I've no taste for that kind of senselessness."

"I've known Edgar longer than you ever did. I came to court when both of you weren't even teenagers. I've practically raised the boy these last few years. I'm telling you. He doesn't have it in him," Havilan said. "Listen. If you want to still be King, you can say so."

"And then what?" Fabrian sneered. "You and Mom go back to your old unspoken animosity? You go back to your quiet jockeying?"

"You can tell The Queen everything you know, if you prefer." Havilan said it with such confidence, it made me wonder why he hadn't.

If Fabrian knew his uncle's younger branch of the family was allying with my brother to stage a coup, why the hell hadn't he said anything about it? Hell—why was he intervening when I tried to question Havilan? Whose side was he on?

"We've been over this. I don't want you to get killed, Uncle. I'd miss you."

"Spare me," Havilan groaned. "Just pick a side and spare me."

309

"Why is it always about *sides* with you people." Fabrian had to hiss to avoid shouting. "You. Mom. Anoïse. Everyone here always has to figure out what side everyone else is on. Life isn't as easy as a game of factions. I don't want Mom dead. I don't want Guindolin as Queen. But I don't want to see you hanged either. And anything I can do to get you out of court would put you on the receiving end of a noose. So what the fuck am I supposed to do?"

Was that why he'd intervened earlier today? To get me off of Havilan's back? He didn't want me catching on to Havilan Reacher's involvement in Ed's plans, but he also didn't want his uncle to stage a successful coup? He was trying to play every side from the middle.

I was annoyed at the degree to which I could sympathize with that.

Oh, shit—was that why he'd brought me here? Did he expect I was going to relay all this to Anoïse? I wasn't sure how I could do that without getting Havilan Reacher killed.

"I don't want to get more involved than I have to," Fabrian went on. "That doesn't mean I want you to win or stage a coup. Or that I think Mom was right to make me King. This isn't about right and wrong. I don't fucking care who does what. I just don't want anyone to die. And if you can't do that, just leave me out of it." He sniffed. Oh god, was he about to cry?

To my surprise, Havilan didn't say anything for a long while. The only sound was the muted fanfare drawling out from the painted windows in the feast hall. "Ah, kid," he said at last. "Come here."

Fabrian's voice was muted, pressed against his uncle's chest. "I don't know what to tell you people. I don't want you dead. I don't want to be a party to any of this. I don't want any of this."

"You did good enough. And I appreciate your help. You stopped him before he could ask me about The Blackheaths. So I suppose your help wasn't a total wash."

"Fuck you," Fabrian said. There was no venom in it. He just sounded tired.

"You heard he's been asking after them, yes?" Havilan said.

Frustration built in me. I wasn't sure how much longer I could stay quiet. What did he know about The Blackheaths?

"I've heard. It's a shame, really. Everything with Mercedes. I'd like to speak with her at court again, you know."

"There wasn't a lot of *speaking* between the two of you last time you hosted her, from what I hear."

"I mean—" Fabrian shrugged. "We used our mouths."

Fuck. Did Fabrian expect me to just sit tight while they talked about all this, as if I didn't need to know what had happened?

I was sick of it and sick of sitting still. I itched all over and I was tired and I was hungry because I'd missed dinner and now from the sound of things I'd missed Anoïse's coronation, and I'd only seen her once since coming back here, and I couldn't believe that I'd managed to squeeze all of this into however many fucking days it had been.

I leapt to my feet. "What the *fuck* is this about Mercedes Blackheath?"

Fabrian rolled his eyes. "Great. Phenomenal work, Petre. Unbelievable."

"Fabrian," Havilan growled. "What is he doing—"

"I thought I told you to stay put!" Fabrian roared.

"What the fuck did your uncle do to Mercedes Blackheath?" I knew that didn't make sense. I didn't care.

"What was that you said about picking sides?" Havilan growled at Fabrian.

"I keep telling you it's not about that!" Fabrian screamed. "It's not about sides. I need you out of Mercy House before someone kills you!"

"Happy to oblige!" I drew Dad's dagger from my coat.

Havilan ignored that. "How much have you heard?"

"Enough."

"Petre—stop." Fabrian stepped between me and Havilan. "Mercedes isn't fucking dead. Calm down."

Havilan Reacher laughed in my face. "And how will you explain my corpse? Will you tell your sister you *overheard* something? You think that would help your case? Do you think I've survived a court environment this long without learning how to keep a lid on things? You can't hurt me. You can't prove a goddamn thing."

"I'll tell my sister, then. See what she thinks."

Fabrian grabbed my coat. "No," he said. "You won't."

"And why the fuck not?"

"He just got done doing an assignment for Anoïse yesterday. He's served your family loyally for years, as far as any of us can prove. Whereas *you* nearly dragged a secretary through a hallway *twice* now in the four days since you've been back, if half the rumors are true. Think for just a fucking second, Petre. Which of you two will Anoïse believe?"

An empty aperture opened up inside my stomach when I realized Fabrian was right.

I was sick of this. Sick of everything. I put the point of my dagger to Havilan's throat.

Havilan tilted his head to one side. "Are you going to kill me, Petre Mercy?"

Fabrian's fist tightened on my free wrist. "Don't."

"Why shouldn't I? He wants us dead."

"He wants his daughter on the throne."

"Is there a difference?"

"There is to me!" Fabrian shouted.

I took a step forward. Havilan stepped back. Put his hands up. "Come on, kid. You can't even lock me up without jump starting this war. Do you really think you can slit my throat and sue for peace?"

"Then for your safety, Lord Reacher, I should hope this war never comes to fruition."

Havilan laughed. "That's the spirit, Mercy! You're getting the hang of this."

Despite everything, or perhaps because of it, I laughed too.

And then I felt flashlights train on me. Voices shouting that the King was here. "Search party," I said. My stomach dropped. But I kept my dagger level with Havilan's neck.

There were shouts to get the Queen, to bring her here to see what had happened. I couldn't hold back my laughter. The situation was ludicrous, right? That's what you do with ludicrous things, you laugh at them.

Anoïse emerged from the crowd an instant later, wearing a crown of shining metal and glinting jewelry. "Petre," she said, gravely. "Fabrian. Havilan. Would you like to explain what I've walked in on?"

I heard Desmon shout from the back of the crowd. "Let me through, let me *through*." He pushed his way beside Anoïse.

I gave Desmon a lame wave. I still hadn't lowered the dagger. I debated explaining the situation to them. But I had no doubt Havilan could run rhetorical laps around me in front of everyone. Reduce all my fears to a vapid and self-centered paranoia—a need to be the center of attention.

So I decided to wait and see if I couldn't explain things when I got Anoïse alone. To Desmon I said, "It's nice to see you, too."

"What's happening here?" he barked, "What are you three doing?"

Fabrian's whole composure darkened. "Leaving," he said.

"Don't worry about it." I jammed the dagger back into its sheath and put it in my coat.

"There's nothing to worry about, Your Grace," Havilan said. "Your brother has just lost his temper. Nothing I haven't come to expect from him. You know how sensitive he can be. I'm sure he didn't mean anything by it. Isn't that right, Petre?"

"Yeah." I fought the urge to roll my eyes. "Yeah. Nothing by it. For sure."

I spotted Jerim and Teya stopping Fabrian's exit.

All eyes turned to Anoïse. "I'm going to need the three of you to come with me."

CHAPTER

NINETEEN

S unlight had bleached the sky by the time Anoïse was ready to speak with me. She'd left me locked inside her personal chamber for hours.

I did a couple hundred pushups to get my blood going. Keep my mind from going insane. All I could do was replay everything I knew in my head. I practiced building my case. Going over what I would say to her.

She had a servant bring a tray of breakfast when it was time to speak with me.

The servant set it down in front of an abandoned chess board, and Anoïse trailed in after. She was on white's side of the board. And from the look of things, if she'd been playing that side earlier, she had been losing.

She looked exhausted, and I doubted she had slept. Her hair was floating with frizz. She took a bite of her toast. "I've been taking statements all night," she said, mouth full, not looking at me. She downed a mouthful of coffee. I smelled the cinnamon. "I hope you're happy."

I closed my eyes and took a deep breath. I could trace

the outline of the banter to come, along with all the vaguely hidden threats behind her coming words. I didn't want to take the bait. Not here. Not now. Not this early in the morning, laden as I was with drowsy weight.

But my thoughts were clogged, congealed inside my mind. Early morning calculations were slow and ponderous things. So my second guesses only arrived *after* I smirked and said, "Not remotely. How are you?"

"Go fuck yourself." She braced her elbow on the chessboard, fingers sifting through her hair, holding her head up like she was clutching at marionette strings. "Seriously. Go fuck yourself, Petre. What the hell is *wrong* with you?"

"But you *just* got here." I twisted to look at the door, then turned back to her. "Should I leave to go do that, or...?"

Anoïse scowled. "You're not funny."

"I'm hysterical."

"Shut up."

"Should I shut the fuck up or go fuck myself?"

Anoïse glowered at me. "Go fuck yourself," she said, as a smile fussed with the corners of her mouth. "Quietly."

I offered her a tin soldier salute. "Happy to serve."

The circlet on her head seemed suddenly dull. A bathroom sink color, empty and meaningless. It left an indentation in her hair when she freed it from her head. "I got you some food. And coffee. With caramel."

"You shouldn't have."

She rubbed her temples. "I'm well aware."

"Right," I said. "Right." I was surprised. I figured she would've taken the food away after a back and forth like that. I forced myself to eat, to get some food in me before I said anything. But before I could think of how to introduce her to the situation I had found myself in last night, she started resetting the chess board. "Are we playing?" I asked between bites.

"Yeah," she said, eyes down. "I'm curious."

"About what?"

"It's been a while since we played."

I couldn't even remember the last time we did. I was certain we had, but these aren't the sort of things that stick in your mind. You usually don't memorize your last game of chess with your sister if you don't think it will be. Hell, wasn't she in the middle of a game anyway? Why didn't she want to play anymore? And who was she playing against. "Where's Fabrian?"

"Out," she said. "He left in a hurry after I took a statement."

"What did he say?" I asked. "About everything, I mean."

"Why?"

"Only curious," I murmured.

"He's out," she said again. She advanced the pawn, two rows forward.

I wrapped my focus in the feeling of my lungs expanding, and unraveled all the thoughts cluttering my head. There had to be some common ground to walk towards. I mirrored her move on the opposite side of the board. "Fabrian got me out before your coronation started."

"I noticed." Her tone was dry. She didn't seem very amused. "You still owe me an oath of fealty, you understand?"

I knew that, but I was feeling petty. So I ignored her. "He took me to the fire pit. Told me not to move, then he and Havilan started arguing. He's been planning a coup for some time now, I think. He wants his daughter and Edgar on your throne."

Anoïse's face contorted, but she did not take her eyes off

of the board. "Interesting." She moved another pawn. "Neither of them told me that."

I shrugged. "I dunno why they wouldn't."

"Well, it's a very serious allegation. Especially without anyone to back you up. Is this anything you can prove?"

Dammit. "Well..." I trailed off.

"Well?"

Where to start? "You know how Mercedes Blackheath has been quiet for a while?"

Anoïse sent her knight out. She could snatch my pawn up in the next move. Unopposed, that knight would take my king two moves later. The most direct threat. "I remember."

"From what I hear something has happened to her." I took a sip of my coffee and another few bites of my toast. I moved my own knight. "I don't know what—but I want to go to Bullion. Ask around. If that doesn't work I could try Blackheath House. People know me there." Avram, for one. I promised him I'd be back soon. Had I been gone too long? "I think I can get in. I think I can get us a clearer picture on why she's silent."

Anoïse just sighed. "Don't waste my time, Petre. I can't let you do that if you can't prove anything is wrong."

"This would be how I went about proving it." I huffed. "You said it yourself. Fabrian and Havilan won't back me up. But I *know* what Havilan said last night. And part of it involved meddling with The Blackheaths. So if Fabrian won't back me up, maybe Mercedes knows something. But I can't get proof if you won't let me go looking."

She chewed it over. "I'm not sure. You know what happened when I moved against Edgar, right?" She moved a bishop. "Did Desmon tell you he walked out with half our people?"

I advanced my own bishop row. "Listen," I said. "Even if Havilan Reacher *wasn't* involved in something happening to Mercedes, don't you want to know why she's not answering? Why she's got Bullion on lockdown? Does that mean anything to you?"

"Do you think I'm sitting on my ass here?" Anoïse shot back. "Just because I'm not talking to you about it doesn't mean I'm doing nothing. I just want to make sure I have proof of things before I act. And if you're only reaching out to Mercedes so she can help you with The Reachers—"

"I'm plenty worried about her too, thanks."

Anoïse winced. "I just want to make sure you're doing this right. That you're not being hasty in your anxiety to get out of here. I want to make sure you can prove your suspicions about The Reachers. Because what if you're wrong? Then I've got Mercedes Blackheath worried about Havilan, and it's all over nothing."

"But what if I'm right?" I wasn't sure if I could convince her without Fabrian's help. But I saw no way he could help me without guaranteeing his own uncle's execution. "Like —you want proof about The Reachers' treachery?" I had very little. I'll admit. So I had to stretch what little I did know. "Havilan wouldn't bring Guindolin here. Which means he's worried about his daughter becoming a hostage. Right?"

She took my bishop with hers. "The thought had occurred to me. Though it wouldn't explain why he brought so many vassals."

"And he's in charge of The Mercy Guard, right? Ed walked out of here without a scratch on him. And nobody found out until the morning. How does he do that without Havilan pulling some strings?"

"The investigation cleared all the guards on duty at the time," Anoïse insisted. "I saw the reports myself."

"Did Havilan *do* the investigation?"

"It's not like there was no oversight, Petre. The whole thing was above board."

I moved a pawn on the other end of the board. "Well, yesterday in the stables he said he'd ask you about bringing me to his estates, too. Which—why would he do that? What does he stand to gain?"

Anoïse considered that as she stole up my pawn, threatened the knight I'd been landlocked with. I brought him back behind my lines. "You *would* be valuable as a hostage to Edgar," she said. Sipped her coffee. "*If* Ed and Havilan were actually working together. But...I don't know. What makes you so sure that you're right?" She moved her other bishop in line with her pawns.

I put another pawn forward. Freed up space for my adjacent bishop to move. "I'm not sure how many times I can explain it to you. I overheard it last night. Havilan and Fabrian all but told me."

"Why would Fabrian stay quiet about a coup attempt his own damn uncle was orchestrating?"

"The same reason I would want to be left alone after I learned my brother was planning one, I expect."

She didn't respond at first. She seemed to shrivel up a bit. All I got from her was a quiet, "Oh." And I wasn't even sure if she believed me.

"Listen—why else would Mercedes have missed this feast? She's reliably on our side. You know that. I know that. Either she's busy with another emergency and I go down to Bullion or Blackheath House, or wherever she is, and we deal with it there. Or she's being kept out of these affairs due to some external threat. I mean, because otherwise she would have told you *why s*he couldn't make it, right? And has she said anything at all?"

For a moment I worried my concerns were misplaced, that maybe she did have a reason, and Anoïse was just humoring me. "No. You're right. She hasn't said anything. I did think that was strange."

"So," I said, "what do you want to do about this?"

She looked down. Examined her board. Took one of my pawns with her bishop so that she was directly threatening my king on white. "Checkmate."

I looked at the board. "Check."

"No, it's—"

I took her bishop with my knight to demonstrate. I held the bishop up between two fingers then set it on the table. "What do you want to do?" I asked again.

I didn't dare to hope she'd give me leave to check on Mercedes. Though the desire for her to let me was like a physical pressure building beneath my chest. I had to see her again, had to make sure she was okay. And if she was, a few other things wouldn't be the worst idea.

"Let's pretend you're right about this," Anoïse said.

"Right." I wasn't sure if I was imagining my eye twitch. "Pretend."

She didn't catch the sarcasm. Or if she did then she ignored it. "If we don't figure out what's happening with Mercedes then Havilan Reacher's side of the family teams up with Edgar's half of our household, and…what are the odds he gets the throne?"

It was as near an even split as I could imagine. "Closer than I would like," I said.

Anoïse fussed with her pieces but didn't commit to a

move before she spoke. "So. If you're right. We'd need to bring Mercedes here, right? To strategize. Keep her safe from external threats. Make sure they can't get to her?"

"And to do that I'd have to go see her. In person. I can move quietly. You could send a small party with me if you're worried. Maybe there are reasons she's unresponsive that we're not seeing. But we need to make sure she's okay."

"Right," Anoïse said. "Right."

"So you're saying you believe me?" I asked.

"I'm *saying* I've been thinking about what you were telling me the other night about trust," she said. "I'm saying I don't like the way things started off between us last night, with all that arguing. And this is me trying to be a better sister. Trying to start over. Try again. Because believe it or not I don't want to chase you away again."

I bit back the first few responses that leapt to my mouth. "I believe you," I said, as I waited for the *but* to come.

"But this doesn't make much sense to me. I am doing my best to take you seriously. Because I don't think you'd just *lie* about what you overheard. But this doesn't fit in with what I know about Havilan. Especially with the work he put in at Bullion just a few days ago."

"What was he doing there? Am I allowed to ask?"

The question took her a bit off guard. "I—I'm looking for a helmet," she said.

Was that why she was interested in Ed's pursuit of a helmet when I mentioned it last night? "I'll reach out to Mercedes," I said. "I've got some channels at my disposal from when she hired me. I can head to Bullion. See if she's there. Quietly." I took another sip of coffee. Felt the heat of it sliding down into my chest "We don't want to alert anyone."

"And again. Maybe it's nothing."

"Maybe." But I didn't trust that. After all, if it was nothing then why would I be so terrified?

"It's like a wellness check or something. A checkup." She sounded like she was trying to convince herself it was a good idea. "Something like that. Yeah. Just to make sure. To strategize. How are you getting a hold of her?"

"Through Avram Maunders. I can reach out to him. Let him know I'm coming. Maybe we can bring him back here? Make him Mercedes's ambassador or something?"

"Maunders?" Anoïse echoed. "Why the hell do you want that freak back here?"

"Freak? Anoïse, what do you mean? He's a friend."

"A friend? Petre, he was exiled! You know what people say about him. The only reason he's with Mercedes was because he swore a holy fucking oath not to try that shit again."

I squinted. Was she talking about the human experimentation? Those stories had been floating around the capital for ages. "I thought that was a rumor. Wasn't he exiled to punish Mom? That was supposed to be a handy excuse Dad made up. Or something?"

"Well. Punishing Mom was certainly part of it, but—"

"I'd like him here. If you don't mind. I—please. I promised him I'd see him soon."

She breathed out slowly. "I will leave that up to Mercedes's discretion."

"Right." That was fair. And I could make a strong suggestion that she bring him. Which meant we had to move on to other things I needed to take care of. "We should probably do something about Havilan, too."

"What do you recommend?" A note of caution edged in on her voice.

"Putting him in a cell, for one thing."

Anoïse let out a slow breath between her teeth. "That's off the table, I'm afraid."

"What the hell do you mean?" It took genuine effort to keep my voice low. "He can move against us but we can't move against him?"

"Yes. He doesn't need evidence to move against us. I've made too many mistakes rushing to judgment as it is. And that's *if* you're even right about this. You haven't exactly given me concrete evidence."

"What you're doing right now isn't a mistake, Anoïse. It's just flinching."

"Flinching?"

"You're worried because of what happened when you detained Edgar. You're scared to do it here now because of how things went last time. But we can't just leave that man to roam about as he pleases."

"He's one of the best generals in the nation. I'd like him where I can see him, thank you. And I'd like to think he's on my side. Or would you rather our antagonism scare him off? If not put him on the field for Edgar?"

Was that what she was afraid of? Did she think taking action without all the information might scare him away? "I just *said* I'd like him detained. Please try to listen. I know you're dealing with a lot but—"

"More than you'll ever know."

I'm sure that wasn't meant to sting as much as it did. But I guess it was my turn to flinch.

"I'd love him detained, too. If he's done anything wrong. If." God. I hated her hedging. "But throwing him in a cell right now with no evidence that anything is even wrong isn't going to win me allies." She sighed. "Even *if* what you say is true. It isn't exactly a politically advantageous move, you know? I just—I'll get the rest of it taken care of, okay? But I can't help you with the stuff with Havilan. I'll send word to Blackheath House just like you asked. You go check on things. Make sure Mercedes isn't being pressured into doing anything stupid. Or sidelined. Or whatever. I'll get it sorted out. It'll be fine. I'll figure it out."

I wanted to push harder. If I'd had more sleep I think I might've. But I was just fucking. So exhausted. I wanted to be furious about Havilan. That he was so untouchable. But I was too tired for fury.

And if I was tired I couldn't even begin to imagine how Anoïse felt.

I wondered if she had the strength to do this. It was what Dad had always been training her for—to bear the weight of nations on her shoulders. To make all the decisions no one else would.

But was the world so draining when Dad was young? When he was our age? It couldn't have been. That felt impossible, somehow.

I wondered what the difference was between Anoïse and Edgar. Did it truly matter which of the two of them sat on the throne? They were both raised the same way. Could their temperament truly be that different? I sighed. "Would it really be so bad if Edgar ruled?"

Her glower chased my breath back down my throat, but the quiet that came after unnerved me the most. The steady ticking of the clock, and her patience. For a brief moment I dared to hope for contemplation.

"I'm trying real hard not to scream at you right now."

Shit.

"So I need you to know how thin my patience is when I ask you to elaborate on that."

"I—I just. Never mind. It was a thought exercise."

"I don't have time for thought exercises."

"Right. Sorry." I chewed my food. Tried to find a comfortable silence and failed to.

She took advantage of the fact that I had food in my mouth. "If I'm going to agree to let you go, I need a favor."

Panic clenched inside my stomach. I raised my eyebrows.

"I don't want to arouse suspicion. I'll need to make this look official. You know the way Dad used to send Desmon out to conduct political meetings?"

I swallowed. "Where are you going with this?"

"Well—you already know Mercedes. But you've never handled political arrangements. That's Desmon's job. But Desmon would need security on a meeting like this. I'll think of an excuse for him to meet with Mercedes. I've heard that there are more people without access to masks lately. Supply chain issues surrounding everything with Edgar."

"So you're sending me *and* Desmon out to meet her?"

"You two can meet up with her, bring her up to speed. See what she knows." She shrugged. "Hell. After last night's outburst you could probably use the time away from court to cool off, right? I'm sure you've got some people angry at you after you were seen putting a dagger at Havilan's throat."

I chewed over her request. Was it a request? I *did* need some time to cool off. But with Desmon? His company would hardly help me keep cool. "Just me and Desmon?"

"You have a better way to keep all this a secret?"

Fair. "That's a good point. Less chance of word getting

out about any of this if it's just the two of us. Less fanfare. Makes it look a lot more low-key, right?"

"Right. It'll only take a few days."

Just a few days. I would get Mercedes and Anoïse into the same room. They could strategize. Get on the same page. On the same side. And we'd avert a brewing war.

Simple, really. How hard could that be?

PART THREE

CHAPTER

TWENTY

D esmon and I left quietly before sunrise. He had no shortage of curses and insults for me as I all but dragged him out of bed at predawn hours. We packed in a hurry. Med kits. Spare clothes. Some experimental painkillers Mom had been devising with her chemists for some time.

We were out of the capital before the shops had even opened for the day. The fewer people who observed us, the better. I barely had time to bring Desmon up to speed with the situation.

We traveled within sight of the shoreline. The first few days of travel to Bullion would occur parallel to The Bay. Travel would be slower with Desmon, largely because he was not used to this kind of environment.

"Can't believe Anoïse signed me up for this," Desmon grumbled, as we passed through scattered bayside villages.

I wasn't sure what to say to that. The silence between us was underpinned by the subtle sound of churning gears inside our horses. Hooves stamped the uneven asphalt. I tightened my legs around its ribcage, then worried I'd crush it like a tin can.

"Damn things always feel so fragile," Desmon groused, when his first complaint failed to procure a rise from me.

I rolled my eyes. "You don't get used to it, either." These things were held together with a cartilage of gears and spinning gyros that dragged us down the cement veins of the earth.

"If we're on a sensitive diplomatic mission the very least you could do is acquire us a coach." Desmon said.

I blinked at him. "I'm sorry? Were you expecting that the roads to come would be paved?"

Desmon looked down at the asphalt. Then back at me. "*These* are," he insisted. "I thought surely—"

"Not if we're interested in making good time."

A soft whine escaped Desmon. "I hate this. I can't believe you brought me with you. I hate this."

"At least this way we've got a decent view," I said, as we passed dull gray, one-story homes with old vehicle doors inset into front entrances. Some of them relaxed upon support beams of corroded steel. Occasionally I glimpsed an envious eye peeking out from between the bars of plastic blinds.

"The view is fine. It's everyone who can see *me* that I have a problem with."

"Well, yeah. Obviously. I mean, who wants to see that?" I cleared my throat. "No wonder there's nobody out here. You've probably scared everybody off."

Desmon rolled his eyes. "If you're going to insult me you could at least be clever about it."

"Oh, like you're any—"

Before I could finish, someone stirred in a small cabin corroding beside the road. I tugged on my reins until I heard the click from inside the hollow of the horse's throat.

"What's in there?" Desmon asked. "What was that? Is it Gaunts, do you think?" Desmon asked.

"Probably not." I adjusted the way my gun sat in its holster. Loosened things up. Just in case.

The cabin door slid open sideways like a curtain, revealing a young boy in the wide doorway, all alone.

"Is it Gaunt?" Desmon asked out of the side of his mouth. "Can you tell?"

He seemed clean enough. Alert. Attentive. I didn't want Desmon to know there was no real way to tell. Not right away at least.

"Oy!" The boy shouted. "You got any money, highnesses?"

But that sure clinched it.

Desmon rolled his eyes. "Oh, God. Don't make eye contact, Petre."

By the time I registered what Desmon had said I was already swinging down from my horse. I walked up a pathway made of fossils and seashells. I could feel the unseen eyes on me from other houses clustered on either side of the road.

"Petre," Desmon hissed. "Get back here. You said it yourself. We have to make good time."

I ignored him and knelt in front of the kid. "You have a name?"

The kid took a step back. "Lukyas. Sir."

"Well, Lukyas—" I discreetly showed him my coin purse. "You guys have any masks?"

I doubted the boy had ever seen that much money in his life. He was transfixed by my purse. "N-no, sir. We bought one a ways back. But it broke."

"That's a shame. How did that happen?"

He was silent for a while. I think he wondered if I was testing him. He weighed the value of an honest answer. "Roughhousing," he said, quickly. As if he hoped if he said it fast I wouldn't hear him.

I wondered if his parents could afford a new one. "If I give this to you, will you buy more masks?"

The boy nodded.

I held out my pinky. "Promise me."

He didn't seem to understand at first. Then he wrapped his own around mine.

"Good man." I pressed the coin purse into his hands. "Get as many as you can. People will need them. I'm trusting you. Don't make me regret that because I'll be coming back this way."

"I-I won't," the boy croaked.

"Thank you." I made my way back to my horse, jump-started it with a tug on the reins while Desmon glowered at me.

"You know—" he began.

"Don't." I cut him off. "Let's just keep going."

Desmon nodded. "Right."

But he could not bear the silence for too long. "Petre?"

"Desmon?"

"What do you think Dad would say if he could see us now?"

"He'd tell you to stand up straight," I muttered, and was surprised to find he actually obeyed. Like Dad's name still held some sway over him. Like he still sought the approval of a corpse.

Desmon seemed to notice what he'd done. He wrung his hands over the reins and slumped into a relaxed slouch. "And he'd tell *you* to dial things back. As usual."

"That's what Mom would say, thank you," I said.

"It's the one thing they agreed on, actually."

I wondered how Mom felt, being saddled with us longer than Dad. He ruined her life. It was the only thing she ever said about him.

I wondered if that's why she behaved the way she did. Subjected me to her cruelest calculations. All those obscure punishments, the corrective behavioral treatments. All the hot oil and pinching, the needles, all the attempts to keep me in line. Was that her true self, or was that just the outrage coming out?

I wish I had an easy answer. Instead I shelved those thoughts. There was no time to think about it. "I don't get why Anoïse decided to send you with me anyway. I don't need help."

Desmon affected a mock pout. "Come on, Petre. I'm disappointed in you. Do you think I'd play my hand like this so quickly? She has her reasons. I'm as thrilled to be here as you are to have me, but unfortunately I happen to be very good at what I do."

"I'm well aware. You're good at talking politically. I'd hate for you to be obvious about anything. You have to obfuscate. That's all you know how to do."

"Oh, spare me. I know what I'm doing. The last thing I need is lectures on being obvious from *you*."

That stung more than it probably should have, but I tried not to focus on the anger rifling through my stomach. "Whatever you say."

Something in my tone must have betrayed the disquiet in my mind. "Oh, come on. Don't be so sensitive."

"I don't know what you're talking about." A lie, but one I hoped he would let pass without comment. It wasn't a big enough lie to capitalize on.

That's all anything we did came down to. Capital. Not coins or money but *information* and *favors* and supplies for war efforts. Small goods and services, unconnected to economy. We were constantly wringing each other out.

All this came to me in the time it took Desmon to sigh. "You're not making this very fun," he groused. "Give me something better. Something I can work with. Something I can use."

I was getting tired of this. "Why can't we stop treating this shit as a game, do you think? Why not talk to each other directly?"

Desmon just shrugged. Then sighed and stared off into space. "We'd have to take a lot of things seriously if we did that. And how would we live with ourselves then?"

I have to admit, I was not expecting an honest answer. But he really seemed to believe it.

"Fair enough," I said. "Joke away, then."

For once, it did not seem he had anything to say.

WE CROSSED The Rill early in the day and stopped on that first night in a trading village called Salttown. A place with sharkskin walls and slanted buildings with roofs of thatched baleen that leaned into the street on unstable structures. A couple tenements visibly swayed in the wind. The whole town seemed a living, lurching thing. A body of uncertain, packed-in architecture that groaned against the seething wind.

Our entrance was welcomed with the kind of sideways rain that makes hoods useless, and a wet wind that could get its fingers into your coat.

I put my head down, focused all my attention to the

steady up and down carousel-movement of my horse's passage through the road.

"I hate this," Desmon whined, for the eleventh time since we had arrived here. "My hands are cold. I can't open them all the way." He raised his hand to demonstrate. He peeled it open until he'd formed a half-closed claw, and gritted his teeth. "That's as far as it will go, see?"

I didn't have the patience to hold his hand through these discomforts. The wind and rain and cold were only shortening my temper. "I don't know what you want me to do about it."

Desmon shrugged. "Nobody told me it would be this cold."

I sighed. "It's a seaside town, Desmon. What did you expect?" I wanted to hit something. Release some of the pressure building in me. Sensory input was something that had weight, to me. The smell of salt, the wind, the cold. Processing it was like a physical pressure moving around in my belly, or the back of my mind. There's only so much a man can carry, and only for so long.

"Well, *you* look fine." Desmon stuffed his hands into his armpits. Slouched in his saddle. "I thought you must be doing something to—"

"Desmon. Shut up. I've got the same problem. I'm just not complaining about it."

He shifted in his seat. "This isn't working." He took his hands out of his armpits, tugged his mask down and breathed on his fingers.

"Don't do that," I said.

He glared at me. "Why not?"

"The moisture on your breath will only make you colder in the long run. And in a place like this it's risky. There could be ghostfog."

"How would you know?"

I could've told him I knew from experience, but I wasn't sure I wanted to talk about my experiences at the moment. I doubted Desmon would understand much of it anyway. Because while Ed had seen my autism as an experiment, Desmon had only ever seen it as an inconvenience he needed to navigate. So I shrugged. "Dunno. I guess I must've read it somewhere."

Desmon rolled his eyes and went back to breathing on his hands. "Well, I say it helps."

"Whatever you say." I just wanted a few seconds of silence.

Instead, Desmon asked me, "How did you know that boy wasn't Gaunt? The one from earlier?"

It was not the first time he had asked the question, and it was not the first time I'd told him, "I don't know." I hoped he would leave it at that this time. "I just knew."

"Well yes, but *how* is my question."

"There are ways of telling, okay?" I didn't want to spell it out for him. He'd never let me hear the end of it if I gave him the honest answer.

"Next turn up ahead, Petre."

I tugged on the reins, fiddled with the controls on the saddle, and steered my horse down an adjacent street, where the architecture was just as wonky, but now the stink of fish and saltwater was more pervasive.

Desmon wheeled his horse around the turn and rode up beside mine. "I was ambushed by Gaunts, once, you know. That's why I'm asking. It might've helped."

I had not expected the conversation would veer off in this direction. Desmon rarely ever left the safety of a chamber unless it was to travel somewhere else on family business, and even then it only happened under guard.

Even this excursion must have been new to him. "Desmon, what?"

"I didn't tell you?"

I wasn't sure if he was being sarcastic, and I didn't have the energy to guess. "Not that I remember."

"It was about a year after you left. Me and Ed and Anoïse were headed to Reacher House to see if we could iron out some kind of deal with Orianna Reacher. There was a Gaunt woman faking a leg injury on the road there. Ed dismounted to go help and a few others sprang out from the trees."

"Ed tried to help?" I asked.

"I know. Even at the time I told him to let a labcoat handle it. Someone who knows how to set a leg at least. But he said the injured lady would have to be carried somewhere until they could figure out what to do about—"

"No but—was he okay?"

Desmon's mouth quirked down. He was quiet. A minute ago I would've relished that, but now I wanted an answer.

"Did he ever show you the scar on his forearm?"

"He only showed me the one on the back of his hand."

"Well. The one who sprang the trap had a knife. A small one, fortunately. Edgar made quick work of it. He told me afterwards, as the wound was oozing blood, that you could never go into a knife fight without expecting a little scratch. Damn thing was bad enough to give him a red sleeve, and he was trying to laugh it off. He was lucky Anoïse was there to take care of the other ones."

Against my better judgment I asked, "Which arm had the scar?"

Desmon blinked surprise at me. "Hm? Oh. Left."

A ball of heat was sinking through my stomach. The same one I'd removed a few days ago. I wasn't sure what to make of this. Some stubborn, unexamined part of me missed Ed. "Desmon, why are you telling me this?"

Desmon shrugged. "Dunno. They just seem so *real*." He made a tiny gesture with the reins, sped his cyborg horse up just a bit. It ate up the space between the street, and a small stable at the end of the road. Squatting in the space between both street and stable was a two-story tavern with electric red lights that buzzed softly, like that device that kills flies.

"It's easy to forget what's happened to them," Desmon said. "To Gaunts, I mean. Or to not know what happened to them until it's too late."

I followed Desmon into the stables. "They are real. They just...they're not exactly fully...*there*. You know? They've got all the memories of the ghosts infecting them. They're obsessive about it." I thought of the woman from a few days ago. The one who could never get warm. How would I feel if I was stuck like that forever? Always feeling like I was now, in this rain.

Suddenly I didn't want to talk about this anymore. "Do you know where we're staying for the night? Are we close?"

Desmon stared up at the sign glowing on the tavern. "Well, gee. I wonder." He shrugged theatrically. "Anyone's guess, really."

ANOÏSE HAD SET us up with a room for the night. I shouldered my way in first, and Desmon had not even finished bolting the door shut before I sloughed like a semisolid to the floor, in front of the fireplace, and took a deep breath.

"You going to sleep there?" Desmon stepped over me, dropping onto the only bed provided.

"It's warm down here." I had wet clothes to get out of. And a fireplace to nod off in front of. I was accustomed to occasionally spending nights on the road. Desmon needed a featherbed more than I did. I didn't want him tired and cranky on the way out of Salttown tomorrow morning. "I don't have the energy to argue over who gets a mattress. I just want to sleep." I hadn't done so since the night before Anoïse's coronation. That was all I wanted.

And for a while, I think I managed it.

I must have, because by the time the fire had smoldered out and the world was dark, the clamor of iron hooves outside jolted me upright.

The tatters of a dream about Ed's arm still lingered like starspots in the insides of my eyelids, but as the boundaries between dreams and reality began to reassert themselves, it dawned on me that there should be no horses that were not ours. This was not a city with many people who could afford to purchase them.

I used the fireplace as a lever to drag myself up and crossed the creaky steps as quietly as I could. Who the hell was out there at this time of night?

"What are you doing?" Desmon asked.

His voice jolted me. I'd thought he was asleep. "Fuck! Don't scare me like that."

Desmon was a vague shape sitting up somewhere in the dark. "That doesn't answer my question."

"I heard a noise. You hear it?"

Desmon listened. The sound of cyborg hooves was getting louder on the cracked stone pavement below. In the low light, I could see Desmon's eyes go wide. "I hear it."

"Lower your voice." I hissed.

"I hear it..." he said, more quietly, as I trudged past him, to the window. I peeked through the blinds, peered through the shimmershield. I could just barely see riders coming around the corner. I pressed my cheek to the windowpane and strained to get a better look.

"Who is it? Anyone we know?"

That was *possible*. Just not very likely. Though I didn't want to worry Desmon. "I don't know."

"Are you seeing anything out there or not?"

"Shut up. I'm trying to get a good look."

"How does me *talking* prevent you from doing that?"

"Because it's hard to stay focused when I'm thinking about how bad I want to hit you." My anger died when the riders came into view. I got as close as I dared. I couldn't see them clearly in the low light. It looked like they were wearing armor, but I wasn't sure.

"Are they friendly?" Desmon asked. "Can we go greet them? I could use some better company."

"Shut up," I said. "Shut up shut up shut up." I wanted to go back to sleep.

Maybe it was Havilan. Was he fleeing, after everything? No. It couldn't be. That would just make him look guilty. And I trusted Anoïse was at least keeping an eye on him while I was going—plus who would he have left with? Fabrian did not seem like the sort to go willingly. And neither of the figures seemed, in the low light, to have Fabrian's build.

"Is it anyone important?" Desmon asked, as they passed us, trotting down the street. I debated following them. Everything in me burned to catch up. See who they were. Even if they were nobody we knew.

I probably should've, in retrospect. I wish I had a decent excuse. Given everything that could've been avoided if I had. That big of a mistake usually demands a good excuse. One worthy of the size of the blunder.

But I was just...tired. I'd just nabbed my first two hours of sleep in as many days. I told myself there was no way I could've caught up with them. Even if I did go after them. That was a lot of energy to spend on someone who was, in all likelihood, a complete stranger.

So I watched as the two riders vanished down an adjacent street.

"No," I told Desmon. "Nobody important. It's probably fine. I'm sure it's nothing. Let's just get some sleep."

I had more pressing things to worry about. I was just being paranoid. That was it. That had to be it. So I went back to sleep.

TWENTY-ONE

"So," Desmon said, when we hit the road the next morning. He was still scarfing down the breakfast we'd nabbed from the tavern. He ate out of a styrofoam bowl, without utensils. "You never told me how you classify a Gaunt."

He was at this earlier than I'd expected him to be. "That's because I said I'm not doing this with you."

"Right, right..." He drifted off, with the tone that indicated he had no reason to believe I wouldn't tell him eventually, if he kept asking.

He waited just long enough that I dared to hope he would drop the subject before he spoke again. "Those people you saw last night, out the window. Were *they* Gaunt, do you think?"

I wasn't sure what to make of that question. "Of course not."

"Well, but how could you tell?"

My molars pressed together while fingernails made space in the heels of my palms. "Dammit, Desmon."

Desmon raised his hands. He looked like some kind of

mocking effigy of a surrender. "I'm just saying! I'd like to know! I think it would come in handy out here. You were gone a long time. I just want to know what you know."

"I don't fucking know, man! I just—I don't fucking know." He had to have an ulterior motive here. There *had* to be one. There always was.

"What do you *mean* you don't know?"

I'd had enough. "Fuck it. You want to know how you can tell? You really want the answer so bad? You *can't.*"

Desmon blinked at me. "But you just said you'd tell me."

I had to retrace my steps to figure out where I'd gone wrong in telling Desmon. "No, no. I *am* telling you. I'm saying you can't tell. I'm saying there's no surefire way to know. Not on sight at least. There are guesses you can make. Things you can intuit. But there's no surefire way to tell, man. Not until they're already dead and you get to check whether or not they spit a soul out when they die. I don't know what you want me to say. I got nothing, okay? Just stop. Stop asking me. God. Fuck."

"Lord." Desmon ran his hands through his hair. "Alright. Alright. It wasn't a big deal. I was only curious. That's all."

I said nothing. I just wanted to not talk for a little bit.

But Desmon spent the next few hours complaining at me. The saddle was hurting his thighs. There were too many bugs. It was too cold out. This place smells funny. Why hadn't I thought to tell him to pack gloves?

Like it was *my* responsibility.

I'd packed us a battery-brazier, at least. I'd figured that might keep Desmon's complaints at bay when we made a camp that night between two tall plants with blooming petals that were dripping tongues.

The brazier was a big unfoldable campfire cube, the size of a man's stomach. It glowed with blue light and radiated heat. I set it up just to shut him up. We could've gone a couple more miles before we lost the light. But I was sick of him whining.

When it was done, he stretched his hands over the brazier and blinked a few times. "Where's the smoke?" That's what he said to me.

Like—what do you *say* to something like that? "Desmon. It's a battery-brazier. It's electric." That was the best I could come up with.

He stuffed his hands under his armpits and muttered something about how that wouldn't keep the bugs away. "Can't you make any fires?"

"Fire won't be warm enough for you," I said.

He slapped his neck. "It's like they know they're irritating."

I bit down hard on my lower lip. I needed something else to focus on, so I dragged the science-sword out of its scabbard. Debated if it was worth it to get some practice in tonight. "Mhm. Something like that."

Desmon tilted his head, then leaned forward to examine the sword. "Isn't that thing a little, um. Short? For you?"

I blinked. "Desmon. It's a saber model. This is the standard. Why were you asking me this? Is something wrong with it?"

"I just—why do you use it?"

I shrugged. "Mom and Dad said I had to learn to use a sword when we were kids."

"I suppose that makes sense," Desmon said. "It's odd, though."

"What's odd about it?" I laughed.

"It's—it's curved. And the damn hilt looks like a teacup handle."

I nodded. "It's a stirrup guard," I said, "Keeps my hand safe, saves on production costs. It's *economical*. What's wrong with that?"

"But isn't it a woman's weapon?"

I wasn't sure at first how I ought to answer. I couldn't shut him down completely. We were still on the road. I still had to deal with him. I couldn't have Desmon in one of his moods. There was no telling what stupid shit he'd get up to. I don't even know if he meant it. I think he was just trying to get under my skin. But still. What do you *say* to that?

"Is there something wrong with a woman's weapon, Desmon?"

Desmon flushed bright red. "You know what I mean." His voice was clipped, annoyed.

"I'll wear a sundress and a flower crown if that's what I want to do. And unless you want to do the fighting, I suggest you keep your opinions on it to yourself."

"You know what I meant!" he said again.

I rolled my eyes. "Man, you said something stupid. You can just own it. Like—that's an option."

"It's not stupid," he insisted, in a stubborn tone, like he just didn't want to admit it. "It makes sense!"

"Desmon how could that *possibly* make sense?"

"I mean—okay. It's single edged. It's short. The length of a leg. You wield it in one hand. It's an oversized kitchen knife with a pirate's hilt on it, so—"

"No, but literally what does any of that have to do with *women*, Desmon? Walk this one out for me. Take it point by point."

"I'm telling you—" Even he didn't seem to believe it. He just didn't want to admit he was wrong.

"—and I'm listening. Convince me. Let's start with single edged. Curved, even. If you want to onboard that part."

"I mean, women are..." a blush climbed up his face. "Um. Sleeker?" He winced as the word crawled out of his mouth, shut his eyes tight and shook his head. "Nope. That was not the right word. I don't like that. I don't like that at all"

"Sleeker," I nodded. "...Right."

"You know what I meant!" He put his head in his palm as he went redder. "Like—I mean on the whole...like on average...?" He made a few slow and meaningless gesticulations into empty air. "Y'know?"

"You cannot possibly know enough women to average that out. And wouldn't women want to wield a longer weapon? Since they're usually shorter? Better reach, y'know?"

"How do you know what the average height is," Desmon echoed. "You can't possibly—"

"No, but that's different," I said.

"Is it?"

"You can track height. You can't track *sleek*."

"You know what I meant!"

"But—" I wanted to keep things going. The outrage was giving me an easy foothold to better faculties. I could focus on anger instead of exhaustion.

But before I could mount a proper protest, I smelled something acrid on the air. It was intense enough to shred my concentration. "Do you smell smoke?"

Desmon looked around and sniffed the air. "Oh, Lord. Petre—*look*." He pointed out across the shoreline.

I whirled and spotted a dull orange glow. It was getting brighter as I watched. The skyline gave birth to a worm's trail of fire slowly writhing across the edge of the world. The blaze hemorrhaged shapeless clouds of firefly-embers. Refractions of the flames bathed in gloomy pools of infected seawater, far off.

"Where are we?" I asked. "In relation to—like—the rest of the world, I mean?" I wanted to ask where that fire was. I wanted to know what was burning. I just couldn't fit the right words into noise.

"I don't have a clue," Desmon said.

Was something blazing on an outlying island some-where? Had some factory caught fire? Or blown up? That wasn't unheard of. But I had no idea if we were looking at the islands or the mainland. It was too dark to tell. For all I knew we were looking across the other side of The Bay.

"Is that on our way, do you think?" Demson asked. "Will we have to ride through that to get to Bullion?"

"We, um. We should get a move on," I said. "I—I'll bet someone on the road ahead can tell us what's going on. They'll be able to tell us what that is."

Desmon turned to balk at me. "Are you crazy? Get a move on?"

I paused halfway through strapping my swordbelt on. "Did you have a better idea?"

Desmon straightened, and lifted his chin. "We should go back to Anoïse. Let her know what's happened here. Warn her—"

"Of what?" I snapped. I didn't like the way he flinched. "Even we don't know what we're looking at. We just know it's a fire! We at least need to scope out the area first." I wasn't going to leave. I had to get to Mercedes. I had to make sure she was okay. I was the reason she was in this situation in the first place. I brought Ed to Bullion.

"You want to go *towards* the inferno?"

"Y*es!* We ought to at least report back with some information, Desmon!"

Desmon tore away from me, made for the horses. "Well. *I'm* leaving. We need to make sure Anoïse knows. And when we send someone to investigate what's happening here, we'll need to make sure we have a team of people equipped to deal with whatever the problem is."

"You can head back if you want," I said. "But I'm not going." I made for my own horse. This was ridiculous. I told Anoïse I was going to bring back Mercedes Blackheath, and that's what I was going to do. I swung up into the saddle. "I'm heading out for more information. The only way I'm going back is *after* we find out what's going on with Mercedes Blackheath. If you want to go back on your own, be my guest. I'm finishing what we started when we set out."

Desmon just looked at me for a very long time. A muscle in his jaw twitched.

"We don't have all night, Desmon. Are you coming with me or going back alone to Anoïse? Make a choice. What's it going to be?"

TWENTY-TWO

W e came upon a cabin the next day, in the late afternoon.

It came after a full night *and* a full morning of stewing in a seething silence. Desmon said as few words as possible to me before we got there. He spent the whole time looking like he was about to cry.

The only other time we spoke before we reached the cabin was when we rode through an especially dense patch of ghostfog.

"More than usual, this morning," Desmon had said, as he sulked in his saddle.

"Whatever happened last night probably killed a few people. Would've made a ton of ghosts. There will be a lot of newly infected Gaunts in the coming days. It happens during any mass casualty event. We'll be fine as long as we keep our masks on."

"Right," Desmon said through a clenched jaw. "Terrific. Can do."

We moved through the ghostfog as the almost-shapes

of lives long lost failed to finish forming. White smoke-souls made the world a vague haze.

"Do you think that ghosts can sense you?" Desmon had asked, a short time later.

"How would they do that? They don't have bodies."

"*Differently,*" Desmon said. "I don't know. I asked you."

I shrugged. "I dunno. I doubt there's a purpose to what they do. They're no more alive than regular fog." Ghosts were no threat. Not to me. I couldn't be contaminated. I could not suck down a lungful of these undigested memories clogging the road. Not with my mask on.

Not unless they found a body.

Speaking of which.

The cabin.

It was two stories tall and looked like it had room for a family of six or seven. It was shoddily made, a stripped-paint carcass made of thatched baleen and wood that had decomposed to the color of rotten teeth. It hugged the shore and sported a backyard of beached seashells that had been crushed down to a fine white sand. The waves eating up the shoreline made it look strangely placid.

"What do you think?" Desmon asked. "Anyone home who knows what's going on?"

"Dunno," I said. "It looks abandoned."

Desmon craned his neck. "There's a light on. Up there on the second floor."

"There sure is," I chuckled. "No sign of sound or movement though. So who knows."

Desmon fidgeted with the reins of his horse. "Hm. What do we do?"

I tugged on my own reins. Heard the clanking sound of guts and gears rearranging themselves.

"Are we going in?" Desmon brought his own horse to a dead halt.

"*We* aren't doing anything," I said. "You are staying here. I'm going to check things out in there. Maybe there's someone here who can tell us what that fire was about." I made for the house without waiting for a reply.

I'd only just begun to ascend the front steps when Desmon called my name. He said it so softly I'd thought it was the wind at first.

"What's up?" I called back to him.

"Don't wait too long, okay? It's getting dark."

"I won't," I said. Though I gave it maybe two minutes before he decided to slink off and try to explore the place himself. I would need to make a circuit of this place quickly before he found himself some trouble.

I felt a pang of sympathy for Desmon. It had to be hard out here with no assurances for your own safety. I'd had time to adjust to that uncertainty over the last few years. I doubted anyone had ever given him that luxury.

He deserved it—deserved to push himself I mean. To get out into the world and test his limits. To experience uncertainty and learn how to navigate it.

I was sure he would learn it by the time this conflict with Edgar was over. But for now there was very little he could do to help right now. If there was a fight, he would weigh me down. Get in the way—and I didn't want Desmon getting hurt.

"I'll come get you when I know it's safe," I said. "Stay here for now, and don't move." I climbed up the three steps to the entrance and threw the door wide. I stepped through, one hand on my gun.

I was immediately struck by a sick miasma of recent decay. It hit me before I even realized what I'd stepped into.

353

This room was a kitchen, and there was something dead in here.

I kicked the door shut with my heel. Didn't want Desmon to figure out what had happened here. I had to close him off to this before the putrid smell of this place completely voided my ability to think straight.

Something or someone had died in here.

My heart made iambic clamors as it squirmed into the hollow of my throat. It thrummed in every hinge and joint I owned. In the sides of my neck. In my fingertips. My wrists. Like my own blood was searching for an exit strategy.

The kitchen was only slightly less cramped than a coffin. I eased my way across the chess-colored tiles. I saw the first body at the threshold to a living room. A corpse slumped in the doorway. Fingers half closed, body turned green.

I lifted my gun from its holster as I neared the living room. The weapon gave a dull hiss as it scraped free of the holster that contained it. I wanted to be prepared. Just in case.

The corpse looked like a woman. I wondered why she died. Who killed her? Or maybe she was Gaunt?

That'd be lucky. Maybe they'd all turned on each other already. Gaunts worked together out of necessity, but it was difficult for them to care about anything other than the life that shared a residence in their body. That made it difficult to plan anything into the long-term.

I stepped over the corpse and into the living room. The white carpet on the floor absorbed all noise. The room was decently sized. I had space to maneuver.

I spotted a small dining room to my right housing a collapsed table. It was folded in half, its tablecloth askew. The mess was littered in a confetti of broken glass plates.

I didn't have time to think on it too much. Even a cursory glance redirected my attention to the backyard. I could see it through the sliding glass door—and what a sight it was. Nausea made itself at home inside my stomach.

A corpse, face down. Pitchfork skewered through what could generously be called his head. His coat stirred in a breeze like a trampled flag. Near him languished something that was probably once human. It was slumped, face first, ass up, in what used to be a campfire. Both face and fire had long since withered to cold ashes and vague shapes. My lunch squirmed through my stomach. It wanted out, but I was going to need it.

I wondered if they'd been cooking food. If there were more Gaunts than usual on these roads, the smell of it could have brought them in numbers. And any of them could still be around for all I knew.

I squeezed the grip of my gun and cycled through what I knew about it, if only to keep the other thoughts from surfacing. Caterwauler. Type IV. Handheld. Leather grip. Vocal cord battery. Fully charged. One shot. Caterwauler. Handheld. Leather grip. Vocal cord battery. Fully charged. One shot. Caterwauler. Type IV.....

To my left, the stairs squealed. I whirled towards the noise, lugging the iron barrel in line with the target who approached.

Then I saw who it was, and I lowered my weapon an inch.

She was a girl. Thirteen years old at *most*. Mired in filth. There was something heavy and burdensome in her hair. Sludgy and dark like shit or decayed organs. I wondered if she noticed. Had she gone Gaunt?

"What happened here?" I whispered.

She looked to the backyard, and then stared back at me. "They couldn't make me stop burning," she said, flatly. "Can you make me stop burning? It hurts. Please."

She was Gaunt alright. Probably newly made, infected from some ghost in last night's fire. I figured it was better to put her out of her misery, so I squeezed the trigger.

My gun screamed. A jet of angry sound roared from the barrel. The vocal cords in the hollow grip vibrated. Even my hand was buzzing. The sonic shot shimmered through the space between us and slammed through the girl's chest, painting the wall behind her in red mist.

I winced at the impact as my mind conjured up a sympathetic pain. I gave weight and texture to the intrusive thoughts making themselves at home in my stomach, unwillingly. A dull ache sat in the center. The imagined hurt from such a blast. How would my chest feel shuddering apart?

I shelved the sympathy as best I could.

It took three tries to holster the gun. My hand was still all impact-numb from the blast. But it needed to recharge. I fitted the barrel to the prong that was waiting at the bottom of the holster and thumbed the switch on the outside to juice it up. It'd be a few more minutes before I could use it again.

Then I realized how much sound that scream had made, and I wondered if that girl was the only one here.

The sound of boots above alerted me. Two pairs. Coming closer. I backed into the kitchen, hoping I could hold my ground. Maybe the threshold would create a bottleneck.

I saw a spear before its wielder came into view, and I realized this was going to be trickier than I'd anticipated. So instead of bracing for a fight, I slid behind the entrance to the kitchen.

I waited.

The spearman kicked the girl's corpse, and she spun down the staircase. The spearman grunted. "Fucking kids," he muttered, coming down the steps. "What killed her?"

"Does it matter?" A deep voice rumbled.

"Suppose not," the spearman said. "Helps to be prepared, though."

"Don't tell me what to do." There was an edge of ire to that low voice.

I heard them coming closer. I wished I could've taken off my mask.

Before I had time to think, I heard another scream. Outside, this time. In the backyard. "The hell is this? What's going on? Petre!"

Fuck. It was Desmon's voice.

"Over there," one of the Gaunts barked.

"Petre! What's going on here! Petre? Where are you? I don't—"

I heard the sliding door open. Desmon went silent.

I sprang forward while their backs were turned. I had to kill the spearman first. I juiced up the science-sword as I lunged, turned my wrist to bring the weight of the saber to bear.

He turned right before the heated blade slammed home, and I realized he was an old man. Frail and gray. Took almost nothing to slice through him. An ounce of pressure. Gravity did most of the work, tearing into him, burning through him in a wash of blood and black vapor. He was down by the time his companion had just started turning around. It was only as I turned my attention to him that I realized just how massive this man was.

He was taller than me. Had to finish him quickly. Wasn't sure I had enough room with the sword, so I reached up and slammed his head into the glass door. Reduced the glass to a web of ice-white knives, just barely held together.

He went down, and I stepped through to face Desmon.

"Lord alive! Desmon! What are you doing here? I told you to wait!"

"I—" Desmon fumbled for the right words. Any words, I expect. His eyes ticked between me and the bodies. "I heard a noise—" Desmon said. "I thought—"

"Desmon you have to get out of here. I—"

"Behind you!"

I whirled in time to see the big man rise. I was stupid. Too worried about Desmon to remember to finish this asshole off. Now he'd rallied. Stupid. Stupid.

His nose was a mess of pulp and rearranged bone, drooling worms of blood through askew nostrils. He took a wet breath through them as he slammed the print of his sneaker into my stomach. Knocked the wind out of me as I stumbled backwards.

I felt the half-cracked windowpane shards wrap themselves around my spine, slicing into me as I fell through.

My back slammed against granite steps. Hard. I hadn't even realized there *were* steps in the goddamn backyard. Angry red pain sent me onto my stomach. I had dropped my sword. I wasn't quite sure when. Damn gun was still charging too. My hands were too empty. I couldn't move. Couldn't breathe. Couldn't think. Too many pains. Too many sounds. Too many smells and calculations yet to come. Too much warm stinging my back. Wet, too. There were red tears weeping. Shards of glass were housed between my shoulder blades. Not sure how many, but I could feel the slivers. Like tiny knives of angry glitter in my back.

I sat up, palms braced on the seashell shore as I scrambled back on all fours, away from the big man's advance.

"Petre!" Desmon shouted.

"No talking!" I shouted back. I felt a vein standing out on my neck.

The big guy had an axe. Did he have that earlier? He'd been facing away from me. I hadn't had a chance to take stock of him. Maybe he'd had it the whole time.

He led with his sneaker first. Probably wanted to flatten me out. Get me on my back.

When his shoe came down, I caught the sole and ankle in my hands. I yanked down, hard. Thought that would bring him down to my level. But I only succeeded in prizing the damn sneaker from his foot. I tossed it at his ruined nose, but he swatted it aside.

That was okay. I only needed it to occupy his attention long enough to climb to my feet. Get some distance. Figure out what I was going to do next.

From there it only took two steps to close the space between us. But he blocked my advance with the side swipe of his axe. I jumped back, out of reach of the crescent moon blade as a surprised breath sliced from my throat. I'd had to buck my hips back just to avoid it.

I ducked beneath the backhand follow up blow—then realized my mistake as the axe sailed past me and I felt the worms of his huge fingers crawling through the roots of my hair. My scalp felt tight. I fumbled with his hands. Raked white lines of dead skin down the backs of his knuckles. But the asshole wouldn't let go.

I saw his knee headed for my face and braced for impact.

Everything went white, then the world slowly bled back into my perception, though star spots still cannibalized my vision. I was dizzy. My eyes had developed a pulse, a heartbeat. The world swam and thrummed around me. Did I taste blood? I wasn't sure.

Well. He clearly had no interest in letting me up any time soon. So I had to bring him down to my level.

I sprang forward, with his hand still in my hair. I dug my fingers into the backs of his thighs. Pressed my ear sideways against his hip. It startled him enough to shake his grip. It gave me room to drag his thighs up, twist him sideways, bring him down.

He grunted as his back slammed against the beach. I pressed my knee into his stomach as I came down on top of him.

He was trying to climb up, arms reaching for my wrists. So I put my hands on his chest. Threw all my weight there, planted him back down. I ignored the ribbons of pain spiraling out from between my shoulder blades and set to work.

He was still flailing as I hemmed him in with my legs. I dug my knees up under his armpits and fed him my fists. Felt his teeth break under my knuckles, and my knuckles split open on broken teeth. I heard him gurgle on his blood and my blood and his own damn teeth and I kept hitting him until he stopped trying to buck me off.

What was left of his mouth had chewed through my fingers. The cuts stung. Blood welled more than it really had any right to. They were just fingers. Why did they have to bleed so much? My right hand was far worse off. That pinky was completely sideways, though a few on each hand had twisted to odd angles.

People talk about violence, sometimes, and the way they talk about it—it's with this utter ignorance. They use a tone that hollows out the word. They don't get it, you know?

You hear it a lot from people who haven't been in a fight before. Who are only vaguely aware of everything that goes into this. All the blood and pain packed into violence. The burst bellies and sideways fingers. The opened, weeping lips, the taste of coarse air, thick as steel wool.

They don't get it.

They don't know what it's like. Getting so wrapped up in what you're doing and just having to be *sure* the other guy is down that you don't realize he isn't breathing anymore and you can stop hitting him but you're doing it anyway because you just have to be *sure*. You've got to have that certainty. To know that when it's time to stand you're the only one getting back up.

By the time I realized it was okay to stop punching him, I had become a vessel for pain. Heat and angry wounds lit up my body. I braced my hands on the corpse's chest and turned to the side to puke, an acid slurry that burned on its way out of my throat.

"You okay?" It was Desmon's voice. He sounded very far away.

I didn't answer him. I felt like I was going to puke again. My throat felt full. He seemed to notice, because his closed fist came down on my back, and the rest of the vomit found its way out. I was heaving. Sweaty. Bleeding. He hit me one more time. I didn't even know I had more to expel, but it crawled out without permission anyway.

The glowing-hot end of my science-sword dipped into my view while I was catching my breath. I traced the length of the blade up to where Desmon pinched the grip as though it were a pencil. "You, um. Did you need this?"

By some miracle I managed to get to my knees. "Might need some help putting it away," I showed him my hands. They were still vibrating with adrenaline. "They're not cooperating."

Desmon paled. "Good Lord, Petre. What did you do?"

"Don't ask. Just put the sword away, Desmon."

He had to crouch to grab the scabbard on my hip. His brows came down with concentration as he lined it up and doused the blade when he slammed it home.

"You could've helped. Back there, I mean. Thank you for putting the sword away." I was not sure that had come out in the right order. Adrenaline still made pain into an abstract mess, but I wasn't sure how much longer that was going to last. I wasn't sure if I ought to try moving yet.

"You asked me not to," Desmon said, quietly.

"I asked you not to *talk*," That wasn't true, but I was too angry to admit that I was wrong right now.

"I didn't want to get in your way."

"So you hit him from *behind.* Or from a distance. Hell. There's a pitchfork right there!"

Desmon flinched. His jaw was a tight line, barely moving. He spoke like he owed an apology to the ground. "It—" He grabbed the sides of his head. "It was in a *skull.*"

"YEAH AND I'M SURE HE'D REALLY MISS IT!" I shouted.

Desmon blinked very quickly. "Well," he scoffed. "I'm sorry we don't all know how to react as perfectly as you do."

"I didn't need perfect. I needed *anything*." I wondered

if I was being unfair to Desmon. But my irritation was as easy to access as my pain. One fed into the other. Was I still shaking? Why couldn't I stop shaking? Adrenaline? Still?

"Can you stand, at least?"

"Let me try." I managed to get to one knee, put one foot under me, and the world reeled around my skull. I felt glass shifting, lodged in my back. I fought down a wave of nausea that made the world hazy.

"Nope," I squawked, and the vertigo pitched me to the ground. I was eye to eye with my reflection in the big man's axe. I realized abruptly that it looked like military hardware.

Where the hell did he get *that?*

I tried to move, but my hand wasn't working with me. Fresh flows of blood were dripping over the dry, brown layer that had congealed to my skin. "Desmon. Man. I think you've got to make a splint."

Desmon laughed nervously and dragged his fingers through his hair. "Right." He paced to the shore. I wondered where he was going. There were no materials to make a splint out on the water.

I think my mind went away for a bit. It had been swallowed up in just managing my injuries without passing out. I only came back to myself when I saw Desmon's boots in front of me. "Can I help you?" I asked.

He crouched. "So, um. You said make a splint."

"Yes."

"How do I do that?"

If I could've got my fingers to work I would've strangled him right then and then, I swear to God. Somehow I managed to get to my knees. Lances of pain sprawled out from impact sites all up my back. I looked up at him, though just doing that sent flares of pain flagging through my body.

Desmon caught me by the collar. "Stay with me," he said, quietly. "Come on. Don't pass out on me. I need your help."

You know the kind of pain that makes it hard to think? That just crowds your mind with *noise* and makes it hard to sort out how to communicate properly? That was the kind of mental tangle I had to negotiate just to squeeze out the word. "Pitchfork," with a vague, limp gesture to the corpse.

His mouth made an instinctive disgusted smear that shifted his mask. "A-are you sure—?"

"Pitchfork!" I said it again, more forcefully.

"Okay, okay! God." I watched him approach the corpse hesitantly. Like it was some feral animal on its back haunches, snarling at him. He greeted it with his hands framing his hips, palms up, braced for anything.

I'm not sure how long it was before he actually gripped it.

Desmon gave it an experimental tug, then let go when the corpse shifted. I heard a startled scream, then he turned to me. "Petre? What do I do?"

"You pull!" I shouted back.

"But!"

"*Now!*"

"Oh. *Oh.* I hate this. I hate this. I hate this." He put his boot on the dead man's skull and winced as he pried it free, screaming like it was his skull that felt it.

He lowered the point as quickly as he could and examined it in an outstretched arm. "Okay. That was easy." He brought it to me. "Okay. What now?"

"There's a knife in my outer coat pocket. It's Dad's. We don't have time to discuss how I have it. Just take it out and cut the pitchfork into planks of wood. I need a brace for my fingers."

I felt his hand in my pocket. He got the blades spinning faster than I thought he would. I wondered if he'd ever used that knife before.

"Wait," Desmon said. "Your back."

"What about it?"

"That's a lot of fucking glass, Petre." Without warning, he was straddling me. "I'm going to try to get the biggest pieces out."

"Don't cut yourself."

"I won't. I'm going to talk to you while I do it, though."

"Why are you—" He ripped the first one free without a thought to how much it would hurt sliding out. "Fuck!" I screamed.

"Stay calm."

"No problem," I groaned.

"Just so you know," he said, as he peeled another piece free from my skin. "There was someone else here."

"Several someones," I groused. "Including the someone with a fucking pitchfork through their skull. A pitchfork that you couldn't be bothered to use to—" I felt a splinter of glass sliding free between my shoulder blades and a burning white sting under my skin as it moved.

"No, not that. I mean—someone got away."

"Desmon, what—?" I twisted, and the shards of glass made their reminders in pain and heat. "What are you talking about?"

"As I was coming around the side of the cabin, I found a scrap of linen," he explained. Each time he pried the glass free, burning pain lived in the empty space he'd left behind. "Polka dotted. One edge had these flaky lines of unspooled string."

I wondered if Dad had taught him to recite that kind of detail. He often asked Desmon for incident reports. Desmon was good at making connections. Buttering people up. He was the most polite, well-mannered out of the four of us. The most unobtrusive. He could pry secrets out of you with a wink and a smile.

"There's a small skeletal whalebone lifeboat around the corner, too. You didn't see it. But it's scorched."

"How do you know what a recently beached whalebone lifeboat looks like?"

Desmon rolled his eyes. "The iron around the skeleton isn't rusty yet. And the heart inside the engine is still pumping."

Asked and answered, I suppose.

"So," Desmon said, "let's assume I know what I'm talking about, shall we? Dad sent me down to The Bay to deal with The Reachers enough times to know what recently beached lifeboats look like. The dirt on the bow hasn't even had time to dry. Whoever left it here landed recently."

"How recent are we talking?"

"Probably sometime last night."

I frowned. That meant if there was a survivor, they would've had almost a full day to run by the time we *got* to this goddamn cabin. They could be anywhere by now.

"There were tracks, too," Desmon added. "Around the corner." He pried another bloody sliver out of me.

I wondered if the boat and the survivor were related. Desmon had drawn the connection, but it seemed arbitrary. For all we knew, whoever had showed up in this ship was one of the corpses currently littering this yard. Then again, nobody here was wearing polka dots. Nobody I could see, at least. Though maybe they were busy rotting on the second floor.

"Okay," he said. "I think that's the big pieces. I'm gonna cut up that pitchfork. Make a few planks of wood. Just like you said."

He said nothing this time. Left me to deal with my pain. I wasn't sure how long it took before he had it ready. "We're going to start with the worst finger." He pointed to my sideways pinky. "Okay. Okay. Okay. Brace yourself."

I learned in that moment sometimes pain has a heartbeat. And it beats far faster than your own ever could. Pumped right up my forearm, and into my shoulder. It took me another moment to even register that I had puked again. I didn't even realize until Desmon retrieved a pristine pocket square to wipe my face. He wrapped up that finger with the one next to it, sandwiched a brace between two planks of wood and tied it off.

My shirt was soaked in blood and vomit that was drying to a crust on my skin and my clothes. It made my skin feel taut. God. Fuck. That was going to drive me crazy.

The world was hazy around me. Distant. Inaccessible. "Desmon. I think I'm struggling to stay conscious."

"Well," he said, "at least then you won't feel anything." He straightened out my middle finger, and the pain dunked my awareness into inky black.

I CAME to in the shelter of trees that were made of mammoth tusks, atop a bed of yellow leaves. I could see the cabin through a lace of branches. We were right next to the house, and my fingers were all splinted.

Desmon was slumped against a tree, looking at me.

"Oh, thank God you're alive. Are you awake now? I need help."

"What happened?" I asked.

He shrugged. "You passed out."

"Anything interesting happen while I was out?" I asked. "Why are we hiding here?"

Desmon leaned forward conspiratorially. "Okay. So I need you to know. There was someone here. While you were out."

It dawned on me that we were whispering. "Why are you being so quiet?" I asked.

He made a few irritated gesticulations at the volume of my voice. "There—are—more—*Gaunts*," he said, slowly.

Fuck. "In the house?"

"No. They came after. I...I think the commotion brought them here. Either that or your screaming.

"You're not about to pin this one on me," I said.

He glared at me. "*I* wanted to go back."

I was too tired to find a way to refute that one. Maybe I couldn't. "Did you happen to come up with a plan while I was out?"

"I'm honored you think I know what I'm doing here."

"Right." We were going to die. Fuck. We were going to die in a hovel in the middle of nowhere. "Show me."

He nodded once and led me around to the side of the house, where the narrow path was filled with scrub and foliage. The dirt and macadam road on the other side of the cabin corroded into dust and clumsy patches of yellow grass as big as crowns.

The boat was languishing to the side of that path. It was a withered thing, made of fossils and old iron, beached near the trees he'd hid us in. Black claws of char raked down the hull. It was wearing scabs of wet dirt and seashell fragments.

Desmon took me through all of his observations as he helped me around the house. A footprint made of blood—the sole of a bare foot, stamped around a half-submerged stone. Vague impressions of toes pressed into the dry earth. Trampled patches of grass. "We know they got as far as the road," Desmon said. "It's harder to see any tracks in the macadam. So unless there's a corpse a little way ahead, we have a survivor on our—"

Our horses came into view, and I saw two Gaunts huddled around mine, their backs to me. A boy and a girl, with hair as cherry black as a raven's eyes. They had turned the cyborg machine into a mess of meat and scrap metal. Stranger still—they were not just tearing it apart. They were actively, methodically, disassembling the armor. Which was odd, to say the least.

There was another figure overseeing them who was shrouded all in burnished armor. He wore a pot of steel shaped with a visor as dark and opaque as a one-way mirror, and the gas mask was pricier than any layman could afford.

"Right," Desmon whispered. "So. Do most Gaunts know how to take apart a horse like that?"

"Absolutely not."

"Then how have they managed it?"

"Beats me."

"The guy in the helmet said something about experiments earlier," Desmon added. That was *that* question answered. "Apparently he's been picking up Gaunts as he travels. What do we do?"

I frowned. How many options did we even have to make a getaway? "You see the gun in my holster?" I asked.

"Hard to miss."

"Take it out."

"You trust me to shoot them?"

"Do you have a better idea?"

Desmon leaned forward and pried my gun out. "It's heavy. How do I—"

"*Point* first. Then dial the hammer back. Till the whine is at its highest pitch." That was the highest setting. It was enough to kill most people.

"Where am I pointing?" He asked.

I did the math as best I could. "Try the guy in the helmet."

"Will it get through all that armor?"

"Worth a try."

"*Is* it?"

"Do we have time to debate this? Just go for it."

Desmon scowled. Hauled the heavy iron handgun up in both hands. Squinted. Dialed back the hammer just like I said and fired.

The shot shimmered in the air, like a humid summer heat. It slammed into the armored man as he was turning. The breastplate turned concave, and he collapsed.

Immediately, the Gaunts he'd brought with him turned on each other. The girl who had been taking apart my horse pounced on top of the boy.

Desmon dragged me out of the chaos and confusion. Fuck. Did they all have the Violent Dead in them? How can you have the Violent Dead in you and still be patient enough to disassemble a horse? What the fuck? How the fuck?

Desmon dragged me to his horse. I felt his arms squeeze my thighs together, and he lifted me up.

"Shit," I said. "You're stronger than you look."

"You've lost a lot of blood," he said. "Maybe you've lost weight."

I couldn't bend my hands with the splints. And it still hurt to move with all the small splinters of glass still in my back. Everything ached, and it took all I had in me just to figure out how to wriggle on top of the horse.

As soon as I did, the world started reeling. "Desmon. I'm gonna fall off."

"Hold on." He swung up behind me and took the reins. His forearms pinned me in place.

I heard the clink of metal moving as the horse churned to life. When I turned to check, I realized that the man in all the armor was getting up. The black visor flashed orange for a moment, the Gaunts around us snapped to attention.

I remembered that Ed and Anoïse had been looking for helmets, and my bowels turned to slurry.

The Gaunts were closing in on us. I couldn't summon up the energy to turn around and see how many were behind us.

Desmon did.

"Shit," he said, between clenched teeth. "Shit shit shit." Desmon hurried with the horse's reins. "Shitshitshit-shitshit."

"Desmon. What the fuck is going on?"

"Don't worry about it." The world started sliding by me. The wind was in my face. Drying out my eyes. Everything smelled like blood and vomit. I bounced uselessly in the saddle.

Everything was dizzy. And either the world was moving sideways, or I was.

"Oh, no you *don't*," Desmon said through clenched teeth. I felt his knuckles on the back of my shirt. The front of my collar snagged on the lump in my throat, and my tongue lolled out of my mouth and smeared against the confines of my mask. He righted me, and I squeezed the horse with my thighs.

"*Stay*," Desmon said.

I heard voices and shouts behind me. Desmon looked again. "Dear Lord, there are a lot of them."

I wasn't sure what he meant. All I could focus on was dealing with my pain.

CHAPTER

TWENTY-THREE

P ain ensured I was in and out of consciousness throughout the day. My only sense of time was the brief glimpses of the sky I could gather up when my faculties returned to me.

We traveled a high slope, with hills and trees and sparse clusters of skeleton houses without settlers in the lowdown landscape to our left, and a view of grass as tall as my waist to our right.

Desmon's voice drifted in through the haze of hurt. "You awake again?" The horse seemed to keep us going at a more reasonable pace.

"I think so."

His hand was close to my face. It blocked my view of the grass and the horizon, like a giant stretching out over the landscape. He had pills cupped in the palm of his hand. "You know how to dry swallow?"

"You know I do."

"Take these." He pressed his palm to my mouth.

"What are they?"

"Painkillers. Mom made them for us. They're still experimental, and she hasn't perfected them yet. They're potent, but short acting. They can only work for a few minutes at a time. Longer if you take a lot. But best we avoid that right now. We don't know how long we'll be out here. Don't want to drain them all in one go."

"Makes sense." The pain was there. But it was damp. A little muted. I could put it aside for a bit. Relief flooded me. "Shit," I muttered. "How many of these have you got?"

"I'm trying to ration them. But we've got a few minutes."

"How are we holding up?" I asked.

"Every time I slow down, they catch up. There's no time to explain. I can't outrun them without breaking this stupid horse. But these Gaunts—they can maintain a consistent pace. There are a dozen of them. And the one guy in all the armor, too. I think he's...maybe he's controlling them? Somehow? I dunno. I managed to shoot a few of them, but there are more."

"I don't suppose there's anything I can do to help?" I asked.

"Honestly? Just stay alive. That's all I need from you right now. And don't get mad at me if I have to borrow your science-sword."

"Are those two mutually exclusive?"

"Shut up, Petre."

I twisted to look at him while I still could. Before I felt the pain. At some point he'd acquired a black eye. "Oh, Lord. Desmon."

"One of them had a quarterstaff," he explained. "And they tried to pull me off the horse, okay? I had to flail with your science-sword. It scared them off for a bit, I think. I'm worried I just got lucky, though."

The latter option seemed more likely to me. "I need to

374

do something. Desmon. I have to help. I can't just sit here like dead weight."

Desmon twisted me back around. "The hell you can't. I said sit still. You need to rest."

"But—"

"Just shut up and let me handle things for once. I think the pain will be back soon."

He was right.

It was nighttime when Desmon's hand appeared before my face again, tugged my mask down and shoved three pills into my mouth. As the pain receded and I came back to myself, somewhat, I realized the stars had crawled across the sky and we were traveling to the tune of whining metal and the squishy sound of gears straining to make ligaments work.

"How are you doing?" I asked Desmon.

"Oh." He tried to laugh, but breathlessness squeezed everything but a faint wheeze out of it. "You know?"

"Do you think we should stop?" The fight, the thousand pains I was facing, the smells from earlier today—they all conspired to void my ability to function. I twisted around to face him. Ribbons of pain conjured up a wince.

His face was pale as bleached bone. He scowled. "Stop it." He turned me around, forced me to stare down into the lowland hills. They were a bed of knuckles wrapped in thinning grass. I heard him lick his lips. "I don't think that's a good idea."

"Me turning around or us stopping?"

"Both," he said. "I saw them behind us not long ago. We're going to have to speed up soon. I keep having to stop so I don't put too much strain on the goddamn horse. But I can't let them catch up again."

I turned my head to one side. I thought I could see them. Small shapes in the low light, off in the distance, coming closer over the hilltop terrain. I studied them. Couldn't get a good look in the dark.

"Do you know what they want with us?" Desmon asked.

Neither of us moved. Not for a while. "I'm not sure." It would take them some time to catch up. And we couldn't stop for long. "If they're Violent Dead they'll want to kill us because we killed those other Gaunts back there."

"How does that work? I thought Gaunts didn't have friends."

"They don't," I agreed. "Remember the time you slammed my head into the floor after I broke your action figure when we were kids?"

Desmon snorted. "That was funny."

I let that slide. "This is like that. We took their resources. Broke their toys. And the only thing they can obsess about is their next chance to hurt someone. We represent that chance. And now they're after us."

"What are the odds they turn on each other before they reach us?" Desmon asked.

"Usually pretty high with The Violent Dead. But they've got a handler now, you said?"

"I think so. Sometimes his visor glows and the Gaunts will do something."

"Do you think they know we're trying to get to Mercedes?" I asked. "Maybe they're working with Ed."

"How do you work with Gaunts?" Desmon asked. "I thought you couldn't convince them to do anything?"

I tried to shrug and failed. I hated that. "Mercedes said

that Ed was looking for a helmet," I admitted. "Maybe it's the one this guy has."

Desmon's voice was shaky. "We'll have to reach The Blackheaths quickly. Yeah?"

"Well. What's one night without sleep?"

Desmon chuckled, dryly. "Best get a move on."

The horse hit a bump, and I bounced hard, hit my hand. My nerves went haywire. Pain engulfed me, sucked me back down, away from everything.

I hated that my hold on consciousness was that slippery. I'm not sure how long it was before I came back to myself.

I swallowed the pills again sometime later and felt like I was eating out of a trough. My senses expanded to a vague awareness of mechanical hooves, heavy breaths, and distant screaming.

No.

Not distant.

Desmon. Right in my ear. "The hell is happening?" I groaned.

"We're trying not to die. Don't look behind us."

I heard shots. A bright orange bolt radiated heat as it sailed past us. Slammed home in a nearby boulder and reduced the rock to drooling golden sludge. My stomach dropped. "Who gave them *slag guns?*" I shouted. I wanted to shoot behind me. But I felt stiff. Leaden. And I wasn't sure if I could take a decent shot under these circumstances.

Desmon did it for me. "I think I'm getting better aim at least," he said. "And we'll get out of range of them soon. Just stay put."

I did my best to sit still and remain quiet while my heart slammed into the sides of my neck.

I was in and out for a while, to the tune of Desmon panicking.

Things had quieted down around the time he put his closed fist right in front of my face. "Take off your mask. Open your mouth. It's been long enough that you can take your next dose."

He fed me the pills. The relief from pain made me feel a little stoned, a little giddy. Part of me wanted to go back to the semiconscious place where all I could do was think up songs to fit the travel rhythm.

Instead, I started thinking about that survivor.

"Hey, Desmon?"

"Huh?"

"You said something about a survivor, back at the cabin? You remember? There was one you said got away. Shouldn't we—y'know—should we do something about that? Make sure they're okay?"

Desmon scoffed. "Petre. Come on. Did you see any bodies on the road? Whoever it was, they got out of it in one piece. They're probably fine now. We have to hurry. We've got a lead on those Gaunts, I'd bet. We're not far from the Forest Wall. From Bullion. We have to get there before those guys catch up with us."

I felt like there was probably something to that. And if I had enough brainpower to think clearly, I probably could have put myself in his headspace. But when I tried, every attempt to do so was rebuked by my own exhaustion. Desmon's worldview was muted and inaccessible to me. "I'd hardly call wandering these places while barefoot in a hospital gown good odds for anything *fine*."

Desmon exhaled a ragged sigh. "Petre. You can't be serious right now. Fuck, man. We're being tailed by a coterie of *Gaunts*. Give it a rest, I'm begging you."

Ire and outrage flared in me. The beginnings of a temper tantrum. It was clear we were not going to divert course from this conversation anytime soon. "I just think—"

"I shouldn't have given you those pills." He sighed. "I'm sorry. That was mean. I just—all I'm saying is that we've got long enough odds right now. Our job is to get to Bullion as quickly as possible before that gang of Gaunts shoots us between the eyes. Whoever survived that raid is not our problem."

I wasn't sure what to say to that, really. "Desmon?"

"Yeah?"

"We're Princes. Everything is our problem. It kind of comes with the territory."

Desmon rolled his eyes. "What we *will* be, when we listen to you, is dead. Or are you saying you'd prefer that?"

That hardly sounded like the worst thing in the world. Not to me. "I just feel like we ought to do *something*, you know?"

Desmon massaged his temples. "Petre, do we have to do this right now? I'm exhausted. I'm hungry. I'm tired. And I'm only human. Not everything has to be our problem, alright?"

"But—"

"How many ways can I say this?" He groaned. "If we follow your suggestion, we're as good as dead. Like, *actually* dead. Really dead. Extremely dead. A cold home for worms and maggots kind of dead. We'll be staring up at daisy roots in no time. Am I being clear enough or should I keep going?"

"I just think we should do something," I said, in a low voice.

Desmon rolled his eyes. "I'm going to kill *myself* at this rate. Save the people chasing us some trouble. You seem very determined to make sure it happens anyway, so." He squeezed his eyes shut and pressed his thumb and forefinger into the corners. "Look. If we find the survivor on the way to Bullion we'll revisit this then. But in the meantime, getting out of here should be our primary concern."

That seemed like a decent compromise. But I was too annoyed to give him an easy victory. I felt useless, like I was dead weight for him to carry. I was tired, and I felt petty. I wanted some kind of victory. So. "When we get to Bullion, can we have them search the area? Make sure whoever got out of there is okay?"

Desmon groaned. "Ask me again when we get there, alright? I can't debate this with you, Petre. Not right now."

Uncertainty and the pain in my back made ire curdle into fear.

I focused on my breath. On the steady, slow expansion of my lungs, jailing all my attention beneath my ribcage.

All the while I wrestled with the terror my mind conjured up from the heavy-animal-noises sounding in the eyelid-dark. I couldn't see. Only my mind's eye was full of awful clarity. Filled with potential dangers. I wished I could hear something other than the cracked-bone sound of snapped twigs, the crunch of road grit that seemed to come from all directions at once.

Dry coughs of nighttime air spilled down the road, underpinned by hissing waves avoiding the sand, white foam dragged by the heel back to the ocean.

Then the pain came back, and consciousness fled from me again.

～

WHEN DESMON SUPPLIED my next dose, we were going at a slower rate.

"I'm back. How's it been since I've been out? You miss me?"

I looked at Desmon's hands on the reins. They were a mess of bruises and blood. "Shit."

"I'm okay," Desmon said. He sounded trancelike. "I'm okay. Just a *real* close call. We're doing great."

"You sure?"

"I have to be," he said, frustrated. "One of us has to be. It's always me who has to be okay. Just go back to sleep."

"No. Come on. Tell me what I've missed. You wouldn't have drugged me if you didn't have anything to share, right?"

Desmon sighed. "We've been traveling all night. It's been hours. I just wanted something new to do. I just needed to talk."

I sighed. "My thoughts right now don't make for decent company."

"I figured. But you're the only one here, so."

I wondered if he was being intentionally difficult. I couldn't think. I wasn't sure I wanted to, but I would've appreciated having the option to decide that for myself. "Are you okay—?"

"We're still being tailed. I'm still exhausted. And we won't meet Mercedes Blackheath in Bullion until morning. What do you think?"

I shrugged. Or attempted to. "Could be worse," I joked.

Desmon was quiet for some time. "We're a few hours from The Forest Wall, though. For whatever that's worth. Though I'm not sure if this stupid horse is in any shape to complete the journey at this point."

I let the silence linger between us. For a moment I was

tempted to drift off again. "We can't keep doing this," I said. "We have to stop moving. We have to fight them."

"We?" Desmon laughed. "If *we* stop running, *I* will do my best. But the only thing *we* will be doing is dying in excruciating pain."

"Right." I rolled my eyes. "Because up till this point I've been having such a swell time, huh?"

"You know what I meant." His voice was clipped.

"Would you rather prolong the time it takes for us to die? Because I don't know how much longer we can do this. I don't know if we'll make it to Bullion at this rate."

"I would rather buy you enough time to recover so you can help me out here."

I realized I was not exactly sure how much time had passed. "How long has it been since you last slept, Desmon?"

Desmon brayed out nervous laughter. "I mean. We've been riding all night. We've probably hit the early morning by now. But what *is* time anyway?"

"Has it really only been *one* night?"

"I'm the one who's had to be awake for all of it. You think I wouldn't know? I'm the one trying to get us to safety. Trying to act responsibly. After everything I've had to put up with while you pass in and out of consciousness all night."

I flinched. "Stop it."

"No!" He screamed. "You want to talk about this? Fine. Let's talk. Because unlike some people I can't rush in and swing a sword around until everyone's dead and I don't have to worry about anything anymore."

"Is that what you think I do?" The words had their own current. Like anger had yanked them from my mouth before I was done thinking them.

"That's certainly what it looks like."

"Tell me how you really feel. I dare you." I wasn't even sure if that made *sense*. I would've crossed my arms if I could bend my fucking fingers without pain.

"You want to know how I really feel?"

"Yeah. Sure. Let's get this over with."

"Shut the fuck up! No. Shut up. Fuck you. You want to know how I feel, Petre? You want to fucking know how I feel? I feel like you've spent so long being a fucking piece of shit mess that everyone just kind of *expects* that of you. Nobody ever expects you to have your shit together. Dad let *you* run away because he was sick of dealing with you. But do you have any idea how badly he would have fucking crucified me if I had even *thought* about doing what you did that night? You got to ride around the countryside for five years while I got shopped around from court to court being Dad's perfect little fucking ambassador, having to do every-thing exactly as intended, never being allowed to get caught making *one* mistake. And what fucking thanks do I get? None at all. Because you three were always such a fucking handful, okay? But since I was quiet, reserved, I didn't get in trouble, I always had to be the one to do it perfectly. Anything other than perfect was what counted as acting out for me. That's what was fucking expected of me, while you three were off fucking around all day long. And now we're not at court. We're thoroughly in *your* element, and I don't know how to fucking handle that because nobody ever fucking *let* me, and all of a sudden you're making it your pride and joy to *mock* me about that every chance you get? Fuck you. Go fuck yourself. I'm sick of it, man. I'm done with you and I'm sick of it."

Well.

I—

Huh.

I wasn't sure what to say. Like what do you say to that, you know? Where do you start?

Probably by taking a minute, and a few deep breaths. "I wasn't trying to mock—"

"Don't lie to me!" Desmon said.

Right. Shit. Maybe he was right about that. But man, he was reading too deep into it, you know? He had to be. But I guess if this was how he wanted to play it I was happy to oblige. "It—it was only because you tried to mock *me*. You always try to make fun of me at court. About what I notice and what I don't. Hell. You fucking lied to me to get me back here, and suddenly when I want to let off some steam—"

"But that's *all* you ever know how to do, Petre. That's what I'm trying to tell you. Hell. That's why we're in this mess. And don't fucking pretend there was something else I could have said that night at The Bucket to get you to listen to me. You threatened to leave. You were on your way out. I—I had to think of something, alright?" I heard him swallow. "We were on the brink of war and I—I just. Maybe I just wanted you back. Is that so bad?"

"But like...why, though?"

"I don't suppose *because I love you* sounds believable enough? Because I fucking miss you? Is that so bad?"

"I mean...I love you, too. But I don't know if I get how that explains it."

"If war *were* to break out, don't you think I'd want to know if you were safe?" Desmon asked.

"Is that why you and Anoïse ignored me for three days? After saying you needed me back so urgently?"

"It's not that I didn't want to make good on my prom-

THE FALL IS ALL THERE IS

ise, Petre. I swear to God. I was just—I was trying to figure out how to do that without alerting you to—"

I thought of a point I had forgotten to make earlier. "You know, if you wanted to leave with me—when we were kids, I mean—if you wanted to get out with me these last five years, all you really had to do was ask. I would've kept you safe."

"I was in the middle of a different point but okay. I just. I couldn't go with you. Dad would've come after you if I left, too.".

"He would've *tried*," I said. But I wasn't sure how to follow it up. How do you break the silence when it's shot through with that kind of sharp tension? There's always that risk you're going to get hurt, I think.

"Come on, Petre. We both know that's not true."

"Isn't it?"

"It's like you were saying about that survivor. It's tempting to run. But we have a responsibility. I couldn't just abandon everything. I had to stay. To at least *try* before I cut and run."

My pain was coming back more keenly. And I didn't want to say anything I regretted. So I hedged. "Does that mean we might look for that survivor?"

"I'm not even sure where we'd start looking. Or when. If you want to start looking though, I might need your help when the Gaunts catch up again."

"I'm not sure how useful I'll be," I said.

"Maybe if you hadn't brought a woman's weapon," he muttered.

I doubted he was serious this time. "If only I packed a sundress. We'd be out of here by now."

"If only." He chewed on his lower lip. "Petre?"

"Yeah?"

"We're not exactly getting less tired, you know."

"I know, Desmon." I scanned the horizon. "Looks like the Forest Wall is getting closer at least, though."

"That's something, at least."

"We just have to keep pace."

"Yeah," Desmon let out a breath. "Keep pace. Right. We can do that. Keep pace or fight."

Or fight? That had not been an option earlier. I wasn't sure what to make of things if Desmon was warming up to the idea. The night was languishing on and so were we. What were our odds? Or did odds matter?

I suppose at a certain point you have to dig your heels in. When everything gets too much, you can't keep running away, can you? Not forever.

But we could certainly try, just for a little while longer, in the hope that we could make it without incident.

Yeah, *right.*

So we rode in silence. Desmon gave me more pills before the last dose had finished wearing off. Slowly we were swallowed up by The Forest Wall. Trees of rotting enamel and foliage with animal furs leered over us. Occasionally statues or the corroded remains of scientific architecture loomed in the distance, surrounding us on either side of the path.

As we traveled, I realized the horse had slowed without Desmon doing much of anything. It was just not meant for two riders, and he'd been pushing the damn contraption past its limits. By the time we were halfway through The Forest Wall it could barely canter.

I'm not sure how long, or exactly how slowly we traveled before Desmon elected to break our silence. "Hey. Um. Petre?"

"Yeah?"

"Do you hear that?"

"Hear what?" I was too tangled in my own nerves to fully hear the outside world. I was home to too much irritation. Too much angry red pain. To the point where it took specific thought and intention to even parse Desmon's words. I had to consciously remember what each word meant and string it together.

He wheeled his horse around, so that it was facing sideways, facing a row of jagged tree stumps that reminded me of fractured teeth. "Just off that path," he said.

I peered forward. There was a scrub of crimson foliage behind it. Wet red moss stretched over rocks that made it resemble the surface of a tongue.

A soundscape introduced itself to me. The crack of branches stamped in half. Gemstones trampled into soil. Breath shuddering in and out. Grunting.

"It's getting closer." Desmon's voice procured a tremor. "What do you think? More Gaunts?"

I chewed it over. "How fast can this horse get us out of here?"

"This thing can barely even walk at this point. Whatever's out there is coming closer. It'd catch up."

Tentatively, I climbed down from the horse. My whole body was wrapped in a haze of pain. I moved awkwardly. But the drugs muted most of the torment and allowed me to climb down without *too* much issue. I could balance fine. Honest. It was all the trees pinwheeling around me that were giving me a problem. "Hand me my gun."

"Petre," Desmon breathed. "Petre, I see it. It's coming for us." He swung down from the horse, raised the barrel of the caterwauler.

I peered into the forest. "I can't see it."

"I'm going to shoot it."

My hands were trembling. "Wait. Not yet. I can't see anything. I want to know what it is first."

"Petre. This isn't funny. I'm just going to shoot it, okay?"

When the hell had Desmon become such a trigger-happy little bastard? Had the last night of violence provoked some change in him? I wouldn't have expected this when we set out. "Don't—" I began.

He ignored me and was taking aim, when I heard a woman's voice go, "Oh, thank God," just as she hurtled clear of the forest.

The voice was familiar.

I realized who Desmon was aiming at.

Mercedes.

My injections jerked my mangled hand towards Desmon, pressed the backs of my knuckles up against the underside of the gun. It fired into the air just as Desmon squeezed the trigger. Making a signal flare out of a sonic pulse that shimmered above us.

The gun squealed, then Mercedes squealed, and she vaulted over the white trees to fall on her knees in front of us.

She was wearing what could generously be called a nightgown. It was made of polka dots. She was barefoot and looked like she had been through hell.

She looked up at us, mute horror widening her eyes. Her gas mask shifted. "Petre. That *is* you, right?"

"Mercedes, I—what are you doing here? What *happened?*"

"What happened to me?" A ragged laugh tore free from her throat. "I could ask you the same thing, Petre Mercy."

Dread filled my stomach, and the blood drained from my face.

"What happened to you? Both of you?" She demanded. Her gaze ticked between the two of us. "Desmon Mercy, what the hell are *you* doing here? I would've expected this from your brother, but—"

Desmon looked like he was going to implode. "We—"

"Good Lord," Mercedes went on. "You two look *awful*."

"I—" I wasn't sure what to say. I stared at the road. "We got into a fight and—"

"Oh, did you indeed?" An undercurrent of incredulous laughter clung to the tide of each syllable. "Is that, in fact, what happened? This wasn't something you just tried for fun? Well, in that case—"

"Mercedes—"

"For a moment I was almost worried about you."

"Listen, Mercedes, I'm fine—I just—"

"You just *what?* I'm sorry. Maybe I'm missing something?"

"We—we got in a fight. We had to hurry—"

"Hurry? Honey, you look about ready to curl up and die."

"We don't have time for this." Desmon rolled his eyes.

"How long have you two been like this?" Mercedes asked.

"I feel fine." That was not true, but I didn't want her worrying about me.

"Bullshit," she spat. "You look terrible." She turned back to Desmon. "He looks awful. It's like he's waiting to keel over any second now."

"Thanks." I rolled my eyes.

"Do you want me to lie to you?" Mercedes shot back.

"No, but—look at yourself. I just—" I shrugged out of my coat and held it out to her. "Here. Take this at least, before you scold us. It looks like you've been wearing that nightgown for a while."

She wrenched it out of my splinted fingers, radiating fury. Shrugged into it with the mannerisms of an angry parent taking their aggression out by folding laundry.

Desmon cleared his throat. "You know I hate to interrupt but you two should know, this horse does not exactly seat three."

I wondered if this was where the fighting Desmon had been talking about was going to kick in. "So what? We dig in and fight?"

Desmon shrugged. "We can't outrun them if there are three of us. This whole plan hinged on Mercedes being in Bullion."

"What plan is this?" Mercedes asked.

"I'll tell you later," I said. "There's no time. There are an awful lot of Gaunts on our tail, and we have to—"

"Gaunts?" Something in her demeanor changed. She stiffened. "How far ahead are you?"

Desmon performed the calculations in his head. "Half an hour." I guessed he was lowballing his number. He wouldn't want us wasting too much time.

"Great. Perfect. Fantastic," Mercedes said. "We have loads of time to figure out how to deal with them, then. Don't we? It's just like when you were working for me, Petre. Isn't it?"

"Fuck it," Desmon said, "I guess we're doing this then."

"Are you sure?" I didn't want him getting himself killed on my account.

"You said it yourself. We can't keep going like this forever," he said. "We're Princes. Have to deal with it eventually. Let's try it your way, Petre. Let's fucking figure something out."

"Well, then what do we do? Do you have any ideas?" I shot back. "Mercedes hardly even has clothes on, I can't use my hands, and you look like you can barely open your eyes by now."

Mercedes cut in, jabbed a finger between the two of us. "Can we *please* figure this out in a place that's not right in the middle of the path?"

Desmon and I just stared at each other. "Right," I huffed. "Lead the horse into the trees, Desmon."

"But that'll break it!" Desmon whined. "It's not built for offroad. It's got the wrong design for rugged terrain!"

I rolled my eyes. "Right, I forgot we were getting such great use of it right now. I wouldn't want it to go to waste!"

"If it's useless anyway then why waste all the trouble hauling it off the road? Are we going to have a use for all that blood and scrap metal anytime soon?"

My stomach dropped. I thought of Edgar. My eyes went wide. "Desmon. Holy shit. You are a genius."

CHAPTER

TWENTY-FOUR

I have a theory: this whole predicament was my fault.

And no, that's not me pretending I have to be responsible for *everything* that goes wrong, okay? Just think about it, alright? Humor me for a sec.

These Gaunts all had the Violent Dead in them. All of them, chasing us overnight, after we wound up on that beach. Everyone else there had been dead for a few days. I bet they were killed on the day of the fire. And you know what else? I bet the people chasing us had turned Gaunt *that day*.

They were probably ordinary people just a few days before. Decided to spend their time maskless on the shoreline. Spend time around that fire pit, when the wind off The Bay invited dead miasma into their lungs.

And well. If I had just gone with Edgar instead of trying to cut and run as usual, I highly doubt we'd have this many Gaunts on our hands. So when you think about it, I bet it's my fault, yeah?

I just wanted to get that out of the way upfront. This was my theory on what had happened. Obviously I can't prove it, but I just want to mention it now, because once they caught up to us—well. I guess it'll look kind of stupid when you get there.

I just wanted you to know. I figured it was my fault, so I had to make it right.

That's why I did what I did.

What you're about to see, I mean.

THE PLAN I came up with was the kind of thing you only envision when all you have access to is agony for hours on end.

I had no clue if my suggestion would *work*, but it was worth a shot. If I could get the damn thing rigged up by the time the Gaunts caught up with us.

The only problem was, with the state of my hands—I didn't think I could do it myself.

So the three of us walked our shared horse over into a hidden stretch of foliage just off the path, behind the white enamel tree trunks. We tipped the horse sideways and set to work on the bed of red moss.

I sat on the stump, watched while Desmon retrieved a wrench and started peeling it out of its armor, then Mercedes opened a hatch beneath its belly and set to work.

"You having fun back there?" She called to me, as she bent over the horse.

"Is now a bad time to admit that I'm admiring the view?"

"Petre!" Desmon shouted.

The only noise for some time was the wet sound of steel moving through organs, and the small shrieking noises of armor pried apart from a false flesh.

"You know, Petre," Mercedes said, "I'm going to be very upset with you if I'm dead in half an hour."

"You don't sound too terrified," I observed.

"I'm using humor to cope with the existential dread."

Desmon's mask shifted, and I could see the grin in his eyes. "I like her."

"Me, too." I wasn't sure what else to say to that. I couldn't exactly tell her we *weren't* going to die. The odds were likely. The second the medication wore off I was going to pass out. The only thing keeping me standing and conscious was the fact that I was too drugged up to feel my own nerves.

It was fortunate we'd run into her, if only because of the better odds as a numbers game. Though I wasn't sure how this had even come about. "Is now a good time to ask what you're doing here, Mercedes?" I asked.

"Edgar and I had an, um—a disagreement. When the two of you arrived in Bullion."

"What happened?"

She was silent for some time. Even her work had stopped. "...I got caught. I went to intercept him, and suddenly three men were on top of me and I..." The sound of her work resumed. "Anyway. It's not important. I got captured. Covert-like. Most of my Guard didn't even find out about it until after your...exit. The next day. Ed might've secured a munitions deal if you hadn't done that. He was very upset with you after."

"I'm sure that was the least of it, from what I hear," Desmon added, dryly.

"I'm sure," Mercedes said.

Guilt swam through my stomach. I wanted to cry. I should have found a different solution, back at Bullion. Snuck out a different exit. I don't know. Something.

"So he took you as a hostage?" That would explain why no one from Blackheath House was talking to us. They were busy scrambling.

"Hm." She came out from the horse's belly wearing blood and grease. Her hair was a piebald pattern of red and black. "Orianna Reacher, too. He took Reacher House, actually. Not long ago."

I balked. "How?"

"Guindolin Reacher made sure it was staffed with his supporters. All he had to do was waltz right in. He brought me with him from Bullion."

I couldn't believe it. "How...how did you get out?"

She stared into space for some time, then reached up with her forearm to wipe the grease from her forehead. But her forearm was also smeared in bloody black. She looked at it, laughed a bit and set her arm down. "Your brother was convinced he had to make the first move. Before Anoïse. He wanted to cement his position that God was on his side. And his advisors told him that he needed to make sure that if war *did* break out, it would be a brief one, and he would come out the victor."

I did not like the sound of that. "What did he do?"

"I...It happened a few days ago. I'd been confined to a chamber for some time. Then a few nights ago I smelled smoke. The whole place was in an uproar. Some kind of pitched battle was going on. No one thought to send reinforcements to guard me. So I slipped out. Went to look at what was going on and..." She stopped to give the horse a once over. Make sure her alterations were set, and ready. There were clockwork sounds and squishy wet things working together. "How much do you know about what's happened to your family's fleet?" Mercedes asked.

My guts shifted. I felt the sudden and oncoming need to take a shit. "My *what*?"

"Our what?" Desmon looked up. He was almost finished shedding the horse of its steel skin.

"You saw the fire, yes?" Mercedes asked us.

"It was hard to miss," I conceded.

"*I* wanted to go back," Desmon said. "See. I told you we should've—"

"But Mercedes, are you saying—"

"Edgar and his supporters were setting your family's fleet alight," Mercedes said. "Massive frigates of whalebone and sinew and steel. They all went up in smoke. A few of The Reachers' ships were there, too. Assisting in the attack."

"Damn," Desmon said. Slowly he set back to work with his wrench. "Damn."

I hoped Anoïse would accept *that* as proof that Havilan Reacher was working with Edgar. Now that it was too late to do anything. Fuck. Shit. Goddammit. I swallowed.

But I still had unanswered questions. "How did you get out of there?" I asked.

"I ran," she said. "Quickly." Her hands were shaky. "There was chaos and confusion. I don't think they even noticed. I knew I would never make it away on foot. So I went for—"

"—the boat," I finished for her. "That was your boat."

She nodded. "I never got near the fighting. I stuck as close as I could to shore. And just followed the coast, until I —hang on. How did you know that?"

"We stopped by the house you stayed at," I explained. "The cabin. Or what was left of it. Part of your nightgown was torn. But we didn't know it was you." It made no sense to be retroactively mad at Desmon for suggesting we forge ahead without concerning ourselves with whoever survived, but my feelings never made sense. They couldn't do that, so I was angry anyway.

"I got a small whalebone boat," Mercedes said. "One of the few there that still had a working heartbeat engine. I skimmed The Bay until I found the cabin. But there...there was a lot of fog. White fog. It hid me, I think. While the ships burned. I thought it was smoke at first. Something to do with the fire mixing with some chemical, maybe? It sounds stupid when I say it now. I don't know. I don't know. It was only when people at the cabin started getting infected with the Violent Dead, I realized. It—it wasn't smoke, was it? It was people. Ghostfog. It must've drifted out. Infected them. If I hadn't had a mask on, I don't know what would've happened."

"Good Lord. That's..."

"Yeah." Mercedes looked down at the horse. "Yeah. Anyway. I just hope this works."

"It will." I managed to muster a confidence that I didn't really feel. I had to keep them safe. That was my only option.

"Right," Mercedes said. "That should be everything." She closed up the horse's stomach.

"Should be?" I asked.

"Should be."

"Right then. Desmon," I said, "help Mercedes get the horse upright."

"And we're *sure* about this?" Desmon asked, as the two hauled the creature to its feet. "The way you describe it—I just—what if something goes wrong?"

The sound of boots stomping down the path were distant and getting louder. "No time to rethink it," I said. "They're coming. You said you didn't have a few more hours in you. I'm in no shape to run. I can't handle this trail." I could hear footsteps on the road. Voices in the darkness, as the three of us settled near the enamel tree trunks, on the precipice of the path.

"Mercedes," I whispered. "I've got a caterwauler in my holster. If you don't want to die, it's all yours. Fish it out and be my guest."

"Right." She nodded. "And your brother?"

"I've got a knife in my pocket. Give that to him."

She did it, with some hesitation. "How are you going to defend yourself?"

Sometimes your ideas ambush you. One minute you're trying desperately to think. The next it's like something has slammed home inside your chest with physical weight. Like it's a living thing. Like there's some kind of idea-space separate from you. You have your own house to build your thoughts in. And your ideas are intruders from someplace else, breaking down the door. No idea where they came from. But suddenly they're there and you've got to deal with them. "Desmon. How many doses of those drugs do you have left?"

"I—"

"You know what? I don't care. Give me what you've got."

"But—"

I glanced at the road. The sound of Gaunts was getting louder. I could see an orange glow of the armored man's visor, far off in the dark. My stomach dropped, and I turned back to Desmon. "No time. *Now.*"

Desmon dumped the pills into my open palm. I tugged down my mask and swallowed them in a couple of mouthfuls.

I kept my head down. I had to focus, had to act quick. I tugged down my mask again and took my splints off my right hand with my teeth. My fingers were clammy, my flesh slick and pale like the skin under a cast. The top two knuckles on my right pinky tipped back further than they were supposed to. In a way that reminded me of a loose baby tooth. I could've twisted it right off if I wanted to. A couple other fingers had bubbles of pus around the sites of injury, and there was a stretch of skin that looked black in a way I didn't like. I couldn't tell if that was dirt or infection. How fast did fingers get infected? I wasn't sure. Probably not this fast, right? I sure hoped not.

Fuck. What kind of dose had Desmon hopped me up on that I couldn't *feel* that? I wasn't sure yet what I was going to do when they wore off. Why had I thought it was a good idea to take them all at once? Guess I had to act quick. I'd bottomed out on pain and fear and second guessing. Or maybe that was the drugs that bleached away all my emotions.

I had to sandwich the hilt of my saber between the heels of my palms to get it out. Awkwardly, I guided my broken fingers around the grip with the back of my hand.

"Fuck!" Desmon turned towards me. "Petre—what the hell do you think you're doing?"

"You gonna stand there or are you gonna help me tie my hand up? We don't have much time." I could hear the coming Gaunts breathing by now. We had a minute at best before they were right on top of us.

Thankfully, Desmon didn't hesitate. He immediately reached for the bandages he'd used to dress my wounds, wrapped them around my hand and the grip of my sword faster than I ever thought he could.

I looked at Mercedes. Lifted my eyebrows. "Miss me?"

She snorted. "You're an idiot. We're going to die."

"Right," Desmon murmured. "That ought to hold long enough."

I heard noises on the trail. A sound of heavy iron, steel and breathing. The clink of armor in movement. They were close enough to resemble shadowed shapes in the dark.

"Mercedes. Ready to start the horse?" I whispered.

She tugged the reins, then crouched behind the white enamel tree stumps. "What are you waiting for? Both of you. Get down here."

Desmon ducked down into our hiding spot, and I joined, the three of us crouched in the cramped space. I stared around the corner.

The horse juddered to what could generously be called *life*. It moved on an uncertain structure. Machinery wheezed beneath the saddle. The creature screamed.

Well—not from its *mouth*. It was a screech of faulty machinery, grinding itself apart in ways it wasn't supposed to. Its torso spiraled out like a drawn accordion, just as the pack of Gaunts closed in on us. It curled apart in pencil-shaving patterns as it shredded itself to pieces, making a bridge of dripping guts and clockwork metal.

"Lord have mercy," Desmon swore. "The hell did you do?"

"Just hold tight," I said. Damn, but there were a lot of Gaunts, too. At least a dozen. They crowded around the mess of steel and machinery as it shredded itself apart.

"It's still got to hit the mainspring." My jaw was tight enough to give me a headache. I didn't even breathe. This had to work. This had to work. This had to work.

The horse went up without warning, erupting like a firework of white sparks. Steel and shrapnel flew in all directions like a living nail bomb. Iron and oil and blood flew out in ribbons. A piecemeal cog of clockwork took the nearest Gaunt through the throat. Another one was instantly reduced to a pincushion before he had a chance to scream. Shrapnel sliced through a woman's sundress, and her stomach. A man beside her took a foot of uneven steel right through the center of his chest, while an old man was lifted off his feet when struck by something I couldn't even see. The world instantly became a confusion of blood and violence and screams.

The silence afterwards robbed me of my breath. That was the most unnerving part, I think. The world should not have been so quiet after watching that many people die at once.

"Holy shit!" Mercedes screamed.

"Petre," Desmon's voice was small and quiet. "What the fuck?"

"Don't thank me just yet," I said dryly. "Some may have survived the blast." I could still see the orange glow of the armored man's visor through the throng of bodies. I wasn't sure if that meant that he was still alive or not.

Slowly, a couple bodies stirred. A few Gaunts staggered to their feet and helped the armored man up.

"Fuck," Desmon whispered. "We're going to die."

I tried to sort through the mess of bodies and figure out who was who. "How many left alive?" I asked.

Mercedes squinted. "Six?" She guessed.

"Shoot one."

"Got it." Mercedes turned and raised the caterwauler, squeezed the trigger home. The sonic shot shimmered through the air and struck a big man in a torn vest right through the chest.

"They'll have heard that. Time to go." I climbed to my feet, as the Gaunts clambered after us. The world just off the path was a scrap yard of concrete, steel girders, and horned trees bristling with ox furs. It was a cramped space, but I could make this work.

Desmon and Mercedes clambered through bloody moss and concrete. The wind howled, and a gentle rain of leaves made from horn and ivory drifted down on them.

I didn't follow. I stood there and waited for the five Gaunts left to come to me.

Desmon twisted around to check on me. "Petre?" He shouted. "What are you doing? Come on!"

"Shut up!" I shouted. "They can hear you!" I didn't want them to find him in the dark.

"I'm not leaving here without you!"

"You wanted to run away so bad?" I shot back. "Now's your chance! Get out of here!"

"This is different!" Desmon shouted. "It's not like when we were eighteen! This is life and death!"

"That's what it was to me!"

"We weren't going to kill you!"

"Some wounds aren't skin deep, Desmon. I couldn't— listen. We don't have time to do this now. Get out of here!"

"No! Fuck you! You always *do* this! I'm not going to leave you alone to die like some hero, you idiot!" Desmon screamed.

"I really wish you would!"

"Well, you wouldn't do it if it were me, so—"

Mercedes appeared over Desmon's shoulder. "PETRE! BEHIND YOU!"

I whirled. Mercedes fired before I could get my science-sword up. The Gaunt's face broke apart. The shot was so close I could feel the shimmer in the air.

It was only then that I realized I should have felt the heat suggestions of my injections when Mercedes warned me. Why didn't I feel them? Could I not feel my injections in the numbed drug haze?

Fuck fuck fuck fuck.

Footsteps were coming closer. I lifted my sword, vaguely aware of the hot, angry pain spilling through my hands. It radiated up my arm every time I moved it. There was a wall between me and agony, but it wouldn't hold forever.

I had just turned around, braced with my science-sword, when I realized that the surviving Gaunts had fanned out. They were all going to get past me. I couldn't reach them before they got to Desmon and Mercedes.

Dammit. So much for *protecting* them. God. Fuck.

I knifed out breaths as I fishtailed through the animal trees. I dragged my mask down and pressed my tongue into the science-sword's thumb ring to activate the thyroid battery. Heat radiated from the blade as I scrambled to catch up with the fanned out Gaunts. I couldn't pull my mask back up without stopping. It bounced as I ran. Against my better judgment, I let it dangle. Maybe the motivation to not go Gaunt would motivate me to keep Mercedes and Desmon alive.

At least Gaunts didn't vomit up ghosts after you killed them. Small mercies, right?

I'd like to describe what I did as hustling. But without the injections, *uncoordinated stumbling* would've been more appropriate.

I spotted someone with a chewed-up pitchfork lunging for Mercedes. She was pinned against a tree, atop a hill of leaves and concrete, fumbling with a Gaunt for control of the haft, boots scuffing on the stone. Her gun must've still been charging. Goddammit.

I hurtled for the Gaunt, kicking up sheets of leaves. I

was almost there when I hit a marrow tree root and slammed my shin onto the concrete as I went down. It was odd not feeling that pain, though I figured the damage it did was probably real. I threw out my sword arm, tried to make the stumble into an awkward lunge.

That got the Gaunt's attention, at least.

He turned on me before I could find my feet. I tried to put my sword up, but he slammed his weight into my shoulders first. The world turned into a tangle of stone and stars and sky all coinflipping into a featureless blur of color as we rolled downhill.

He was on top of me when we stopped. I didn't feel his knuckles on my forehead, though the drugs did not stop the dizziness.

I was on my back. I tried to angle the point of my science-sword, but I couldn't even figure out how to get the space to take a swing with him on top of me. Goddammit. I needed to feel the goddamn injections. I couldn't line anything up right.

His knuckle slammed into my head again, and the world flashed white, even when I couldn't feel the pain. What the fuck? That wasn't fair. I wanted to puke.

His fist came down again, and for a moment I went completely blind. It took a minute for my vision to right itself. While panicked, waiting and wondering if my vision would come back, his fist came down again.

When my vision *did* come back an instant later, the world was still blurry. Or was that the tears? I couldn't tell. Good Lord. I was going to die.

I tried to push at his shoulders with the heel of my hands, and the guard of my sword. But he barely budged. One hand closed around my collar as he dragged his fist back again. Everything in me screamed to get my sword up, but my only instinct was to close my eyes and wince, as his knuckles hurled me right back to the ground.

I wanted to scream. I was pinned under a goddamn Gaunt and the best I could do was flail at him. I had all the fighting prowess of a fucking five-year-old, and—

Oh. I knew what I had to do. I just had to figure out how to fucking coordinate myself for just a brief second.

"Petre!" It was Mercedes's voice. I heard her grunt, and an instant later the pitchfork slammed home in the Gaunt's calf. He reeled up, screaming, and I found my opportunity.

I sat up, wrapped my hands around the back of his neck and dragged him as close to me as I could manage. I opened my mouth and bit down hard on the front of his throat. Right on either side of the lump. I squeezed my teeth together as blood and gristle filled my mouth. I closed my eyes and kept chewing. The Gaunt screamed—until he didn't. I spat out a scrap of skin when he stopped moving.

"Right." I staggered to my feet. The world was woozy, spinning like the last mad spirals a coin makes before it flattens. "Right."

I looked to Mercedes, who was breathing as hard as I was. "You good?" I coughed.

She gestured at her mouth, lazily. "You got a little..."

What came out of me was closer to a wheeze than laughing. I wanted to droop forward. I wanted to hit the concrete floor. I wanted to melt. "Right," I said. "Okay. Where's Desmon?"

I heard him scream somewhere in the dark. "FUCK FUCK FUCK!"

I looked in the direction of the noise. Desmon was struggling with a surviving Gaunt.

Before I could react, someone's shoulder slammed into

my chest and drove the breath from me. A body had just plowed me into a tree. The whole world smelled like fur.

A cold hand closed around my throat. I looked for a face and found a helmet staring at me. "I'm sure you thought you did something with your little trick." A mechanical voice droned through the featureless metal. Where was Mercedes? Had a surviving Gaunt tangled up with her?

I tried to find something funny to say. But my head was swimming, and it was difficult to breathe.

"All you've succeeded in doing is giving me a test run, Mercy. I don't need any of these Gaunts to survive."

I wanted to tell him that I never thought he did. But before I could he raised his fist.

Had there always been spiked knuckles on his gauntlet?

I swung up blind with the saber, my eyes squeezed shut. I couldn't feel if it made contact, because I still couldn't feel a fucking thing, but I felt the pressure leave my throat, and when I opened my eyes the man was staggering. Though it didn't look like he even had a scratch on him.

"You sure showed me," I said, as I dropped. My body smeared the ground. Fuck. My limbs weren't working with me. I had to get up. I had to get up. Goddammit. Goddammit. Goddamn.

The armored man dragged me up to my knees. I tried again to take some blind swings. I wasn't sure how many I'd thrown before I realized they all had failed to hit hard enough to even form a dent. He wasn't even *singed*.

His fist slammed into the space above my collarbone. I couldn't feel the spikes. That was funny. Huh. I was still marveling over that when he kicked me onto my back. This was going to hurt as soon as the drugs wore off.

He clawed up a knife, so I tried to kick him. The first

shot missed completely, and the second hit his breastplate, though I'm not sure if I managed to kick him or slide away.

In an instant, the armored man was standing over me again. A bloody wail clambered out from my lungs without permission. Part of me wanted to let him win right there, as he climbed on top of me.

Instead I took my sword and hammered it into his helmet. Again. Again. Again. Surely I was getting somewhere with this. No matter how uncoordinated it was. Goddammit. Fuck. There had to be a few scratches by that point, right? A couple black streaks of burn? Maybe—

Nope. The damn sword snapped.

"Fuck shit fuck goddammit holy shit fuck fuck goddammit I swear to god."

I used the guard to take shots at his chest. It must've felt akin to a toddler with brass knuckles.

He wrapped his hands around my wrists and pinned them over my head. I dragged my knees into his crotch. But all I did was hurt my knees. I don't know why I expected different.

"Your sword is broken," the mechanical voice said. "Your brother is either dead or will be soon. And then I will take the girl back with me, to Edgar. You're alone. Don't worry, Petre. I'll tell them all you've run away."

He had a knife held downward in an icepick grip. I had no way to stop him with my hands in their current state. I sucked in a breath. Had to think of something. Fuck. Fuck. I was fucked. I was—

Hands closed around the sides of his helmet. Someone behind the armored man muttered something. His neck craned back. Armor there too.

But not under his chin.

I yanked myself upright. From this close it was impossible to miss. Even for *me*. I slammed the stump of my saber up through his jaw. His body jerked, hands spasming for my wrist, panicked fingers scrabbling as I pushed the ruined blade up through his head. Black blood sluiced down my blade. The whole world was made of sticky, suckling sounds.

His corpse yanked me sideways when he fell. I was too jittery to get the sword out on my own. I levered the stump blade, heard it scraping on the inside of the helmet, and felt it moving through his face. I smelled his skin smoking on the science-sword, but I couldn't let it go. I was tied to it.

"Petre." It was Desmon's voice. He was crouched beside me. His hand around my wrist. "Breathe."

That's what Avram would have told me to do

I let out a deep breath. He guided the sword out of the dead man's skull for me. "Desmon. Desmon. Fuck man thank God you're alive. Where's Mercedes?"

"She's alright, Petre. It's over now." His voice was shaky. He sounded like he was about to cry. I couldn't see the extent of his injuries clearly. But he was out of breath. "She's alright. You did good, Petre. We're alive. We're alive."

"Huh." I cackled and felt a little deranged. "That's good." I realized abruptly the drugs were wearing off. I didn't have much time. "G-get the helmet off. I want to see who I killed." I didn't. I just wanted to make sure it wasn't Ed. "Make sure to keep it. Anoïse wants it."

He didn't even ask a question. He just knelt over the corpse and removed the helmet.

His face had been pulped up and burned by my attempts to remove the science-sword from his helmet. I could barely even discern who he was, I had only one concern. "Don't be Ed don't be Ed don't be Ed."

I leaned in close. Blue eyes. I granted myself a breath of

relief. It wasn't him. That was all that mattered. It wasn't him.

Then all the gathered pain flooded back into me in an instant.

Somewhere distantly, someone was screaming.

Or perhaps it was just me.

I DON'T REMEMBER ALL the details between hitting the concrete and waking up again. All that remains are vague afterimages.

I remember Mercedes and Desmon with hands on me. A trail. A couple travelers who had heard a signal flare in the air—the caterwauler Desmon had shot when we found Mercedes.

There were shouts. Some kind of train lumbering through The Forest Wall. The cars were as shiny as polished coffins, with blue tarpaulins hauled over corroded rooftops. The head of the train was crowned in swordlike spires, and the furnaces that powered it were breathing like heavy animals, guttering smoke from iron teeth.

I remember black grate steps and automatic doors that sighed. There were hands on me, fingers digging under my armpits, hauling me up.

I blinked in and out of consciousness. I don't remember being placed on a makeshift stretcher, but at some point I must have been. I remember the sag of heavy linen under my weight. The world was a confused tangle of noise and pain all limned in an eyelid void.

Alarms blared. People shouted. A floodlight switched on.

I opened my eyes, and then thought better of it. And

then I opened them again, in what I thought was an instant. But in that time the scene had changed.

Avram was over me, wearing a surgical mask, and I felt gray and weak. He was speaking, but I couldn't hear his voice. It hit me like some dream-impression. No words, just ideas. He was going to get me help. He was going to take care of me.

At some point, my head lolled to one side. Desmon was on some kind of hospital bed beside mine. I hadn't seen his injuries in the dark. Was he in worse shape than I had thought?

That was okay. We were on the train. We were getting help. We were moving. I knew it because I could hear the wind passing by us.

The two of us were bleeding together on our backs.

Desmon's head had lurched to look at me. As if he sensed me staring. We made a hazy, half-lucid sort of eye contact. I could not read the expression on his face. Maybe he wanted to murder me, or maybe he wanted to murder himself. Or did he want to hug me? I wasn't sure.

His arm spilled from the bedside, his hand suspended in the air between us.

All around us physicians swarmed; a seething froth of white coats surrounded us, corroding my vision—except for glimpses of Desmon's eyes, and his hand.

It took me a while to realize he was offering it to me. I'm not sure how long it took me to decide to take it. Probably a mere few seconds. But it felt like much longer.

His hand was cold. Or maybe that was mine. I couldn't tell. I think he tried to squeeze. Our grip was clammy, but mine was the one that had most of the blood.

I know I tried to squeeze back, but my fingers weren't working with me. It was like they weren't even there. Just lumps of flesh tied up in dead nerves and unresponsive sinew.

I might have been missing some. I wasn't sure. I couldn't get a clear view through Desmon's hand, enclosed around mine.

At some point a physician came and pried our hands apart, stuffed mine against my side and went on with his task.

Desmon looked over at me. Then at the ceiling. And he smiled. And he *laughed*. A mad cackle, filled with glee.

Then suddenly I was staring at the ceiling, too. The world tilted all around me. My eyes refused to sit still, and the world was swallowed up in black again.

I think I made a few return visits to consciousness after that, but I was always a little fuzzy around the edges.

At one point I remember Avram more clearly. His voice, underpinned by the clink of metal, and a sound like strummed wires. He was working with wires. The sounds were part of his work. I just wasn't sure what it was, or how I knew that.

"You gotta wake up eventually, Petre." That was it. That was what he'd said. "Anoïse wants to see you. I want to see you. Mercedes wants to see you. Even Desmon wants to see you. Everyone else is alright. It wasn't that bad out there, was it? Come on, kid."

I could not make myself move or speak.

"All your readings say you should be awake by now."

I wondered if there was some part of me that wanted to shut down longer. Maybe my brain needed a break from me. A respite for a while. I'd been taking psychic damage for some time now. I wouldn't be surprised if somewhere deep in my subconscious, I'd decided I'd take any opportunity to rest.

CHAPTER

TWENTY-FIVE

The most shocking thing about waking up was not the fact that I'd lost a hand.

It was the relief that snagged in my throat when I saw it.

That's not the reaction you expect, right? You expect a bit of mourning first, y'know? And maybe I'd do that too, once things calmed down. But by the time I was able to maintain consistent consciousness, the best that I could manage was, "Oh? Is that the worst of it? Well. That isn't so bad."

My left hand was wrapped in splints and gauze, sticky with medical ointments. But the right—well. It was a mesh of steel and rubber, with knuckles each made of three wheels—dials, maybe? They were through with spinning gyros and clockwork contraptions. My fingers were more metal and axis points, with pale yellow wires ribboning through intertwining steel. I wanted to count the points of articulation, like an action figure.

It was a thing of rubber fingertips stretched out over

scrapyard metal, ligaments held together with fine piano strings. I almost wanted to use them as a harp.

First thing I did when I saw it was put the hand I had left to the back of my neck. The base of my spine. There was a square of plastic squirreled into my skin—some kind of corpse technology connection there that made the hand work. That had to be it.

Funny. I thought it would feel more...noticeable. But I wouldn't have known to look for it if I hadn't known about Havilan Reacher and his missing fingers. I was reminded of a time I woke up from a surgery to find someone had closed up the openings with a shirt button and forgotten to tell me. It had been there for weeks, and I never even realized.

"Don't pick," Avram said, when he walked in on me touching the back of my neck.

"What happened to it?" I had asked.

"The hand was in rough shape," Avram explained. "You were going to lose too many fingers anyway. And I had a few spare parts lying around. So...." He shrugged. "Used what I had."

I recalled the rumors regarding why he had been exiled. *Human experimentation*, Anoïse had said. I was sure she meant it in a darker way than this, but how was something like a new limb hurting me?

It did not occur to me to bring it up. After everything, I didn't have the energy.

"Now," Avram said. "How are you feeling? You staying awake?"

"Mostly," I said. "I think I'm getting better. I—"

He crouched over my hospital bed. "You'd better," he said. "I swear to God, if you don't keep improving, I'm going to kill you, boy. You can't scare me like that."

"I—I didn't mean to."

The hardened edges of his features seemed to soften. "Ah, kid." He grabbed the back of my head, tucked me against his chest. The whole world felt and smelled like him for just an instant. "I was just worried about you, alright? I'm glad you pulled through. And I'm sorry about your hand."

"Don't be." I gave my fingers an experimental twirl. The hand made a clockwork ticking sound when it moved. "This is....um." Fuck. I wanted to cry. Why did I want to cry? "It's... it's cool." You ever say something and in retrospect you can't even find the path you used to get there? That's how I felt in that moment. That wasn't what it was. It was worse things, I think. Emptier things, at least. I was not prepared to acknowledge those just yet, though. I wanted to pretend for a while that everything was alright.

"If you're more conscious," Avram said, "I should have something for your back." He crossed the room. Snapped on blue latex gloves. His back blocked my view of what he was doing. "You have no idea how hard it was to get all the glass out."

"I thought Desmon took care of that," I admitted. Was that why it still hurt on the horse ride?

"He got the biggest pieces. No idea how, with all the wounds he was dealing with when we picked him up. But we patched him up a couple days ago and moved him out of the intensive care car as a thank you. He's spending time with Mercedes."

"His wounds might have happened after the glass. I got the glass in my back a while before Desmon fought anything. I think." I was still getting the whole timeline sorted out. "But I—thank you, Maunders. I appreciate—"

Before I could finish he crossed the room, scooped his

salve in two fingers. A thick, grainy paste, white and dripping. "Get on your stomach."

I obeyed. A drop landed on an unmarked area of my
back. I winced. "It's cold."

He nodded. "It'll sting, too. Try not to scream."

I swallowed. "What happens if I do?"

He started the application before answering. My back
felt hot and sharp as the salve slid over irritated wounds.

"I'll have a headache," Avram said.

I took deep breaths. I could feel my heartbeat in each
wound. A warm thrum beating slowly. I had to concentrate
on my breath.

At some point, blackness swallowed me while I was
horizontal. I'm not sure how long I was out. But Avram
woke me up. The first sensation to bring me back was him
gently slapping me awake.

"Come on, kid," he was saying. "Don't doze off on me
yet."

"Were we not done?"

"We're almost there." He crossed the car, rifled through
medicine cabinets. "I know I shelved them *somewhere*," he
said to himself, as he retrieved what he'd been looking for,
and crossed the room. There were pink pills cupped in his
palm. "Take these," he said. "And chew them carefully."

I scooped the pills from his hand with my false one.
Took it for a test run. It was a little shocking, being able to
pick the pills up with rubber fingers. Though it felt strange
to realize I couldn't actually feel them. I examined them.
"What are they?"

"Pain relievers," he said. "And antibiotics."

I obeyed. They were bitter and tasted like chalk. But
they went down easily enough with a bit of water. "How's
everyone holding up?"

Avram crossed the room with bandages. Reached them under my shirt, started rolling them around me. I wondered if Avram's hands were always that big? Or had I just reached a stage of exhaustion where I started noticing old things like it was the first time I'd ever seen them. That philosophical, 3AM headspace. You know what I mean?

"I'm fine," Avram said. "Your brother's fine. Mercedes is fine. Don't worry about us right now."

"You're sure?"

He cinched my bandages a little tighter, which felt like a punishment. Though I wasn't going to complain. "I'd whine about something if I wanted to. But seriously, Petre. Just look after yourself right now. Focus on that. You're hurt. You lost a fucking hand. Now's not the time to be worrying about others."

Right. I could do that. No problem. "Am I allowed to sleep soon?"

"You already had half an hour. How much more do you need?"

"I can't tell if you're being serious. I don't feel like I slept."

"No, I'm not." Avram wrapped an exhale of laughter around his words. "You can get some sleep soon. Just promise me you'll start worrying about yourself, kid." He finished wrapping me up. It was difficult to take deep breaths. I had to do it through my chest, which was going to take some getting used to.

"I don't know if I know how to stop worrying about everybody else," I admitted.

Avram leaned back and crossed his arms. "Best learn, right? You know how they treat empathy where we're going."

My eyebrows shot up. "You're coming?"

"Your sister invited The Blackheaths," Avram said. "Why wouldn't I be?"

There was the whole exile issue. Though I supposed Anoïse had said it was up to Mercedes' discretion. "Fair point."

"Now get some rest, Petre. And put on some trousers."

I had not realized I was only wearing boxers. Damn. I really was out of it, wasn't I?

At some point, amid the heat and hazy pain, I slept. The world was quiet. I think I dozed off. I don't remember what I dreamed, or if I dreamed at all. I think I was too tired for that. I couldn't get consistent sleep. Which had to be a sign I was recovering, I think.

I just kept thinking about the new hand. It was a bizarre change to wake up to. When you're going to lose something that important, I mean—you figure it's the kind of thing you're awake for, right? This life changing shit isn't the kind of thing you expect to jump you while you're out. It makes you worried what else you'll lose next time you wake up.

I didn't want to think about it. I wanted a distraction.

So. With that in mind. Once Avram left, was I *planning* to spy on my brother instead of going to bed? No. I wanted to go to bed more than most things I'd ever done in my life.

But did I hear his voice in one of the nearby boxcars, and figure if I could hear it, I might as well?

Absolutely I did.

It had been a while since I'd done any eavesdropping.

Well. I guess it was more like half a week at most. But it *felt* like a long time.

I pressed myself against the door, and I listened.

"What do you mean? Of course I'm sure," Desmon was saying.

"He's very resourceful." That was Mercedes.

"Petre? I mean listen—I'll give him credit. He knows how to make the most of what he's working with."

"He definitely does." Mercedes said it with a tone that made my face turn bright red. I was glad neither of them knew that I could hear them.

"But he can't work miracles, Mercedes." I felt as though there was something *off* about Desmon's voice. He seemed a little more relaxed than he usually was. Had they put him on pain medication? "I'm telling you. There's no way he's found out. The Recollection Helm is in safe hands."

The what now?

"I just...I worry what he'd do if he found out what it's for."

A noise of consideration squirmed through Desmon's throat. "I doubt there's much he could do, except be mad."

And to be sure, I was very good at that, just hearing him talk about me.

"The plan here doesn't seem like something he'd be opposed to *that* much," he went on. "And anyway—Mom still needs to get the damn thing working the way she wants it to. Do you not trust him to go with the plan?"

Mercedes was quiet for a long time. Quiet enough that for a moment I was worried someone had heard me. Then in a small voice I heard her answer. "No. It's not that."

"Well, then what is it?"

"It's...it's because I trust him that I'm so worried about this. I'm worried he won't agree with what we're doing. And I'm worried he'll have a point."

"It's too early to worry about this, Mercedes," Desmon said. "We don't even know how much of this is possible yet.

We'll have to see what scale Mom can engineer this thing on."

I caught myself nodding off a moment too late—right after my forehead hit the door.

"What was that?" Mercedes' voice was muted on the other side.

"I'll check on it." Desmon said.

My injections yanked me out of the way of the open door and around the corner. I waited until he was just about to look around the hallway to pounce on him. I wrapped my false hand over his mouth so he couldn't scream. "I'm not here," I said in his ear.

"Desmon?" Mercedes called from inside the room.

Desmon spun to face me. He did not break eye contact with me as he said, "It was nothing. I'm gonna go take a piss while I'm up, though. I'll be back in a sec." He dragged me around a corner. "What's going on?"

"Did everything that happened out there count for nothing? You're keeping secrets already?"

"Me? You're the one spying."

"I'll have you know I was only passing by. Mercedes wanted to speak with me." It was a filthy lie. But what was he going to do? Call me on it?

"I thought I smoothed things over with her." Desmon said.

I wasn't sure what that meant, but I didn't have the energy to question it. So I said, "I...I'm sure you did. You're good at that. A lot better than I've ever been at least."

Desmon tilted his head. Like he was expecting a trick. "I. Um. Thank you?"

I wasn't sure what to add to that. Maybe I hadn't been clear with him. "Look, I just—I'm trying not to jump to conclusions. But what is this about a Recollection Helm?"

Was this related to the corpse technology about memories that Mom had been telling me about? "What is it that Mercedes knows? What don't you guys want me to figure out?"

Desmon frowned. "Okay so—would you believe me if I said I do want to tell you?"

I had to chew on that for a second. "I should hope so. If after all this we couldn't trust one another I would be very—"

"So I need you to trust me when I say this isn't my secret to spill."

"Desmon—" What did that *mean?* "But—" Was he—was he talking about Anoïse?

"It's not my place to tell you," Desmon said. "I don't want to take that from her. She'll let you know when she's ready. We have a lot to catch her up on anyway."

"No kidding." I managed a small chuckle. "Do you...do you think she does? Trust me, I mean."

Desmon had to think about it. "I think she wants to."

I thought she wanted to go back to the way things were when we were eighteen. I wasn't sure yet if that was the same thing as wanting to trust me. "So I take it you and I aren't running away?"

"I don't think so." Desmon rubbed the back of his neck.

"You sure? There's really nothing to it. Just open the window, tuck and roll."

Desmon had to cover his mouth to keep from laughing. "It's like you were saying earlier. We're princes. We can't outrun that. We have to try to make this work."

"And by 'this' what you mean is...?"

Desmon shrugged. "This family? This country? I don't know, Petre. It's late. It's been a long few days, and I'll bet you're more exhausted than I am."

"Man, you think you're exhausted, I—oh. Right. Yeah." I coughed. "You, uhh. You did good out there, Desmon." I clapped him on the shoulder. "Thank you for saving my life. I owe you one."

"You don't owe me shit, man." Desmon punched my arm. "I did what I had to do. You would have done the same. Now get some rest. We arrive home tomorrow morning."

I turned to leave. "Yeah. I should get some rest."

His hand closed around my arm. "Wait. I almost forgot. Stay here."

Frankly I was so bewildered that he'd ruined his chance to get rid of me that staying there and looking dumbfounded was about all I could do, while Desmon ducked back inside. He kept his voice low, so I couldn't hear his conversation with Mercedes. But when he came back, he was holding Dad's knife in both hands. "I kept this for you." He proffered it.

I peeled it from his hands. "I..." I swallowed. Why did that choke me up? "I'd thought you would try to keep it."

"Hey," he said, "you stole it, not me."

I put it in my pocket. "Could've stolen it back," I admitted. "Those are the rules."

"Careful." He winked at me. "You'll give me ideas."

"Can't have that. No but seriously, I—thank you."

TWENTY-SIX

W e got to the courtyard at some point the next morning. Maybe a few mornings later? I wasn't sure. Time was blurry, considering how much I was sleeping.

I woke up to the lurch of our stop and hustled to armor myself in the clothes Avram had brought with him. The ones I'd left behind in Blackheath House.

Nobody had taught him how to properly fold clothes. Either that or he didn't care to. So I tugged on a wrinkled dress shirt with lace on the wrists and shrugged into my chameleon coat. It was still sliced up in the back. Mom would have to repair that at some point, I realized, as I put on trousers.

They were tight enough to make my ass look great, but I was worried you could see the outline of my cock through them. Nobody had ever said anything about it to my face. But also? Who *would?*

Maybe that's the measure of someone you can trust. Someone's who's willing to tell you they can see your whole cock through your trousers, and could you maybe wear something else to the occasion?

I strapped on my mask and headed down the black grate steps into the pandemonium.

The courtyard to Mercy House was swarming with crowds of people. I was immediately wrapped around a sea of glittering jewels, waves of fur and fabric slashing through the disarray.

If there was such a thing as white noise, there had to be white vision too, and I think I experienced it in that instant. It didn't take very long for the yard to blur into a visual soup of absurd and garish colors. Rainbows knifed through crystals that sparkled on coruscant clothes. Large dresses, big coats, suits, all wrapped in a plumage of primary colors.

People squeezed each other's forearms all around me as sights and sounds conspired to vex my mind. I couldn't find firm shapes amidst the chaos. Everything was an indistinguishable muddle of confused noises and hazy shapes that could've been human if they could quiet down with the intensity of their clothes so I could actually *process* what I was looking at.

I searched the crowd for Mercedes. I couldn't find her, though I spotted Desmon ahead of me, cutting through the crowd, eyes on Anoïse.

I tried to figure out how to get through the press of people all around me, but the noises made my head fuzzy. Which made it difficult to think and move and remember how to arrange myself in three-dimensional space. My breaths kept snapping short before I could finish exhaling. Panic engulfed me.

Then I felt a warm hand pressing down on my coat. I felt warm breath as Avram's voice spilled into my ear—an anchor that I was trying not to get aroused by. "Stay calm."

"I am calm," I murmured. He didn't hear me and had to dip his ear against my mouth so I could say it again.

"You're not good at keeping your thoughts from showing up on your face, Petre." Avram gave my shoulder a gentle squeeze. I wanted to groan, wanted him to do that again.

"Just take my hand," Avram said. "Follow me. You'll be ok."

I obeyed. His hand entombed mine. I squeezed my eyes shut and followed him, peeking out occasionally through my eyelashes to make sure I didn't have to maneuver around anyone.

Talk swallowed me. Rumors. Words like *blaze* and *fire* and *conflict* jumped out at me. The crowd was buzzing with the vocabulary of warfare. Until, after long protracted moments of breathless anticipation, we emerged on the other side of the throng.

This was not a sudden thing, like a bubble popping. This was slow as a pustule draining. We slowly oozed free from the mass of people as the crowd corroded and we neared the door-bridge.

Anoïse stood in the center of it, already occupied with Mercedes and Desmon. Mercedes was shoving councilors out of her way, thrusting index fingers at anyone who wouldn't let her get a word in. She looked like she wanted to smack the next person who interrupted her.

I was tempted to go try it. See what happened. Might be fun. She had a good slap. It made a nice crisp sound.

I realized I should not think about that. Not here. Not now. I tried to put my focus elsewhere, on other things. Things that were less distracting.

Unfortunately, before I could, my gaze settled on Fabrian.

He stood beside Anoïse, fidgety as a puppet jerking on a string. He looked like he couldn't decide if he wanted to be bored or miserable, or both.

I hated how much I wished I could comfort him. I didn't *want* to think about sitting on his lap, about pressing my mouth against his. I didn't *want* to think about the scrape of his fingernails against the roots of my hair. This was my sister's husband. I had no right to entertain these thoughts.

And *yet*—okay, I know that doesn't sound good—but hear me out, I'm going somewhere with this—another part of me, loath as I am to admit it, *wanted* to do what I was doing. With Mercedes. With Fabrian. Because as involuntary and intrusive as the initial inklings were—and they *were* intrusive—I still harbored some resentment that I was back here. This felt like some small, harmless defiance. After all, my thoughts couldn't exactly hurt anyone. Not on their own.

I mean, I won't defend them. They weren't good thoughts. But they were *mine*. And I was sick to death of giving everything up to these people and this place.

"Petre." Avram dipped his head to whisper into my ear. His voice incised through my inattention.

I yelped. "I—I can hear you clearly now," I said. "You don't have to do that."

"I just wanted to check. Are you doing okay?"

"I—I should be fine now." I realized Fabrian was looking at me. I had a moment of bizarre worry that he had read my mind or glimpsed what I was thinking somehow. "Thank you, Maunders."

Avram stepped sideways to move past me, blocking my view. "I think we'll be here for a little while," he said. "You need anything, you come to me, okay?"

"I'll be okay."

425

Avram laughed. "It's been a while since I saw this place with my own eyes. I've heard stories about what it's been like since I've left. You got *me* nervous, kid. So don't go acting tough on my account."

I couldn't let him do that. He'd already done too much for me. "I just—you've got enough on your plate without me. I can handle these things. These people. This environment. I've been here before. I don't need help."

He let go of my hand. I hadn't realized he was still holding it. "You know—it doesn't take a lot of strength to decide to do these things on your own. It's the easiest thing in the world. You're *expected* to. The actual doing of it can get pretty rough. But the decision? That's nothing. You know what's harder?"

"Is it asking for help?" I asked, tonelessly.

"It is in fact that!" Avram punched my shoulder playfully. "That's not expected of you at all, is it? You're risking more by doing it. So don't conform to the kind of person they expect you to be, alright? I'll be here if you need me."

I hugged him. I had to. The sentiment was too saccharine for any other kind of gesture. I pressed him against me, held him tight. "Thank you, Avram."

I felt his hand on my back. He made a small circle between my shoulder blades. "You're doing alright."

I let him go. "If you have anyone else here you need to talk to right now feel free. I don't want to eat up all of your attention."

"It looks like everyone is headed inside actually." Avram thumbed back to my siblings. "Are we allowed to join them? I don't quite know yet how it works here."

I wasn't sure how to feel about the fact that Avram was turning to *me* for advice. "The hell if I know."

"You're their family. Why wouldn't you be?"

426

"You'd be surprised how well some siblings can exclude each other."

"Petre," Fabrian called to me, as the others headed inside. "Get over here."

Avram grinned at me. "He doesn't seem to mind."

"Technically he's not a sibling," I said.

"And, *technically*, he is."

"Quiet, you." I did not want to think about that. It only made me feel guilty.

Avram hustled to catch up with Mercedes, to talk with her about what she and my sister had discussed.

I lingered behind the group, and—quite accidentally, I promise—fell in step with Fabrian, who tucked his hands behind his back and kept his head high. "Welcome back, Petre."

"Nowhere else I'd rather be." It came out as more of a sneer than I intended.

To my surprise, he looked genuinely shocked at the tone of my voice. I was worried I had upset him. "I..." he swallowed. "I understand how you feel."

The doors to Anoïse's court lurched open. The sentries needed to lean their weight against the massive frames to move them.

Anoïse had packed the court for this impromptu session. Clerks were sitting at desks in corners with fountain pens and quills, writing notes that would go into history books. What was moments ago a bustle of movement and activity went immediately pond-placid as we came through.

Burnished armor all around me winked to still reflectiveness. I became quite suddenly aware of all the ways in which my court clothes constrained me. I could not move to adjust all the discomfort I was hyper aware of.

"This way." Fabrian led me to the front of the hall, to a clustered crowd at the base of Anoïse's throne.

The throne's steps were wrought from old devices, machines that brought fire and iron artillery shells and napalm, after The First Annihilation. The whole throne was framed between two massive tusks. She climbed the wreckage of old chaos to plant herself atop it. The product of two catastrophes, and her, sitting on top of what was left.

I watched Anoïse as I took up residence among the hall's attendants. I realized that her dress was our house colors. Red and black. Bronze mastodons fastened her skirts together. Pins chewed through the cloth-of-gold, which accented the red that seemed to shimmer, shiny with silk.

A train of magistrates attended her. The Book of Law, its cover plated in gold leaf, was wrapped in old, gnarled hands. They kept their heads high and their suits pristine. The Keepers of the Faith soon followed, manacles chafing at their wrists. They were dressed in robes as simple as potato sacks. Some of them were not even wearing shoes.

The labcoats were last. Mom chief among them. Straight white coat, yellow embroidery, branching jaundice-veins all down the length of it. They settled into predetermined spots.

Once everyone was settled, she called Mercedes before her, and asked her to give a statement about what had happened.

Mercedes went to one knee. She bowed her head, red hair obscuring her face. I was trying to pay attention to what she was saying. Even if I'd heard it all before. But there was too much sensory input all around me. It was too difficult to grasp what her account was.

"I know how you feel," Fabrian whispered, as Mercedes

spoke. His voice was electric, right beside me. It felt as if he radiated heat. I tried not to think about him. Tried to focus on Mercedes. But I could not extricate his words from hers.

He'd said that already. I raised my false hand at him. "Are you sure?"

His eyes went wide. "Oh, shit." He covered the rest of his surprise with a cough. "Alright. Maybe not that part. But the rest of it—"

"You're quick to write that part off." I wanted to tell Fabrian it wasn't even about the hand. I wanted him to know he didn't know what I was feeling. Because he hadn't grown up here, hadn't lived here long enough to understand.

"I trust you enjoyed The Blackheaths' comforts on your way back here, though," Fabrian said, beneath his breath.

Unfortunately, that got my attention. I turned to scrutinize his face. "Fabrian. Hey. Hey. *Look* at me, Fabrian. You saw the hand, right? And my face? And all the rest of me? Does it look like I've had a swell time out there to you?" What was he even doing down here? Wasn't he supposed to be on the throne with Anoïse? Or was this a calculated move? Maybe Anoïse wanted the spotlight for what was to come.

I wasn't sure if I liked the sound of that.

"Oh, absolutely not," Fabrian said. "You look like shit." His smile jacked my heart rate right up. I felt sweaty. Even grosser than I was. It wasn't fair. How did he look so easily presentable?

"However bad I look, trust me, I feel worse. You haven't even seen my back."

"I'd certainly like to."

I felt a pit of dread beginning to form inside my stomach. This boy was going to get me killed. "The wound is covered in bandages, I'm afraid. There isn't much to see." I wasn't sure why I was sparring with him. I suppose it was easier to entertain myself with this than turn back to face the recounting of everything I'd *just* dealt with out there. I didn't have to relive all the exhaustion. All the violence. I could just engage Fabrian.

And yet—

"What was it that happened?" he asked.

I wasn't sure how to answer. Where could I even start? How much did he know? "Nothing you didn't anticipate that night at the fire pit, I'm sure."

Fabrian chewed on his lip. "I had no idea what was going to happen at the fire pit. I just had to get my uncle out of here. Before he got himself or somebody else killed."

"And how did that work out?"

"Oh, splendidly. He left some time in the night, shortly after you and Desmon did."

That turned my guts to jelly. "He what now?"

"That's why I'm asking you what happened out there," Fabrian said. "I want to know what he did after I left."

I thumbed over to Mercedes, still kneeling, giving testimony. "Are you listening closely?" I asked. "She's telling you."

Fabrian's mouth quirked halfway to a grin. "I think she's finishing up, actually."

Oh. How did I not know that? How bad had my attention been? I had thought I could multitask. How much had I missed?

"The crown calls Petre Mercy," a herald called.

I nearly choked. "I'm being called to witness?"

"Oh, right. I was supposed to tell you about that." Fabrian chuckled. "Anyways, go knock 'em dead up there.

I'm sure you'll do great." His hand came down on my ass as he shoved me forward. I nearly yelped.

The last thing I needed was my face turning bright red in front of Anoïse's whole court. But Fabrian ensured that as I made my way through the crowd before they could call my name a second time. I moved past men and women burdened in heavy fur. Through a scintillating hailed greeting of bladed light lensed through diamonds and jewels.

My mouth was dry. I could not remember if I was supposed to make a vow. I had not stood in this place for a long time. Nobody was speaking. Everyone waited. Was there something I was forgetting to do?

Anoïse's mouth squirmed. "Petre," she said.

My heart slammed into the sides of my neck. "Anoïse."

"You missed the oaths at the coronation."

My stomach dropped. Was that what this was about?

"Is there something you would like to say to me?"

My mind went blank. Panic swallowed it up in white noise and ambience. She needed an oath of fealty, long overdue.

I dropped to my knees. How long had the hall been silent? I wasn't sure. Goddammit. What were the words? I'd seen people speak them a thousand times before in front of Dad. Why couldn't I remember them?

I fought back the memories of old fights dredging themselves through me. Half-remembered arguments between me and her that I needed to discard to speak the words. *What were they*—oh.

The memory ambushed me. The words of oath came back in a rush. "I swear," I breathed, as I studied the stone ground, "on my Faith, and all that is Holy...to serve my liege in every action, word and deed. I shall love all that she loves, abjure all she abjures. I offer up my counsel, my sword, and my life to the endurance of her person, work and legacy."

"Amen," she said. "Rise."

I got to my feet. Was I shaking? Why was I shaking? I felt as if my face were hot, but I wasn't sure if it showed. My mind was clammy, and I could not find focus through the morass of emotion making my mind into a tumult of noisy thoughts.

"Now," she said, "you believe our brother, Edgar Mercy, is conspiring with Havilan Reacher to take the throne? Is this true?"

I nodded. "Yes, Your Grace." I wasn't sure if I wanted to grow accustomed to that form of address. For a moment I thought the murmurs rippling through the crowd pertained to calling Anoïse *Your Grace,* and not y'know, the accusation of treason.

"Are you willing to swear it on any holy relic, book, or before any Keeper of the Faith?"

"I am." I said. "Your Grace. I know what I know. I heard what I heard. I saw what I saw."

"Thank you, Petre. You are excused."

Relief made its weary way into my body as I fled for the relative safety of the crowd. More men and women were drawn up to give statements.

It was determined that Edgar had taken Reacher House from Orianna, and her immediate court staff were being kept as hostages. We could expect splinter branches from her loyalists to arrive at court soon, flocking to Orianna's child, Fabrian.

Havilan Reacher's branch of the family was sending their navy out to claim Outlying Island territories that belonged to other families, and they were relatively unopposed, thus far. They'd burned our fleet and consolidated the forces of Reacher House. There was no clear plan of defense for our resources. Some rumors claimed they were planning a blockade.

More statements came. Reports of towns within our holdings declaring for Edgar. Housing Ed's forces. Helping these rebels. Someone was in the midst of explaining a skirmish in a place called Magtown between a couple different vassals who had declared for Edgar and Anoïse. I would've tried to listen more closely if I could have just retained the information. But it was too late for that. Details slid away from me. I wanted to be free, to soothe the ambient seething in my thoughts.

A hand closed around my upper arm, far too tight. Someone spun me around to face that lady from The Mercy Guard. Jerim's friend. Teya, I think. "Petre." She filled the space between us with as much of a bow as she could muster through the press of bodies all around us.

"I just wanted to let you know, your sister would like to speak with you. Privately, in her office, once she's done here. I'm told that you can go there now if you need."

I sketched a small bow for her. "I will," I said. But as I turned to go her fingers snagged on my wrist, nails digging in over the space where I felt my pulse.

"One more thing," she intoned, slowly. "I've been asking around. I need to know if you've seen Jerim. It's important. He's been missing for a few days now. I want to make sure he's not hurt."

I wondered how many days he'd been gone. Tried to think if I'd seen him anywhere. "Not a sign since I got back. I've been gone for a while, though. You might have better luck asking someone else." I didn't wait for a reply. I just twisted out of her grip, and fled for the safety of an empty room, for the first time in what felt like a long while.

~

ANOÏSE HAD TAKEN Dad's old office. I'd never *thought* about what this place would look like after Dad was gone. What Anoïse might do with these walls, this room I thought I'd known so well.

I thought she would've made more changes, you know what I mean? A new administration comes in, you sort of expect there are going to be a few cosmetic differences. But it was like she was afraid to shake things up, like swapping out a color palette would dishonor Dad's memory. How hard was she trying to imitate him?

Was that how we'd ended up here? Imitation? Was that all a monarchy was? A generations-long game of telephone with a concept called *Kingship*? A game of Divine Right playing homeopathy?

All this to say, she'd left up all the family portraits. The cluster of vaguely concerned tempera faces crowned the four walls. The room still smelled like newly minted money, though it had lost the underpinning of what I can only call *Dad-smell* after all this time—an old familiar musk I had associated with him.

That was funny. I had thought it such a permanent fixture of his office. I'd never accounted for the fact that even such tiny details like that could fade in time.

The only thing that was different about the office was the desk itself. Sheaves of paper were strewn in uneven piles of precarious stacks just barely balanced.

The window behind Anoïse was supposed to have a

434

THE FALL IS ALL THERE IS

screen projecting nature imagery. But something had gone wrong, and it was just an idle screen, with a logo bouncing around the edges of a black void. I wanted to see if it fit neatly in the corner. But Anoïse entered before I had that chance.

She leaned the door shut with her back, closed her eyes and sighed. "God. Are you okay?"

I chewed on my bottom lip for a minute. Tried to take a headcount of all my aches and bruises. "Never better," I said.

Her gaze hardened, and she didn't blink for quite some time. "Answer honestly."

Anoïse was many things, but she was not Dad. She couldn't scare me. And after all we'd been through, I wasn't sure if honesty was what I owed her. I dunno. It would depend on how this conversation went.

Not until she fessed up about the Recollection Helm. I wasn't sure how long it would take for her to do that, and I did not want to be the one to bring it up. "Honestly? I'm just grateful to be back home." I gave her a fool's grin.

She rolled her eyes. "I have a favor to ask of you."

"It's good to see you too, Anoïse."

"Fuck. I'm sorry I just—I've had a long day."

"You're telling me." I waved hello to her with the hand Avram had made for me. A patchwork thing made from scrapyard steel, piano strings, and clockwork.

She laughed. It didn't seem so bitter. "I'm not getting any sympathy, am I?"

"Afraid not. How did things go?"

"Well." She fell into her chair. Even the cushions sighed. "Edgar's burned our fleet, captured Fabrian's Mom, controls the resources of Reacher House and half our family, Havilan Reacher's fled to go join Edgar, and I've declared war. So." She shrugged. "I'm sorry I didn't believe you earlier."

I took a deep breath. It would have been really useful if she had. "You sent me out to make sure Mercedes was okay. That seems like apology enough." It didn't, but that was more than I thought I would get from her, after all this.

"I, um. I tried to trust you. But if I believed you, I would've been more quick to put him in a cell."

I shrugged. Wasn't sure what to say. "We all make mistakes. How are you feeling about the coming war?"

She stared down at her desk. "I'm still deciding." She pressed her lips together. "You let me know if you need anything, alright?"

She was angling for that favor. I knew it already. "Of course."

"I have a few things *I* need," she said. "And I hope you know—I'm asking this because I trust you. You wanted something to do earlier that would help." She flexed her hands around her desk. "I'm trying to listen. I'm trying to make good on what you told me."

I nodded slowly. "Just let me know what you need." My heart jackhammered. I felt as if it rattled in my ribcage.

"Right." She sighed. "I should just get it out then, huh?"

"That's usually the best way to go about it."

She sighed. I started counting the seconds. I got to five before she blurted. "I'd like to make you a part of The Mercy Guard."

I stifled my laughter with a closed fist over my mouth, turned it into a cough. "You have an opening?"

"I do. And you're taking it. I'm putting you in charge."

The only thoughts housed in my mind were wordless exclamation marks. I wasn't sure what to do, what to say. I just stared at her, mouth open. "You're serious."

She tilted her head. "Were you under the impression that I was in a joking mood?"

"It's not that, I just...I—wait. Hang on a minute. Hold up. Just a second. You just said you were making me a part of The Mercy Guard. Not putting me in *charge* of it." I'd never been in charge of anything before.

"It doesn't hurt to be cautious," she said. "And I want someone I can trust in the organization. I need to know how many people there are in there that I can count on, and I need you to find that out for me. I want to know if anyone in the group helped Edgar escape."

I had to make sure this was more than empty words. That she wasn't doing this because she needed a body to take up space. I had to be absolutely certain she'd thought this through. So I leaned forward. "You want my cooperation? That's fine. I'll cooperate. Just so long as you can cooperate with me. I did what you asked. I want a release from my status as a hostage. I want to be working here under my own volition. Because I want you to understand that if you give me a good reason to leave, I'll take it. Not because I hate you or I'm a traitor or I'm going over to Edgar, but because you will have left me no choice but to go back to fucking off and doing my own thing, away from all of you. Believe me, I want to stay here. But that does not happen unconditionally. And I'll need some indication from you that you want me here as much as I do. Going forward. So let me ask you, Anoïse: do you trust me?"

"Yes," she said, immediately. I was surprised by just how little hesitation, how little consideration, she had to give the subject matter. "I do. I trust you."

"Alright," I said. "Don't think you can stop here, and I'll put up with anything. Don't just tell me this because you think it's what I want to hear. I want to work with you to put an end to this. Hell. Maybe I have to." I remembered what Desmon had said about princes. "But I am willing to leave if you can't work with me."

"I understand." She breathed a ragged sigh.

"So. With that out of the way—is the war official yet?"

"I plan to announce it in a few days. I'll want it to be big, with vassals and holy oaths and everything." She shoved her hand through her hair. "Fuck. We're going to get through this. Will I see you there?"

If she needed support so badly, if she could work with me, I was sure I could deal with the mental agony of such a public gathering for a few hours. It was the least I could do, if that was what it took to help build trust between the two of us.

"Yes," I said. "I will be."

I sucked in a breath and braced myself for the world to come.

Acknowledgments

It takes a village to build a book, and I couldn't have done this without the help of friends and family. So I want to thank my fiancée Kira for providing for us in the year and a half it took to write this thing—and for all the stuff before and after that, too. This book would not exist without her constant help and support.

I want to thank my godfather Ron, for the years of guidance that shaped me into the kind of person who could write this book—and for introducing my parents to each other. I owe you a life debt and if this book ever takes off, I promise you'll see a check in the mail paying that off.

While I'm at it I want to thank Sara for her support, and the fact that she let me live with her for four months while I put the finishing touches on this. I am literally sitting down to write this acknowledgment they day after I moved out of your place. I definitely owe you one.

Thanks to Quenby Olson for the proofread, and for telling me to stop using "murmured" so many times, for God's sake, to Krystle Matar for the last year and a half of pushing me to level up, and to chase the whys in my worldbuilding, to Angela Boord for the support, the encouragement, and also the most brutally painful, most phenomenal dev edit I've ever had the honor to receive, to Fiona West for the support, the helping me come up with this title, and for one kick-ass cover—and to Noah Sky for one hell of a copy edit.

Additional thanks goes to one Mr. Hermes, as well as Thomas, Justin, Tori, and Alistair, and the rest of the community I've found for the last year and a half of guidance, support and friendship, cheerleading and challenging that made this book possible, and made writing this thing a lot less solitary than it could've been.

Final thanks to Tim Quigley, who read Petre's first story when I was eighteen, and absolutely refused to allow me to ever stop writing him, even when I was discouraged. Thanks for pushing me to finish the stories I started, Tim. I finally finished one of Petre's books, just like I promised. RIP.

ΛBOUT THE ΛUTHOR

C.M. Caplan is the author of *The Fall is All There Is*. He's a quadruplet (yes, really), and is disabled. He has a degree in creative writing, and his short fiction won an Honorable Mention in the 2019 Writers of the Future Contest. You can subscribe to Caplan's mailing list by following this link to receive, updates, information, and sneak previews into future projects.

facebook.com/thecmcaplanauthor

x.com/cmcaplanwrites

instagram.com/thecmcaplan

patreon.com/thecmcaplan

Printed in Great Britain
by Amazon